UNFLAPPABLE

SUZIE GILBERT

To Russell Galen

CHAPTER 1

Adam Matheson stood by the front door of a sprawling beach house, and watched the elegantly-dressed guests part for his wife. Ignoring the stares, smiles, and proffered hands she slipped through the crowd quickly and cleanly, a skyscape of diaphanous silk trailing from her slender frame. As she approached him, he felt a burst of desire; but when she drew closer he saw that her eyes were not on his, but on the open door. Once again, he thought she might bound past him and disappear into the night.

"Damn, Adam," breathed Jay Sheinkopf. "You are one lucky man."

She stopped before them, her face impassive, and Jay rested his hand on her shoulder. "Great to see you, Luna," he said. "Seriously, when are you going to ditch this guy and move in with me?"

Luna glanced at his hand, then gave him a level gaze. Adam grinned as he encircled her with his arm and ushered her away. "You keep trying, Jay," he whispered, and winked.

The inside of the limousine was silent. Adam poured himself a Scotch as Luna lowered her window. "You didn't say five words all night," he said. "I didn't think you were going to come out of the bathroom."

"You know I hate those things," she replied, her eyes on the passing streetlights.

Adam stared at the slope of her cheekbone, the curve of her shoulder, and ran a hand through his greying hair. "Tell you what," he said. She turned toward him and he felt a rush of vertigo, a surge of all the emotions he had always claimed but never actually felt until he met her. "Let's throw a benefit for the Sierra Club. Would you like that?"

He watched her anger subside, replaced by a coiled despondency that alarmed him. He silenced his buzzing phone.

"It's not working, Adam," she said. "I can't deal with all these people. The parties and the questions and the media and your friends hitting on me all the time."

Adam felt a sense of foreboding. "I'll take care of it," he said, reaching for her hand and kissing it. "I promise it will get better. We've only been married six months."

She took a breath. "You can have it annulled," she said. "You don't have to give me anything."

Adam was proud of his mastery of facial expression and body language, two of the arsenal of skills he had used to amass his vast fortune. But suddenly, unthinkably, his grid went down. He felt his eyes widen, his lips part, and his hand clench tightly around hers. The car stopped, the door opened, and Roland Edwards — impossibly big, dark, and wearing a perfect suit — stood waiting. Luna slid out of the car and headed not for the ornate, wrought-iron front door of Cielo Azul, but for the stucco archway that led to the ten acres behind it.

"Wait!" said Adam.

A young man in khakis and a blazer stepped forward, holding a phone. "Mr. Matheson," he said. "Don Besko. It's urgent."

"I'll be ten minutes," Adam said, touching her hand. "Please. Can we talk about it? Can you wait for me in the sun room?"

Luna hesitated. She glanced at the driver, at Roland, and at Adam's assistant, all waiting; and at Adam, his dark eyes boring into hers. "All right," she said. Adam gave her a relieved smile, and she followed him into the house. Beneath the heavy chandelier he angled toward his office, and Luna turned and walked down the long hallway to the south wing. She passed a heavy oak door, and entered the sun room.

Discreet spotlights illuminated the soaring glass panels, the rare orchids, and the murmuring marble fountain. Luna crossed the room and gazed through the delicate glass door leading to the veranda. From where she stood she could see part of the enormous Spanish-style villa, the patio overlooking the ocean, and the stairway leading to the pool.

Directly across the lawn Adam stood in his office, gesturing as he talked on the phone.

Luna briefly settled on a couch, then rose and circled the room. She trailed a hand through the fountain, and inspected a new orchid in its ornate pot. Finally she glanced at the clock and then at Adam, still framed by his office window. She started into the hallway and nearly ran into of one of Adam's longtime security men, who was standing outside the door.

"Evening, Mrs. Matheson," said Paszkiewicz, who was tall, solid, and wore a brown linen suit.

"Hi, Paz," she answered. "Could you excuse me, please?"

Paszkiewicz's broad face flushed slightly as he moved forward, nearly filling the doorway. "Would you mind waiting a few more minutes? Mr. Matheson said he's very sorry for the delay, but he'll be right with you."

"I've waited long enough. Could I get by?"

"I'm sorry."

Luna blinked, confused. She tried to squeeze between him and the door frame, but he shifted his weight.

"I'm sorry, ma'am," he said quietly, then reached for the door and pulled it shut.

She flinched at the click of the latch. Turning on her heels, she crossed the room and reached for the glass door. It was locked. She turned the twist button and tried the knob once more, to no avail. Her stomach clutched as she tried to recall what Adam had said about the automatic locking system.

Luna scanned the empty room. Her adrenaline rose like a wave, and a sheen of sweat appeared on her skin. When she rattled the knob the sound screamed around her, thudding against her chest and blocking the air from her lungs. Seizing an antique chair, she swung it against the door. The glass shattered into an icy cascade, and the broken chair sailed into the night. Shards and splinters fell to the stone patio as Luna slipped from the room, her ethereal dress floating behind her.

• • •

Celia Jenkins sat in the office of the Western Pennsylvania Wildlife Center, staring at the computer screen and curling a strand of pale hair around her finger. The newsletter was due. The 638 people on her donor list were waiting for her stories about orphaned fawns, rescued raccoons, birds injured, healed, and set free; for news of just-completed cages, recently-won grants, and second-hand medical equipment topped with bows and left at the clinic door; for tales of panic-stricken people who found themselves racing up the long dirt driveway with something alive in a box, unaware of how their lives might be about to change.

Do you think this is any good, Dad? she had asked him six years before. Do you think if I wrote one a couple of times a year, we might get some donations?

Lord, Celia! Elias had replied, astonished, looking up from her computer. I didn't know you could write like that!

Celia knew she should get to work, but instead she left the office and headed up the hill toward their biggest flight cage. Twelve feet high, twelve feet wide, and a hundred feet long, it had been built with donated lumber and erected by revolving groups of volunteers, Girl Scouts, Boy Scouts, Audubon and Lions Club members, even minimum-security prisoners on work programs. The splendid slatted structure was for two unreleasable Bald Eagles, a bonded pair who had raised orphaned eaglets four out of the last five years.

The eaglets were delivered by wildlife rehabilitators as far away as Maine, all happy to make the drive knowing the orphans would be raised by their own kind. By summer's end they were as large as their foster parents, and had learned to catch the live fish volunteers supplied in rubber tubs. The young eagles were skillful, strong, and healthy, and every year dozens of people met at one of the lakes to watch them fly away.

Celia peered into the flight cage, at the two regal birds resting side by side on a high perch. From her own perch on the hill Celia could see the office, the clinic, the pens, the smaller flights, and the storage sheds. She gave a contented sigh. It was rare for her to be here alone, but her daughter, father, and all eight of the Sunday volunteers were at the wildlife festival in Ellington. So far this year there had been no orphaned eaglets. She smiled up at the birds, wondering if they were enjoying their solitary tranquility, as well.

Celia heard the sound of an engine, and opened her eyes as a black Suburban rolled to a stop by the office. Two men in suits emerged from the front seat, and two men in jeans from the back. The men in suits spotted and started toward her.

Celia scrambled to her feet. "Ms. Jenkins?" asked the first, a white-haired man in sunglasses. "We're here on behalf of Adam Matheson."

"We're here for the male eagle," said the second, who was young and tanned. "Here are the papers."

Celia watched the two men in jeans pull out a large animal crate, a heavy, long-handled net, and two pairs of elbow-length leather gloves. She felt sick with dread, and cursed herself for believing she could handle the center alone. "No!" she shouted, but when her voice emerged it was little more than a whisper.

"No," she tried again, staring at the papers. "You can't have him! It's not legal!"

The younger man regarded her coldly. The two men in jeans passed by, carrying the crate between them.

"Sign here, please," said the older man, handing her a pen. Behind her, the flight cage door opened with a soft creak.

"No! I'm calling the police!"

Celia reached a trembling hand into her pocket, but her phone was on the office desk. The high perch groaned, and there was a rush of feathers. Celia peered through the wooden slats as a huge dark bird hurtled toward one of the men in jeans, the man raising his net in defense but not in time. Swinging its legs forward, talons outstretched, the eagle slammed into the man's shoulder and knocked him off his feet.

"Stop!" sobbed Celia and ran for the door, but the young suited man blocked her way. Tears blurred her vision as she stumbled down the hill and into her office. She seized her phone, shaking so violently she dropped it twice, misdialing as through her window she saw the flight cage door swing open. The men in jeans emerged, carrying the animal crate between them; one's shirt stained crimson, the other with a bleeding gash on the side of his face.

"911," came the dispatcher's voice.

The white-haired man leaned in the door. "Thank you for your cooperation, Ms. Jenkins," he said, and Celia wept as they drove away.

• • •

"Dammit," murmured Luna, as three-quarters of a pound of regurgitated mackerel landed on the lap of her cotton pants.

The otherwise healthy adult Brown Pelican had come in with a broken humerus, mid-shaft, perfectly fixable. He had been found dragging a wing along Schooner's Cove by a family from Vermont, a can-do group of five who had each manned a beach towel and eventually cornered and tackled the very large bird. They had sensibly wrapped one towel around his beak, another around his wings, and sandwiched him in the back seat of their car. The mom had located Starfish Key Wildlife Center on her cellphone, and the dad had driven like a bandit.

Miss? the smaller girl had asked, her face aglow with concern. Will you take care of him and make him better?

Yes, Luna had replied, then x-rayed, set, and wrapped the broken wing. Two days later the patient was better, but unable to keep his food down. "Hey, Kelly?" called Luna. "This guy needs a shot of Reglan. You have any? He's 3.7 kilos."

"Hang on," came a voice.

Kelly appeared, wiry and sunburned, her sandy hair just turning grey. She gave the bird the injection while Luna held him gently but firmly. "Listen," said Kelly. "I know you said a week, but you can stay with me as long as you want." She grinned. "And not just because you rock at pelicans."

At two o'clock Luna collapsed onto one of the Adirondack chairs behind the wildlife center. She tossed her baseball cap onto a nearby table, put her feet up, and closed her eyes. Immediately her thoughts turned to Adam, and to where she would go from here.

"Luna."

She opened her eyes to find Kelly standing next to a man. He was brown-haired, ponytailed, and wore horn-rimmed glasses, shorts and a t-shirt. He stood with his hands in his pockets, slouching and looking noncommittal. "This is Ned," said Kelly. "Potential volunteer. Can you quiz him? I got a beached dolphin on Vero."

She disappeared, and Luna gestured to the chair beside her. Ned sat down on the edge, glanced at her briefly, then stared at the palm tree in the yard. Luna waited, but the man stayed silent. "Have you worked with wildlife before?" she asked finally.

"No."

"Why now?"

"Because." The man frowned at her. "You look familiar," he said.

"I'm not."

"Is that your roadster out there in the parking lot? I thought animal people didn't have any money."

Luna gave an exasperated sigh. "Why do you want to work here?"

The man grimaced, as if he were about to do something he truly didn't want to do. "Because wildlife are valuable…and free…and filled with free…things…and they have wild lives…and…"

Luna held up a restraining hand. Ned removed his glasses and rubbed his eyes.

"Is this a condition of your parole?" she asked.

"No."

"Too many speeding tickets? Part of your community service?"

"No."

"You work for one of those high-tech computer companies that are all touchy-feely and have gyms and day-care centers and don't want their staff to be a bunch of nerds with no social skills, so they require everyone to do volunteer work."

Ned pointed an affirmative index finger at her. "Listen," he said. "I'm not exactly an animal person. I mean, I have nothing against them. Except for birds. I don't like birds."

"Then why volunteer here?"

"Because I drew the short straw!"

He gave her a pained look. "I'm not criticizing you or anything," he added, "but there's this really nasty smell coming from your pants."

She grinned. "You seriously have no social skills, do you?"

"None," said Ned, shaking his head. "Sorry. I have none."

"Welcome to the world of wildlife," said Luna. "We're the poster group for people with no social skills."

The new volunteer spent the afternoon industriously cleaning empty aquariums, having preferred it to unpacking the just-delivered boxes of live mealworms. "Live worms?" he'd asked, in a tone that made her respond, "Never mind," and lead him to the outdoor shower with the hose attachment.

Later that afternoon she pulled a ringing phone from her pocket. "Harper?" she said, after glancing at the screen.

"New arrival," came a woman's voice, clearly angry. "It's Mars."

"What?" said Luna.

"He's here at the zoo. Just came in. Adam sent a crew to Celia's, and they took him."

"What do you mean, 'they took him?' They can't just…"

"Two lawyers, two handlers. They timed it so Celia was the only one there. You know Celia, she practically had a breakdown."

"Is he all right?"

"Mars?" asked Harper, and snorted. "He ripped them up. Nearly took the eye out of one of them."

Luna hurried out of the building. "But why did Adam take him?" she asked, her fingers digging into her palms. "What's he going to do with him?"

"Evidently he's your welcome home present. I gotta go. Do something!"

Luna disconnected, and a bead of sweat trickled down her back. She tapped her phone again. After three rings, there was a faint click.

"Luna."

"Adam!"

"I'm in a meeting, can you give me a second? I'll be right with you."

His voice was low and modulated, unlike the staccato bark he used when things weren't going his way. This was the voice he used to soothe, to reassure, to convey the illusion that even though he held all the cards, he was still, somehow, on your side.

"Luna?"

"What have you done?"

"I brought Mars down to see you. I thought it would make you happy."

"Are you kidding?"

"Babe — you've been gone almost a week. I gave you your space, just like you asked. I haven't called you, I sent you your things. How else can I show you I'm sorry? It was a miscommunication. A system fail. You know I'd never lock a door on you." He paused. "And I'm still completely in the dark, I have no idea why you would…"

"You took Mars," she interrupted, gripping her phone.

"I took him for you. He's right here. Just come home, and you can see him."

Luna stood immobile, her eyes on the sliver of ocean just visible beyond the sandy yard.

"Luna?"

"I'll be there tomorrow morning."

"Oh, that's great," said Adam warmly. "I'm so glad. I can't wait to see you."

Luna hung up, a fiery ember in the pit of her stomach. Her expression darkened. She spun toward the clinic and nearly banged into Ned, who took a quick step backward.

"I need a big car!" she snapped.

"I, uh…I have a big car," he stammered.

• • •

At midnight Ned eased to a stop by the southeast entrance of Cielo Azul. He had no idea why he had agreed to meet this crazy animal person outside the compound of Florida's wealthiest financier, any more than he knew why he had agreed to volunteer at a home for wounded iguanas, or wherever he'd spent his whole stupid afternoon.

"Neddy, honey," his mother had said during her last visit. "I don't want to keep sounding like a broken record, but you're twenty-six. You need to get out more."

Maybe after he told her about this little foray, she'd leave him alone.

He rested his arm on his car's open window. Beyond the property's eight-foot wall, the roofline of a huge Spanish-style villa seemed to ripple in the moonlight. Adam Matheson was in his mid-fifties, charismatic, wildly successful, and, so it was said, very much a dick. Ned puzzled over the connection between the famous financier and the smelly young woman who had ranted for twenty minutes about plastic six-pack holders and their effect on marine life.

"Ned! Ned!"

Luna and a second woman struggled toward him, each carrying a duffel bag and one end of an enormous covered box. As they placed the box on the ground, Luna regarded Ned's car with astonishment.

The classic old Cadillac convertible was impossibly long, sleek, and low. The forward-canted, stacked dual headlights made it look like it was in motion, even though it was parked. It rested by the curb like an elegantly grounded battleship, its dark blue paint pristine, its shining hubcaps encircled by spotless whitewalls, its massive front grille buffed to a high sheen.

"Wow!" she whispered. "What year?"

"1968 de Ville," Ned whispered back, relieved to see she'd changed her clothes. "472 cubic inch V-8 Turbo Hydra-Matic, 4-barrel carburetor with a ...."

"Would you two shut up about the fucking car?" hissed the other woman. "I've got exactly four minutes before all hell breaks loose! This is not going to fit through the door, can you put the top down?"

"But what's in there?"

The two women exchanged looks. "Top down," growled the woman. She was very tall and solid and wore a ferocious expression, so he opened the locks, flipped the switch, and the roof folded neatly into place. The women lifted the box onto the back seat, then tossed the two duffel bags onto the floor.

"Thank you, Harper," whispered Luna, giving the woman a tight hug. "I love you. I owe you."

"Damn straight you owe me," replied Harper, kissed her on the cheek, and returned to the compound. Luna slid onto the front seat beside Ned.

"Hit it," she ordered.

"Wait a minute," he said, frowning. "Did you just steal something? Because I know who lives in there — it's Adam Matheson, and he's a major big shot, so if…"

"Will you go?" she snapped. "And no sharp turns."

Ned crossed his arms, steeled himself, and gazed into her blazing blue eyes. "No. I'm not going anywhere until you tell me what's in that box."

The sound of an alarm pierced the night. Luna flinched, then seized his arm in an iron grip. Oh God, thought Ned. She's going to eat me.

Instead she loosened her grip, clasped her hands in prayer, and lowered her voice until it was ragged and husky. "Please, Ned — it's a living being in need of help! Please! I'm begging you!"

A police siren wailed. From within the crate came the sound of a heavy thud. Ned winced, and stepped on the gas.

• • •

The covered box sat innocently in a corner of Ned's living room.

He had continued to circle Key West long after it became clear that Luna had no plan. Silently he rehearsed questions, then rejected them as potential sources of conflict. I used to work for Adam Matheson, okay? she had finally blurted. And what's in that box does not belong to him.

He stood in his apartment a few feet from the box, daring himself to walk over and lift the cover. He watched Luna slide the plastic-wrapped contents of a duffel bag into the refrigerator, envisioning health inspectors arriving in the morning and wrapping the entire appliance with biohazard tape.

"This is nice!" she said, standing in the doorway and surveying the minimalist two-bedroom. "How long have you lived here?"

"What's in the box?" he replied. "And what did you just put in my refrigerator?"

"Can I use your bathroom?" she asked.

Ned watched the door close. Cursing his inability to bend women to his will, he went into his bedroom. When he returned, Luna looked up from the couch and smiled. He held up a freshly printed photograph of her in a silver evening gown and a million dollars' worth of emeralds, hand in hand with a handsome, tuxedoed man. Her smile disappeared.

"Bet you didn't get that job on Craigslist," he said.

Luna sighed. "It's not like I lied to you," she said. "I did work for him. And then I...you know. Married him."

Ned grimaced. "How old is that guy?"

"Listen," she said haltingly. "I can't...it's just that..."

She stopped, and a flush rose to her cheeks. Ned watched silently, unsure if she was about to burst into tears or demolish his apartment. She crossed the room, unzipped one of the duffel bags, and pulled on an elbow-length leather glove. "You'll understand when you see him," she said, as she knelt in front of the box and reached inside. "Don't worry, he's really gentle."

Ned's blood turned cold. Gracefully she rose, her glove gripped by the bear claw-sized talons of an enormous Bald Eagle. The bird spread its dark wings, turned its snowy head, and raked him with malevolent yellow eyes. The room spun, and Ned dropped to the floor.

When he regained consciousness, his head was cradled by a pillow and there was a glass of water by his side. He sat up and gazed at the slight, curly-haired woman wearing cargo pants and a t-shirt, a silver bead on a leather cord hanging from her neck. As she rested her cheek against the razor-sharp beak of a bird the size of a St. Bernard, her husky half-whisper sent a pang through his heart. "It's okay," she told the eagle. "It'll be all right."

Delicately she stroked the massive creature's chest feathers. "Ned," she said. "I need to take him to a safe place. Can you get us out of here?"

Holy shit, he thought. I'm heading for a road trip with Adam Matheson's wife and her stolen pterodactyl.

CHAPTER 2

Adam dove into the turquoise depths of his Olympic-sized swimming pool. For the briefest of seconds he was still, then he exploded into motion.

For a full 50 meters he swam with mechanical precision, every toned muscle, every measured breath propelling him forward until his fingers reached the far end of the pool. He stood, breathing hard, then turned and rested his arms on the cool surface of the tiles he commissioned and had flown in from Mykonos.

Stars shone in the night sky. His house gave off a warm glow. Once again he heard a crash, splintering wood, and a hailstorm of glass, all lodged in his head like an unwanted song.

Jay's party was six nights ago, though it felt like six years. You can have it annulled, she said. He had watched her through his office window as she paced back and forth across the sun room. The phone call shouldn't have lasted that long; had the deal not been so complex, none of this would have happened.

He remembered it as a fever dream. The wave of glass rose, crested, and fell, and Luna emerged with her diaphanous gown swirling around her like sea foam. Her steady stride quickened until it matched the shrieks of the burglar alarm. As she passed the office, she met his eyes.

Roland appeared by his side, and saw her expression of incredulous fury. What the fuck, he rumbled, as she disappeared beneath the stucco archway. From the driveway came the sound of her car purring to life and skidding away.

It had taken every ounce of Adam's self-control not to sprint after her, to keep the staggered expression from his face. Call Enrico, he said to Roland.

Enrico had followed the tracking device beneath her front bumper to a palm tree-lined community of small, brightly painted houses. Eventually he pulled over, parked, raised his phone, and snapped a series of photos: a lavender house with a front porch, a mailbox with "1725" in large black type, an old grey Subaru parked outside the garage. Squeezed beside the Subaru was a bright red quarter-million dollar Tesla Roadster, three awestruck teenagers peering into its windows.

Enrico texted the photos, followed by some basic information: Kelly McPhee. 1725 Hobart Avenue. Age 37. Single. Director of Starfish Key Wildlife Center, Key West. Ten minutes later, he sent a video.

Adam ran a hand through his wet hair. Another lap, he commanded himself.

Instead he walked up the pool stairs, dried his hands on a towel, and reached for the cell phone resting on a table. Three taps, and the video appeared.

Luna stood on the porch of the lavender house. The teenagers looked up from the car. When she raised her hand, they waved in return. She walked past them and stood at the curb, barefoot, wearing track shorts and a faded T-shirt. She spotted and marched toward the camera, and the picture tilted.

"Enrico," came her voice.

"Hello, Mrs. Mathe…"

"Give me the phone!"

Once again the picture tilted. Adam sank slowly onto a pool chair, eyes fastened to the screen. Luna's face appeared. "Adam?" she said, managing to look rattled and defiant at the same time. "I'm staying with Kelly for a week. If you don't give me some space, I swear to God I'll disappear. And this time, it'll be for good."

The picture tilted, a street light appeared, and Luna walked back into the house. The video ended, and Adam placed the phone back on the table and stared into the pool. I don't make mistakes, he told himself again, but locking that door was a big one.

He thought back to the following morning, after she parked the Tesla in the garage and she and Kelly drove away in Kelly's car. Enrico had installed a tiny wireless camera in a bougainvillea across the street, and the image of the lavender house appeared on one of the monitors in the surveillance room of Cielo Azul. The same image appeared on Adam's phone and computer, and he received an alert whenever the motion sensors picked up activity. One of Enrico's colleagues, driving a battered Hyundai, kept an eye on Starfish Key. She's doing yoga in the Seychelles, Adam told those who asked.

She had emailed him from the wildlife center, requesting a small list of supplies: her phone, some toiletries, shorts, pants, a few t-shirts, sneakers, and her silver necklace. He had them delivered, along with a beautiful vase of flowers. No note. No more mistakes, he thought. Each night he watched the two women sit on the porch, their feet on the railing, drinking beer from bottles.

A week, she said, and he tried. He made it to six days, then he dispatched the Gulfstream to Pennsylvania. All he wanted to do was prove to her that he knew her better than anyone; that while other men might show their regret with jewelry or cars or houses, he alone knew the way to her heart was through the bird whose small downy feather she kept inside a silver bead on a leather cord. He would present the bird to her. She would understand.

And if she didn't understand, well, then, he'd have the bird.

But she *had* understood. It worked. She agreed to come home. He had been so triumphant he'd told Enrico we're done, shut it down. Wait a day, then retrieve the equipment.

When the alarm went off two hours ago he was in his office, clearing his schedule so he could welcome her home properly. Enrico rebooted the camera and the lavender house appeared on Adam's computer screen, the garage door open, the Tesla gone. Later they found it parked at a public beach half a mile away.

Adam rose, jaw clenched, and stood at the edge the pool. He launched himself forward, thinking, the eagle. The fucking eagle.

• • •

Roland Edwards was not happy.

It was 1:00 in the morning and the Monroe County police were still asking the same questions. Harper Napinski sat in her office chair, one ankle resting on the opposite knee, regarding the officer with the death's-head stare of a linebacker. She was built like a linebacker, too, which had earned Roland's grudging respect, as did the way she could sling a Burmese python over her shoulder and lug it to wherever she needed it to go.

"And why was the back door unlocked, again?" asked Officer Peters.

"I told you why it was unlocked ten minutes ago," replied Harper, "just like I told you why it was unlocked ten minutes before that. I came in late to give one of the gibbons some meds, and it didn't occur to me that there might be an eaglenapper in the neighborhood." She narrowed her eyes at the cops. "I'm beginning to think you don't believe what I'm telling you."

"No no," said Officer Peters quickly. "This is standard procedure. Just one more time? The camera was off because …?"

"Because when I came in it was flickering, and I turned it off thinking it would reboot. Once again: I work with animals, not electronic equipment. I turned the camera off, I checked around, I turned the camera back on, and I texted Gus, who works with the electronic equipment. I didn't see the need to hurry, because I knew Carlos was somewhere nearby."

Carlos, the night guard, rested his head against the back of the chair and closed his eyes. "I was checking the tennis courts," he sighed. "It was not me who took the eagle."

"Gentlemen," said Harper, rising and holding out her formidable arms. "Would you like to frisk me to see if I am concealing an eagle on my person? If not, I have to be back here by seven, so I'm ready to call it a night."

This is bullshit, thought Roland.

He left the room and stepped back into the night. He took off his jacket, loosened his tie, and walked toward the pool. In the distance, he could hear the sound of thrashing water.

Harper's flat, virulent gaze had triggered a blaze of images and a series of audio flashbacks: the whir of automatic cameras, the roar of a stadium gone wild, the crunch of a career-ending tackle, and the voice of a man he'd seen on the cover of *Time* magazine.

His cell phone had rung when he was still on crutches. I've followed you since you were a freshman at Ohio State, Adam Matheson said. I'm really sorry about that tackle. I'm making a lot of money, and they say I need to hire more security. Would you consider working for me?

Fuck you, Roland had snapped, and hung up.

Eleven months later it was clear no miracle would return him to the field. Two hours after his final orthopedist appointment he'd been sitting on a park bench in Chicago, staring bitterly at Lake Michigan and swigging a pint of Jack Daniels, when his phone rang.

I was wondering if you might reconsider, said Adam Matheson.

There had been money, gadgets, custom-made suits, and private jets; training in weapons, boxing, martial arts, and evasive driving; and late nights on the road drinking high-priced Scotch with a man who became more famous by the year, but never lost his teenaged-boy fascination with his football hero. This is my friend Roland Edwards, he said to captains of industry and owners of teams. Roland Edwards! they beamed, and shook his hand.

Come on, baby, said Lyllis, as she curled against him. It's not your dream. But it's a damned sight better than most folks get.

I know, he replied. But whenever he heard a sportscaster's voice, his hand slid toward his left knee and his latent rage returned. It flared during the playoffs, or when he spotted another gridiron biography. Eventually he developed a sense of gratitude, but its focus did not please Lyllis: he was grateful there were so many people in the world who hated Adam Matheson.

There were stockholders blindsided by hostile takeovers, insurance policyholders left dangling when the company moved out of state, homeowners whose wells were contaminated by the new factory. The list went on and Adam, a fixture on the social circuit and usually pleased to see his picture in the media, was not difficult to track. Roland's earliest encounter was with three men who were waiting in the dark outside a restaurant in New York City.

Adam had bought the manufacturing plant where they worked, fired everyone, and was in the process of selling off the pieces. The men, in their 30s and burly, were slightly inebriated and intent on confronting Adam with his crimes. Roland had seen his boss defuse far more volatile situations; he wouldn't have been surprised had Adam invited them into the restaurant and bought them six or eight rounds of the best Scotch in the house. Instead, Adam taunted them until one threw the first punch.

How did that make you feel? he asked, sitting next to Roland in the back of the limousine, after Roland beat all three men so viciously that the ambulances called ahead to check the hospitals' blood supply.

Roland held an ice bag to his split lip and blackened eye, fully expecting to be fired. It made me feel damned fine, he answered belligerently.

Good, said Adam.

Fourteen years later Roland stood next to Adam Matheson's pool. He watched as his boss climbed the stairs, water streaming from his taut body.

"Cops are leaving," said Roland. They'll be in touch."

"Anything?"

"No."

Over six feet himself, Adam had to tilt his head back to meet Roland's eyes. Roland noted the jut to Adam's chin, the rigid set to his fingers even as he gestured downward with a calming motion.

"All I want to do is talk to her," he said. "So find her."

"Got it," said Roland.

• • •

Squinting in the morning light, Ned let himself into his building and entered his apartment. He found the giant box empty and the guest room door slightly ajar. Cautiously peering through the gap, he saw the enormous eagle standing on a giant perch.

"I thought while you were getting used to each other it would be better to have a door in between you," said Luna, emerging and closing it behind her. Although he had no intention of getting used to a predator he knew could take him down without ruffling a feather, Ned found himself nodding in agreement. "I put a plastic tablecloth on the floor," she added, "so you won't have to worry about your rug."

Ned hadn't even considered his rug. "Listen," he said. "Remember last night I told you the less I knew, the better? Can you just tell me who the eagle belongs to? And, like, what the penalty might be for stealing it?"

"'It?'" repeated Luna, with an offended lift of one eyebrow. "His name is Mars."

"Sorry. Stealing *him*."

"He doesn't belong to anyone. He lives at the Western Pennsylvania Wildlife Center. That's his home. He has a mate. He can't be released."

"Why not? He looks awfully healthy to me."

"Because some shitty guy took him from his nest and raised him in captivity. He doesn't know how to be a wild bird."

"And why would your husband ..."

Luna frowned, and Ned stopped. "Never mind," he said. "Like I said — I'll get you to Immokalee, but that's as far as I can go."

"That's fine," she said earnestly. "I really appreciate it. Thank you."

Ned pulled a plastic bag from the pocket of his cargo shorts. Earlier she had put down her coffee cup, grabbed her wallet, and announced she would be right back. He asked if she would be taking the bird with her; when she said no, he quizzed her and bolted from the apartment.

"Here," he said, pulling out two burner phones and some change.

"Thank you," said Luna, and held up one of the phones. "This one's for Harper. We'll leave it someplace for her before we get on the highway."

"Why?"

"I don't want her calling me from her phone. I'm sure Adam has it tapped."

"But that's not legal."

Luna gave him a look of amusement, then pulled her own phone from her pocket. "You're an IT guy," she said. "Can you transfer all the numbers from my old phone to my new one?"

"Because he's listening in on you, too?"

"Not only that. He tracks me through it."

"Do you think he's tracking you right now?"

"Nope," she said, smirking. "Because when I don't want him to track me, I turn it off. He put a tracker in my car, too, so I left it at the beach."

Ned took both phones and disappeared into his bedroom. When he returned Luna had cleaned his kitchen, made a fresh pot of coffee, and was sitting on his couch, intently scanning *Gaming World* magazine. The eagle sat majestically on its perch in the box.

"Great, thanks," she said, when he handed her the phones. "I put Mars in his crate, so we're ready whenever you are."

"His 'crate.' That's what you call it?"

"Yes. See, the front has that metal grate, and there are little windows on the sides, but the rest is hard plastic. If the whole thing were made of metal, he could hurt himself or damage his feathers. And I cover him with that dark sheet when we're moving, so he doesn't get freaked out by the things passing by."

"Hmm," said Ned, filing it all away for future reference. The metal screen door, he noted, had a squeeze spring which could only be opened from the outside. He's not really that scary, he thought, and sidled forward for a closer look.

"You might not want to..." Luna began, as he crouched down and peered inside. There was a rush of feathers, a huge and sinewy yellow foot hit the door with a heavy clang, and what looked like four curved black bayonets burst through the metal grid not far from Ned's face. He scrambled backward as Luna shot off the couch, grabbed the dark sheet, and draped it over the crate.

"Sorry!" she cried.

"'Don't worry, Ned!'" he quoted, his voice filled with outrage. "'He's really gentle!'"

"He is! He just..."

"He just what?"

"He just doesn't like men!"

"He doesn't like *men?* What do you mean, he..."

"Let's go into the kitchen," she said, grabbing her new phone and beckoning energetically. Once there she faced him, her voice low and urgent. "Ned — it's not his fault! I promise you I'll keep him covered all the way to Immokalee, if you can just get us there. Okay? Do you need more coffee?"

For a moment he was silent, struck dumb by her beauty, then he pulled himself together. "Do I look like I need more coffee?" he demanded.

"Let me show you," she said determinedly, furiously typing on her phone. "Look." The text was addressed to "Group."

777-388-0021 Everyone, I need help. This is my new number, PLEASE DELETE last one from your phones/computers. Heading north. Need a bed & a flight cage, or as close as you can get. Details on arrival.

"They're rehabbers," said Luna. "Rehabilitators. They're my friends. They take care of injured and orphaned wildlife, like I did at Starfish Key. They'll help me."

"Help you what?"

"Get where I'm going. I can stay with Warren in Immokalee, but that's just my first stop."

"Where's your last stop?"

"Not sure."

"Doesn't your husband know your rehabber friends? How do you know he won't hack their phones?"

"He doesn't know them. I only know them through the internet. Except for Warren and everyone at Celia's, I've never met any of them in person."

"You're like gamers."

"I guess we are."

A silent minute passed, and then another. Luna stood holding her phone, staring intently out the window, agitation rolling off her in hot waves. Ned knew he should say something comforting, but for the life of him he couldn't think what.

"They're not answering me," she said finally, her voice increasingly hard-edged. "Maybe they're busy. It doesn't matter, I can do it alone. I don't need anyone's help."

She narrowed her eyes, as if daring him to contradict her. Ned quickly looked away and into the living room, where her huge and bloodthirsty bird stood inside its sheet-covered crate. Luna followed his gaze and once again her expression transformed, her icy eyes infusing with color, her clenched jaw softening, her lips rising into a small, devoted smile. Ned watched this facial sleight of hand with fascination, unable to fathom how a creature so terrifying could provoke it.

Her phone pinged.

It pinged again, and kept pinging. She grinned with relief, and held the phone out so he could read along with her.

> squirrelsrus@gmail.com Sending you directions to my place. Let me know, or just show up.
>
> bearwithme@hotmail.com What did you do this time? Is it juicy? Door's always open.
>
> meadowlark@outlook.com You need supplies? Will send interns to meet you.
>
> carnivorous@gmail.com Mi casa es su casa, babe. Bring wine.
>
> blossompossum21@att.net No flight cage, but can clear out the bigger possum run. Tell me when.
>
> chiroptera@gmail.com Fuck you, Luna, you bitch! Everyone knows you do jack shit for wildlife!

"Oh, that's just Esther, sometimes she hits the bourbon," Luna chortled. "She does that to everyone! She's always really sorry when she sobers up!"

"But ..."

"I still haven't heard from Warren," she said, looking concerned. "The thing is, if he doesn't have anyone in rehab sometimes he goes into Big Cypress without his phone."

"You mean the swamp? Aren't there alligators in there?"

"He's a panther rehabber. He likes alligators."

"Ha ha," laughed Ned, the sound more high-pitched than he'd intended. "Very funny."

"No, really. He lives on the edge of the Panther Refuge, and he knows more about them than just about anyone on the planet."

"Wait a minute! Panthers are mountain lions, right? Cougars? Same thing? He has them walking around his house?"

"Of course they're not walking around his house! They're wild animals!"

"Oh, wild animals! You mean like the one standing in my living room?"

The phone pinged. "Warren!" she sighed with relief, and turned the phone toward Ned.

PRIVATE CALLER Come on up. Got one kitty and a fine collection of dildos to show you.

"No," said Ned, holding up a restraining hand. "Allow me. 'Don't worry, Ned, it's not what you think.'"

Luna gazed at him in surprise, then slowly she smiled; a big, genuine smile that lit up her face, flashed through her eyes, and sent shafts of light, he was sure, beaming into the dark corners of every swamp in Florida. Ned gazed back at her, thinking, no wonder the guy took her eagle.

"That's exactly right, Ned," said Luna. "It's not what you think."

CHAPTER 3

F ederal Wildlife Officer Erik Gunderman stood on the porch of his
cabin, holding a cup of coffee and watching the mist rise from the
Arthur R. Marshall Loxahatchee National Wildlife Refuge. He had
done the same thing nearly every morning for the past eight years.

The Loxahatchee was all that was left of the northernmost area of
the Florida Everglades. It comprised almost 150,000 acres of wet
prairies, sawgrass ridges, tree islands, and cypress swamps. It teemed
with white water lily and floating heart, least bittern and great egret,
river otter and bobcat, alligator and cottonmouth; all just a tiny
fraction of the species trying to co-exist in what little remained of the
once-vast River of Grass.

Gunderman protected it from poachers, smugglers, illegal traffickers,
polluters, and visitors who didn't follow the rules. He gave education
programs, rescued capsized boaters, and assisted staff biologists battling
invasive species. He received awards and citations for the skill with
which he dealt with people awed by the refuge, those unwillingly
dragged into it by their families, and those who tried their best to
plunder it. Surrounded by highways and houses, airports and strip
malls, the refuge — like every other refuge in the country — was
unique and precious. Gunderman grimaced as his cell phone disturbed
his morning reverie.

"Gunderman!" said his Regional Supervisor, who instructed him
to leave his post immediately and drive south to the estate of the
financier Adam Matheson.

"Sir?" said Gunderman, puzzled.

"Just get going. Sinclair will cover for you. I'll call you back in half
an hour, when you're on the road."

Gunderman put on his olive slacks and tan dress shirt, poured the rest of his coffee into a thermos, and lifted his broad-brimmed ranger's hat from its hook. There were six National Wildlife Refuges closer to Key West; why he was being asked to drive four hours to the house of this infamous environmental hit man was a mystery.

By the time he drove through the gates of Cielo Azul, Gunderman's mouth was set in a tight line. Two local Florida Fish and Wildlife Conservation Commission Officers waited for him beside their SUV, both clad in tan slacks, shirts, and caps. He parked his vehicle, slid out, and shook their hands.

"We'll file our state report but you can take the lead, since it's a Federal case," said Hayes, the older officer. "It's just more billionaire bullshit. Whatever he's actually done, he'll buy his way out of it."

"Jesus, look at this place," said Bianchi, the younger officer, as the three of them followed a suited man down a hallway lined with paintings and covered with Oriental rugs. "I gotta tell you — I'm just hoping Roland Edwards is in there."

Adam looked up from his mahogany desk as the three officers entered his office. "Gentlemen," he said, rose, and offered his hand. "My associate, Roland Edwards," he added, as Bianchi tried and failed to conceal his delight.

"Mr. Matheson," said Gunderman, his expression deadpan. "According to Elias Jenkins of the Western Pennsylvania Wildlife Center, yesterday afternoon four of your employees removed a Bald Eagle from their facility. Is this true?"

"Yes, that's true," said Adam. "Would all of you care to sit down?"

"No, thank you," answered Gunderman. "Removing a a protected bird from a permitted facility is a violation of both the Migratory Bird Treaty Act and the Eagle Protection Act. The penalties are two years in jail and fines of up to $250,000."

"Officer… Gunderman, is it?" said Adam, peering at Gunderman's name tag and looking concerned. "I'm afraid there's been a misunderstanding. My wife has an emotional attachment to an eagle in Pennsylvania, so I had her eagle brought here. I wasn't aware that I needed special papers, considering I have a state-of-the-art zoo run by professionals."

"Mr. Matheson," said Gunderman evenly. "This is not your wife's eagle. All American wildlife belong to the National Public Trust. Licensed facilities can host them, but only with proper permits. You have broken the law. Ignorance of it is no excuse."

Adam glanced at the two state conservation officers. Both were listening attentively, the younger one sneaking starstruck looks at Roland. "I see," said Adam. "I truly regret the situation, and I'll do whatever it takes to remedy it. I would be more than willing to return the eagle, but as of last night, it's no longer here."

Gunderman maintained his impassive expression, but the state wildlife officers were not as skillful. "No longer here," Gunderman repeated. "Then, where is it?"

There was a knock on the door, and the suited man ushered two uniformed police officers into the room. "Good morning, Mr. Matheson, Mr. Edwards," said the shorter of the two. "I'm Officer Nichols. I know you usually deal with Officer Reinhardt, but he's away." He offered his hand to the three wildlife officers and introduced his partner. "Monroe County Police Department," he said. "I expect we'll be working together on this."

Roland watched them from behind his sunglasses. "To answer your question, Officer Gunderman," said Adam, "I have no idea where the eagle is. When it was taken last night, I was in my office. The police arrived almost immediately."

Police officer Nichols spoke up. "Mr. Matheson, last night Officer Peters found your wife's name, a phone number, and "Starfish Key" written on a pad in your zoo's office. We made a routine call this morning, and spoke to Starfish Key Wildlife Center's director Kelly McPhee. She said your wife stayed with her for six days."

"That's right," said Adam.

"She said Ms. Burke left her house last evening, and… "

"Mrs. Matheson."

Officer Nichols paused. "Ms. McPhee referred to her as Luna Burke. That's the name on her driver's license. Is her legal name Luna Matheson?"

But I don't want to change my name, she had said.

Her reaction both puzzled and annoyed him. All he had to do was glance in a woman's general direction, and she started trying to figure out how to change her name to Matheson. It would make it easier for me to transfer funds into your account, he replied.

I don't need funds, she answered.

"You can refer to her as Mrs. Matheson."

"All right," said Officer Nichols. "Ms. McPhee said she didn't know anything about a missing eagle. She said Mrs. Matheson left her house last evening. She didn't say where she was going, and Ms. McPhee hasn't heard from her."

"That doesn't surprise me," said Adam. "You'd have to know my wife. But I spoke to Mrs. Matheson late yesterday afternoon, and she said she was coming home this morning. Are you telling me something may have happened to her?"

The room grew quiet. "I'm not saying that, though it's a possibility," said Nichols. He looked uncomfortably at the floor, and then back at Adam. "I'm sorry if this is a sensitive subject, but according to Ms. McPhee, Mrs. Matheson said the two of you were divorcing and she planned to move out of state."

"Really," said Adam.

"Are you and Mrs. Matheson in the process of a divorce?"

Adam regarded the five men standing before him. "Officers," he said, "Mrs. Matheson and I have only been married for six months." He paused, then smiled. "That would be pretty fast, even for me."

The police and the state wildlife officers hesitated. Every environmental crime in the book, thought Gunderman, not to mention accusations of securities fraud and insider trading, and all he gets are fines and slaps on the wrist. He watched Nichols and Bianchi smile back at him. And that, thought Gunderman, is how you make a billion dollars.

"Do I have this straight?" asked Gunderman. "Yesterday you removed a federally protected bird from a licensed wildlife facility. Last night the bird — as well as your wife, who has an emotional attachment to the bird — both disappeared. Your wife, who may or may not be in the process of divorcing you. Is that correct?"

"If Mrs. Matheson is in the process of divorcing me, she hasn't let me in on it yet," said Adam. "As for the eagle, I made a mistake. Tell me what I can do to rectify it. I'll write you a check for the fine today. What about a reward? A million dollars for its safe return?"

The state wildlife officers looked alarmed. "Don't do that," said the older one. "Every zoo and wildlife sanctuary in the country will get hit. You'll end up with eight thousand Bald Eagles, and I guarantee none of them will be yours."

"Do you think your wife took the eagle?" asked Gunderman.

"I'll know when I talk to her," said Adam.

"What's your educated guess?"

"We're talking about my wife. Legally, I'm not required to give you an educated guess."

Gunderman pulled out a card. "My office will be in touch with you regarding your violation," he said, handing it to Adam. "May I speak with your zookeeper?"

The door opened, and the suited man appeared. "Mr. Matheson," he said. "You have a meeting."

"Thank you, Lloyd," replied Adam. "Will you take these gentlemen to see Harper? Officers, let me know if there's anything else you need."

The men nodded, filed from the room, and Lloyd closed the door behind them.

"That one with the Smoky the Bear hat is a pain in the ass," said Adam.

"They're all a pain in the ass," said Roland, and tucked his sunglasses into his pocket.

• • •

Ned eased the Cadillac onto the highway. His passenger sat beside him, clad in cotton pants, a T-shirt, and sneakers, her curly hair framing a large pair of sunglasses. Her bodyguard perched in the covered crate on the back seat.

Luna looked approvingly around the car. "What do they call this color?" she asked, gesturing to the hood. "All these classic car colors have cool names."

"Spectre Blue Firemist," he answered.

"See? I knew it!"

She removed her shoes and crossed her legs. He waited for her to make the first conversational move, but she continued to gaze silently out the window. Normally this would be the answer to his prayers, but after a half an hour he began to wonder if he should take a stab at communicating. After all, he certainly wasn't going to be in this position ever again. The problem, he knew, was that he needed to start off with something interesting, unusual, and deep, otherwise she would think he was an idiot.

"So, what's it like being married to a billionaire?" he asked, then immediately cursed himself out.

She regarded him with an inscrutable expression, and he forced his eyes back to the road. "Never mind," he said.

"Did you ever go to a county fair when you were a kid?" she asked. "At first you're blown away by how much stuff there is to do and see and buy. But then everything becomes a blur, and then you start feeling sick, and then you want to leave."

Ned nodded. "Got it." She turned toward him, rested her head against the seat, and promptly fell asleep.

Ned drove in silence, occasionally turning on the radio when he grew tired of questioning his own sanity. He pondered the connection between Warren and dildos, concluding that if this person did, in fact, collect plastic penises, it would hardly be the strangest thing that had happened to him in the last two days.

Three and a half hours later he passed the sign for the Florida Panther National Wildlife Refuge, slowed down, and found an unmarked break in the thick vegetation. You're driving toward lions, he thought, with a meat-eating bird in your car. This sequence is flawed.

Luna opened her eyes. She gazed groggily out the window, and regarded Ned with surprise. "We're here already?" she asked. "I'm sorry, I didn't mean to sleep the whole way!"

Ned pulled up beside an old cabin surrounded by a riot of plant life. Pale lime to forest green, slender stalks to jagged fronds, they all seemed to be trying to elbow each other out of the way; no doubt wanting to be the first to engulf the unsuspecting blue Cadillac which had just blundered into their midst.

"Look how beautiful!" said Luna, when she emerged from the car. "Look at the orchids. Look at that cypress over there."

Ned regarded the bursting vegetation. He turned slowly, head tilted backward, and suddenly found himself staring into the penetrating dark eyes of a man with shaggy grey hair and a full grey beard.

"Gah!" cried Ned, heart thudding.

Luna hurried over and threw her arms around the man, who regarded Ned with amusement. "I keep telling you not to do that," she said with mock severity, as he encircled her with a tanned, muscular arm and kissed her forehead.

"Sorry, man," he said lazily, and extended his hand.

"It's okay," said Ned, impressed by his grip and fitness, estimating he had to be in his mid-sixties. "She warned me. I just...y'know. Didn't see you coming."

"No one ever does," drawled Warren.

Luna opened the Cadillac's door and reached for the covered crate. "Sweet," said Warren, eyeing the car. "So, what have you got?"

"Mars," said Luna.

"Mars!" he repeated, mystified.

Luna's crystal eyes filled and her lower lip trembled. Ned was so thrown by her gust of emotion that his gaze returned to Warren, to see how he would react. Warren stiffened, then gave him a look of such intensity that Ned's stomach plummeted.

"What'd you do to her, man?" he demanded, his voice an octave lower.

"Ned was a lifesaver," said Luna, regrouping. "I owe him big-time. Please, Ned, don't go yet. That was a long drive — stay the night! At least stay for dinner." She addressed Warren. "Right?"

"Oh, yeah, sure," said Warren, appeased. "Come on. Let's get the birdie out, then we'll all have a beer."

Ned's heart slowed as he watched them pull the crate from the car. The dark sheet slipped and revealed a side window. Behind it hovered a cold yellow eye and a great hooked beak.

"Go on inside," called Warren, as they disappeared into the underbrush. "We'll be five minutes."

• • •

Harper stood before an ornate water trough with a hose, the head of a Bactrian camel resting on her shoulder. Absently she scratched the camel's chin, wondering how long she'd be keeping her current job.

I don't want to be a reporter, she had told her father. I want to work with animals.

That's not a profession, replied her father, the managing editor of The St. Louis Post-Dispatch.

Harper had grinned as she drove north on the Pacific Coast highway, her degree in Animal Biology from UC Davis tucked into the side pocket of a battered suitcase. She had loved her job at the wildlife rehabilitation center in Alaska, loved the crystalline winters, the exuberant explosion of life in the spring and summer, and the palpable restlessness of the migratory wildlife just before the leaves began to turn.

That's called *Zugunruhe*, said her caribou biologist friend, and it's why you won't stay in Alaska.

Three years later Luna called, told her she'd married her boss, and asked if Harper would move to Florida and replace her as Adam Matheson's zookeeper. Harper found the offer irresistible for two reasons: it would allow her to give in to her pent-up *Zugunruhe*, and it would get her closer to her goal, which was to study the difference in communication patterns between Spinner and Bottlenose Dolphins.

Harper's left pocket fluttered. She eased the camel's head off her shoulder and moved to his other side, effectively placing his body between her and the camera installed on a palm tree. A few hours earlier she had stopped by a coffee shop and picked up the burner phone Luna left for her. Harper pulled the vibrating phone from her pocket and read the text.

777-388-0021 We're at Warren's. This is my new number. Thanks again! More later xx

Harper glanced at the time, pocketed the phone, and headed toward a long building ringed by azaleas. Once inside she passed the Honduran Curly Hair, the Brazilian Black, the Green Bottle Blue, and the Chilean Rose Hair, then stopped at the Mexican Red Knee. She reached in, carefully picked her up, and placed her on her open palm. Most tarantulas didn't like to be handled, but this Red Knee was a honey.

Harper was standing in front of her office window, her back to the door, when Adam and Roland entered. She waited until they were fairly close behind her and then turned around, the thick, hairy Red Knee calmly clasping the front of her shirt.

"Christ!" said Roland, slamming on the brakes.

"What can I do for you, gentlemen?" asked Harper.

The quintet of tarantulas, as well as the rest of the zoo, had been the brainchild of Adam's third wife. I don't know why he keeps the spiders, Luna had said, shrugging at Harper's initial query. Must be some macho thing. They scare the shit out of him *and* Roland.

Adam's outward composure didn't even waver. You have to hand it to him, thought Harper, if it's possible to hand anything to a soulless ecosystem serial killer.

"What are you doing?" he asked, in a conversational tone.

"Routine arachnid check-up," she replied.

"Where's Luna?"

"No idea."

"You called her phone yesterday afternoon at 4:23."

"I suspect the way you obtained that information is illegal."

"I suspect that really doesn't matter."

"Cut the shit, Harper," growled Roland. "Where is she?"

Harper cocked her head. "You know something, Roland?" she said. "You could take me down, but I'd hurt you on the way."

"And it would be your last act on earth."

"You have a bad attitude, Harper," said Adam, without changing his tone. "The only reason you're still here is Luna, so it's in your best interest to cooperate."

"Oh," she said, as if this were news to her. "In that case…"

"Did you help Luna take that eagle?"

Harper delicately touched the tarantula on her chest. A moment later, she leveled her assassin's eyes at Adam.

"No," she said.

• • •

Warren, Ned, and Luna sat in a row, beer cans in hand, facing four video screens. The cameras focused on a two-acre enclosure surrounded by a fourteen-foot heavy-gauge wire fence. From his cabin Warren could make the cameras swivel, lighten and darken, zoom in and out, and take videos. Four microphones picked up the sounds.

"There's a barrier on top of the fence, too," said Warren. "Fourteen feet is not much of a deterrent when you can jump eighteen from a standstill."

"There he is," said Luna, pointing to a lean form stretched on the ground, perfectly camouflaged by the sun-dappled soil. The panther flicked his long tail into the air, rolled onto his back, then curled onto his other side, yawning.

"Good kitty," said Warren.

The cabin was filled with outdoor gear, camera equipment, and stacks of books and outdoor magazines. Photographs of wild panthers hung haphazardly from the walls.

"What happened to him?" asked Ned.

"Hit by car, like most of 'em," said Warren. "Unless they get shot by those limp dicks who call themselves hunters. Panthers used to range all across North America. Forests, mountains, deserts. Now they're only in Canada and the west, down to Mexico. Florida panthers are a subspecies, you used to find 'em across nearly the entire southeast. Now? They're gone. The only breeding population of Florida panthers is right in this area."

He shook his head. "They're the toughest, most beautiful wild athletes this country has ever known. They're the embodiment of the free spirit of America. Settlers called them Ghost Cats. They're innocent killers …"

He gave a grunt of disgust. "And they're gone. Maybe a two hundred left in Florida. All thanks to the vermin hordes of fuckheads that come here so they can drain and build, like that scum-sucker prick husband of Luna's. Our girl here did not do her homework before making a major life decision."

Luna gave a rueful sigh. "I did not."

Ned looked back at the screen, anxious to absorb the comparative tranquility of the lone mountain lion, but it was no longer there. He scanned the monitors, startled when the cat's head suddenly appeared directly before the screen.

"Now you see him, now you don't," said Luna. "Just like Warren."

Warren turned up the volume, and a bass purr filled their ears. "You know why they can purr?" he asked Ned. "Because they have hyoid bones, which are tiny little bones that run from the back of their tongue to the base of their skull. When the smaller cats — say, bobcats, lynxes, ocelots, or panthers — want to purr they vibrate their larynx, and that makes the hyoid bones resonate. The hyoid bones of the big cats — lions, tigers, jaguars, or leopards — are reinforced with cartilage, so they can't resonate. But the cartilage makes their larynx flexible, so they can roar. Big cats can roar but not purr, and small cats can purr but not roar."

"Wow. I thought a small cat meant a house cat."

"A house cat is a *toy* cat."

"He has a nice sound," said Ned, cocking his head. "Like a '74 Barracuda 408 with a 6.51 V8."

Warren stared at him, and Ned froze. What had he done? He had insulted the panther man's panthers by comparing them to the machines that ran them over. He pictured a fist as it flew toward his face, felt the thump of his own unresponsive body as it hit the ground of the pen, heard himself renounce his atheism as the cougar approached him, licking its chops.

"No shit!" said Warren. "I always thought they sounded more like a '68 Mustang with a 4.71."

Ned exhaled. "Got them both on my phone," he said, pulling it from his pocket.

"I'll be right back," said Luna.

• • •

Luna passed the Cadillac, the pickup truck, and the clinic, then she slid through the underbrush and reached the slatted wooden enclosure. It was eight feet high, ten feet wide, and twenty feet long, built in a day by a crew of twelve after Warren fished an injured Wood Stork out of the swamp, paid for by a minuscule portion of her husband's ill-gotten gains. Mars preened himself from the top perch. The remains of a large catfish lay on the ground beside a rubber tub half-filled with water. Luna entered the enclosure and he called to her in his high-pitched giggle, a sound which always astonished those who had never actually heard a Bald Eagle's cry.

Luna whistled, matching his descending call note for note. She knew he wouldn't leave his perch after a meal, so she curled up on the ground nearby.

Babe, Adam had said. When you're in finance, you get cornered into doing things you don't want to do, things that violate your moral code. But I promise I'm listening to you. I'm pouring money into new technology. Don't you think I lie awake at night, obsessing about the world I'm leaving to my kids?

Bullshit, said Harper flatly. You want to know what he's pouring money into? Gutting the carbon tax proposal. Read *The Wall Street Journal.*

Luna walked back to the cabin, grabbed a beer from the refrigerator, and found Ned and Warren on the back porch grilling hamburgers. Conversation ceased as Warren stared at her.

"I'm gonna take that guy out," he said matter-of-factly.

Luna's eyes widened. "No, you're not," she said. "That would only make things worse."

"How would it make things worse? I'd say it would solve a hell of a lot of problems, and not just yours."

"I'm going to get Mars to a safe place. I'm going to get both eagles to a safe place."

"And you don't think he'll be looking for you?"

"Come on, Warren, he can replace me in a second! He can have any woman he wants. I told him he didn't have to give me any money."

Ned watched as Warren sighed and gave her a surprisingly tender look. "You don't get it, do you?" he asked her. He turned to Ned. "She doesn't get it."

Ned attempted to assume an expression of wisdom, but the whole situation reminded him of lying on the floor of a friend's apartment, smoking way too much hash, and watching a foreign film with no subtitles.

"It's not just him," said Warren. "Fish and Wildlife'll be after you, too. And state conservation. Not to mention the cops."

"Fish and what?" asked Ned.

"Wildlife," said Warren. "The government. Eagles are a protected species. You can't just help yourself to one."

"The government protects eagles? Then why don't you call them?"

"Because the government knows shit about eagles," said Warren. "Goddamned government's half the problem."

"Thanks to the government, it's against the law to touch these birds without a license," said Luna. "But some of the government wildlife people are great and some are not, which means I can't trust any of them. If they get a hold of Mars, there's no guarantee they'll reunite him with his mate. There's no guarantee they won't put him down for being a dangerous bird."

"A *dangerous bird*," repeated Ned pointedly.

"Where can you go where they won't catch you?" asked Warren.

"They won't catch me. And I'm going to Canada. To Hélène's."

"What?"

"Who's Hélène?" asked Ned.

The dining room table was piled with hamburgers, containers of deli food, and beer. Grace Slick's clarion voice emerged from a pair of speakers on either side of a turntable, slicing through the chorus of crickets on a warm summer night.

"Hélène de la Croix," said Warren, drawing the syllables into a seductively long growl: *Hel-ennnne de la Quaaaaaaa.* "She's a warrior queen. Gotta be 85 by now, and everyone's still scared shitless of her."

"She has an eagle sanctuary in Ontario," said Luna. "If I get Mars and his mate there, no one will be able to touch them. Not Adam, not the police, not the government. No one."

"But…" said Ned. "He's a billionaire. He can do whatever he wants. And the government — can't they extradite eagles?"

"Let me tell you about Hélène," she said, putting down her hamburger.

"Hang on," said Warren. "I'll get a visual." Ned watched him rise and disappear down the hallway, relieved to have something to focus on besides Luna's unnerving blue gaze. Warren returned and handed him a framed black and white photograph. Ned had once watched a documentary about iconic protest images, and now a series of them flashed through his mind.

Police dogs in Birmingham, Alabama. Kent State. The Stonewall Riots. Women marching down Fifth Avenue. And now, in his hands, the most powerful and celebrated photograph of the early environmental movement.

Thunderclouds loomed. The rain slashed sideways. Propped before a brick wall was a large wooden cross, and chained to the cross was what appeared to be a woman with outstretched wings. The wind whipped ropes of drenched hair across her high cheekbones, her feral eyes, and her expression of wild fury. As she struggled to burst from her chains, a perfect bolt of lightning bisected the roiling sky.

"The Canadian Bird Woman," said Ned.

"Hélène," said Warren.

"It was the 1960s," said Luna, her voice hushed, as if she were telling him a secret. "People were just beginning to wake up to the environmental devastation taking place all over the United States and Canada. There was that huge oil spill in Santa Barbara. You couldn't breathe for the smog. DDT was legal, and so was using lead in paint.

"A man named Kevin Dean owned a big paint factory in Michigan, on the southern shore of Lake Huron. He'd dump the paint he didn't want into the lake. On the northern shore of Lake Huron is Ontario, where many of the lead-poisoned eagles went to die.

"Back then Hélène was running a small clinic out of her house. She scheduled a meeting with Dean. She brought vet reports and photographs, and described exactly what happens to a lead-poisoned bird. Dean was not sympathetic. Things escalated. At the end? He told her to go fuck herself."

Warren closed his eyes and chuckled.

"She had planned to stage a protest at his annual company party, which was held on the top floor of a building in Grand Rapids. But a big scary electrical storm was supposed to hit late that afternoon. Hélène called one of her First Nation friends, and asked him to bring her his ceremonial eagle feather jacket. It was a hundred years old. Four of them managed to get the cross to the roof of the building across the street from the party, and they attached it to the stairwell. They covered what they were doing with a black tarp until six o'clock at night, when the storm was raging and the party was in full swing. And then they pulled the tarp away."

"Then what happened?"

"*That's* what happened," said Luna, gesturing to the photograph. "All those bigwigs saw a woman with wings, hanging in chains. They unrolled a banner that said KEVIN DEAN - EAGLE KILLER. The guy who took the photos wasn't even a pro, he just took a bunch of pictures with his second-hand camera. She made him leave before the police arrived. Look at the lightning! Any one of them could have been killed."

"Two days later that photograph was in every newspaper in the country," said Warren.

"And Dean's life took a turn for the worse," finished Luna, with a grin.

"Look at her," said Warren. "She was cursing him out in three languages. She was just a little bitty thing, and they say it took four cops to get her off the roof."

Warren and Luna tapped their beer bottles together, and Ned regarded the famous photograph. Whoever designed this game was a master, he thought. I'm on a completely alien planet, yet there are recognizable historical elements.

"But how will you get the eagles across the border?" he asked. "Don't you need documents? And Mars…"

"Named after the Roman god of war," supplied Warren.

"What's his girlfriend's name?"

"Banshee."

Ned grimaced. "It's because she's really loud," Luna explained.

"I know what a banshee is!" said Ned. "It's an Irish spirit, and they're really loud because they're announcing that somebody is about to die."

"If anybody dies it'll be thanks to Mars, not Banshee," said Warren.

Ned sighed, determined to follow at least one thread to its conclusion. "So back to Banshee, who currently resides in Pennsylvania. How are you going to get her to Canada? Don't you think if you swing by to pick her up, someone you don't want to see might be waiting for you?"

"See, that's the…ahh!" Luna jumped backward, nearly toppling her chair.

"Ha ha!" laughed Warren. "What is it about the sudden sight of a great big dildo that just sets people off?"

Ned gave Luna a reproachful look. *That's* what you were talking about?" he asked, as a large armadillo sauntered out from beneath the table.

Warren frowned. "Did you lead this young man to believe I was trafficking in sex toys?" he asked.

That volunteer program was a big mistake, thought Ned. This is a textbook example of what happens when computer people decide they need to work on their social skills. "Don't panthers eat armadillos?" he forced himself to ask.

"Oh sure, all the time," said Warren. "But not here, because all the injured or orphaned ones are either in the clinic or the bird cage. There's nothing wrong with Jacques, though, that one there, he just walked in one day and I never had the heart to kick him out. But he ever takes a stroll into that kitty pen, he's gonna get the surprise of his life."

"Look at him!" chortled Luna, sitting cross-legged on the floor as the armadillo rose on its hind legs and peered into her face. "If you're wondering why he likes them so much," she said to Ned, "there's no real reason."

"Awww, 'course there is," said Warren. "They're tough little guys. I'll tell you what, couple years ago some douchebag shot one in his yard with a .38, and the bullet ricocheted off the dildo and hit his neighbor. Neighbor was just sitting there in her trailer, minding her own business. She was pissed. I expect the dildo was, too."

The dishes had been cleared from the dining room table, replaced by a battered map of the United States. Luna traced a route with her finger.

"I'll need to drive northwest, past the Great Lakes, and head for the Minnesota border. He shouldn't be in the crate for more than five hours at a stretch, so we'll just go from rehabber to rehabber. Whoever has a flight cage, and is willing to take the risk."

"An eagle underground railroad," said Warren.

"Exactly. I'll line up a different ride each time, and cover my tracks."

"Give me three days," said Warren. "I have to release that guy, make sure he's okay, then I'll take you."

"I can't wait three days," said Luna. "Ted's picking us up tomorrow morning, and taking us to Carlene's in Tallahassee." She reached into her pocket and pulled out her phone. "Oh good, here he is. I didn't hear it ring."

She read the text, and her face fell. "Shoot," she said. "He can't do it. He's trying to line up someone else."

"Ned'll take you!" said Warren.

"No, he won't," said Ned.

"Ned has to get back to work," stated Luna. "He's done more than enough."

She smiled at him warmly, bravely, sadly, her eyes like summer skies, her fragile frame buffeted by the harsh winds of fate. Her long legs were tucked beneath her. Her flawless skin was dusted with rose.

"I'll get you to Tallahassee," blurted Ned.

"Good man!" said Warren, clapping him on the shoulder. "You are a valiant knight, rescuing both the errant bride *and* her winged companion! Damn the Federales, full steam ahead! I'll catch up with you in a few days."

"I'm so grateful to you, Ned," said Luna. "More than you know."

"Gotta do my rounds," said Warren. "Bedrooms are that way." He saluted, took another beer from the refrigerator, and left.

Luna picked up one of her duffel bags. "Yours is the second door on the left," she said. "Have a good sleep."

Ned watched her go, berating himself for agreeing to drive Luna and her eagle to Tallahassee. But once he delivered them, he vowed, he would stay exactly five minutes, then he'd get back into his car and return to his life. If he was lucky, it would be without fanfare, arrest, or prosecution.

Ned dropped his bag on the floor of his room, then wandered back through the house and onto the porch. In a small clearing stood Warren and Luna, bathed in moonlight, looking at the sky. They were focused so intently he followed their gaze, expecting to see a comet, fireworks, or at least a low-flying plane. He scanned the sky, but saw only the moon.

CHAPTER 4

Adam sat behind his desk, coffee in one hand, a contract in the other. Roland lounged in a big leather armchair, scrolling through the news. There was a soft knock on the door. Darcy entered, green-eyed and black-haired, her perfect body clad in leggings, sandals, and a tank top. "Morning!" she said, and waved a manila envelope. Roland nodded, and returned to the news.

"How'd you do?" asked Adam.

"Those wildlife people are a tough bunch!" she said. "I waited until Kelly McPhee left, then I went in and said I was Luna's cousin. I said I couldn't reach her, and they said they didn't know where she was. I even started crying, and they didn't care! But then I met up with another one in the parking lot, and evidently she wasn't in the loop. She said the last time she saw Luna, there was a new volunteer. Long hair, glasses, mid to late twenties, drove an old blue Cadillac. She figured he was fairly local, because he signed up for once a week."

She handed him the manila envelope. "It's a start. I can widen the search."

"Thanks, Darcy. Good job."

"Anytime. Can I do anything else for you?"

"Nope. That'll do it."

"You sure?" she asked. She raised an eyebrow and gave him an inviting smile, but he smiled back and nodded toward the door. Darcy sighed, shrugged, and closed it behind her.

Adam opened the envelope and pulled out photographs of three young men, each stapled to copies of their driver's licenses and registrations. Thomas J. Tyler, age 29, wore wire-rimmed glasses, his hair pulled back, and owned a blue 1963 Cadillac Coupe De Ville.

Ronald P. Smythe, age 35, wore rimless glasses, had a balding mullet, and owned a blue 1959 Cadillac Sedan De Ville. Edward K. Harrelson, age 26, wore horn-rimmed glasses, his shoulder-length hair in unruly waves, and owned a blue 1968 convertible Cadillac De Ville.

"Look at this," said Adam, exasperated.

Roland rose and surveyed the photographs. "I've got that conference call," said Adam, gathering the paperwork and returning it to the manila envelope. "Do me a favor and give this to Lloyd. Tell him to call Nichols and read him the three plate numbers, and I want to file a Missing Person Report."

Roland raised an eyebrow. "What the hell is she doing?" asked Adam.

"You know what she's doing."

"No, I don't!"

"She doesn't want to be here."

For a moment Adam met his gaze, then he lifted his suit jacket from the back of his chair and pulled it on.

"Then we'll just have to find her," he said, "so I can change her mind."

• • •

Ned cruised along Interstate 75, heading north, listening as Luna crooned to her eagle in a husky half-whisper. "It's okay," she said. "It'll be all right."

Ned's neighbor walked her Chihuahuas by his window each morning, spouting such high-pitched, rapid-fire baby talk that he was regularly tempted to race from his apartment and bludgeon her to death with his oversized coffee cup. Luna, on the other hand, spoke in a voice so soft and warm that he felt a foreign, wistful pang in his heart. He wondered how he could get her to keep it up.

Luna glanced at Ned. He piloted the enormous blue car unhurriedly, one arm resting on the window, the tendrils of hair which had escaped his ponytail blowing in the breeze. What luck, she thought, that his company's nerd squad had sent him to Starfish Key. She leaned her head back, and curled a leg beneath her.

"So, um...I meant to tell you," he said, adjusting his glasses. "Yesterday I gave your former phone to a friend heading for Miami."

"Why?"

"When he got to his hotel, he used it to call a few airlines. This morning he dropped it off at my company's Miami office, and today one of my co-workers will put it in the mail being overnighted to our office in Denver. Tomorrow a co-worker in Denver will use it to call a few airlines, then he'll put it in the mail being overnighted to our office in Portland. So according to anyone who's hacking your phone, for the next several days you're on your way out west."

"What!" she gasped, and punched him on the arm. "That's brilliant!"

"Ow," said Ned, pleased.

"Didn't your co-workers want to know why?"

"I said it was part of a Treasure Hunt."

"But I didn't see you give the phone to anyone!"

"You were out like a light."

"Thank you," she grinned, then looked down at her pinging phone. "It's from Harper," she said, and read it aloud.

689-333-2150 Your cousin stopped by Starfish Key with a lot of questions and somebody told her about the new volunteer with the Cadillac. Since I know you don't have a cousin you better ditch the car

"What do you mean, 'ditch the car?'" said Ned, alarmed.

Luna bit her lip. "Did you give Kelly your real name?"

"Uh...yeah?"

"Adam's looking for me. He must have had somebody go to Starfish Key and pretend to be my cousin, to see who I could have left with. Let me thank Harper and ask Warren." She typed, then read the response aloud.

PRIVATE CALLER A DMV check will get his plates. Cops will be out. Don't go through any tollbooths, they have cameras.

Ned snorted. "You can't just call the DMV and get somebody's license plate number!"

Luna regarded him sympathetically, as if he'd said something stupid but wasn't fully to blame. The phone pinged again.

PRIVATE CALLER Maybe they think you're still in the area. How far are you from Tallahassee?

"About an hour," said Ned.

"We need to pull over," she said, after she read the reply. "Someplace inconspicuous, with dirt."

Twenty minutes later they were back on the highway, Ned's face set in a scowl, the car filled with strained silence. Her phone pinged.

wildatheart@outlook.com **I had everyone check in with me after they deleted your old contact info. Have 112 so far, will run the others down. Be careful!**

suwanneeangler@msn.net **You need fish?**

meadowlark@outlook.com **Can't wait to see you!**

chiroptera@gmail.com **Oh damn, Luna! I'm sorry I insulted you!**

shelley@eastshorerescue.org **Forget about it, Esther!**

carnivorous@gmail.com **Esther, get back to work! We need you!**

rackocoons@hotmail.com **So does Jim Beam!**

dorsalfin28@att.net **Shut up, Bob! Ignore him, Esther!**

Luna laughed. "It's from the rehabbers," she said. "Esther's sorry she called me a bitch who does jack shit for wildlife! Didn't I tell you she'd be sorry? You want me to read them to you?"

"No," said Ned. They had stopped at the edge of a deserted rest stop, poured their water onto the ground, scooped up the resulting mud, and flung it all over the lower half of his formerly pristine 1968 Cadillac De Ville.

"Listen," she said. "I really am sorry about the mud. As soon as we get to Carlene's, I promise I'll help you clean up every bit of it. But don't you feel better knowing no one can read our plates?"

The GPS guided them through back roads and a maze of subdivisions. Ned rolled into the driveway of a neat raised ranch and stopped beside a Toyota hybrid. As he and Luna slid out, the front door opened and a stout woman in her early forties barreled toward them, her glorious, waist-length brown hair streaming behind her.

"Luna, darlin'!" she cried, enveloping her in a bear hug. "What a kick in the pants it is to meet you in person after all these years!"

A smiling blond man appeared behind her. "Derek," he said, and offered his hand. "Carlene's other half."

"I'm so glad to meet you both!" said Luna. "This is Ned!"

"Hello there, darlin'!" said Carlene, enveloping him in another hug. "Now, not to be pushy or anything, but let's get your bird out of the car and your car into the garage, because Harper says people are looking for you."

"That is one beautiful automobile!" said Derek. "I'm kinda surprised you take it off-roading."

"You said you needed a big flight cage, so I figured you had one of those raptor bastards with you," said Carlene, peering inside the Cadillac. "Holy shit, I guess I was right, look at the size of that crate! So Ned, I only do songbirds, and I hate those raptor bastards because some of 'em eat my little guys. But if one of 'em gets hurt, then even if he is a raptor bastard I'll try to fix him, because what am I supposed to do? He's still a wild thing! Come on, bring him in."

"I'm just dropping Luna off," said Ned. "I have to go."

"I promised to help you clean up your car!" said Luna.

"Use the bathroom and we'll show you around, then you can get back on the road," said Derek.

The right half of the backyard was ablaze with flowers. The water in three birdbaths shimmered, bright feeders hung from the trees, and all were alive with small, darting birds. On the left half of the yard stood four medium-sized wooden flight cages, all lined with soft green mesh. Visible through three of them were more small birds. In the fourth one Mars stood alone, Gulliver among the Lilliputians. He hopped into a large black rubber tub filled with water, ducked his head, and let the water run down his back.

"This is like the Garden of Eden, Carlene!" said Luna. "I can't thank you enough."

"We can't thank *you* enough!" she cried, throwing an arm around Luna's shoulders. "Those two flights on the left? Those are thanks to you. I don't know if you know this, Ned, but Luna here's like Santa Claus for rehabbers."

"There's a lot I don't know," said Ned, gazing at the bright turquoise streak running from the top of Carlene's hair all the way down the left side.

"You know why I did that? Because I talk a blue streak, so's I might as well wear one. And this way if Derek ever goes deaf, he can find me in a crowd! You got quite a head of hair yourself. Anyway, come on, we'll give you a tour and then say farewell."

The sunny living room was as colorful as the garden, with cushions and pillows in primary colors and floral prints. Vying for space in the den were two big easy chairs in front of a flat screen TV and a long, wide table piled high with what looked like the contents of an entire craft store.

"Derek works for an insurance company, and when I'm not doing birds I make crafts," said Carlene. "Why people want this kinda crap cluttering up their homes is beyond me, but they do. Now come on and I'll show you the bird room, and don't forget there's no talking except a whisper. Which is obviously a bigger problem for me than for any of you."

Ned and Luna followed her into a large, bright room and stopped in astonishment, as they appeared to be standing in a long-leaf pine forest. The sun's rays illuminated knee-high ferns, wiregrass, and cabbage palms, while a delicate mist crept toward a cluster of pitcher plants. Gauzy clouds drifted in the blue sky. The sounds of birdsong, crickets, and tree frogs emanated from an iPod set up in the corner.

"Look at the myrtle oak and the gopher apple," whispered Derek appearing between them and pointing to each tree. "Sweetbay magnolia there, and Atlantic white cedar over there. You'll find every one within ten miles of here. That woman can paint!"

"Carlene did this?" marveled Luna.

Resting on a long table were a half dozen cages made of black mesh stretched over metal frames. Each one was edged with greenery, contained a small branch for a perch, and held a single adult bird, most sporting a bandaged wing or leg. Carlene stood at a second table, holding a pair of forceps in one hand and a jar with live mealworms in the other. Before her were six plastic containers, each home to a small padded bowl containing several nestlings. She went down the line, plucking mealworms and pushing them into gaping mouths, each tiny nestling squirming and squeaking in its frantic effort to outmaneuver its siblings.

"I don't talk at all when I'm in the bird room because it'll scare the adults and I don't want my babies growing up thinking it's normal to hear human voices," said Carlene, when they were back in the kitchen. "I can't even whisper 'cause I'm like a bowling ball rolling down a hill, before you know it I'd be yelling my head off. I do know my own pros and cons."

"I had no idea you could paint like that!" said Luna.

"Well dang," said Carlene, waving dismissively. "'Course I can paint, I'm a crafty kind of a gal. And y'know something, Ned, since you're not a rehabber? If I get an injured or orphaned bird in, I'm not going to drag 'em into my world. I'm going to take care of 'em in a world that's as close to theirs as I can get it."

"Thanks for the tour," said Ned. "This is a great place, but I have to go."

As Luna opened her arms to give him a hug, Carlene reached for the phone chiming on the kitchen counter. "Thanks, Ned," Luna whispered in his ear. "I'll let you know when I get there."

Ned was so overcome by the feeling of her body against his that for a moment he lost track of his surroundings. "What!" cried Carlene and Luna jumped, wrenching him back to the kitchen. He looked up to find Carlene wearing a thunderstruck expression. "Waxwings!" she bellowed, and rushed from the room.

"This is awesome!" said Derek, close behind her. "We're releasing five of them!"

"A release?" cried Luna, her face lighting up. "Oh Ned, I'm sorry you'll miss this! It's why we do what we do!"

Ned sat in the back seat of Carlene's small SUV next to Luna, listening to Carlene describe how the five Cedar Waxwings she had just raised needed to be released into a flock of wild ones. Her birder friends had been searching for two weeks for a flock, but the flock always disappeared before Carlene could get there. All five birds rode in a covered crate — a tenth the size of Mars's, and with a handle — in the storage area behind the back seat. Computer people are so sane, thought Ned, once again regretting his decision.

"So Luna," said Carlene. "Last October I saw Janie Beckendorf! Did you ever meet her?"

"No, but I've talked to her a bunch of times! How is she?"

"Well, she's just fine! Still flying wildlife around in that old bush plane of hers. Wiscasset Wildlife in Maine had a Cerulean Warbler who hit a window and missed migration, so Janie picked him up in the plane and flew him down here. She hung out with us for a few days while he acclimated, and then we let him go. With any luck he didn't meet up with any more windows on the way to Costa Rica!"

"What's a Cerulean Warbler?" asked Ned.

"Gorgeous little blue songbird. You gotta see 'em to believe 'em."

"Are they endangered?"

"Nah, there's a bunch of 'em out there."

"But... you're saying this woman flew the bird from Maine to Florida and then let him go? Just a regular bird? A common, five-pound bird?"

"Five pounds!" cried Derek, wearing a theatrical expression of alarm. "Can you imagine a five-pound warbler?"

"Oh, mama, that'd scare the bejeebies outta me," said Carlene.

"A warbler made of *lead* wouldn't weigh five pounds," said Luna.

"They're, like, ten grams soaking wet," stated Derek.

Ned regarded his fellow travelers, who did not seem to understand his point. "But how much did it cost in fuel to fly this ten-gram bird in a private plane to Florida?"

"Got me there," said Carlene. "Sometimes these warblers have secret bank accounts."

As Derek and Luna chortled, Ned shook his head. "I'm just not getting this. One single ten-gram, not-endangered bird? What does it matter?"

For a moment the car was still, then the others exchanged good-natured smiles.

"Well hell, it sure mattered to that bird!" cried Carlene.

"There! There!" said Derek. He pointed to the edge of a field, where a woman standing between two parked cars waved her arms. Three people stood close by, and four more were halfway across the field.

Carlene stopped the car and jumped out. She opened the back door, grabbed the crate, and, holding it carefully by the handle, took off across the field at a dead run. Ned looked at Luna for some kind of interpretation, but she was already sprinting behind Derek. Ned hustled after the crowd of people, some old, some young, all carrying binoculars, all seemingly beside themselves with excitement. Fifty yards into the field, he heard the sound of tiny bells coming from the top of a tree.

Eight pairs of binoculars pointed in one direction. Ned squinted, and a middle-aged man handed him an extra pair. Lining the branches of a grand old myrtle oak were dozens of striking little black-masked, buff-colored birds, their tails edged with brilliant yellow, a single bright red speck on each wing. Carlene raised the crate into the air, opened the door, and five blurs streaked outward and upward; into the tree, into the welcoming flock.

Ned glanced at Carlene, at the tears streaming down her face. He started toward her, thinking she must have injured herself in her mad dash across the field, only to realize that everyone in the small crowd was in pretty much the same condition. The tough ones were only blinking rapidly; the emotional ones were practically sobbing. Almost on cue, everyone started hugging each other. What fresh hell is this, thought Ned, then Luna turned and wrapped her arms around him.

How have I gone this long without knowing about Cedar Waxwings, he thought.

• • •

Federal Wildlife Officer Erik Gunderman entered the U.S. Fish and Wildlife Service building in Falls Church, Virginia, filled with a sense of unease. The previous morning he had met with Adam Matheson, then with Matheson's far more forthcoming zookeeper. After he returned to his office he wrote a report to his Regional Supervisor, struggling to edit his sarcasm and disgust. Three hours later he received an email from the assistant of Daniel Whittaker, Fish and Wildlife's Chief of Law Enforcement for the entire United States. It requested he meet with the Big Kahuna himself at 4:00 the following afternoon, with a round-trip ticket to Washington attached.

Gunderman grew up within walking distance of the Loxahatchee, the refuge he now dedicated his life to protect. He snuck into it in his youth, volunteered there in his teens, then attended the University of Miami, only two hours away. He followed his meticulously planned career path with determination. He graduated with a degree in Ecosystem Management and Policy, then spent eighteen weeks of Special Agent training at the Federal Law Enforcement Training Center at Glynco, Georgia, four weeks of Advanced Wildlife Officer training at the National Conservation Training Center in Shepherdstown, West Virginia, and ten weeks of field training in Alaska, Texas, and Vermont. Eventually he returned to the twisted pines of Loxahatchee, this time wearing the uniform of a Federal Wildlife Officer.

For years his supervisor had encouraged him to become a Special Agent, one of the elite team of undercover wildlife officers who crack big-money poaching and smuggling rings and nail major polluters. Gunderman always promised to consider it, then he dismissed it in under fifteen seconds. Special agents lived on the move, and he was not about to leave the Loxahatchee.

Gunderman landed, rented a car, and drove to the Fish and Wildlife Service office in Falls Church, Virginia. He rode the elevator to the 10th floor, his thoughts jumping while his demeanor stayed calm. What did Whittaker want? There was no precedent for this.

"I have your report here, Gunderman, and it's very astute," said Whittaker, after Gunderman had been seated in his spacious office.

"Thank you, sir."

"This Matheson mess could be media hell," said Whittaker, who had crew-cut grey hair, a solid build, and a level gaze. "That arrogant asshole! What did you call the bird? A 'marital bargaining chip.' That's exactly right. Some rich loony on the lam with a Bald Eagle? Jesus Christ! What the hell is going on in this country?"

"I don't know, sir."

"And of course, the public doesn't give a shit about permits. All they'll care about is Mr. versus Mrs. Billionaire fighting over the symbol of America. And then every moron in the country will want an eagle, just like every moron in the world wanted an owl after Harry Potter."

"I agree, sir."

"I expect the police will pick her up within a few days, if they haven't already, but I'm not taking any chances. I want that bird back in the possession of Fish and Wildlife. I want it done yesterday, and I want you on it."

Gunderman blinked, dismayed. "But why me? I mean, why me, sir?"

"Your Regional Supervisor is a good friend of mine. I told him the problem, he recommended you. Your record is exemplary. You have the instincts and skills of a undercover agent, but you wear a uniform. That's exactly what I need."

"But what about my duties at the refuge?"

"I'll temporarily transfer another officer." Whittaker leaned forward, arms on his desk, and looked at him intently. "Listen to me, Gunderman. This is way bigger than John Q. Public wanting a pet eagle. You officers are out there risking your lives and what do you get? Couple inches of type. You want to send a message to the lowlifes shooting eagles out of the sky, *and* to the rich bastards who buy their heads on the black market? To the poachers netting endangered species, *and* to the rings grinding them up for traditional medicines? *Then find and arrest Luna Burke.* If she took that eagle, then she has committed a Federal offense. Once we've got her, we've got a better shot at her fucking husband. This is our chance to show the public that when it comes to environmental crime, nobody is above the law! When the shit hits the media, I want them to report that crossing Fish and Wildlife is a big mistake."

Gunderman nodded. This was big picture stuff. It wasn't what people normally thought of when they thought of an environmental crime, so perhaps therein lay its effectiveness. It would mean he'd have to leave the Loxahatchee — at least, temporarily — which did not make him happy. But in the end, it would be worth it. Plus, it didn't seem as if he was being given a choice.

"Rent a car, book a flight, whatever you need, just keep an expense report. Got it? Since we don't have a trail on either one of them, I'd start at the wildlife center in Pennsylvania. You on board?"

"Yes, sir!" said Gunderman.

• • •

Warren leaned back in his chair, feet on the deck railing, listening to the occasional lazy snarl. The beer was cold, the sun was warm, and soon Florida's resident population of panthers would increase by one.

Maybe I should paint a bullseye on him before he leaves, he thought.

Bastards.

He could spend hours, if he let himself, obsessing about all the greedy, rapacious scumbags who had invaded Florida. They felled the trees, fouled the skies, polluted the water, killed off entire populations of wildlife. For what? Another house? Another car? How many did they need? When would it end?

Adam Matheson: one of the worst. Industrial parks. Airport expansions. Golf courses. His lawyers had snatched a ten-acre piece of land next to Big Turkey Swamp right out from under a local Land Trust; instead of open land it was now a cluster of high-end condos, right at the edge of prime panther habitat. Less than two weeks after those yuppy douchebags started moving in a radio-collared panther had been hit by a Lincoln Navigator.

And then there was Luna.

Matheson could have stuck with the socialites and the bimbos, but no. He had to land an orphaned girl who'd never been out of Pennsylvania, whose idea of a heartthrob was an imprinted eagle. And now she'd left him, but he would bet Adam Matheson wasn't going to take it lying down.

Warren rose and paced smoothly back and forth across the deck, stripping the label from his beer bottle. Basically, her plan was good. The rehabbers would close ranks, and she'd be hard to track. But It was a long way to Canada, and a lot could go wrong. How long before

Matheson sent his psycho football player after her? Both of them were nuts, and Roland had guns. Not the type of men he wanted focused on Luna, a child of the wind and sky.

Warren walked through his house, pulling a ring of keys from his pocket, cursing American gun laws. Every pea-brain in the country owned a gun. You didn't have to know a damn thing about them, you didn't have to be a decent shot, you didn't even have to not be a paranoid schizophrenic.

He unlocked the basement door and descended the stairs, feeling the cool stillness rise to greet him. He flicked on the light. Warren stood in the middle of the small room covered with pegboards, stroking his beard, his gaze traveling past the Glock, the pair of .38s, the .45s, the trio of Berettas, the Super Blackhawk, the Ruger, the M-16s, the AK-47s, finally settling on the Heckler & Koch PSG1.

He took it down from the wall. He stroked the barrel, then raised it to his shoulder and squinted through the scope. Finally, he smiled.

The only thing better than a good sniper rifle, he thought, is a wild kitty just set free.

Chapter 5

Police Sergeant Louis Garrity sat at the table in the garden room, eating a caviar blintz. "More coffee, sir?" asked the uniformed maid, and he nodded. She turned to Adam. "Would you like anything else, Mr. Matheson?"

"No thanks, Carmela," he replied.

"Adam, at this point there's not much more we can do," said Garrity. "We filed a Missing Person Report, issued APBs on the three Caddys, and put it on our Twitter feed. We had to link her with the missing eagle because they both disappeared the same night, and the media got a hold of the police reports. But we're saying she might have information about the missing eagle, not that she stole it. You don't know anyone she could be staying with?"

"No."

"That incident seven, eight days ago, where we responded to an alarm. It was a broken door - in this room, right? Be straight with me, Adam, because it'll make my job a lot easier. Any connection?"

Adam shook his head. "It would make a better story if I told you we had a fight and I smashed the door," he said. "But my son was visiting. He's into skeet shooting, and he was messing around with his new launcher." He paused. "In a glass room." He paused again. "I think he's heading for a career in finance."

The sergeant chuckled.

"Lou," said Adam. "She's young. She's impulsive. I just want you to find her."

"Thanks for breakfast, Adam," said Garrity, rising. "I'll turn up the heat."

Adam stood, and offered his hand. "Appreciate it, Lou."

He returned to his seat, thinking, no woman leaves a man worth ten billion dollars.

How long ago had it been? Back when he actually believed that making a million dollars would make him an undisputed success. Certainly no one in the crappy North Dakota town where he grew up ever dreamed of such wealth, let alone obtained it. But a million dollars, he discovered with dismay, simply opened doors to rooms where he was once again at the bottom of the heap. Just stay out of those rooms, said his mother, who at that point hadn't left her trailer park.

He gazed through the restored glass door and out over his perfectly manicured estate, one of six. Fifty million. A hundred million. Five hundred million. Ten fucking billion dollars, and he was still one of many. But then she arrived, and things had changed.

Seventy floors above midtown Manhattan. For the first time, he entered a room filled with men of enormous wealth with Luna on his arm. And she mesmerized them, just as she had mesmerized him. She entered the huge room in a blazing red Dior gown and stiffened, her eyes sweeping the crowd as if assessing its risk, returning admiring gazes with hostility. She smiled tightly, shook hands, and murmured a few pleasantries; she pulled at her rope of diamonds as if she couldn't wait to be rid of them, her eyes on the door. It was impossible to predict when or how the energy so obviously roiling beneath her straight-backed self-control would erupt, and the men all regarded her with collectors' eyes.

She had nearly left him that night.

Roland entered the room. "Breakfast?" asked Adam.

"Already ate."

Roland wore the same tie he'd been wearing the night Luna burst through the glass door, the night they'd gone to Jay Sheinkopf's party. Adam remembered the way the steel magnate had watched her cross the room in her misty dress, nearly drooling with desire.

"You think she's at Jay Sheinkopf's?" he asked.

Roland snorted. "I think there's a better chance she's on the moon."

"What about Joe Montego?"

Silently, Roland shook his head. "We still going to Atlanta?"

"Yeah," said Adam, glancing at his watch and rising. "Twenty minutes."

• • •

Luna, Derek and Carlene sat at the kitchen table by a picture window overlooking the backyard, drinking coffee and eating Danishes.

"I was volunteering at Celia's wildlife center," said Luna. "One day the Department of Natural Resources brought us a confiscated eagle. A guy had stolen him from a nest, and kept him in a cage in his garage."

Ned appeared in the doorway, blinking, crowned by a tangled head of bed hair. "You and I oughtta start a hair metal band," called Carlene.

Ned frowned. "Ned needs coffee in the morning," said Luna. "I know that about him."

"Aren't you glad you stayed over?" Carlene asked. "You got a nice clean car again, and now you get to eat raspberry Danishes and hear Mars's story. I mean, unless you've already heard it."

"Nnnn," said Ned. He poured himself a cup, and settled into a chair.

"By the time DNR confiscated him, he was almost three years old," said Luna. "He was sick, all his feathers were broken, and he hated people. Everyone. I thought they were going to make us put him to sleep, but the DNR guy gave us a chance.

"The first time I handled him, Celia made me wear hockey pads and a helmet with a face shield. I named him Mars, after the Roman god of war. You know, in Greek literature the god of war is a jerk. But to the Romans, he was strong and wise and and only used his power when it was needed. Mars came around — well, sort of — and I wanted so much to release him, but we couldn't."

"You can see how releasing a homicidal eagle could be a problem," Derek said to Ned.

"Since he was imprinted we didn't think he'd ever accept another eagle, but then he bonded with Banshee and every year they raised orphaned eaglets together."

Luna sighed. "He came at me a couple of times in the beginning. He was pretty scary. All I did was fend him off. I had to prove to him that no matter what he did, I would never hurt him." She turned toward Ned. "Now do you understand?" she said. "It's not his fault."

"Those two eagles were as content as they could be, and now they've been split up!" growled Carlene. "It's like Romeo and Juliet, only Romeo's been kidnapped to Florida by some rich dickweed instead of getting dragged into the middle of a family feud."

"But *this* story's gonna have a happy ending," said Derek.

"Thing is," said Carlene, "there's a kink in the plan. I was so dang sure that giant crate of yours would fit in my car, but Derek measured it this morning and it just won't fit. And it's not even close to fitting in Derek's, which means I can't take you to Esther's, goddammit. So I called Peter, who does small mammals in Shady Grove, and he'll be here at 11 o'clock to pick you up. Okay? You've been such a peach, Ned, you get on back down to the Keys and Peter will take over from here."

The phone on the counter beeped insistently. "Uh-oh," said Carlene. "That sounds like a red alert." She picked it up, regarded it, held it to her ear and said, "Phyllis?"

Carlene listened, growing visibly perturbed. "Check," she said. "Thanks. Gotta go." She turned to Luna. "Darlin'," she said. "This ain't good news. There's an official Missing Person Report on Adam Matheson's wife, they're saying you might be connected with the missing eagle and traveling in an old Cadillac. Phyllis's son is a cop, and he's on his way over. They got three license plate numbers, I don't know if one of 'em is yours."

"Damn it!" said Derek.

"Wait a minute," said Ned. "Do they have a warrant? Because they can't come into your house without one."

"Honey, you gotta understand about being a rehabber, especially one who works outta the house," said Carlene. "You want the police to stick up for you, not make your life hell on earth. So if they knock on your door you're gonna say 'come on in,' no matter who you may be hiding in your flight cage."

"When they get here, Carlene and I will go out the front and stall 'em," said Derek. "Luna, go get your bird. Get him on your glove and head into the woods. There's a thousand acres of state park back there, you keep on going until you can't see the house. Ned, if one of 'em comes in here you'll have to distract him, and everybody start praying they don't look in the garage and find that Cadillac."

"You see why I love this man?" said Carlene with an admiring smile. "When the chips are down, he knows just what to do." She reached into her pocket and tossed Ned a rubber band. "Here, darlin'," she said. "You're gonna need some credibility."

"They just pulled into the driveway," said Derek.

Ned stood in the empty kitchen, harnessing his hair into a ponytail and wearing a look of dismay. He smoothed his clothing, and looked up just as a uniformed police officer entered the room.

"Good morning, sir," said the officer.

"Good morning," Ned replied.

The officer shook his hand, turned, and looked out the picture window. "Sure is beautiful here," he said. "I hate barging in on Derek and Carlene like this, it's just something we have to do."

He turned his back to the window and continued. "We're looking for a woman named Luna Burke. She's the wife of Adam Matheson, and he's afraid she may have come to harm. Also, she might know something about the disappearance of a Bald Eagle."

A slight motion caught Ned's eye, and he glanced over the officer's shoulder. Through the window he could see Luna emerge from a flight cage with Mars, who seemed to be having a fit. He lurched from foot to foot on Luna's glove, pulled at the leather jesses attached to his legs, and slapped his massive wings against her head; Ned was sure he was about to seize her by the back of the neck and carry her into the sky. The officer saw his gaze and began to turn around.

"Doesn't Adam Matheson live in Key West?" Ned asked suddenly. "I"m heading that way now! What does she look like?"

The officer turned back. "She's five foot seven, slender, curly auburn hair. The bird's the size of a hang glider."

Ned tried to appear as if he were about to divulge key information, but once again the officer began to turn toward the window.

"Eyes!" cried Ned. "Does she have eyes?"

The officer regarded him suspiciously.

"I mean, what color are her eyes?"

"They're blue. Have you seen her?"

"Uh …" said Ned, as Luna and the eagle disappeared into the forest. "Sorry, I haven't, but I'll make sure to watch out for her."

• • •

Earl Baedeker pushed a lock of black hair out of his eyes and squinted at the alternator of a red 1963 Corvette Sting Ray. Pulling a rag from his pocket he gave it a swipe, then straightened up and announced, "This is going to cost PJ a lot more'n he counted on."

Julie Marie lounged in a recliner in a corner of the garage, her voluptuous body encased in a tank top and shorts, cracking gum and reading *Us* magazine. When the landline rang from the top of a dusty table, she extended one leg and lifted the receiver with her toes. "Baedeker Auto," she said, then squealed, "Nedeeeeee!"

"Put him on speakerphone!" said Earl.

"Yo, Oil," came Ned's voice.

"Inter-*nedt*," called Earl. "When was the last time I heard from you, man? Where the hell have you been?"

"Busy," said Ned. "Lot of work. Listen, I'm in a rush and I need a big favor. I need you to meet me about 20 miles outside Marietta in my Chevy. I'll switch cars with you and give you the Cadillac to drive home. And this is really important — you need to bring a set of temporary plates to put on the Caddy."

"Is this another Treasure Hunt?"

"Yeah, it's a Treasure Hunt."

"Do you have a crew with you?"

"Mmm, just one person."

"A female person?" yowled Julie Marie. "Is it a girl? Is she your *girlfriend?*"

"No, just a friend."

"What does she looked like?"

"She's…uh…regular."

Julie Marie curled her hands into paws, stuck her tongue out, and panted. "Arf! Arf!" she stage-whispered. Earl gave her a look of irritation, and leaned against the Sting Ray.

"Ahhhh, Net...I'm kinda backed up here and Marietta is like, three hours away."

"Buddy, World War Dead Zone 3 is coming out in five weeks and four days."

"Like I don't know that."

"Do this for me, and instead of standing in a parking lot at midnight behind 400 other gamers, you'll have yours delivered to your doorstep the day before."

"Done!" cried Earl. "Let me finish up here and I'll call you back for directions!"

"Bye, Nedeeee!" caroled Julie Marie. "Can't wait to meet your *girlfriend!*"

She hung up the phone and threw her magazine on the floor. "Ned's so cute but he's such a dork," she said. "Remember that one he had with the braids and the braces?"

• • •

Ned stood in the kitchen with Derek and Carlene, all of them expressing great relief. Luna appeared, her face drained of color. "How far is it to the Georgia border?" she asked.

"Less than an hour," said Derek. "But don't worry. The cops are gone, and Peter's on his way."

"Peter won't be here for two hours," said Luna. "The police might come back. I have to go."

"How?" said Ned. "You mean in my car?"

"Can we?"

"But that doesn't make any sense — they're *looking* for my car!"

Luna glanced at the floor. After a moment she looked up, a hunted look in her eyes. Carlene gave a maternal scowl and pulled out her phone.

"Don't you worry, honey," she snapped. "I'm calling my sister and telling her to rent me a van. It'll take a half hour tops."

Ned opened his mouth to speak. "Well, good luck," was what he meant to say. "Can I borrow a set of plates?" was what came out.

Minutes later he knelt by the Cadillac's grill, switching the front plate while Derek did the same with the back. He wasn't sure which was more disturbing: his continued willingness to flout the law, or the fact that he'd rather face another serious violation than cover his car with more mud. Luna and Carlene appeared, and settled the covered crate onto the back seat.

"Just mail the plates back to me," said Derek, sliding Ned's plates under one of the floor mats. "Forty-five minutes you'll be out of Florida and into a less conspicuous car. You have your GPS? Don't take the highway, take 137. Fewer cops."

Carlene enveloped Luna in a hug. "We're all behind you, darlin'. You just tell us how we can help. All right?"

"You already have," said Luna. "Thank you both."

"Ned," said Carlene, wrapping her arms around him, then holding him at arm's length. "You are one fine man."

Ned flushed, nodded, and pulled out of the driveway. He followed the GPS's directions while Luna sat with her knees to her chest, fingers entwined in her hair, staring stonily out the window. Ned had always found body language confusing, but this one seemed fairly simple. How to bring up the cause of it, however, was still beyond him. Twenty minutes later, Luna spoke up.

"You know something?" she asked, staring at him with open antagonism. "It's not like I can pay you back for any of this."

Astonishment loosened his conversational block. "Pay me back!" he said. "You can pay me back by making sure the next stop is my last! And if you can keep me from getting arrested, that would be a bonus!"

Luna bit her lip. Mars stood placidly on his perch, the opposite of his angry, combative self that morning. She touched the small metal bars on the side of his crate.

"I'm sorry, Ned," she said, speaking with difficulty. "I saw what you did...you know, in the kitchen, distracting that cop. And the license plates and...and now getting us to Esther's..."

"Well," he said, mollified. "It's okay. I just don't get why... what was the reason... what you..."

"I… it's that sometimes… it's just… when things…"

Luna's phone pinged, and they both sighed with relief. "It's from Harper," said Luna, and read it aloud.

689-333-2150 That local online gossip rag just said you went off your meds and stole a bald eagle

Luna looked puzzled. "But I'm not on any meds."

"You're not?"

Luna returned his surprised look. "Do you think I should be?"

Ned suspected he might be sailing into treacherous waters, so he quickly came about. "I think you should join the team."

"What team?"

"Any team. Join the team, and your life will be golden."

"Are you on a team?"

"Obviously not."

"Not even at work?"

"No. Sometimes they trick me into going into a room full of people, then they lock the door and call it a meeting. No, I work alone. It's better."

"Sports?"

"Don't talk to me about sports."

"Why not?"

Ned wondered why he had brought this up. He glanced at Luna, and found her wearing an expression of both interest and encouragement. He had never seen the point of discussing his family history, but for some reason he continued.

"Everyone else in my family is a jock. They're loud and in your face and all they do is shout at each other about who won the game what a bonehead the ref was. That's, you know, when they're not mocking the family geek. I used to think one day they'd appreciate that I was smarter than all of them put together, but…no. My mother would put down her tennis racket for five seconds and say, "That's nice, honey," and my father would say, "Good work, Neddo, but what about the team? Next semester *are you gonna make the team?*"

Luna's encouraging expression faded, and Ned instantly regretted his admission. He glanced at her again, expecting the worst. "I would have been really proud of you," she said, her azure eyes filled with such sympathy that he held her gaze, suddenly wanting to admit more. The sound of a car horn forced his eyes back to the road.

"Whoa!" said Luna. "Sorry. But you want to hear something? Once I tried out for the softball team, and the ball hit me in the face and knocked me cold."

Ned returned her smile. "Look," he said. "We're over the Georgia border."

County route 46 meandered for miles, and eventually led to the Dennings County Shopping Mall. Ned drove to the back of the movie theater, found a relatively deserted, shady area, and parked. He and Luna slid out and stretched. She lifted the sheet. "You'll be out of there soon," she told the eagle.

"Earl should be here any minute," said Ned. "He's never late. Oh look, there he is."

Luna turned her head and gasped. "*That's* your idea of a less conspicuous car?" she cried.

The enormous, bright red 1957 Chevrolet Bel Air convertible cruised regally through the parking lot, a swan among sparrows, a unicorn among burros. Hooded headlights gleamed above its enormous grill, sweeping tail fins flowed past pristine white wall tires, and the top was down and tucked beneath a perfect canvas cover. Impossibly, it saw the Cadillac and raised it one.

"I like classic cars!" Ned retorted. "Had I known I had a future in wildlife smuggling, I might've made a different choice!"

Luna watched it roll toward them wearing an awed expression. "Oh my God," she hissed. "That is one gorgeous piece of machinery. What do you call those colors?"

Ned grinned. "India Ivory and Matador Red!"

Earl coasted to a stop. Julie Marie jumped from the passenger seat and tottered toward them, breasts bouncing, jewelry jangling, balancing precariously on her high heels. She halted at the sight of Luna, who stood beside the Cadillac in her cotton blouse, safari shorts, and flat leather sandals, a single silver bead hanging from a leather cord around her neck. Luna returned her stare with her celestial blue eyes, a sudden shaft of sunlight glinting on her cap of curly hair.

64

"You're Ned's friend?" asked Julie Marie incredulously. "Seriously?"

Luna's gaze turned icy. "Maybe Ned has friends you don't know about," she said.

"Hey, man!" Earl exclaimed, throwing an arm around Ned's neck. "Long time no see!"

"You look so familiar," said Julie Marie, peering at Luna. "I feel like I've seen your picture in magazines. Are you a model?"

"Shit, man, she's a fuckin' babe," said Earl in an undertone, whacking Ned on the back. "So what's in the box?" he asked, eyeing the inside of the Cadillac.

"It's a mystery," said Ned. "We don't know and we can't look, because that's part of the Treasure Hunt!"

"What if I just lift the corner of the sheet and take a little peek?" asked Julie Marie.

Ned threw Luna a look of alarm, and instantly Luna beckoned Julie Marie away from the car. "Why don't we let the boys do the dirty work so I can ask you about those shoes?" said Luna. "Where did you get them?"

"Oh!" she replied, smiling. "There's this cute little shoe store down at the Roxbury Mall outside Asheville! I also got a pair in lilac. Dontcha love 'em? Y'know, they'd look real good on you, too."

Luna glanced at Ned and Earl as they lifted the crate out of the Cadillac and settled it into the Chevy. "Is there something alive in here?" asked Earl.

"Speaking of models, you're the one who should be a model," said Luna, stopping Julie Marie in mid-turn.

"You really think so?" she asked. "I mean, people tell me that all the time, but …"

"Absolutely," said Luna. The roof of the Chevy settled into place, and Ned and Earl locked it down.

"Sorry this is so rushed," Ned told Earl, closing the back door, "but if we're late we'll lose the game! Don't forget — before you leave, put on those temporary plates. Okay?"

"Yeah, no problem!"

"Lovely to meet you, Julie Marie. You too, Earl!" said Luna, hurrying around the Chevy and hopping into the front seat.

"World War Dead Zone 3!" called Ned, starting the engine and easing it into reverse. "You'll be the first!"

"Awesome, man!"

Luna watched them grow smaller as the Chevy pulled away. She scrutinized the interior, then leaned back in her seat. "You could have borrowed a normal car," she said.

"You could have not committed Grand Theft Eagle," he answered.

• • •

Warren sat on a summit beneath a blue sky. He gazed down at the majestic pine forests, the meadows ablaze with wildflowers, the crystal lakes dancing with dragonflies, and was filled with blessed exhilaration. The wilderness throbbed with life unbound. Untouched by human hands, it rejoiced in its splendor. The very air was singing.

He wanted to remain on the mountain, in a world of perfect grace, but his inner clock told him an hour had passed. He said a prayer of gratitude, took a deep breath, and opened his eyes.

He rose from the bare floor of his deck, stretched, and bent forward from the waist until his grey hair touched the floor. Holding his arms out to the side, he lifted one leg at the knee, extending it both forward and backward, then repeated it with the other. He walked to one end of the deck, did three backflips, then cracked his knuckles, walked into his house, and put on Creedence Clearwater Revival's "Run Through The Jungle."

Warren walked down the basement stairs and pulled an oversized black guitar case from a closet. He placed it beside the PSG1, which had been disassembled and lay in pieces on the table. Humming along to the song he opened the lid, picked up the barrel, and carefully fitted it into a customized compartment. That Stu Bechnikoff! he thought, as he snuggled the stock, the recoil buffer, the cheek piece, the sling, the night scope, and the silencer all into their own little travel seats. The man had created a rifle case only the most compulsively discerning would notice was just a bit too large for a bass guitar. A true craftsman!

When the song's bridge began, Warren seized a harmonica from a shelf and wailed a duet with John Fogerty. Most people thought the song was about the Viet Nam war, but Fogerty himself said it wasn't: it was about the fact that there were too many guns in America. Amen! Where were the goddamn rules?

At the end of his duet, Warren put the harmonica back on the shelf. He closed the lid of the case, snapped the latches shut, and rested it on the floor by the stairs. The PSG1 was a heavy gun. Unloaded, it weighed almost 16 pounds. The updated versions were far lighter and more portable, but Warren didn't care; sacrificing one micrometer of accuracy just so some wussie didn't have to carry a heavy gun was just another example of the insanity of the modern world.

He opened a velcroed pocket and checked the straps which would allow him to wear the case like a very large backpack. Satisfied, he tucked them back in and mentally traced his route, which would begin in a parking lot and end at the top of a 60-foot West Indian Mahogany tree approximately one-eighth of a mile from Adam Matheson's pool.

Soon he'd have a light dinner, then change into black climbing boots, black track pants, black baseball cap, and a black T-shirt with a darkened image of the Grateful Dead's *American Beauty* cover. Should anyone ask, he was just an aging rocker returning from his tribute band gig, and no, after decades of 120-decibel concerts he was practically deaf and hadn't heard a thing.

For now, though, all that remained was to wait for night to fall.

CHAPTER 6

Roland turned away from the cockpit, still chuckling over his exchange with the pilot. He started down the aisle of the Gulfstream and spotted Adam sitting by the window, Scotch in hand, staring at the afternoon sky. Roland stopped at the bar, poured himself a drink, and settled in the seat across from Adam. He raised his glass. Unsmiling, Adam raised his in return.

"What's the matter with you?" asked Roland. "You've been working on that deal for a year."

Adam shrugged. "Got things on my mind."

"How many times have you been through this?"

"This is different."

"Yeah, it's different, this one doesn't want any money! It'll be the easiest split you ever had."

"I don't want to split!"

"No woman's ever left you. You need to separate that from the reality of the situation."

"One, she hasn't left me. And two, what exactly is the reality of the situation?"

"She's not cut out for your life."

Adam drained the rest of his drink. "Zoey!" he called, and held up his glass. He gave Roland a baleful stare. "This isn't over until I say it's over. Now leave me alone."

Roland sighed, rose, and returned to the front of the plane. A smiling blonde took his glass and supplied him with a fresh one. I should have stayed with Vinnie, thought Adam.

He pictured her: dark-haired, dark-eyed, brilliant and beautiful. A sarcastic sense of humor, an encyclopedic knowledge of post-Renaissance art, and an adventurous attitude in bed. He remembered their college graduation, their hurried morning kisses as he left for his job with Goldman Sachs, she for hers with Sotheby's. Their wedding. The births of Craig and Caroline. The apartment on 57th Street, the estate in Bedford, the sprawling summer house in Maine.

Why didn't I stay with Vinnie? he thought. But then came Kendall.

He sighed. Kendall, the blonde über-WASP, whose old money, Ivy League, Social Register family looked at him with horror; the ultimate club which had no intention of allowing him to join until the public scandal and ensuing marriage forced their hand. He pictured her, every hair in place, wearing her grandmother's triple strand of pearls while she performed extraordinary feats of social manipulation, orchestrating dinner parties from which deals would flow and spouses' friendships would blossom. He remembered her in a white beach dress and a striped visor, building sand castles in Bermuda after the births of Amelia, Blake and Taylor.

I should have stayed with Kendall, he thought. There was no earthly reason for Shannon.

Young and vapid and built like a cartoon. A mid-life crisis on steroids. Why had he done it? The moon in Saturn. Unresolved mommy issues. To prove he could do whatever he damned well pleased, so he could watch important people struggle to appear fascinated by every monosyllable she uttered. Why the hell did he have to marry her? He could have just kept her on the payroll, like Darcy and Kit and whatever the other one's name was.

Eww, Caroline had said when she met her. Eww. One word, then his own daughter didn't speak to him for a year.

And the sonofabitching zoo. Out of all the hot babes coming out of the woodwork, he had to pick the one who thought she was some kind of animal whisperer. Monkeys. Camels. Flamingos. He'd finally find an hour to lay on a hammock and suddenly there'd be screaming elephants or a kangaroo stampede and Shannon would appear, angry and disheveled, demanding he replace the animals with more cooperative ones.

And the sex. Her attempts to clinch her position with a pregnancy hadn't worked, so he'd ended up forced to have scheduled intercourse with a woman most men would have given their left nut to screw once. He winced at the memory. He could still hear the consoling voice of the fertility specialist. I'm afraid adoption is your only choice, he said. Then I want a baby from Sweden! Shannon had screeched.

He called it quits four months later. What about the animals? he asked.

I don't give a shit about the animals! she shouted. I want half your money!

Despite the pre-nup she had taken a fair amount of cash, the silver Lexus, the black Bentley, two safes crammed with jewelry and 40 metric tons of clothing, then she left her Ark without a backward glance. Unless his kids were visiting, he had simply ignored the existence of the zoo. But then Tom announced he was retiring, and suggested a replacement zookeeper: a young woman his daughter had met at college.

He could still see her waiting in the sunlight, her curly hair auburn, her eyes Caribbean blue, wearing khakis and a white sleeveless shirt. When she turned toward him something he couldn't identify blazed through his chest so powerfully it stopped him in mid-stride. Hanging from a leather cord around her neck was a silver bead. Eventually he learned that the bead had a clasp, and inside was the small downy feather of an eagle.

He closed his eyes and there she was, beneath a starlit sky. I'm sorry, Adam, she said, but I don't want to marry you.

He picked up his phone and tapped it. "Garrity," came the sergeant's voice.

"Anything yet?"

"Not yet."

• • •

"You know something, Ned?" said Luna, as they followed a country road toward Esther's. "Mars isn't really that big a bird."

"Oh, please," said Ned.

"No, really! Most female birds of prey are bigger than the males. Female bald eagles, about 25%."

"Why are you telling me this?"

"I'm trying to make you feel better. How much do you think he weighs?"

"IA hundred pounds."

"A hundred pounds! You've lifted his crate, he doesn't weigh that much."

"That's what he looks like he weighs. At least, that's what his claws look like they weigh."

"They're not claws, they're talons. And he only weighs about ten pounds! Birds are deceptive. They need to be light so they can fly, so their bones are hollow."

Ned slowed and turned. Luna looked surprised as they coasted up a long, perfectly tended driveway lined with mature sweetgums dripping Spanish moss. In the distance stood a stately Southern plantation house.

"Nice digs," said Ned.

"Really," replied Luna, looking impressed. She touched his arm. "Before we get there, I just want you to know…"

He turned and found her regarding him earnestly: skin glowing, curls shimmering, lips parted as if she were about to say something that would change his life. "I just want you to know," she finished, "that in some species of soaring birds, their feathers weigh more than their skeletons."

The front door was opened by a tall, elegant woman wearing an immaculate white lab coat over cream-colored slacks. Her grey hair was gathered into a neat bun. Her dark green eyes were tired but sharp.

"Luna," she said warmly, and held out her arms.

Luna hugged her tightly. "Esther," she said. "This is Ned."

Esther shook his hand with a firm grip. Ned had expected to find her staggering out of a bird cage, shouting expletives, gripping a half-empty bottle of bourbon; instead she looked like the head of Neurology at the Mayo Clinic.

"What a stunning car!" she exclaimed, circling it and beaming in admiration. "Juan," she added, as a young man appeared behind her. "This is Luna and Ned. Juan will help you with the crate."

A brick path led around the house, past the patio and the formal garden. To the left, semi-circled by buckeye trees, was a guest house.

To the right, surrounded by azaleas and maidengrass, stood a barn with large windows. Beyond them stretched endless fields of rye. The guest house door opened and a dark-haired woman appeared, smiling, flanked by two excited young children. "Isabella!" Esther called, and they all followed.

A one-room structure had been added to the side of the barn. Juan and Luna carried the crate through its door and into an office, passing floor-to-ceiling bookshelves, an intricately carved desk with a matching chair, and several framed landscapes. Facing the desk was a picture window and another door. When Juan opened the door they entered the spotless barn and walked across its polished wooden floor.

"My late husband was an art collector," said Esther, coming up behind them. "He especially loved large pieces of sculpture. As you can see, from his office he could look through the window at his collection. It's climate controlled, and there's a sound system. At the end of each day, we'd meet in the barn and have a drink. If he acquired a new piece, we'd have our friends over. We hosted openings and invited the artists." She paused. "Two years ago I donated everything to the museum In town, and the barn has been empty ever since."

Silence fell. "Empty until now," said Isabella, watching her carefully.

Esther met her eyes, and her smile returned. "Yes!" she replied. "Until now!"

The two large windows were covered with dark strips of duct tape at three-inch intervals, creating what appeared to be a slatted flight cage. A thick standing perch rested on an eight-foot square of Astroturf. One rubber tub was filled with water, the other held a large fresh bass.

"Juan has worked so hard on Mars's hotel room," said Esther, patting him on the shoulder.

"This is perfect!" said Luna. "Ned, you and Juan can watch from the office!"

"Why?" asked Juan.

"Mars doesn't like men," said Ned. Isabella and the kids regarded him with interest.

"Why does he not like men?" asked Juan, when they reached the office and shut the door.

"He had a bad experience with one," said Ned.

"Ah, well, then that is understandable," said Juan, with a shrug. "I have had a few bad experiences myself. I am happy to watch from here. *Señora* says you have to respect the nature and needs of every living thing."

They watched as Luna pulled on her glove, opened the crate's door, and rose with Mars gripping her forearm. He raised his dark wings and glared at his unfamiliar surroundings, and the barn resounded with gasps. *"Madre de Dios,"* whispered Juan.

Luna circled the barn slowly, talking softly. Eventually Mars spread his wings and lifted into the air, circling the barn twice before settling on the perch.

"Where is your lab?" asked Luna, after Juan and his family had disappeared and she, Ned and Esther were walking toward the house.

"Up there," she said, pointing to the second floor. She turned to Ned. "Luna texted me that you're dropping her off, then you have to leave right away. Would you like a tour before you go?"

"Sure," said Ned, relieved they were all on the same page. "What are you working on? And what kind of birds do you do?"

Esther gave Ned a look of amusement. "The furry mammal kind."

"Ned is new to wildlife," said Luna, regarding Ned apologetically. "Somehow I neglected to mention what kind of…"

"Bats," said Esther. "I do bats."

Ned gave Luna a long-suffering look. "Of course you do," he said to Esther.

The lab was bright and spacious. Resting on the desk were two computers, stacks of journals, and an open copy of *Captive Care and Medical Reference for the Rehabilitation of Insectivorous Bats*. The bookshelf overflowed. A refrigerator/freezer stood in one corner. On the countertops flanking two sinks were microscopes, Bunsen burners, racks of test tubes, and several open notebooks. Pinned to the walls were charts, graphs, maps, and photographs: small bats, large bats, bats with wide eyes and short ears, bats with faces like foxes.

"It's called White-nose Syndrome," said Esther. "It's caused by a fungus, *Pseudogymnoascus destructans,* which invades their skin when they hibernate. People don't realize how vital they are to the environment, and we've lost millions. The mortality rate of a winter roost can be 90-100%."

"Esther is our best hope," said Luna. "She's a grant-winning machine. Everyone gives her money because she's brilliant."

"Including Luna," said Esther. "My lab is cutting edge, thanks to her."

Ned watched them exchange warm smiles. "Are there bat caves nearby?" he asked. "Or," he added, wanting to show his mastery of the lingo, "do you have bat flight cages somewhere?"

"Behind that door over there is the hospital," she replied "I have two Big Browns, three Grays and two Eastern Small-footeds, all in various stages of the disease. I'd show you, but we'd all have to put on hazmat suits. I take no chances because I have healthy populations — so far — in both the attic and the basement."

Ned's eyes flickered to the ceiling and the floor. He imagined a sudden gust of wind hurtling through the house, blowing open doors and windows, and sweeping thousands of bats into a furry, toothy cyclone that engulfed him in their squeaky, flappy midst. He felt a flash of vertigo as they pulled him into the sky, swung him like a lariat, then dragged him into the depths of Esther's dark, inescapable basement.

"Ned, who is new to wildlife," said Esther. "You've turned a bit pale."

Luna's phone pinged. "It's from Carlene," she said, and read it aloud.

bluestreak@juno.com Are you at Esther's yet? Tell Ned to come back this way and spend the night with us

Esther looked at her watch. "It's getting late. Why don't you leave first thing in the morning?"

"Because he's been trying to leave for days!" said Luna. "He was only supposed to take me to Warren's. I'm his tar pit."

Esther gave Ned a solemn gaze. "Then you'd better go," she said. "Because once I break out the bourbon, nobody leaves."

Esther and Luna exchanged smiles. Ned looked at the lawn, the gardens, and the fields, all bathed in golden afternoon light; at the famous, elegant biologist, deep in conversation with the most beautiful and perplexing woman he'd ever known; and at the classic old plantation house, exquisitely maintained and filled with bats. And he saw with clarity that none of this was sustainable, and the odds against it ending well were astronomical, and once Luna left she'd be gone for good, and that nothing like this would ever happen to him again.

"Excuse me," he said, interrupting their conversation. "But I'd like to drink some bourbon. Actually, I'd like to drink lot of bourbon."

Esther stood at the bar in the library, pouring a rich amber liquid from a decanter into three short glasses. "My late husband was a bourbon drinker," she said. "They used to call him 'Batman,' even though he wouldn't go anywhere near the bats. He was a wonderful man."

She held up her glass. "May you reach my dear Hélène without mishap."

"Do you know her?" asked Ned.

"Of course," said Esther.

The fiery liquid had a rich afterglow. "Yum," said Luna, looking down into her glass.

Three drinks later they entered the dining room, where Juan's wife was setting a steaming plate of corn onto a food-laden table. "Thank you, Isabella," said Esther. "Did Rodrigo finish his homework?"

"Yes, he did," replied Isabella, nodding. "I told him you would be very disappointed if he does not finish."

"Good. I am always willing to play the bad cop." Isabella left, and Esther continued. "So, please, help yourselves. How long can you stay?"

"Just the night," said Luna. "Phil Cassava is picking Mars and me up at 10:00 tomorrow and taking us to Paul and Anna Lee's in Kentucky. And Ned will go back to Florida. He's been the best. "

She threw him another grateful look. Ned was suffused with delight, then with a sense of impending loss.

"Why did Adam do this?" asked Esther.

"Because he's in love with her!" said Ned loudly. He glanced around in surprise, as if the statement had emerged from one of the potted palms.

"Aha," said Esther. She topped off her glass, then lifted the decanter inquiringly toward them.

"Yes, please," said Luna.

"Yes, please," said Ned. "Though neither one of us are doing a very good job of keeping up with you."

Esther gave a mirthless laugh. "No one can keep up with me," she said.

After dinner they sat on easy chairs on the patio. The garden was dotted with lanterns, the lawn flecked with fireflies. The decanter sparkled in the moonlight.

"You 'member when Meryl Streep played Isak Dinesen in *Out Of Africa?*," asked Esther, proceeding in a breathy Danish drawl. *"'IIIIII had a faaahm in Aaaahfricaaah.'* Well, tha's me, 'cept *IIIIII have a baaaatcaaave in naaawthernnn Geooorgiaaaa."*

Ned and Luna hooted, their ribs aching from the past hour of increasingly garbled story-swapping. "Look!" said Luna and pointed to the half dozen bats catching insects above them. Esther gazed upward, and the joy on her face faded.

"Ned," she said, her words only slightly slurred. "Luna understands, but you don't. You think bats are creepy, nasty things. Rats who fly and get tangled in your hair. They're not. They're beautiful. They're *so beautiful.* I watch them fly, and I see miracles. Their eyes. Their bones. They care for each other, they feel the same pain we do. This disease is killing them all, and I can't stop it. I've been in caves where the colony is strong and healthy and ready for winter, and I go back in the spring and they're all dead. Maybe two or three survivors out of hundreds. I'm trying my best. But I look at them and I see all the wonder of nature inside one small creature, and sometimes I feel as if all I do is watch them die."

Ned looked up, trying to map their intricate patterns as they fluttered and zigzagged, swooped and reversed, disappeared into the silhouette of a sweetgum, and emerged again. He pictured Esther sitting alone on a distant summer night, her face lined, her hair white, remembering when she could still look into a starry sky and see the tremulous flight of a bat. To his surprise he rose, sat beside her, and put his arms around her. She started, then hugged him back.

"Thank you," she said.

Finally she pulled back. "Y'know," she said, regarding him. "White-nose exists in Europe, but it doesn't kill them. Maybe the bats and I should all move there."

Juan and Isabella appeared. "Is time for sleep," said Isabella.

"No fucking way," replied Esther. "Where's my phone? I have to text Bob and tell that syphilapic…syphilonic…syphilitic little boil that I'm going to kick him and all his muskrats right square in their uropatagiums."

Isabella shook her head firmly. "If you stay up late you can't work," she said, as she and Juan each took one of Esther's arms and helped her to her feet. "You know the alarm goes off at six."

Esther turned to Ned and Luna. "You must accompany me to my chambers," she said grandly, "or I shall deem you rude."

Esther sat on the edge of her bed, her eyes nearly closed, as Isabella gently pulled off her cardigan. She leaned back into the pillows, and Isabella removed her shoes and tucked her beneath the sheets. "We know she will win," said Juan, standing in the doorway between Ned and Luna. "She will save the bats."

They followed Juan and Isabella down the stairs. "She said to remind you to watch the eagle movie," said Juan, as he and Isabella headed off to their house.

"The eagle movie!" said Luna, holding onto the wall for support. "I forgot! Whoa, that bourbon packs a punch!"

"Hell yeah!" agreed Ned, swaying. "But what eagle movie?"

The large screen television in a corner of the library flickered to life as Luna struggled to feed a disc into the CD player. "Patrick filmed it," she said, sitting beside Ned on the couch. "Patrick is an elf biologist in South Dakota!"

"Really!" chortled Ned. "Does he study fairies, too?"

"Ha ha! *Elk!* I meant elk! Okay, so watch this." She lowered her voice dramatically. "It's the eagle courtship ritual!"

Ned blanched in mock horror. "Not the courtship ritual!"

"Otherwise known as the Death Spiral!"

"They sure got *that* right!"

The camera followed an adult Bald Eagle as it flew across a cloudless sky. "Look how clear is is!" cried Luna. "Sometimes this kind of footage is pretty blurry."

A second eagle appeared on the screen. They flew directly toward each other, seemingly on a collision course, but just before impact the first eagle lifted its feet and turned upside down. The second eagle reached out and they cartwheeled downward, each holding the other's talons, tumbling, spiraling, swinging like square dancers, hurtling ten thousand feet through the crystal sky and plunging toward the unforgiving earth. The top of the treeline appeared, and the eagles broke apart, spread their wings, and rose back into the air.

Ned looked at Luna in disbelief as eagles, bats, cedar waxwings, panthers, and armadillos all surfed the amber bourbon wave cresting around his head. He blinked them away and stared at the slight, curly-haired woman, and she gazed back in a way he couldn't even begin to comprehend.

"What happens now?" he gasped.

"They do it again," she blurted.

They reached for each other at the same time, pressing their lips together and grasping each other with delirious need. Luna pulled back and stared at Ned, at the warm brown eyes behind his horn-rimmed glasses, at his sudden expression of concern. She stood abruptly, and he followed her lead.

"I have to go," she said.

"Oh…uh, yeah! Me too!"

"Ok, goodnight," she said, and left the room. Ned sat down heavily on the couch, and watched the eagles whirl through the sky.

• • •

The West Indian Mahogany tree towered over the parking lot of a nondescript office building, the base of its trunk screened by underbrush. The area was deserted, lit only by widely spaced street lamps. Warren assembled his rifle, strapped it to his back, and pulled on a lightweight face mask and thin leather gloves. He grasped one of the strangler figs encircling the tree, and began his ascent.

He could almost climb it with his eyes closed, having done it at least a dozen times before. The last time had been the previous night, when he noted where the branches and vines had flourished, where they had withered or broken, and made a mental map of the best hand- and footholds. When he reached the top he discovered a bit of new foliage which obscured his line of sight, so he had pulled out a small pair of clippers and done a bit of judicious pruning.

Warren climbed silently and carefully. He couldn't understand the need to kill a grizzly, an elephant, a 12-point buck, all living beings seemingly too powerful to be taken down by a mere human. He thought it a particularly disgusting form of sacrilege to cut off a piece of one and hang it on a wall.

A piece of Matheson, however, would look mighty fine mounted in his living room.

He'd almost done this six months ago, right after she married him. But it would have left her in the middle of a billion-dollar feeding frenzy, so, wise to the ways of the natural world, he'd simply waited for her to call it quits herself. Which, of course, she had done.

He reached his spot, and the lights of Key West sparkled before him. The tree provided a solid limb for his feet, a sturdy branch against which he could lean, and another upon which he could rest his rifle. Its leaves furnished additional cushioning, as well as a protective screen. Smooth and light-colored when it was young, the tree's bark had darkened and become heavily furrowed, supplying a coarse, slip-free surface. Warren ran a gentle hand over a branch, and positioned his rifle.

A single bullet. It would be like destroying malaria or dengue fever, and peace and goodness might have a chance in hell of ever reigning over the land.

The pool glittered. Warren checked his watch, and fifteen minutes later Adam appeared alone, stretched, and dove. Warren knew he would swim exactly fifty laps, then pick up a pair of weights and do three sets each of dumbbell, preacher, cable, and hammer curls. Warren watched him churn through the water, back and forth, back and forth, thinking, Jesus, man, you've got an entire ocean at your doorstep and you've probably never stuck a toe in it.

Adam emerged from the pool, and slowly Warren closed one eye. He squinted through his scope, his forefinger perfectly still against the trigger. Adam flexed his arms expressionlessly, betraying no hint of effort. His forehead, centered in Warren's crosshairs, was smooth.

A thought slid through Warren's focus. He hesitated.

A bullet through the frontal lobe produced no suffering. Matheson would die quickly, but his toxic legacy would live on. Still caught would be Luna, linked with murder as well as theft. His mission was to help her. Killing him would set Matheson free, and bind Luna more tightly.

But the sonofabitch deserves to die, thought Warren. He felt a breeze, and voices whispered through the rustling leaves.

Blessed are the merciful, said Sister Mary Catherine.

We lost the final appeal, said Audubon's attorney.

Keep your fingers crossed for me, said Luna.

Warren sighted Adam between the eyes. He slid the rifle a hair's breadth to the right, and pulled the trigger.

The lustrous collection of vases behind the lone figure burst into a thousand shimmering shards. Adam leaped into the air, landed in a crouch, and dove toward the pool house.

Warren gave a snort of amusement. A startled dildo could jump four feet straight up, and damned if Matheson hadn't done just that.

He slid the safety into place, slipped the rifle back into its harness, and strapped it to his back. Pulling a miniature pair of binoculars from his pocket he surveyed the pool area, littered with shattered glass and porcelain but devoid of activity. He imagined Matheson in his poolhouse, the crotch of his suit warm and wet, suddenly realizing the downside of his solitary workouts. Maybe now he'd know what it was like to have his habitat invaded.

A single man rushed into the pool area. That'll change, thought Warren, pocketing his binoculars and beginning his descent. In the future it won't be so easy to take potshots at the damned bastard.

He paused. A nervous billionaire with heightened security — now, that would be a most singular challenge. He caressed the tree, looked up at the stars, and grinned. This was going to be a lot more fun than he thought.

CHAPTER 7

The seedy little club was noisy and crowded. Roland sat alone at the bar, wearing a track suit and sneakers. A shot glass of tequila rested in front of him, two empties beside it. The air was thick with sweat and cheap fragrance. Roland downed his last shot, pulled a twenty from his pocket, and slid it beneath the glass. The front door led to the street, a stretch of road populated by chain-link fences, crumbling buildings, and the occasional cruising SUV. The back door led to a maze of alleyways lit dimly, if at all. Roland rose and made his way to the back.

He took a deep breath, filling his lungs with the humid Key West air. He raised his arms, stretched, and started forward at a casual saunter. His car was parked a mile away.

A few minutes later he heard angry voices. He turned a corner, and found a tall, muscular man towering over a petite woman who wore a miniskirt and stacked heels. When she shouted at him, the man raised his arm and slapped her. The woman staggered backward, regained her balance, and wiped her nose.

Roland approached, and the man scowled at him. "Not your business, bro!" he rasped. Roland stopped and cocked his head. The man reached into his pocket, raised his hand, and with a heavy snap a six-inch blade glinted in the dingy light.

Roland's first kick caught him in the solar plexus. The man grunted and doubled over, and the knife sailed through the air. By the time it clattered to the pavement, Roland's uppercut had shattered his cheekbone, flipped him backward, and left him crumpled on the road.

Roland picked the knife up, folded it, and slipped it into his own pocket. He stuck a foot beneath the moaning figure, and rolled the man onto his back. Leaning over and grasping the hand that had held the knife, he stepped down, yanked up, and broke its adjoining wrist bone.

"Stop it!" shrieked a voice by his ear, as a small pocketbook crashed into the side of his head. "Leave him alone, you sonofabitch!"

The woman stood before Roland, a bloody smear trailing from nose to ear. "You pussy!" she screamed. "I'm going to call the cops! You goddamned mother…"

The slap sent her spinning to the ground. She sat up slowly and Roland reached down, grasped her by the throat, and pulled her to her feet. "I'm not hearing a lot of gratitude," he said.

The woman gasped for air, her eyes wide. Her body began to tremble.

Roland's phone chimed insistently, and he relaxed his grip. He pulled it from his pocket and regarded the screen. Absently he let her go, and she hit the ground with a soft thud.

"What," he said into the phone. "All right. On it."

He pocketed his phone and started walking east. After a few steps, he began to jog.

A crowd had gathered outside Adam Matheson's ornate front gate. Roland drove past a TV truck and lowered his window at the gatekeeper's station. "Evening, Mr. Edwards," said the guard, buzzing him through. Parked in front of the house were four squad cars, lights flashing. Two officers talked on their radios.

"Mr. Edwards," said one. "Need a statement."

"Give me a minute."

"One more thing — we're going to need a list of people who might want to take a shot at Mr. Matheson."

"We'll be here 'til next October," Roland snorted, and walked into the house.

The office curtains were drawn. Carlos stood mournfully beside two uniformed policemen as Adam paced back and forth, clad in a sweat suit. His jaw was clenched, his eyes hard, but the hand holding the tumbler of Scotch was steady.

"Evening, Mr. Edwards," said one of the cops, as they filed out and closed the door behind them. Roland looked at Adam with concern. "You all right?" he asked.

"Yeah."

"What happened?"

Adam gestured to Carlos with a short, violent wave of his hand.

"I came back from checking the zoo," said Carlos. "I was in the monitor room watching Mr. Matheson swim, then he came out and stood with the weights, and then all the art blew up. So I pushed the police station alarm and ran to the pool."

"I've got windburn from a bullet on the side of my head!" Adam snapped. "And $12 million worth of Ming vases all over my goddamned patio."

"You can go," Roland told Carlos, then turned to Adam. "Any ideas?"

"No. Anything on the Cadillacs?"

Roland frowned. "The Cadillacs! Didn't you just get shot at in your own back yard?"

"Yeah, yeah," said Adam impatiently. "I have enemies. So - anything?"

"They tracked down two of them and there's no connection. Still haven't found the convertible."

"What about Enrico?"

"Nothing."

"What the fuck, Roland? How hard can this be?"

"Jesus, Adam! You think finding the shooter might be a little more important right now?"

"Let the cops handle it," Adam replied dismissively. "I want you to take the plane to Pennsylvania tomorrow. I think those damned wildlife people know where she is. Shake them down."

Roland scowled. "You got somebody aiming at you through a night scope and you want me to go hassle the bird freaks? Why? Send the lawyers!"

"You'll do a better job. They've probably never seen a black guy before, I'm sure you'll scare the shit out of them just by standing there."

Roland's frown deepened. "I'm telling you," he said. "You gotta ease up on this."

"You know what she wants more than anything? She told me."

Roland was silent.

"She wants to find a safe place. And I am her safe place."

Here comes the iceberg, thought Roland.

• • •

Celia stood in her office, looking through the window at the eagle flight cage. She thought of the day the Department of Natural Resources brought Mars, starved and vicious, eventually gentled by the quiet girl with the bright blue gaze; the girl who would never have left Pennsylvania and married a billionaire had the eagle not accepted the one-eyed Banshee as his mate. She could see Banshee's silhouette, alone and motionless on her perch. Celia thought of Luna, on the run.

Her phone buzzed. She tilted it toward her, and found a text from Carlene in Florida.

bluestreak@juno.com If that dickweed took Mars there's no reason he won't come back for Banshee so you better be awful careful! Don't you let him take her!

Celia swallowed, her throat burning. The door rattled and a tall, gray-haired man entered, his round, wire-framed glasses glinting in the morning light. Celia dissolved into tears.

"There, now, poor girl," he said, sitting her down on the couch and putting his arm around her. "We'll get him back, and Luna will be fine."

"But Dad…"

"We'll figure it out."

Celia sniffled. "Mom?" came a voice, along with the sound of rapidly approaching footsteps. The door flew open. A young girl burst into the room, her red hair in a haphazard braid, her sneakers, jeans and T-shirt layered with grime, a long scabbed scratch running down one arm.

"Not again!" she cried. "Mom, you gotta pull yourself together!"

"Pipe down, Wizzie!" said Elias. "Your mother's got a lot on her mind!"

"But two people are here, they hit a coyote and knocked her cold but they knew she wasn't dead, so they picked her up and put her in the back of their car and they were halfway up the driveway when suddenly she woke up!"

"Are they still in the car with her?" gasped Elias.

"No, they jumped out and slammed the doors and ran up to the clinic! But the coyote's in the car and I'm telling you, she's hopping mad. She keeps falling over, but that doesn't make her any less mad."

Celia wiped the tears from her eyes and rose. "How big is she?"

"I think maybe thirty-five pounds."

"Dad," said Celia. "Could you talk to the people for me, please? I'll get the 4-foot catch pole, two pairs of gloves and a crate, and I'll meet you at the car. I think Don's in the barn, I'll grab him too. Wizzie, will you go to the clinic and tell Lauren we need Telazol, then ask Ryan to get the x-ray machine ready?"

"I don't see why I can't get the Telazol," said Wizzie irritably. "Jeez Louise, I'm eight years old!"

"It's a controlled substance, and you know it," said Elias.

A small SUV was parked three-quarters of the way up the driveway. The car's petrified owners stood to the side, hands over their mouths, as a shadow moved erratically back and forth within their car. Celia and Elias conferred as three volunteers hovered behind them, and Wizzie waited by the crate.

"One, two, *three*," said Elias quietly, and opened one of the back doors enough to insert a hollow metal pole ending in a rope snare. The amber-eyed, luxuriantly-furred coyote snarled, jumped over the back seat into the storage area, and crashed to the floor when her balance failed. Elias dropped the snare over her neck and pulled; Celia yanked open the hatch, placed a heavily gloved hand on the coyote's shoulder, and plunged a hypodermic into her haunch. Within a few moments, the coyote had gone limp.

"Wow!" cried Wizzie, as several hands transferred the coyote from the car to the crate. "Look how pretty she is!"

The latest patient had been x-rayed, given medication, and transferred to a recovery area in the clinic. The last volunteer had gone home. Celia sat in a chair in her living room, going over intake records. Elias watched the baseball game from the couch as Wizzie leaned against him, transfixed by an old hardback copy of "The Call of the Wild." The phone rang, and Celia picked it up.

"Celia Jenkins?" said the male voice. "This is Officer Erik Gunderman, Department of Law Enforcement for U.S. Fish and Wildlife Service. I'm wondering if I might come by your center tomorrow and talk to you about the missing Bald Eagle. I can work around your schedule, if you could give me a time."

"Oh," said Celia.

"Is there a time that works best for you?"

"Yes."

"What would that be?"

"Um."

"Morning? Afternoon?"

"There."

"Afternoon?"

"Right."

"Two o'clock?"

"Ah."

"Okay, thank you. I look forward to seeing you."

Celia hung up the phone, breathless. As Elias and Wizzie looked toward her, she covered her face with her hands and sobbed.

"Oh, Pop!" sighed Wizzie. "There she goes again."

• • •

Ned opened his eyes, then shut them quickly. But not quickly enough.

Needles of pain shot through his skull. His mouth was parched. He rolled over and groaned.

The bedside clock said 7:48 AM. He struggled out of bed, staggered to the bathroom, and stood before the toilet, cursing the inventor of bourbon. Closing the shades against the sunlight, he climbed into the shower.

Clad in a pair of shorts and his last clean T-shirt, he walked into the kitchen and poured himself a large cup of coffee. Esther's voice emanated from another room, speaking some kind of gibberish. She must be in even worse shape than me, thought Ned. He sipped his coffee and stared out the window, trying to plan his trip home, prevented from doing so by his grievously wounded brain cells.

Esther strode into the kitchen in a skirt, blouse, low heels, and a lab coat, immaculately coiffed, holding a phone. *"Würden Sie mir Ihre neuesten Testergebnisse senden?"* she asked, catching Ned's eye and pointing to a bottle of aspirin on the window ledge. *"Ja, ich würde es wirklich schätzen. Können Sie sich eine Minute halten? Danke."*

She pressed the phone against her shoulder. "New statistics out of Frankfurt," she said, nodding encouragingly. "Is Luna up?"

"I uh, don't know," said Ned. "She wasn't in her room."

"She's probably in the barn. I'll be done in 15 minutes. *Dank für das Halten,"* she said into the phone, and disappeared.

Ned entered the office and looked through the picture window. The barn was bathed in morning sun. Curled on a pair of cushions beneath Mars's perch was Luna, eyes closed, halfway covered by a blanket. On the floor beside her stood the great dark eagle, delicately preening her hair.

Ned watched her sleep. She stirred, and a shadow crossed her face. A dream, thought Ned, and wondered if he should be there when she woke up. The problem, of course, was the creature standing guard over her. He's not that big a bird, Luna had said. Ned wondered if the eagle was like a suburban yard dog, aggressive only when there was a barrier between it and the prospective intruder. Perhaps by now it felt a bit of goodwill toward him, since he'd chauffeured the damned thing at no charge for 850 miles.

He was returning to Florida this morning. He had to say goodbye.

He opened the solid wooden door and stepped into the barn, willing his body to convey confident nonchalance. Mars looked up. Ned took two more steps and Luna stirred, then opened her eyes. "Harry?" she said, her voice filled with hope. She sat up and saw the barn, the perch, and the carefully watching bird; she touched its chest feathers, and her face crumpled with grief. The eagle raised every feather on its snowy head, let out a war cry, and launched itself at Ned.

Ned turned and ran for his life. He hurtled through the office door, slammed it behind him, and a split second later he heard a heavy thud and the ripping sound of claws sliding down wood. They're not claws, Luna had said. They're talons.

He leaned backward on the door, head and heart both pounding. A minute later, or maybe it was an hour, there was a soft knock on the door. "Ned?" came her voice.

"What?"

"Can you open the door? He's back on his perch."

Unwillingly, he opened the door a crack. Luna slipped in and closed it behind her. "Are you okay?" she asked. "Why would you do that?"

Ned sat down on the edge of the desk. "I don't know," he said. "Maybe I'm still drunk."

She gave him a sad smile. "Who's Harry?" he asked, and all trace of emotion vanished from her face.

"No one," she said. "Come on. Let's get you on the road."

Esther put down her phone as they walked into the kitchen. "All hell has broken loose," she said. "Harper says someone took a shot at your husband last night."

Ned's jaw dropped. "With a gun?" he asked.

"Warren," whispered Luna, and locked eyes with Esther. Ned looked incredulously from one to the other.

"You think *Warren* tried to *shoot* him?" he demanded. "You do, don't you? Remember when we were at his house, and he said he was going to take Adam out? I didn't think he meant on a date, but I didn't think he was going to try to kill him!"

"If it was Warren, he wasn't trying to kill him," said Esther matter-of-factly. "If Warren wanted to kill him, he'd have done it."

"But..."

"You both need to get out of here," said Esther. "The hotline's burning. Carlene said the cops in Florida are looking for you and a long-haired guy with a '68 Cadillac. It won't take long before the cops in Georgia start looking for you and a long-haired guy with a '57 Chevy."

Ned hesitated, torn between elation and dismay. "Come on," he said. "Let's go."

They left the stately plantation house behind, cruising between the line of sweetgums dripping Spanish moss. As they reached the end of the driveway, a police car pulled in. It passed them unhurriedly, the two police officers glancing at them and continuing toward the house. Luna turned her face away, and Ned drove on.

The Saturday morning traffic was sparse. The cover had slipped and Ned could see the eagle in his rearview mirror, perched regally in the crate. BOWLING GREEN, KY, read the sign. 392 MILES.

"Ugh, do I have a headache," said Luna, and regarded her phone. "Look, it's from Warren!"

PRIVATE CALLER What do you mean, was it me? That's the way rumors get started.

"He'll never admit it," she said, and texted him back.

777-222-3800 Seriously, don't do that again.

"I'm going to line up my next ride," she told Ned.

777-222-3800 Had to leave Esther's early. On the road to Paul & Anna Lee's. Can anyone help me from there?

"I'm not using your name because I'm trying to protect you," she said.

"That would be nice," said Ned, picturing her giant carnivore hurtling toward him. A moment later the phone pinged, and she read it aloud.

bluestreak@juno.com That Ned is one fine man! Just sayin'.

Luna's eyes widened. "My first name on your burner is the least of my problems," said Ned. Luna continued to read the texts aloud.

bluestreak@juno.com BTW, cops are going nutty in FL because hunting season just opened on rich bipeds.

greenplanet@hotmail.com Damn I wish somebody would take a shot at my ex.

crocodilians@gmail.com Me too, I could pay them good money. NOT!

toby@eastshorerescue.org Honey come to my place next. I'm three hours north of Paul & Anna Lee's.

pacificawild@outlook.com FYI, we're here outside Portland OR and they just showed up looking for a missing bald eagle.

rockymtbighorns@gmail.com Here too. We're near Aurora, CO.

amphibious632@att.net Ditto, we're in Alabama.

"Jesus," said Ned.

"They won't catch us, Ned," she said. "I know how to do this."

Her voice was low, but Ned could actually feel a swirl of adrenaline emanating from her skin. He frowned, puzzled. Mars shifted on his perch and shook his feathers.

annalee@bluemoonwildlife.org Nothing yet here in KY, so y'all keep heading this way.

"Here's something from Harper," said Luna.

689-333-2150 Security upswing in the Sunshine State. Haven't seen Adam yet but Carlos says he's loading for bear.

"Can't you get any of your friends to talk to him?" asked Ned. "Not your rehabber friends, your rich friends."

"I don't have any rich friends. The more money you have, the squishier the definition of 'friend' becomes." She paused, then continued as if the answer were obvious. "If you had to choose between having me as a friend or Adam, who would you choose?"

"You," he said, as if he didn't understand the question.

A flash of distrust crossed her face, then she gazed at him ruefully. "I must have a hundred years on you," she said. "If anyone catches up with us, you're not my friend. You're my hostage."

"I kind of am your hostage."

Luna's expression softened. "You're my friend," she said, and went back to her phone.

CHAPTER 8

The sign for the Western Pennsylvania Wildlife Center was nearly hidden by a sea of trees. Erik Gunderman spotted it, slowed his rented sedan, and turned onto a dirt road. The rolling farmland, wooded hills, and stately mountains of Pennsylvania were beautiful, but he felt parched and landlocked. He missed the Loxahatchee's spongy earth, its slow damp air, and the clattering call of the anhingas as they dried their wings in the sun.

He had arrived in town the previous afternoon, checked into a motel, and spent part of the evening poring over the Western Pennsylvania Wildlife Center's website. It was a carefully created combination of inspirational stories, disturbing statistics, and impressive photographs. It contained instructions to follow if one discovered an injured animal, and ended with an enthusiastic invitation to donate time, money, and/or supplies. He knew the names of the founders and the volunteers, and had read two dozen rescue stories.

"Bunny-huggers," most of his biologist friends called wildlife rehabilitators dismissively, and many of his Fish and Wildlife colleagues agreed. "Spending time and money on individuals is a waste," they said. "Only populations matter."

But Gunderman liked the rehabbers he knew, and always tried to give them the benefit of the doubt. They were a tough bunch, the odds stacked against them, constantly stressed by too many injured creatures and not enough time or money with which to care for them. They lived in an emotional riptide, caught between compassion and pragmatism. He thought of his friend Beth, who kept two baby squirrels alive for three days, syringing formula into their tiny mouths every hour. When they died she sobbed on his shoulder, then fed them to one of her hawks.

The problem with rehabilitators, though, was sometimes they just didn't follow the rules. State and federal laws were meant to protect everyone, especially the wildlife, and there was no excuse for disobeying them. There had been cases of rehabbers simply taking matters into their own hands, and then there was Luna Burke. He understood her situation was complicated, but to actually take a federally protected bird and hide from her own regulatory agency? He shook his head.

Luna Burke. He still didn't have a complete picture of her. So far she seemed to be a mass of contradictions, her life before marrying Adam Matheson not well chronicled at all.

He spotted a mailbox and another sign, and turned onto a dirt driveway leading into the woods. A hundred yards ahead was a young girl, her unruly red hair in a braid, her hands in the pockets of her dirty jeans. As he approached she stood her ground, scowling. She looks like the protester of Tiananmen Square, he thought, and stopped his car.

The girl didn't move. Finally he opened the door and stood up. "Hello," he called. "You must be Wizzie."

"That's Winifred, to you," snapped the girl.

"Ah, Winifred. Okay. I'm Officer Gunderman, from U.S. Fish and…"

"I know who you are," said Wizzie. "I don't want you scaring my mother. And you can't have Banshee, either."

"I'm not here to scare your mother or to take Banshee. I'm here to help recover Banshee's missing mate."

Gunderman sat in the center's office trying not to stare at Celia, who reminded him of the doe who had entranced him when he was five years old. She regarded him from behind her desk, fair-haired, delicately-featured, poised for flight. Don't spook the wild folk with your predator eyes, his grandmother used to tell him. They'll think you mean them harm.

"So you see," he concluded, "U.S. Fish and Wildlife seeks to implement the safe return of the eagle, and we would like your help."

"But return to where?" asked Elias. "Will you bring him back to us? His mate is here. They're a bonded pair."

"I agree that would be the best solution, but ultimately the decision will be up to the agency. I will do my best to reunite the pair. Can you tell me where Ms. Burke is?"

"No," said Celia, in her soft voice. "No one knows where she is." No one, she thought, except the 119 rehabbers who know she's on her way to the Blue Moon Wildlife Center in Kentucky.

Outside, a car door slammed and footsteps approached. The screen door opened. Roland Edwards filled the doorway, wearing sunglasses, a perfectly tailored suit, and a look of intense irritation. Jaws dropped, Celia gasped, and Wizzie bolted from her chair.

"I'll save you, Mom!" she shouted. She rushed to the door and slid to a stop In front of Roland, hands raised, the top of her head just about even with his waist.

"Get off our land!" she cried.

Roland frowned. "You are one rude little girl," he rumbled. "Somebody ought to teach you some manners." Unsmiling, he regarded the rest of the crowd. "Where's Luna Burke?"

Celia swallowed, heart pounding, unable to decide which was worse: the sudden appearance of the nightmarish figure, or the sight of her feral child, snarling and snapping her teeth at a man eight times her size.

Gunderman rose and extended his hand. "Erik Gunderman, U.S. Fish and Wildlife," he said. "We met in Florida."

"I know," said Roland, shaking his hand, annoyed at the unexpected presence of a uniformed law enforcement officer.

Keeping his expression neutral, Gunderman once again assessed Roland's height, weight, and physical condition, which were formidable, and his simmering expression, which upped the ante significantly. His training had provided him with an arsenal of techniques to use against smugglers, poachers, and illegal traffickers; he hadn't planned on adding a professional defensive lineman-turned-bodyguard to his list of adversaries.

"If either one of you think you're taking Banshee, you've got another think coming," announced Wizzie sharply.

"Wizzie!" growled Elias, then he turned to Roland. "Are you going to try to take our other eagle?"

"I don't want your damned eagle," said Roland. "I want to know where's Luna Burke?"

"We don't know," said Elias.

"She's in Texas," said Wizzie.

"Texas!" said Celia and Elias in unison, as if she'd said "Bulgaria."

"How do you know she's in Texas?" said Roland suspiciously.

"That's what the guy who delivers our hay says he heard," said Wizzie.

"We don't have a guy who...ah! The guy who delivers our hay!" said Elias. "Yup, there's a feed store in town, you might want to ask around there."

Roland shook his head. "Here's some free advice," he rumbled. "Don't make me mad."

Gunderman glanced at Celia, who was turning increasingly pale. "Mr. Edwards," he said. "The U.S. Government wants to speak with Ms. Burke. I hope you will respect that and let us do our job."

"Why don't the both of you leave that poor girl alone?" demanded Elias, and pointed an accusatory finger at Roland. *You* won the Heisman Trophy!" he exclaimed. "You should be coaching the next winner, instead of playing hatchet man for some rich sonofagun! Why are you wasting your precious gift?"

Roland flinched. "Why don't I break you in half?" he asked.

"You try it!" shouted Wizzie. She launched herself at Roland, who looked down at her as if she were an especially irritating housefly; Gunderman grasped her around the waist and pulled her backward, her arms and legs still flailing.

"Celia!" shouted Elias. "Call the poli...where'd she go?"

Silence descended as everyone stared at the open window. In the distance Celia raced across a field toward the woods, her blonde hair streaming behind her.

She's so beautiful, thought Gunderman, then checked himself for his unprofessionalism.

"Now look what you've done!" said Wizzie disgustedly, pulling away from Gunderman and glaring up at the three men. "I hope you're all happy!"

• • •

Anna Lee Lassiter leaned against the counter in the clinic, wiped her hands on her faded jeans, and regarded her husband of twelve years.

As usual she was damp and disheveled, her clothing splattered with various wildlife-generated body fluids, her dark hair bursting from beneath its bandana. Paul, as always, looked like he'd just stepped out of a menswear ad. Wearing a spotless T-shirt emblazoned "Blue Moon Wildlife Center, Allentown, Kentucky," he glanced up from the exam table, gave her a blinding smile, then continued syringing worming medicine down the throat of a groundhog.

Anna Lee checked her phone, something she tried to avoid whenever possible. "What the Sam Hill!" she said.

"What is it?" asked Paul.

"Luna's on her way with the eagle, and last night somebody took a shot at her husband!"

"No!" said Paul. "Was it Warren?"

"Don't know," said Anna Lee. "But things are heatin' up out there. All kinds of law enforcement are makin' unscheduled visits."

"This could be problematic. What are the laws in Kentucky when it comes to harborin' a fugitive?"

"I don't know and I don't care, neither," snorted Anna Lee. "Typical political bullcrap! Coddle the billionaire, and make a criminal out of a girl just tryin' to do the right thing by our national symbol! Bless her heart!"

"I don't know how much coddlin' that billionaire's gettin' if somebody just shot at him. We still got room in the fourth flight?"

"Yep. He can go in with the three other balds for camouflage. We're gonna git that girl and that bird to Hélène's, and not back to some damned goober in Florida."

The door opened and in swept Iris, perfectly made up, clad in tight jeans and a low-cut shirt. "Happy Saturday!" she cried, swinging her jaunty ponytail. "Ready for my party tonight?"

"Why, aren't y'all a vision?" said Anna Lee. She scowled, pulled a half-dozen mealworms from her pocket, and threw them at her best friend.

"Would you quit throwin' worms at me?" said Iris, fishing one out of her bra and throwing it back at Anna Lee. She turned to Paul. "Why's your dearly beloved got her panties in a wad this time?"

"She's in Mama Bear mode," said Paul. "Luna's on the run with the eagle, and last night somebody shot at her husband."

Iris's jaw dropped. "Was it Warren?" she asked.

"Listen," said Anna Lee. "That girl's got everybody and their brother after her, all on account of she made one great big marital mistake."

"Well," sighed Paul. "That big mistake bought us a new Jeep."

"And wouldn't you give it back if it meant gettin' her outta this mess? Anyway, looks like the media's all preoccupied with the shootin', which is good, so she can lay low here for a few days. But we can't let the word out about who she is. How many of the volunteers are on her email list?"

"Let's see," said Iris. "Three. Maybe four."

"Tell 'em don't say nothin' to the other volunteers. She's with a real nice guy named Ned, we'll just say we met 'em at a wildlife conference and they're passin' through. They must be drivin' somethin' nondescript, we can park it in the back in case the police come by."

"Ok," said Iris, "but what about the Paulettes? You know how they live for drama!"

"Will you quit callin' 'em that?" said Paul.

"Sweetheart," said Anna Lee. "That horse has left the barn."

"It's your own fault," grinned Iris. "If you didn't look like the star of a beach party movie, you wouldn't have lovelorn volunteers trailin' y'all around."

"They're *sixteen*," said Paul, looking aggrieved. "They're underage girls, and I'm a 38-year-old happily married father of two! We need a 'no volunteers under 21' policy."

"If you keep smilin' at 'em, they'll keep cleanin' cages," said Anna Lee. "That's all I care about."

"Oh, look," said Paul, pulling out his vibrating phone. "Here's an update from Esther."

"Good gravy," said Iris, peering out the window. "I think Butch and Sundance just arrived in their nondescript car."

• • •

"In three miles, your destination is on the left," intoned Ned's phone. He picked it up and tapped it. "Stop directions," he said. "Call Francine." He glanced at Luna. "I have to call my office. I told them I'd only be a couple of days, and today they've called me…eight times. I can't keep doing this, because I have to get back to work."

The phone trilled and clicked. "Ned?" emerged a voice.

"Hi Francine," he said.

"Ned! Oh my God! Did you kidnap Adam Matheson's wife?"

"What?"

"You were on TV! They showed a picture of you and your car and said you were wanted for questioning! Did you do it? Hello?"

"I didn't kidnap anybody!" he said. "I have family matters! I'll be back in a couple days, gotta go!"

He disconnected, and Luna's phone pinged. "It's from Esther," she said, and read it aloud.

chiroptera@gmail.com Cops have Ned's name and the make of the Chevy. Also the current plates, because the cruiser caught you on camera when you left this morning. I told them I met you at a conference and didn't realize who you were. Said you're on your way to New Mexico.

"Jesus," said Ned. He coasted to a stop on the shoulder, and turned to face her. "You said you knew how to do this. What do we do now?"

Luna twisted her hands in her lap, then clenched them into fists. "They think they have all the power," she said, her voice low and angry. "But they don't! Not if you don't let them. So you wait, and then you beat them."

He regarded her, baffled. "What are you talking about?"

She glanced at Mars, drowsing on his perch, and her features relaxed slightly. "I'm sorry. Just get me to Anna Lee's, then go home. If they try to charge you with anything, tell them I had a gun on you. I'm not kidding."

"But that's ridiculous," said Ned.

"Let's go!"

The rooflines of a row of flight cages were visible behind a neat cluster of buildings. Luxuriant viburnum nearly covered a stretch of chain-link fence, and two small bicycles rested on the weedy lawn of an Adirondack house. The hand-carved sign hanging from a tall post read BLUE MOON WILDLIFE CENTER.

A woman in tight jeans and a flowered shirt skipped out of a building, arms in the air. "Hi, there!" she cried. "Git yourselves out of that awesome car, y'all must be dog tired!"

Ned and Luna emerged, and the woman clasped them both in a quick embrace. "Luna — it's me, Iris!" she said. "It is so nice to finally meet you! And you must be Ned, our hero driver! Are you two all right? You're lookin' kinda iffy, though I s'pose that could be because of the TV sayin' that Ned here's a kidnapper. Oh look, behind me is Anna Lee, and this is Paul."

"Come here, sugar," said Anna Lee, opening her arms to Luna.

"Don't you worry, Ned," said Paul. "We take care of our own."

"We can't stay with you, Anna Lee," said Luna.

"'Course you can!" exclaimed Iris. "Where else y'all gonna go? Ain't no flight cage at the Motel 6."

"They've seen the car," said Luna. "Somebody's going to spot it, and then you'll be in big trouble. Can you just keep Mars overnight?"

Silence fell, then Anna Lee spoke up. "Let's think about this logically, all right? We'll hide the car in Iris's brother's barn, and we'll hide the bird in one of the flight cages. Ain't nobody here ever laid eyes on Luna, 'cept for photos of her in her zillion-dollar dresses, and ain't no pictures of you out there yet, right Ned?"

"I don't think so," said Ned.

"Don't mean to burst your bubble," said Paul regretfully, and held up his phone. From his driver's license photo Ned stared straight into the camera, the long hair brushing his shoulders slightly tangled.

"Is that a mug shot?" asked Anna Lee. "What have you been up to?"

"Oh, here's something from Carlene," said Paul, looking back at his phone. "She says your husband's doing damage control on TV. Lemme see if I can call up this link."

He held out his phone. "Of course my wife hasn't been kidnapped," said Adam, wearing a suit and looking unruffled. "She's fine. I just spoke to her twenty minutes ago. And accusing her of any kind of theft is a little absurd, don't you think? Yes, she has the eagle, and she's going to return it."

Everyone looked at Luna. "I didn't talk to him," she said.

"I hate to say it, but for an old guy he's awful hot," said Iris. "I think of billionaires as bein' short and fat."

"Let him spin it all he wants," said Anna Lee. "You just stay here for now."

"Hang on, I just got the best idea ever!" Iris exclaimed, clasping her hands together. "In case you two don't know, my official title here is Director of Communications and Makeovers. Know why? Because rehabbers never have time to fix 'emselves up, so I do it for 'em. 'Cept for Anna Lee, obviously she won't let me near her, bless her heart."

"Shut up, Iris!" said Anna Lee.

Iris gave the group a triumphant smile. "I'm gonna give Ned a makeover so good his own mama won't know him! That way kidnapper or no kidnapper, he won't be so easy to flag. Come on, Ned, we'll go hide the car, and then afterward y'all come on over for the party."

"What party?"

"My Saturday Night Volunteer Party!" said Iris. "Starts at seven!"

"Ned needs to get back on the road," said Luna.

"Y'all got a long row to hoe if you're goin' to Canada," said Anna Lee. "Nobody around here knows you, and Esther told the cops you're on your way to New Mexico. So come on and chill out with the rehabbers, and forget the damned goober husband for one night."

"I sure as heck need a break from the owls and the bunnies," said Paul, giving Ned a punch on the arm. "And y'all need a break from your life of crime! So why don't we just get us some beers?"

"There!" said Anna Lee. "It's settled. Now let's unload your poor traveler, and let him stretch his wings."

• • •

Adam left back-to-back meetings, climbed into a waiting SUV, and double-checked his schedule: *8:00 ballet - Kaplan.* Ballet, period. Not which ballet. He spent his traveling time on the phone. When the car stopped and the door opened, he looked at the Swan Lake banner and grimaced. More fucking birds! he thought. Accompanied by Paszkiewicz, he met his five guests in the lobby and led them to his private box in the magnificently restored old theater. After they were seated, Herb Kaplan turned to him.

"Do they know who shot at you yet?" he asked, in an undertone.

"Not yet."

"Jesus, Adam, I can't believe you didn't cancel tonight. You're an iron man. What's going on with Luna?"

"The media's making up all kinds of garbage. She's on her way home from visiting her cousin."

Adam glanced at Kaplan's stunning second wife, her head cocked as she listened to her stepson murmur something into her ear. She raised her eyes to Adam's, and deliberately held his gaze. Automatically he filed this away for future reference, and returned to Kaplan. A few minutes later the music began, and the curtain rose.

Adam watched the kaleidoscope of dancers, fine tuning the Electrex merger and debating how to back Florida's irritating new senator into a corner. But then the stage cleared and darkened, and the prince watched the enchanted swan maiden dance with her graceful, long-legged flock. And Adam remembered standing in his bedroom with a pair of binoculars and watching Luna glide among the flamingos and the crowned cranes, disturbed by his own behavior but filled with an eclipsing kind of hunger.

No thank you, she had said, when he invited her to dinner. Not maybe another time, or I have other plans. Just no, thank you.

He thought of the first time he stopped by the zoo and discovered her with his soon-to-retire zookeeper. She and Tom were eating lunch and laughing, and Tom held up a photograph of his granddaughter dressed as a palmetto bug for Halloween. Tom was easy-going, problem-solving, and paternal. The week before Tom left, Adam studied his body language and mimicked it when he was with Luna. He slowed his pace, toned down his gestures, and lowered his voice. He postponed an important meeting the day Tom left so he, too, could say goodbye, shaking his hand and handing him a thick envelope after Luna hugged him and, trying hard to smile, waved farewell.

Whatever you need, he told her when Tom was gone, all you have to do is tell me.

She knocked on his office door four days after he returned from Chicago. Mr. Matheson? she said. I need more shade for the elephants.

How much more shade? he asked, fighting the urge to say, call me Adam. Why don't you show me?

They walked to the zoo, Luna politely answering questions but asking none of her own. In the corner over there, she said. I know a company that makes shade structures.

Would the elephants like something more natural? he asked. Like a tree?

I'm sure they would, said Luna, with a smile. But it would have to be an awfully big one.

Okay, he replied. I'll take care of it.

When she returned from a three-day wildlife conference in Miami he was sitting by the pool, reading a prospectus. How was the conference? he called, as she crossed the lawn. It was great! she replied, then she stopped dead and gasped at the 30-foot ficus tree, the elephants and gazelles basking beneath it. He remained in his seat, wearing a casual smile as he held himself in an iron grip.

I like animals, he said, his heart pounding at the incredulous joy on her face. I want them to be happy. He raised a hand, and forced himself back to his prospectus. Thank you, she called, and hurried toward the zoo.

The glittering ballerinas whirled across the stage, delicate in appearance but made of steel.

He had tossed occasional group invitations her way: dinner at a five-star restaurant, a party on his yacht, front row seats at a pop star's concert, never reacting with more than a smile and a nod when she refused. Eventually she appeared in his office to discuss the zebras, and as she turned to leave he bowed his head and rubbed his eyes. Are you okay? she asked.

Just tired, he replied. I'm going to get through today, then I'm going to have dinner on the patio and relax for the first time in six months. I still owe you a welcome-to-the-neighborhood dinner if you feel like joining me, he added, in a tone that showed he knew she would decline.

All right, she said.

As soon as she left he called one of his techies and asked for a list of all the animals on the property, as well as short descriptions of what in hell they were. Springboks. Gila monsters. Hornbills. This is insanity, he thought, as he memorized the list.

She appeared in a cotton blouse and a pair of khakis, wearing no jewelry but the silver bead hanging from a cord around her neck. He could still see her, poised and polite, yet so guarded that he wondered why she had accepted his invitation at all. I don't drink much, she said, clearly not appreciating the $7500 bottle of Domaine Leroy Chambertin Grand Cru 1990 he had impulsively ordered brought up from his cellar, suspecting if he bragged about it she probably wouldn't drink it at all. He waited for her to speak but she seemed content to sit in silence, looking out over the ocean, occasionally watching a passing bird.

I don't know much about Pygmy Slow Lorises, he said finally.

She looked at him in surprise. She recited a short natural history, then described the galagos and pottos included in the family *Lorisidae*. When he nodded encouragingly, she began spinning tales about the four in his zoo: their mannerisms, their personality quirks, their complicated relationships, until he was so heavily invested in the gripping soap opera taking place in his own back yard that he almost demanded she give him daily updates.

I'm talking too much, she said, breaking the spell. I don't usually do that.

During the ensuing silence he racked his brains, determined to show his interest in wildlife. I was just in Rome, he said. I saw lots of pigeons.

How many? she asked.

After dessert she finished her single glass of wine and stood. Thank you for dinner, she said, and refused his offer to walk her to her bungalow.

He sent no follow-up: no text, no call, no jaw-dropping gift. Instead, he rose in the night and followed an incomprehensible siren's song until he discovered he could see her bungalow from the fourth bedroom in the guest wing. Unable to fathom his own directive, he had Enrico tail her whenever she left the property.

She's walking on the beach, said Enrico the first time.

By herself?

Yeah.

Is she talking on the phone?

No.

Is she wearing headphones?

No.

What's she doing now?

She's just standing there. She's looking at the ocean.

He waited until he returned from San Francisco and, nerves burning, offered another casual dinner invitation. Mystifyingly, she said yes.

Every missile in his dating arsenal — name dropping, offers of career help, hints of a possible invitation to an exotic locale, any reference to his massive wealth — landed with a thud. Halfway through the second dinner, he began to suspect he just wasn't all that interesting. But then she mentioned a Snowy Owl, and he responded with a memory of looking out the window of a hotel room in Manhattan at five in the morning, at the snowflakes just beginning to fall.

What did it look like? she asked, watching him like a bird dog as he struggled to describe in detail something he had looked at for about three seconds. He recalled his early days in finance, when he had neither the skill nor the confidence to pull off a slam dunk; so he winged it, hesitating to cross his fingers and jump, knowing one bad move could sink the deal. Mostly, he waited.

The prince and the swan maiden danced together, bathed in moonlight. Adam watched them, remembering the lengths to which he had gone just so he could say something that might entice her to dine with him again. He lunched with a butterfly biologist in Mexico City. A fog expert gave him a tutorial in London. He added a day to his Vancouver trip so he could see the Northern Lights, knowing if he looked at them on the internet and tried to pass it off as a personal experience she'd be onto him in a heartbeat.

And that was what led to the near calamity.

His trip to Zurich had been so heavily scheduled he never left the hotel. He could have simply come up with an interesting memory, but instead he called Giselle, who took care of his gifts. A bracelet, he said. Stunning but understated. Valuable but not flashy.

As always, they had dinner on the patio. When he pulled the box out of his pocket her smile disappeared. What's that for? she asked.

I thought you'd like it, he said. Open it.

At least he had the sense not to have it heavily wrapped. She tipped the lid with one finger, as if it might contain live ammunition, and stiffened when she saw the graceful swirl of gold. She looked up, her eyes filled with betrayal.

A spangle of dread flashed through his stomach. I'm sorry, he said quickly. That was stupid. I don't know what I was thinking.

She remained immobile, her arctic eyes level, as if she were continuing to look at him only to keep him safely in her line of sight. He reached out, covered the box with his hand, and pulled it back to his pocket. Frantically he regrouped and came up with only one possible maneuver: partial honesty.

I don't have a lot of time, he said. I travel. I'm always in meetings. I was walking by a shop and saw that bracelet and thought of you. I would give a bracelet like that to my assistant or my daughter, so I thought it would be all right.

How do you think of me? she asked flatly. Like your assistant, or like your daughter?

I don't know how I think of you, he said. I think of you as my zookeeper. As someone I enjoy having dinner with. I like that you don't want anything from me. Everyone wants something from me.

After a long moment her stare became less frosty. She took a sip of wine. Well, she said. I wanted a tree from you.

But you didn't know you wanted it, he replied.

A month later she arrived for their ninth dinner with red-rimmed eyes. What's wrong? he asked, alarmed. What happened?

The female toucan died, she said. Her mate is grieving.

I'm sorry, he said. What can I do?

Nothing. He has to mourn her.

Her wine disappeared at a surprising clip, so he asked Maria to bring another bottle with dinner. Alcohol seemed to have no effect on her cognitive function; it just propelled her more smoothly forward, allowing her to glide past questions that normally would have brought the evening to a screeching halt. Did you ever lose someone? he asked, the second bottle gone, knowing full well she was an orphan and personal questions were out of bounds.

No, she answered, then she leaned toward him and said, I'd like to see your bedroom.

His dealmaking prowess vanished. You mean now? he asked.

"This is a fabulous performance," whispered Kaplan's perfectly coiffed wife, her heavy diamond pendant suspended above her cleavage. The dancers leapt and pirouetted through the hovering mist, the music reaching its crescendo as the swan maiden flung herself into a billowing silk lake; and Adam saw nothing but Luna shedding her reticence like snakeskin, leading him into a realm of silent sensation where he, who had seen and done it all, had never been before.

The audience rose to their feet, clapping and shouting. Startled, Adam rose as well, surprised to see the prince and the swan maiden standing together center stage, reunited and smiling for all the world to see. He wasn't surprised, he corrected himself, because luck was what you made it, and life imitated art, and a truly great love surmounted all the odds stacked against it.

CHAPTER 9

Iris's small yellow Cape was brightly lit, the driveway and both sides of the main road lined by cars. Ned's Chevy was nowhere to be seen. Luna followed Paul and Anna Lee inside, wearing a short summer dress Iris's friend had delivered an hour before. "Iris says get gussied up!" the girl had ordered, then handed Luna a bag. "Here are some shoes, one of those sizes oughtta fit you."

The house was filled with people, all chatting and laughing. Glowing in a cloud of chiffon, Iris beckoned them into the kitchen and pointed to the bar in the corner. "Why, Luna, don't y'all look like a prize petunia!" she cried. "Wait 'til you see what I done to Ned! Get a drink first, and there's food in the living room."

Luna made her way to the bar. "You want some wine, honey?" asked an elderly woman, and poured her a glass. "Here, baby, have a cheese ball. I don't recognize you, are you Paul and Anna Lee's friend?"

Soon she was deep in conversation with a circle of people all happy to swap wildlife stories, all asking if her dress belonged to Iris. They handed her plates of food, refilled her glass, and wanted to know if she had heard about the latest treatment for roundworms. Eventually she glanced at the clock and was stricken with guilt, imagining Ned standing alone in a corner, or holed up in a room with a TV. She excused herself, and walked to the deck. He wasn't there, so she tried the living room.

He wasn't there, either. People of all ages talked in pairs and in groups. Five teenagers, exotically dressed and coiffed, vied for the attention of a handsome man. Luna started down a hallway, then stopped and turned around.

The ponytail was gone. So were the shorts and T-shirt. Ned was dressed in a pair of belted chinos, brown loafers, and a white linen shirt. His hair was short and tousled. He finished his sentence, and the five girls burst into gales of laughter. He adjusted his glasses and caught sight of Luna, clad in her summer dress and heels. Slowly his grin disappeared. The girls followed the direction of his gaze, and glared at her.

"Lord have mercy," said Anna Lee, as she and Paul appeared. "Sweetheart, I do believe you lost your groupies."

"Thank you, Jesus," said Paul.

The country western music stopped. There was a hammer of drums, and the scratch of vinyl. "Finally!" cried one of the girls. "Something we can dance to!"

"Come on, Ned!" encouraged another, as they dragged him past Luna and toward the deck.

"But I can't dance!" he protested, and then he was gone.

Luna edged her way around the flailing crowd, and leaned on the railing at the corner of the deck. She spotted Ned: generous, dependable, surprisingly handsome Ned. The song ended, replaced by a low, melancholy beat. He met her eyes, extricated himself from his dance partners, and threaded his way toward her. When he held out his hands, she stepped into his solid warmth.

He wrapped his arms around her. Her spinning world slowed. She began to relax, and knew it was a mistake.

"I'm going to get you to Hélène's," he said.

"No," she said, pulling back. "Thank you for everything you've done for Mars and me, but I've lined up all my rides. You need to go home. We don't need your help anymore."

He looked at her with surprise and dismay. "Like I said," she added. "If you get into any trouble, tell them it was me."

Paul and Anna Lee appeared. "Gotta go," said Anna Lee. "Critters are up early. Who's comin' with us?"

"I am," said Luna. "Ned's staying here."

She followed them through the crowd. Ned watched her leave, until the bright cluster of teenagers hid him from view.

• • •

Gunderman sat at the laminated plywood desk in his motel room, staring at his computer screen and munching distractedly on his cheeseburger dinner. He had spent two hours on the phone, filling folders with information about everyone involved in the case. Luna Burke was not only a Missing Person, but now wanted for questioning in the theft — not disappearance — of a protected species. Gunderman wondered if her husband was responsible for the upgrade. He began reconstructing Luna Burke's route, and dialed the number of a Tallahassee songbird rehabilitator named Carlene Reynolds.

"Officer Gunderman, lemme tell you somethin'," she said. "I meet rehabbers at conferences all over the country, and every time I meet one I say, 'Come on by if you're in the neighborhood.' So how am I supposed to know who's gonna stay a regular rehabber, and who's gonna turn into the runaway wife of some rich dickweed? I don't know beans about eagles, but I do know that she did not steal that bird, her husband did. Anyway, I got work to do, so do you mind?"

He followed Luna Burke's trail to Georgia, where she had been caught on a police cruiser's camera. The grainy photograph showed a shadowed figure sitting in a perfectly restored 1957 Chevrolet, emerging from the driveway of a bat researcher.

"Of course she stayed here," Esther Poparov said briskly. "She and her friend and the bird spent the night, then they left in the morning for New Mexico. I had no idea there were all these issues, as obviously I have better things to do than watch trash TV. What I *can* tell you is this kidnapping story is a bunch of bullshit. Is there anything else?"

Rehabbers had online chat groups and listservs, but they were like secret societies. Outsiders — especially state and federal wildlife officers — never made it past the virtual door. He called the rehabbers with whom he was friendly, but they all professed total ignorance. Even his rehabber friend Beth was uncharacteristically brusque.

"No idea," she said. "Gotta go, I just took in a window strike."

The Chevy was owned by a young man named Ned Harrelson, who, it seemed, also owned the 1968 Cadillac in which she may have been riding through Florida. He tapped his keyboard and a series of photos of a long-haired young man with horn-rimmed glasses appeared on the screen. Gunderman closed the profile he had created of Luna Burke, and opened the adjoining one of Ned Harrelson.

Well-to-do Ann Arbor family, excellent schools, excellent grades, computer science major, gamer, loner, coder, partner in a growing tech company, Florida resident for the past five years, no record. Not even a parking ticket. Nothing to show he might ever allow himself to become an accessory to a felony. He stared at the rumpled, bespectacled Ned Harrelson, then called up a photo of the dazzling, bejeweled Luna Burke.

Bad luck, he thought. Odds were the guy had simply volunteered at the wrong place at the wrong time, and good luck saying no to her.

Gunderman shut down his computer. He rose and snapped on the television to catch the news. Harrelson could be on his way back to Florida by now. Some of these quiet types take a walk on the wild side, his criminal psychology professor had told him, but normally they don't stay for long.

As for Luna Burke, he thought, she's not going to New Mexico. She's heading north. If she has a personal attachment to the male eagle, she has one to its mate. Either she's going to bring the male home to Pennsylvania and face the consequences, or she's going to try to pick up the female and keep going. If that were the case, her destination was a mystery. He didn't even have a theory. He climbed into bed, snapped off the light, and went to sleep.

• • •

Warren lay naked in bed, laughing uproariously. "You should've seen him," he gasped. "I'm lucky I didn't fall out of the tree!"

Seized by another spasm of laughter he threw out one arm, sending a half-empty bottle of wine thudding to the floor. The armadillo slowly making its way across the bedroom flew into the air and landed on all fours, quivering, then scuttled out the door.

"Ha ha ha!" cried Warren helplessly, doubling over. "He looked *exactly* like that! Awww, sorry, Jacques, I didn't mean to scare you!"

"Admit it — you two have been practicing that all afternoon!" cried Harper, cackling uncontrollably, the bedsheet slipping off one large, rounded breast.

"Hours! We spent *hours,* and now I'm going to have a heart attack!"

"If you were going to have a heart attack, champ," chortled Harper, one eyebrow raised salaciously, "you'd've had it twenty minutes ago."

"Good point!" he replied. He reached over the side of the bed, picked up the fallen wine bottle, and held it up. He poured the remainder into two glasses on the bedside table, and offered one to Harper.

"To the gods of justice and mirth," he said. "And to you, the goddess of everything else!"

They tapped their glasses and emptied them. "Everything except for wine," said Harper. "Page the god of wine and tell him we need more!"

"All in good time, Your Goddessness," said Warren. "First: what else did you bring me, besides your luscious self?"

Harper swung her legs off the bed, rooted through the piles of clothing on the floor, and picked up a bag. She removed several neatly typed pages, and handed them to Warren.

"Untraceable. One of the tech guys doesn't like the boss much, either. Itinerary, addresses, and that's the new security firm."

"Huh! I've got a friend who works there."

"Any late-breaking news will be duly reported. For a price."

Warren put the papers on the bedside table. "You are a remarkable woman," he said, gazing at her appreciatively. "Truly remarkable. What are you doing hanging around with me?"

Harper snorted. "I'm not hanging around with you. I just show up every once in a while to take advantage of your gloriously evolved, lethal self."

In a flash Warren rose to his knees, flipped her onto her stomach, and pinned her arms behind her. She struggled and he settled on top of her, laying one side of his bearded face against hers.

"You're not taking advantage of me," he said. "I'm taking advantage of you."

Harper lay still. Slowly her eyes narrowed, and with a mighty heave she rolled them both off the bed. They crashed to the floor, Warren on his back beneath her. She turned over and slid forward, pinning his upper arms with her knees, then sat lightly on his chest. With a leisurely sigh she reached back, grabbed his scrotum, and squeezed. "Say uncle," she said.

"Uncle!" said Warren, whose eyes were barely visible beneath her lush swath of pubic hair.

"I have just demonstrated one of the many advantages of being a big woman," she said, loosening her grip. "Would you like me to let you up?"

"No, thanks. I like it down here."

"You're lying in a pool of wine."

"It's called *marinating.*"

She rose and offered her hand. He reached for it and they both returned to the bed, leaning companionably together.

"Enjoy me while you can, Panther Man. I'll stick around until you're finished messing with Matheson's head, then I'm going to find homes for all those animals, get a grant, and move to the islands. The dolphins are calling me."

"As well they should. By the way, I notice the god of wine has not responded."

"I'll get another bottle. For a price."

"Heartless wench! Can't you see I'm an old man?"

"Old man!" scoffed Harper, clasping him by the beard. "Sergeant, this is no time to hold your fire."

Warren turned toward her and kissed her neck. "Prepare for a full frontal assault," he growled.

"Don't limit yourself," she replied.

CHAPTER 10

Anna Lee stood in her kitchen, holding a cup of coffee and looking worriedly at Luna. "I swore those three volunteers on your phone list to secrecy," she said, "but dang if one didn't spill the beans, and now everybody here knows who y'all are."

"Even the Paulettes?" asked Luna.

"The Paulettes are now the Nedettes," said Paul.

"The Paulettes ain't the problem," said Anna Lee.

"It's Fish and Wildlife," said Paul. "They've been saying they just wanted you for questioning, which wasn't so bad." He turned his laptop around to face her. "But now they've issued a warrant for your arrest."

Luna stared at the screen. "'Wanted for the theft of a protected species,'" she read aloud. "Does that mean the police have a warrant for me, too?"

"Probably. But it also means if you're caught at a rehabber's, the rehabber could lose their license."

Luna swallowed. "I'm sorry. I'll get out of here fast, and I'll get rid of my phone so none of you can be linked with me."

Anna Lee covered Luna's hands with hers. "Sugar, that's not what we're sayin'," she said. "We ain't givin' you the kiss-off. Y'all got 119 rehabbers on your phone list. We're your family, and we're going to git you and that bird to Hélène's. It's already arranged, your next stop is Sean's."

"Ned called this morning, and he said last night you gave him a mighty clear kiss-off," said Paul. "So he's going back to Florida, but first he's going to bring you another vehicle."

Luna sat on the ground of Paul and Anna Lee's flight cage, hugging her knees and watching Mars on his perch in the sun. She worried constantly that he was becoming stressed by all the traveling, the different flight cages, and the air of tension surrounding him. But his appetite was healthy, and he acted unperturbed. Don't you worry about that raptor bastard, Carlene had told her. He's unflappable.

Her phone pinged.

PRIVATE CALLER How's my girl? How's the birdie?

777-222-3800 Are you okay? Are you crazy?

PRIVATE CALLER Excuse me, but I consider myself the only sane person in this whole operation. Do you need anything?

777-222-3800 I need you to be safe!

PRIVATE CALLER As I will be. And the same for you. Keep me posted and give Sean my best regards. That's all for now.

777-222-3800 Don't go! Are you still there?

Her phone remained silent, as she knew it would. Warren already knew where she was headed, which also didn't surprise her.

Luna climbed to her feet. She needed to grab her duffel bag, then get Mars into his crate. She headed across the parking area just as a battered grey minivan pulled in.

"Morning," said Luna, as Ned climbed out of the driver seat.

"Morning," he responded, without warmth.

She squinted at the van. "Did you rent that under your own name?"

"What do you take me for? It belongs to Iris's brother. He said you can drive it to your next stop, then he'll pick it up next week."

"Okay. Sorry. Thank you. Listen…how are you going to get home?"

"That's my problem, isn't it? Come on. I'll help you load up and see you off, then I'm out of here."

He waited while she loaded Mars into his crate, then helped her carry the crate into the van. Silently they walked into Paul and Anna Lee's house. "Anna Lee?" called Luna. "I'm leaving! Paul?"

There was no reply. The hallway was empty, as was the kitchen. But standing In the living room and looking out the bay window was an extremely tall, powerfully built man in a perfect suit. They slid to a stop.

Roland turned. He took off his sunglasses, folded them, and tucked them into his pocket. Unhurriedly he lifted his eyes to Luna's. "You're not being very cooperative," he said.

Luna scowled as her fright turned to anger. "What do you want, Roland?" she demanded. "How did you find me?"

"Jesus Christ!" whispered Ned. "Roland Edwards!"

Roland looked Ned over, then turned back to Luna. "Adam wants to talk to you."

"Too bad! No deal!"

"Ah, shit, Luna, just talk to him! Why are you making this so hard?"

"I'm not the one making it hard! Tell him to leave me alone!"

"Come on," he snapped. "Let's go."

"'Let's go?'" Luna repeated. "Are you kidding?"

"You heard her," said Ned. "Leave her alone!"

Roland shifted his aggravated stare to Ned. "What happened to the hair?" he asked.

"Same thing that happened to the shoulder pads," Ned retorted.

Luna looked at Ned in disbelief.

Roland stepped toward him with slow, fluid grace, as if he were reaching toward a partner in an underwater ballet. Ned heard a heavy thump, saw a flash of orange, and felt himself sail backward. As the floor slammed against him he heard Luna shout, "Goddammit, Roland!" and Roland rumble, "Hell, I barely touched him."

Ned sat up, blades of pain shooting through his head, his glasses swinging haphazardly. As the room swam into focus, he saw Roland take Luna's arm in a rough grasp. Inconceivably, instead of trying to pull away, she clenched her other hand into a fist. She swung her whole body behind it, and her roundhouse punch landed with a thump just beneath the huge man's collarbone.

"Sonofabitch!" he muttered, pinning both her arms and propelling her forward as if she weighed no more than a hand towel. Ned was halfway to his feet when he heard the unmistakable sound of a ratchet. Standing in the doorway between the kitchen and the living room was Anna Lee, wearing a formidable scowl, and Paul, pointing a shotgun at Roland's face.

"Let her go," ordered Anna Lee, her voice low and menacing. "Go on! Don't make my husband splatter your brains all over this nice clean living room."

Roland paused, his eyes on Anna Lee.

"Don't you screw with me, mister!" she snapped.

Roland released Luna. He let out an irritated sigh, then in a single movement dropped to a crouch, launched himself forward, and caught Paul at the waist. Paul flew backward, and the shotgun ripped a hole through the wall. Anna Lee dove for the gun but Roland rolled to his feet, grabbed it, clamped an arm around Luna, and dragged her from the room. They burst through the front screen door onto the porch, and stopped dead.

Standing in a half circle were nine volunteers, each pointing some kind of firearm at him. "Good thing you're so much bigger'n her," drawled a young man holding a rifle. "'Cause that means I got a clear shot of your head."

"Holy Moses!" said another. "That's Roland Edwards!"

Luna yanked herself away as Anna Lee and Paul appeared in the doorway, each supporting one of Ned's arms as he swayed between them.

"Fuck you, Roland!" she shouted furiously. "You want a message for Adam? Tell him 'Fuck you, too!'"

"Get in the van!" Paul ordered, as he pulled the shotgun away from Roland and limped down the stairs.

"You'd best stay where y'are," a middle-aged woman called to Roland, holding her pistol with both hands. "'Cause besides the guns, we all got shovels."

"Luna," said Roland. "You just made me mad."

"Come on!" cried Anna Lee.

The van was parked nearby, the engine running. The sliding door was open, revealing Mars's covered crate and Luna's duffel bag.

"Thank you!" said Luna, as they helped Ned into the passenger seat and closed both doors. She slid into the driver seat, and shifted into gear.

Luna stopped the van at the end of the driveway. She looked at the broken glasses resting on Ned's lap, at his rapidly swelling jaw, at the shades of violet already blooming beneath one half-closed eye.

"Didn't I tell you I didn't need any more of your goddamned help?" she cried. "Didn't I tell you …"

Ned slid his hand behind her head, pulled her toward him, and gave her a long, deep kiss. "Oh my God!" he said, and sagged against the headrest. *"Ouch."*

"Did I hurt you?" she gasped.

"Just drive," he said, and closed his eyes.

• • •

The heat rose in waves from the sidewalks of Charleston, South Carolina. People moved slowly, hurrying only to cross from the sunny to the shady side of the street. On the outskirts of the city, the grand old Southern architecture metamorphosed into bland modernity. Warren stood on a warehouse roof, snapping a cartridge into his rifle and contemplating the soullessness of modern life.

He had parked a mile away, then jogged to the warehouse. Streams of Five Alarm Chili-fueled sweat ran beneath his filthy shirt and grimy pants. His sneakers, old and rotting veterans of Big Turkey Swamp, bore fresh evidence of the local dog population. His face and hands were blackened, his hair and beard flecked with bits of debris. He lowered his head and inhaled deeply, searching for a trace of Harper; and there she was, rising like an olfactory genie, sinuously winding through sweat and swamp.

He checked his watch. He had accessed the building's stairwell through an unlocked door just off the south corner. The owners didn't seem particularly concerned with daytime security, probably because heavy metal tubing wasn't easily pocketed. He drained the contents of his water bottle, and dropped the empty container into a large black garbage bag. Beside the bag lay an oversized rucksack, as well as his rifle's empty foam traveling frames.

He rested the barrel on the metal rail encircling the roof and focused on the entrance to the office building across the street. Eight minutes later, the door opened and two suited men emerged. They carefully scanned the area, then Adam Matheson appeared.

One of the men opened the door of the waiting limousine. Ignoring him, Adam gazed into the sky's hot glare and pulled out a pair of dark glasses. Warren waited until they were firmly in place, then sited their bridge in his crosshairs.

Smiling, Adam rolled his shoulders in what Warren interpreted as a triumphant stretch. Another 500 acres of prime wildlife habitat covered in cement, thought Warren. He squinted, slid the rifle a hair's breadth to the left, and pulled the trigger.

The door to the office building shattered and crashed, and one of the men knocked Adam to the sidewalk. As the clang of an alarm filled the air, both men dragged Adam into the limo. With a scream of tires, the car raced away.

"Yo!" said Warren. "That had to hurt!"

With fluid precision he disassembled his rifle and eased it into the oversized rucksack. From a side pocket he pulled out a roll of duct tape and a pint of cheap brandy. He ripped off a length of tape, placed the roll and the rucksack into the garbage bag, and taped the edges closed. He opened the brandy and held it aloft.

"Here's to staying positive and testing negative," he said, and took a long swig. "Ugh!" he grimaced, and poured half of it down his shirt. "What I won't do for the cause," he mused, capping and sliding the bottle into his back pocket.

Police sirens wailed. Warren sighed, his eyes half-lidded, and an expanding stain appeared on the front of his pants. Finally he scratched his beard, hoisted the garbage bag over his shoulder, and headed for the stairwell.

The street was ablaze with police cars. Warren exited the stairwell and was ambling along a block away when another cruiser screeched to a halt beside him. Two uniformed officers jumped out and drew their pistols.

"Stop right there!" shouted one, then recoiled.

"Officers!" grunted Warren, raising a hand in greeting. "Can I offer you some assistance?"

"Did you see anyone come out of any of these buildings?"

"Yeah," said Warren, and gestured vaguely down the street. "Down there."

"What did he look like?"

"Like Frank Zappa!" replied Warren.

"Come on," said the other officer, turning away. "There's nothing here."

The police car moved off, and Warren continued down the street.

CHAPTER 11

FORT WAYNE 68 MILES, read the sign.

"Take exit 21 toward Three Pines Lake, then stay left," ordered Ned's cell phone. Luna eased the van down the exit ramp, and left the highway.

Ned lay asleep on the passenger seat, a wilted ice pack on the floor by his feet. Luna had taken a back road away from Blue Moon, passed through several small towns, and eventually stopped in the back of a Walgreens. After donning her sunglasses and one of Iris's wide brimmed hats, she'd swept through the store and grabbed an ice pack, a pillow, a bottle of Extra-Strength Tylenol, and several containers of bottled water.

Luna drove through the rolling farmlands of northern Indiana, keeping a careful eye on her speedometer. She passed fields filled with corn, wheat, and soybeans, and felt a chill every time she saw a police car. Eventually she spotted a solitary green mailbox. The dirt driveway continued for a hundred yards, then curved around a soft swell of land. Luna rounded the curve, made sure the van was hidden from the road, and gently slowed to a stop.

She lifted the crate's cover, and Mars regarded her sleepily. She had silenced her phone during the trip, and now there were a line of texts.

> greenplanet@outlook.com Can't believe the sonsabitches have a warrant out. Careful, doll!
>
> meadowlark@outlook.com You have enough fish?
>
> carnivorous@gmail.com You need Valium?

chiroptera@gmail.com Watch out people, there's a nosy Fish & Wildlife guy on the trail.

bluestreak@juno.com You said it! Tried to grill me last night BUT WE ALL KNOW SHE'S HEADING FOR NEW MEXICO.

689-333-2150 Newsflash: second attempt on the life of the dearly beloved.

Luna inhaled quickly. Beside her Ned stirred, opened his eyes, and winced.

elias@wpwc.org RED ALERT We think Matheson's goon took Celia's phone. DO NOT EXCHANGE ANY FURTHER INFO!

"What is it?" asked Ned.

"Elias thinks Roland took Celia's phone. That must be how he found us." She swallowed. "I guess this means I'm cut off."

"No, you're not. I can fix it. I mean, if I don't have brain damage."

"I'm sorry." She paused. "Warren took another shot at Adam."

Ned groaned, and covered his eyes with one hand.

The house was an old restored Dutch Colonial, carefully painted in slate blue-grey, protectively surrounded by old tulip poplars. Luna parked behind it.

Their knock was answered by a teenaged girl. Half her hair was white and closely cropped, the other black and braided into shoulder length cornrows. Her ears and nose were pierced. She wore dark Egyptian eyeliner, Capri pants, and a tattered shirt reading "Eye Dare U." She looked them over, then scrutinized Ned's face.

"Did you do that to him?" she asked Luna.

"No!"

"You'd be surprised. Anyway, you can come in."

The house had rough exposed beams and old pine floors. A large stone fireplace dominated the living room. The girl led them into the kitchen, past the butcher block island and an old stove from which enticing smells emerged. Dried bunches of herbs, some dotted with delicate flowers, hung upside down from the ceiling, and the wide windowsill was lined with tiny plants. The girl gestured to a pillow-covered window seat. Beyond it was a small greenhouse, its open door the entrance to a jungle kingdom.

"Lie down here," she said to Ned, pulling a set of old lace curtains closed and arranging the pillows. "Luna and I'll get her eagle settled, then I'll fix you up. My dad's busy, but he said you'd be coming."

Ned lay down on the window seat, which was redolent of lavender and bathed in a soft light. He lay his throbbing head against a pillow, and instantly fell asleep. Sometime later he heard voices, and crawled painfully back into consciousness.

"Are they saying first Ned stole Mars and then kidnapped you, or are they saying first you stole Mars and then Ned kidnapped the both of you?"

"Honestly, I don't have a clue what they're saying."

Ned sat up, blinking. His broken glasses rested on the counter next to the window seat.

"This is Bailey," said Luna.

"Hey," said Bailey, and picked up the glasses. "Lucky it only cracked the frame." She handed them to Luna, and pointed to a drawer. "There's tape in there."

A kettle and a double boiler rested on the stove. Bailey lit the pilot lights, then entered the greenhouse. She pinched off a handful of leaves and flowers, returned to the kitchen, and set the small pile on the counter.

The kettle whistled, and she poured the boiling water into a mug and added curls of fresh ginger. After choosing two small eyedropper bottles from a crowded shelf, she squeezed several drops into the mug. She placed the herbs in a small ceramic bowl, then crushed them with a pestle.

"Here," she said to Ned, handing him the steaming mug. "It'll help your headache."

"What's in it?"

"Ginger, St. John's wort, and skullcap."

Ned looked at her suspiciously. "Skullcap?"

"My dad used to look at me exactly the way you're looking at me now. Not anymore. See that greenhouse? He built it for me. From scratch."

Ned sipped his tea. Bailey plucked a square bottle of oil from two dozen lining a shelf, then combined the oil and herbs into a paste. She placed the bowl into the double boiler, and pulled a white cloth from a Tupperware container.

Luna held up Ned's glasses, the broken side piece held firmly to the frame with narrow strips of duct tape. "It'll do for now," she said, and handed them to him.

Bailey reached into the double boiler with an oven mitt, and pulled out the warm ceramic bowl. "Lie back down and close your eyes," she ordered, and with a tiny rubber spatula she smoothed the paste onto Ned's face, carefully avoiding his eyes. She covered it with the white cloth, then over it she stretched a small sheet of plastic wrap.

"It's a poultice," she said. "Arnica, aloe vera, turmeric, and oat straw. A little chamomile. The plastic wrap is to keep in the heat. If you needed antibiotics I'd give them to you, but you don't."

Ned sank gratefully into a warm haze. "Bailey?" he heard Luna say. "We left Paul and Anna Lee's in kind of a hurry…"

"I know," said Bailey.

"Anna Lee said you wouldn't get in trouble if we stayed here. But what about Fish and Wildlife? What about local conservation? What if they show up?"

"Closest Fish and Wildlife office is almost a hundred miles away. Our local conservation officers are Department of Natural Resources, they're the ones who are looking for you. My dad has a friend who works for them."

"You mean the friend won't report us?"

"Not if Dad doesn't tell him you're here."

A screen door slammed and a freckled boy entered the kitchen. "You must be Cole," said Luna. "I'm Luna, and this is Ned."

"Your eagle took a bath," said Cole. "He flew around. Now he's eating."

"Good," said Luna, with relief. "Thank you."

An hour later the four of them sat around the kitchen table, sharing salad and a casserole. "I can't get over how the swelling's gone down," said Luna. "Though you're still pretty colorful."

"Black and blue I can handle," said Ned, wearing his battered glasses. "But the swelling and the headache — you're a magician. Where did you learn it?"

"From my mom's best friend," said Bailey. "Mom died when Cole was three and I was six. So her best friend Vera moved in until Dad learned how to be a single dad. Then she went home, but she still comes over a lot. They're just friends, if that's what you're thinking."

Silence fell. "Paul told me you're a falconer," said Luna.

Cole shook his head. "Not really," he said.

"Yeah, he is," said Bailey. "Not on purpose. People bring their birds to him if they can't control them. He's a bird whisperer."

Cole gave her a look of mild exasperation, and returned to his salad.

"If I want to piss him off, I call him Frannie," said Bailey. "Like St. Francis."

Cole rolled his eyes. "Shut up, Bailey," he murmured.

"Eat some more casserole, Frannie," she said.

• • •

Roland parked his rented SUV in front of a strip mall in Kentucky. He watched the shoppers push their carts, selecting the ones he wanted to grab by the throat and pound into bloody pulp. He tapped his phone, and Adam's voice came through immediately.

"Luna?"

"She's not here."

"What happened?"

"You didn't tell me about the goddamned hillbillies!"

"The what?"

"What about the shooter? Is it the same guy?"

"I don't care about the shooter! He missed! Looks like the two of you have something in common!"

Roland watched the skin along his knuckles tighten as he gripped the steering wheel, observing a disconcerting phenomenon: without any conscious effort, his mind had turned the steering wheel into Adam's neck.

"Did you talk to her?" asked Adam.

"Yup."

"Well? What did she say?"

"You really want to know?" said Roland, the edge in his voice a signal Adam always recognized, and from which he had always backed away.

"Yeah, I want to know!"

Roland felt another surge of fury. "She told me fuck you, and she said to tell *you* fuck you, too! And then while Animal Freak Nation were all pointing their guns at my face, she climbed into a piece of shit van with the bird and the white boy model and laid tracks!"

"What white boy model? What happened to the guy with the long hair?"

"Somebody cleaned him up!"

"It's the same guy?"

"Yeah, and he looked pretty good until I hit him!"

When Adam finally spoke, his voice was low and harsh. "You think she's fucking him?"

Roland rubbed a hand over his eyes, then glanced at Celia's phone on the seat beside him.

elias@wpwc.org RED ALERT We think Matheson's goon took Celia's phone. DO NOT EXCHANGE ANY FURTHER INFO!

He scowled at the word "goon." There was another brief silence.

"Roland. You said it looked like the people on her phone list were from those animal places."

"Looked like it."

"Then it would make sense that she's staying with them on the way to wherever she's going, because they would have a cage big enough for the eagle."

"Right."

"They said she's going to New Mexico. Where do *you* think she's going?"

"North. Other than that, I don't know."

"All right. Come back to Florida."

"I need a day. If you don't care you're getting shot at, I'm going up to see Lyllis."

"That's fine. Take a couple of days, if you want. But when you get to Chicago, do me a favor. Take the phone to the office, get the tech guys to copy the list, then you keep the phone." There was a pause. "Has Lyllis been in contact with Luna?"

"Don't know."

"Find out. I'll call you in the morning."

Adam disconnected. Roland tossed his phone beside Celia's. From his left, two beefy, red-faced men walked toward the car. "What you looking at, boy?" asked one.

Roland's eyes moved behind his sunglasses. A woman with a child in front of him, three teenagers at one o'clock, a single man reflected in the rearview mirror. Too many witnesses. The two men continued past him, unaware of their luck. Roland slammed the car into gear, and headed for the highway.

• • •

Harper pulled into the parking lot of a nondescript motel. She pulled out her phone, found the texted photograph, and smiled at Warren's selfie, his face blackened, bits of debris sticking to his beard. She walked to the back of the building and opened a door. Warren lay propped against the pillows, his chest bare, the sheet tucked around his waist. He looked up from his newspaper.

"Reading about yourself, Grampy?" she asked, locking the door behind her.

Warren peered over his readers. "I'll give you Grampy," he replied.

"That's what I'm counting on." She reached into her bag and tossed a printout onto a table. "New itinerary."

"Hot dog!"

"By the way, why did you clean up? I kind of liked your swamp mammal look."

"Better to be captured on digital than experienced in person. Trust me."

Harper stripped off her shirt, stepped out of her pants, and tossed them both onto a chair. "I had a hard day at work," said Warren, removing his glasses and flipping the sheet back. "Come here and let me bury my face between your spectacular breasts."

Harper unhooked her bra, slid off her panties, then climbed onto the bed and straddled him. "Think of me as your bonus package," she said, as Warren clasped her breasts together and leaned forward. "Good God," he groaned, his voice muffled. "I am so overpaid."

Harper sighed, tilted her head back, and closed her eyes. "Tell you what," mumbled Warren. "I'll be the panther, and you be the dolphin."

"Atlantic Bottlenosed dolphins have between 80 and 100 teeth," said Harper, sliding downward. "They're really sharp. If I were a dolphin, you would not want me to do what I was about to do."

"Return to human form, you water witch! And carry on. Ohhh pleeeease, carry on."

• • •

The last of the sunset faded from the sky. Bailey and Cole cleared the dinner plates and put them into the dishwasher, refusing offers of help, having slipped from polite conversation into tight-lipped silence. The sound of a car engine hummed, then ceased. Bailey glanced at the clock. Cole pushed the hair out of his eyes, his hand trembling slightly. Luna looked out the window into the twilight. A car door opened, and a white-haired man climbed out.

A second kitchen door led to the back of the house, and a man appeared so silently Ned and Luna both jumped. He was medium height, solid and muscular, with dark hair turning gray. A Red-tailed Hawk stood on his left arm.

"Sean?" Luna uncertainly. "Hi. We thought you weren't here."

"I didn't say he wasn't here," said Bailey quietly. "I said he was busy."

"Welcome," said Sean. "I'm sorry I couldn't join you for dinner."

The kids stepped forward. Bailey reached out and touched the hawk's foot, then Cole ran the back of his index finger down her wing. The bird regarded each of them with fierce dark eyes, then she raised and lowered her cascade of feathers.

"I'll be back," said Sean, and left the room. The front screen door banged softly.

Ned looked at Bailey, who was trying to swallow, and at Cole, who was gritting his teeth. "What is it?" cried Luna. "Is she sick?"

Cole nodded, grasping his hands behind his head. "She has a mass next to her lung," he said, as tears spilled down his cheeks.

"She's in pain," said Bailey, curling into a ball on the window seat. "She won't eat. That's why Dr. King is here."

"Oh, no," said Luna, a sheen of tears in her eyes. She sat beside Bailey, and took her hand. "How long was she with you?"

"She was with Dad almost 20 years," said Bailey, as Cole settled on Luna's other side.

"How did they come together?" asked Luna, reaching for Cole's hand.

"She was hit by a car," he said. "It healed but she couldn't fly well enough for him to release her."

"Dad said Mom used to call her 'the other woman,'" said Bailey, futilely trying to wipe her tears away.

"What's her name?"

"Athena."

"Dad said we had to be strong because she's so sensitive," said Cole. "If we were upset she would be upset, so we had to say goodbye from a peaceful place." He looked up at Ned. "Were we okay?" he asked, his voice breaking. "Did we do a good job?"

Ned looked at them, their faces soaked with tears, their fingers entwined with Luna's. "Yes, you did," he said. "You made it a very peaceful place."

A car's engine broke the stillness, and Bailey rose and pulled the lace curtain back from the window. Outside was a patio, arranged with wicker furniture and illuminated by a half dozen small lights. Sean sat alone, his face turned toward the moon. In his arms he cradled the hawk, still fierce and graceful in her stillness.

Cole and Bailey hurried from the room. Luna watched them go, wearing a look of desolation. She beckoned to Ned, and he lifted their duffel bags and followed her up a staircase to a bedroom. One of the twin beds was neatly made and ready for a guest. "Are you okay?" he asked.

"Yes," she whispered, and took her bag. "I'm fine. I'll see you in the morning." She continued down the hallway, and disappeared into another room.

Cole's bedroom was filled with books and video games, the walls covered with rock band posters. Falconry equipment lined two shelves. Ned looked out the window to where Sean sat on the wicker couch, his face in his hands. Cole and Bailey sat beside him, their heads against his shoulders.

Ned stretched out on the guest bed and stared at the ceiling. Lifting one hand he touched his jaw, a place of simple pain.

• • •

The suite at the top floor of the Ritz-Carlton was luxuriously decorated and filled with flowers. The lights of Charleston shone below. Adam lay on the king size bed, physically exhausted but wide awake. Beside him Darcy lay on her stomach, her green eyes closed, her black hair fanned across her back.

Adam rose, pulled on an extravagant white robe, and poured himself another drink. In the doorway he turned and regarded Darcy, her beautiful face resting on a pillow, her sculpted body cushioned by a down comforter. One arm hung languidly off the edge of the bed, a diamond bracelet and stack of rings catching the light.

Shiny objects, Luna would have called them.

Darcy was so cheerful, so helpful, so mind-bogglingly skillful. He had summoned her, livid, immediately after his conversation with Roland. By the time she arrived he had put out half a dozen financial fires, talked to a trio of detectives about the rooftop shooter, and spent the remaining time trying to picture the Harrelson guy with a haircut and a decent set of clothes, his hands all over Luna. When Darcy walked in, he practically ripped off her dress. But then, somehow, his body failed him. His body never failed him. Not that part of it, anyway.

Immediately his rage escalated, and Darcy downshifted. She lowered her legs from his hips, and pushed him away from the wall against which he had her pinned. Steering him into the bedroom, she suggested he remove his clothing. She turned on some music and handed him a fresh drink, undulating slightly to the heavy-breathing blues, then she let her damaged dress slip to the floor.

Adam squinted, unable to figure out exactly what she was wearing. Delicate silver chains began at her neck, crisscrossed her breasts, and snaked around her waist. They disappeared between her legs, rose again between her buttocks, and some kind of wispy black lace held it all together. Adam felt a familiar stirring in his groin.

Who takes care of you better than me? she whispered, after she interrupted his merciless pounding and transitioned him to something more detailed.

He paused in the doorway while Darcy slept. Once she closed her eyes she was like a spellbound princess, untroubled as a child.

Adam, Luna had said. Don't wake me if I'm dreaming.

He wandered through the living area and stood by the window, remembering that first tipsy night when she had transported his body and cracked open his consciousness. He had planned to stay awake and watch her, but sleep fell like a shroud and when he awakened she was gone. He pulled on shorts and a shirt and eventually found her curled in her own bed, asleep in the moonlight. He couldn't remember how long he stood outside her window before retreating to the house.

Why didn't you stay? he asked her the next day, when he made some excuse to stop by the zoo.

I like my own bed, she said. I don't sleep well.

There was no schedule. She refused to accompany him off the property. Women had used every trick in the book to ensnare him, to appear in public with him, but Luna made it clear their relationship existed only sporadically and only within the borders of Cielo Azul. Attempting a strategy of his own, he invited a Brazilian model to have lunch with him by the pool, knowing Luna would walk by. Infuriatingly, she smiled, waved, then never brought it up.

Adam tightened the belt on his robe and swirled his Scotch, picturing her in his bed in Florida, her eyes closed. The first time he awoke to find her sleeping beside him he was exultant, his patience having finally paid off. But she was trembling, the heat rising from her body, her breathing quick and uneven. Don't wake me if I'm dreaming, she had said with no explanation, and he hesitated. But then a sheen of sweat appeared on her skin, and he couldn't stand to see her in such distress.

Luna, he said quietly, touching her shoulder. Luna?

Her backhanded fist caught him on his cheekbone, and snapped his head to the side. She scrambled to the end of the bed and turned to face him, a savage look in her unfocused eyes.

Oh, Adam, she said, when she was fully conscious. I'm sorry.

Every ounce of common sense told him to bail. She said she couldn't remember her dreams, suggested they returned to an occasional dinner, and offered to look for another job. No, he said as calmly as he could, as by then she inhabited nearly every hour of his days and nights, and he couldn't begin to imagine the void she would leave behind.

Adam regarded the lights of the city. Roland had seen her in Allentown, Kentucky, and believed she was heading north.

Those animal people. Wildlife rehabilitators. She had spoken about them, but not in any detail. He had never met any of them, although, thanks to Luna, he had certainly given them enough money. They didn't seem to be players, but the ones in Kentucky had given Roland the slip. They had to know where she was going. Were they all connected?

Adam ran a hand through his hair, reminding himself that he had already done the impossible. When she refused to answer personal questions, he stopped asking. When she dreamed, he waited on the other side of the bed until she opened her eyes and stopped flailing, then he slid over and put his arms around her sweat-slicked body. Finally one night she tore herself awake, scrambled over, and slipped her arms around him. She held him silently, and in that moment he realized every dime he ever made had led to this, to the chance to cherish her, to guard her, to protect her from harm, and maybe even someday, to understand her. And when she adamantly refused to marry him, he'd come up with something so ingenious he'd wished he could market it.

He thought of the swan maiden standing beside her prince. That's the way he and Luna should be, he thought, sharing both joy and tears. He realized he'd never seen Luna cry. It was up to him to make sure that never happened.

CHAPTER 12

Gunderman sat in the neonatal room of Celia's clinic, syringing formula into the mouth of a very small opossum. On the desk was a plastic container, and in the container was a flannel nest and three more opossums. Gunderman stared at the fuzzy little creatures, glad his fellow Fish and Wildlife officers couldn't see what he was doing.

Yesterday he had described how the theft of an eagle fit into the big picture of environmental crimes, stressing that they were really after Luna's husband, not Luna. When he finished Elias nodded, and Wizzie asked if she could shoot his gun. Celia, however, excused herself soon after he began.

"I have a theory," he said to Celia, who now sat beside him. "Would you mind if I ran it by you?"

Celia scooped her opossum back into the nest and picked up one of its siblings. "Not at all," she said. "Go ahead."

"I think Ms. Burke is rehabber-hopping. I think she only stays where there's a flight cage for the eagle. I think she might be on her way here. Would you know anything about that?"

"No."

"I don't want this to turn into something bigger than it has to be. You know, you and I are both on the same side. My job is to recover the eagle and reunite it with its mate, not get rehabbers in trouble."

Celia willed her pounding heart to slow. She refilled her syringe with formula, and offered it to the opossum in her lap. "Not get rehabbers in trouble?" she repeated, an edge to her soft voice. "Then why do you have a warrant out for her?"

All of them, he thought to himself. They take their Band of Brothers thing to epic extremes.

"It's a means to an end," he replied. "I know she didn't mean to break the rules, but the reason they're there is to protect the wildlife. The recovery of this eagle will send a message to all the people who want to hurt them."

"Can you personally guarantee that Mars will come back to us? And that Luna won't go to jail?"

"I don't run the agency. All I can do is give you my word that I'll try my best. But honestly? I think she might be giving rehabbers a bad name."

"And I think what you're doing will backfire on all of you!"

She put the opossum back in the nest, and Wizzie slid by the door. "No running in the clinic," snapped Celia.

Wizzie beckoned, and Gunderman followed her outside. There was an art to obtaining information from people who had no intention of giving it; he thought he was fairly skillful, although he was beginning to look at poachers and smugglers as amateurs.

"I don't think your mom believes what I tell her," he said.

"That's because you're Fish and Wildlife," said Wizzie. "Pop says, 'You gotta take what those critters say with a grain of salt.'"

"Your grandpa called me a critter?"

"Well yeah, because you work for the government. But I mean, we're all critters, right? Look at that one! He just got out of the clinic. Isn't he cool?"

He followed her pointed finger to an enclosure where a porcupine sat in the sun, eating a banana. "He was caught in a trap," she explained. "They said he was too far gone, but we saved him. You know why? Because everyone deserves a second chance."

Wizzie led him to the top of the field. Gunderman sat on the grass beside her, looking down at the wildlife center. "I like it up here," she said. "You can see everything, and the woods are right behind you in case you need them." She split a thick blade of grass down the middle, held it between her thumbs, and blew on it until it whistled.

"So where is your dad?" said Gunderman. "Does he live near here?"

"Dead," said Wizzie.

"Oh! I'm sorry. Do you miss him?"

"No."

"Oh. Um. When did he…pass away?"

"When I was five. Three years ago."

"What was he like?"

"'Blah, blah, blah!' That's what he was like. My mom would try to say something, and he'd get all red in the face and shout, 'Blah, blah, blah!' That big guy with the sunglasses who was here? He said I was rude, but my dad was way ruder."

"What happened to him?"

"Kicked by a horse. Right in the head."

"Really? Gee. Your mom must have been…sad?"

Wizzie raised her eyebrows and slipped into her best detective voice. "She *said* she was sad…but the evidence tells a different story."

She pulled out her phone and found a photograph of Celia, taken from a distance and enlarged, delivering a big kiss to the nose of a grey horse. "That's the horse," said Wizzie. "Her name is Battle Axe. She belongs to my uncle Rick. Scroll through."

Gunderman flipped through the photos: Celia grinning joyously, her arms around Battle Axe's neck; feeding her an apple; industriously brushing her coat; weaving garlands of flowers into her mane and tail.

"My cousin Bobby took the pictures," said Wizzie. "Uncle Rick said kicking my dad in the head was the last straw and he was going to shoot that damned horse, but my mom wouldn't let him. She drives over there to visit her once a week. Mom doesn't know I know this, so don't tell her."

"Oh, don't worry, I won't."

"Bobby takes lots of pictures. He put one of his aunt on Instagram, and a week later a friend his aunt hadn't seen since she was 10 years old called her up! Out of the blue!"

"Really? Wow!"

"I have to go help my mom," said Wizzie, rising. "See you later."

"See you later!" called Gunderman, his mind racing. He pulled his phone from his pocket, and began to text.

• • •

Cole stood in the center of the field, his eyes on the blustery sky. He whistled, then waited.

Sean, Bailey, Ned, and Luna sat on a rough wooden bench at the edge of the field. Bailey's arm was linked firmly around her father's, their eyes glued to the sky. "Is that him?" asked Bailey, squinting.

Sean shrugged. "Peregrines!" he sighed.

"There he is!" said Bailey, pointing to a moving speck on a cloud. "When he first came here, his name was Darth Vader," she told Ned and Luna. "He tore part of Cyrus Miller's face off," she added casually.

"The guy deserved it," Sean explained. "He's a jerk."

"So Cole... like...trains them not to tear people's faces off, somehow?" asked Ned.

"You're either born to be a falconer, or you're not," said Sean. "The bird has to be your partner. Your friend. *Your trusted friend.* You make a mistake and maybe they'll forgive you, maybe they never will. Some of these falconry birds get passed around. They get treated worse and worse, they get madder and madder, and finally they rip someone up. If they're lucky, they land here."

"Cole's famous," said Bailey.

"It's one thing to raise a bird right," said Sean. "It's another to take one who's been ruined, and change his view of the world. Like with Mars, right, Luna?"

"Right."

"Some people just drop off their birds and come back in a few weeks, because they can't deal with taking lessons from a 12-year-old kid." He frowned. "Some people are never going to change the way they treat their birds, so we don't give them back."

"Like that one," said Bailey, nodding at the sky. "We changed his name to Shiva — the Hindu god of destruction, transformation, and rebirth. Wait until you see him with Cole. There's a falconer in Easton, she's been coming here almost every day. In a couple of weeks, we'll send Shiva home with her."

"Look!" said Ned.

The speck in the sky metamorphosed into something slender and horizontal, and streaked over their heads like a rocket. Cole whistled again, and swung a thin dark line over his head. In a flash the peregrine changed direction, hurtled back, and struck the small leather lure at the end of the line. Bird and lure dropped to earth, and Sean and Bailey exchanged grins. Cole walked to the grounded bird. He offered his glove, and the falcon hopped up and dug into a snack.

At the far end of the field, a car pulled up in front of the house. Sean and Bailey rose. "You know Dina Pontillo in Illinois? She's clearing out one of her flight cages today," said Sean. "She's your next stop."

"But she could lose her license!"

"She said to let her worry about that. You can spend another night here, and set off first thing in the morning. It'll be good for your bird to rest another day."

"And I'll make you another poultice," said Bailey to Ned.

"Thank you," said Ned. "You have an amazing talent. Or maybe it's a gift."

Bailey blushed and ducked her head.

"Honestly," said Luna. "We can't thank you all enough."

Ned watched Sean and Bailey walk across the field and join Cole. Luna leaned back against the bench and closed her eyes, her face tilted toward the sun. He remembered her asleep on Esther's barn floor, the eagle delicately preening her hair. "Harry?" she had said, then the shadows crossed her face. Ever since then he had pondered Harry's identity, and debated how to bring it up.

All women do is talk, Earl once told him. If you want to find something out, just wait till they pause for breath and ask it like you don't care. Sometimes they're so busy talking they don't even realize you've asked a question.

Ned had always thought of Earl as a woman whisperer, like Cole with his birds. After all, Earl had landed one as hot as Julie Marie. But Luna was nothing like Julie Marie. Neither was she like any of Earl's previous girlfriends, nor like either one of Ned's. She was perfectly comfortable with long silences, so if he asked her a question, she'd know it. There had been several times on the road when he tried to quiz her about her life, but each time she tensed, her eyes clouding over, and he had lost his nerve and turned on the radio.

"Luna," he said. He opened his mouth to begin the carefully rehearsed query he'd been practicing for the past 650 miles, then blurted, "Who's Harry?"

Luna's eyes opened. She leaned forward as if she were about to rise, but then she paused and eased back against the bench.

"He was my dad," she said. "Rose was my mom."

Ned didn't want to appear astonished, so he glanced at her with what he hoped was a mildly encouraging expression.

"I don't know what happened to my biological parents," she said, looking at the sky. "My dad left my mom, my mom left me. I guess it was a domino effect. What I do know is nobody checks the references of foster parents very well. When I was fifteen I decided to hitchhike out west, and a guy picked me up but he was drunk, so after awhile I made him let me out. It was night and I was tired, so I slept in a barn. In the morning, Harry woke me up."

She hesitated, and he wondered if she would continue. "Harry said I could stay a few days and have some food and maybe help with the animals. And Rose said I was too smart not to be in high school. Mars came to the wildlife center where we were volunteers. And Rose and Harry sent me to college."

Ned glanced at her lowered eyes, at her look of resignation. "We talked about me going to vet school, and then they died in a car crash."

The only sound was the wind rolling across the field. "I'm sorry," said Ned.

The flush rose from her throat, staining her cheeks and filling her eyes with tears. She swallowed, her tears disappeared, and her expression of despair darkened to anger. "Don't feel sorry for me!" she snapped. "Worse things have happened to people!"

"Like what?" he asked incredulously.

She stopped and gazed at the horizon, and he watched her facial alchemy transmute grief and hostility into a desperate determination. "Will you promise me something?" she asked urgently, and grasped his hands. "It has to be a real promise! You can't just say 'I promise' and then not do it!"

"Uh…" he stammered.

"If anything happens to me — anything — will you promise to get Mars to Hélène's?"

"I don't even know where Hélène's is!"

"You'll find it!"

"Bu t what about Banshee?"

"Once you get Mars there, you can come back for her."

He searched her features for any hint of humor or irony, but saw nothing but unblinking resolve. She's one of them, he thought. All she needs are the wings.

"Do you promise?"

Once again, Ned was nine. Fighting terror, vertigo, and common sense, he peered over the edge of the quarry to the glowing green water below. Go on, you chicken! shouted his brother. It won't kill you unless you land flat!

"All right," he said. "I promise."

Luna exhaled, her face suffused with relief. "Thank you," she said. She relaxed her grip, but didn't let go of his hands. "Ned?" she asked. "Do you know why we name some of them after gods?"

"No."

She let go of his hands, leaned back, and stared at the sky. "Because they might be as close as we'll ever get."

• • •

Stew and Selma Lawler sat on the edge of their living room couch, silent and apprehensive. Gunderman sat on a nearby easy chair, wearing his formal summer uniform and a grave expression. Stew passed a hand over his ample belly and winced. "I'm afraid this all's givin' me some indigestion," he said.

Selma patted his knee. "I'm gonna kill that girl," she muttered.

The room was small and cluttered with knickknacks and plastic flowers. Gunderman sipped his lemonade, silently appreciating the invention of facial recognition software. *Can you help me?* he texted his brother's teenaged daughter in Sacramento that morning, along with two photographs. *Sure Uncle Erik!* she responded. Eventually sent him five photos taken at a party in Allentown, Kentucky and posted on

Instagram, all featuring a handsome young man in horn-rimmed glasses and a white linen shirt.

Gunderman had been surprised at Harrelson's transformation. *You are very good at this!* he texted. *Can you tell me who posted them?* Her response contained two hearts, three smiley faces, and *Savannah Lawler, otherwise known to her friends as Savvy.*

The front door swung open, and a 16-year-old girl dressed in a tank top, miniskirt, and heels burst into the room. She took in the uniformed officer and the look on her parents' faces, and stopped abruptly.

"You better siddown," said Selma, " 'cause I'm aimin' to burn your bacon."

Savannah sat on the couch between her parents, all three wide-eyed and silent. Gunderman had quickly ascertained that the elder Lawlers appreciated the Blue Moon Wildlife Center not because of its charitable work, but because so far the four-legged varmints in cages and pens had kept their daughter away from the two-legged ones in bars and pool halls.

"So you see," he concluded, "unfortunately, we're dealing with a federal offense. Everyone involved in this case is facing both heavy fines and jail time."

He was rewarded by three looks of horror, all badly concealed, so he continued. "I know Savannah was not directly involved, but some of these prosecutors can get a little overeager, if you know what I mean. What I want to do is find the responsible party, so innocent bystanders don't end up with serious problems."

When all three Lawlers nodded their heads in unison, Gunderman began to fish.

"Adam Matheson removed a federally protected bird from a licensed wildlife center. He said he didn't realize it was a crime, but that's no excuse. He broke the law."

The Lawlers regarded him silently.

"And now Luna Burke is in possession of the bird. I don't believe she's a hardened criminal. She used to work in a wildlife center just like Blue Moon. She may just be a naïve girl who wanted to protect a bird she was emotionally attached to."

Stew and Selma remained impassive but almost imperceptibly, Savannah's eyebrows lowered. Her chin moved a hair's breadth forward. The second finger of her left hand pressed down on her knee. Gunderman fastened his eyes on hers.

"The thing is, you never know with a woman like that. There's a good chance she knows exactly what she's doing, and she's just dragging Ned Harrelson along with her."

The faintest trace of a blush rose in Savannah's cheeks. Gunderman shook his head, as if he were stymied. "He's never been in any kind of trouble before."

Almost indiscernibly, her eyes narrowed. Her lips tightened. One more ought to do it, thought Gunderman. "I'll bet that poor guy doesn't even know what hit him," he added.

"He doesn't!" Savannah burst out. "He doesn't know anything! It's her fault!"

Stew and Selma both snapped their heads toward their daughter. "Are you messin' around with him?" demanded Selma. "Because I swear…"

"I'm not! I promise, I'm not! I just met him once at Iris's party!"

"Ms. Lawler," said Gunderman, regarding her in a kindly manner. "All I want to do is find the eagle, return it to its mate in Pennsylvania, and make sure no one gets in trouble who doesn't deserve it. Can you help me? You sure don't deserve it, and neither does Paul or Anna Lee. And neither does this poor guy Ned Harrelson, who could be looking at a long prison term. I'll bet you he's out there right now, wishing someone would come to his rescue."

Gunderman could see her wheels spinning. Her parents held their breath.

"I know if I were him, I'd be awfully grateful for some help. I sure wouldn't want something like this to ruin *my* life."

Savannah swallowed, blinking rapidly. Gunderman gave her a sad smile. "Here's the thing," he said finally. "I wish I could help him. I wish *somebody* could help him. But I guess he's just going to have to go to jail, because I don't know where he is."

"He's at Sean Callahan's in Indiana!" cried Savannah. "They're drivin' a gray van belongs to Iris Beemer's brother Ollie!"

Gunderman rose and placed a hand on her shoulder. "You've done a very good thing, Savannah," he said. "You should be proud of yourself. Now, I just need you to promise me not to tell anyone about this for at least two days, until I can help Mr. Harrelson. All right?"

"All right."

He smiled at Stew and Selma. "Mr. and Mrs. Lawler, I want to thank you for your assistance. You've been a tremendous help."

• • •

Luna placed the last fork on the dinner table as Ned uncorked a bottle of wine. Sean closed the oven door, then glanced through the window at the yard. "Look!" he said. "She's up!"

Cole sat on the ground, his back against a hackberry tree, resting a glove on one knee. Perched upon it was a Northern Goshawk. Her wings were blue-grey, her chest pale and delicately streaked, and her eye bands gave her the look of a highwayman. She shifted from foot to foot, her brilliant red eyes fixed on Cole.

"He's still out there?" asked Ned, surprised. "It's been almost four hours!"

The soft leather jesses around the goshawk's legs were attached to a five-foot line. The line was knotted to a stake in the ground, which gave her the freedom to move around but not to fly away.

"Depending on the bird, sometimes he'll stay out there all day," said Sean. "That goshawk doesn't trust anyone, so he's just letting her know that dealing with him is her choice. No bird wants to be on the ground at night, though, so when the sun starts to set that glove looks pretty good, even though it's attached to a human. Bit by bit, he'll go from her enemy to her safe place."

"Dad, you left this in the barn again," said Bailey, entering the kitchen and handing him a ringing cell phone. "There's 32 calls from the same number."

"Hello?" said Sean.

Anna Lee's voice was audible to everyone in the room. "God dangit, Sean, git 'em outta there! Fish and Wildlife guy is on his way, and he knows they're drivin' the van!"

For a moment, no one moved.

"Pack up," said Sean.

The van's engine was running, its side door open. Luna and Bailey slid Mars's crate into the back, and Cole shut the door. "Don't go out the front," said Sean, as Ned climbed into the driver's seat. "Over there, behind the barn — see those tracks? It's the old hay trail. It'll put you out on 52."

"Thank you," said Luna, grasping Sean in a quick hug. She threw her arms around Bailey, and was heading for Cole when she saw his expression. She turned and saw a pair of headlights shining through the twilight.

Luna gasped. "He can see us," she said. "He can see the van!" A flash of panic crossed her face, then she turned her eyes on Ned. "Get out of here!"

"What?" said Ned. "I'm not leaving you!"

"We can't outdrive him in an old van with an eagle in the back!" she cried, her expression as ferocious as the day he'd met her at Starfish Key. "Go! You promised! *You promised!*"

She grasped his face in her hands and kissed him on the lips, then she turned and ran toward the oncoming lights. Ned groaned in frustration, and threw the van into gear.

CHAPTER 13

The loft was spacious and filled with late afternoon light. Two tables stood in a corner, one piled with multicolored fabrics, sequins, beads, and spools of thread, the other littered with tape measures, scissors, and containers of needles and pins. An ornate sewing machine rested on a stand, surrounded by a half-dozen manikins draped with garments in various stages of completion. Tacked to three bulletin boards were sketches, photographs, newspaper clippings, and a banner emblazoned "Amaryllis" in loopy, florid script.

Lyllis wore a brilliantly patterned kaftan, her hair intricately braided and dotted with tiny beads. When the building's front door buzzer sounded she looked up from the hem of a half-finished dress, crossed the room, and pressed the button. For a few moments she stared out the window at her Chicago neighborhood, then she opened her door.

Roland stood waiting. He tucked his sunglasses into his jacket pocket and gave her a careful smile. "Baby," he said warily.

"Baby," she replied, in the same tone. He leaned down and gave her a kiss on the cheek. She stepped aside, and he entered the apartment.

"Drink?" asked Lyllis.

"Beer?"

Roland walked past the flamboyantly-colored couch and stood before the window. To the left hung a wall of framed photographs, each showing one of Lyllis's creations in a star-studded setting. His eyes traveled over the smiling celebrities and socialites and came to rest on Luna, who wore a showstopping turquoise gown and an impassive expression.

Lyllis emerged from the kitchen with two glasses and two bottles of beer. She set them down on the coffee table, one at each corner of the latest *National Enquirer.* LOVEBIRD QUADRANGLE screamed the headline, surrounded by head shots of Luna, Adam, a long-haired Ned, and a white-headed eagle. She sat down on the couch.

Roland approached and surveyed the arrangement. Carefully he lowered himself beside her, picked up a beer, and a poured it into a glass. He offered it to her, then poured one for himself.

"How was Kentucky?" she asked pleasantly.

"Not a place I want to spend a lot of time," he answered agreeably. "How are things at the store?"

"Just fine. Hired another salesgirl."

"Anything new in the fashion world?"

"Not much. What's new with you?"

"Oh, not much."

Lyllis took a sip of her beer, returned her glass to the table, and sat back. Three, two, one, thought Roland, just before she squared her jaw, reached for the *National Enquirer,* and held it up with both hands. Roland returned her gaze, determined to remain silent. "He just wants to talk to her, is all," he said, in less than ten seconds.

"So you're after her again?" she snapped.

The first time Luna disappeared, it was from Adam's Chicago townhouse. They had been married for three months, and the whirlwind of travel, social events, and public appearances had left her edgy and rattled. She played a good game, perfecting an expression of inscrutability even as her rigid posture announced she might as well have been dropped into a cage match. Adam had tried to distract her by pouring money into her account, most of which she immediately gave away to her rehabber friends.

Roland remembered Adam's expression when she didn't show up at the restaurant, starting with a slight frown and steadily morphing into something close to panic. Soon he had twelve men and half the Chicago police department looking for her, and Lyllis knew it. At one in the morning he let himself into her loft and found the two of them on the flamboyantly-colored couch, hammered on margaritas, Chinese food containers littering the coffee table. Their laughter had been audible in the hallway. When he appeared in the doorway Luna regarded him silently, looking younger and more fragile than she ever had before.

You back the fuck off and give this girl some space, Lyllis had said, enunciating each word like a mob boss.

Roland returned an hour later with Adam, who was uncharacteristically subdued. Lyllis? said Luna as she left. Don't forget your promise, okay?

"You know where she is?" Roland asked.

"You want to check my closets?"

"Don't start. I don't need this."

"You don't need this from me, or from Adam?" she asked contemptuously. "The sonofabitch himself denied the kidnapping story, which means she left him of her own free will. And *that* means if you're looking for her, he's turned you into a bounty hunter."

She looked pointedly at a framed photograph. A young Roland stood grinning, wearing a mud-covered football uniform. His arm firmly encircled a young Lyllis, dressed in a dazzling summer dress and beaming, a wide smudge of dirt across her cheek.

"I've been waiting for you for years," she said, spooking him with her quiet deliberation. "Waiting for you to quit beating the shit out of people while that bastard looks the other way. Waiting for you to turn back into the man you used to be. All this time, wondering what would push me over the edge."

Roland maintained his deadpan expression, but it was difficult. He could deal with shouting Lyllis, threatening Lyllis, dish-throwing Lyllis, even torrentially weeping Lyllis. But this was different.

"And this is it," she said.

Roland's frown deepened. "What do you care?"

"You are one blind man when you want to be. I care because that girl doesn't deserve either one of you. You don't even see how much she's like you."

Roland gave a disgusted snort. "What? Why? Because we both grew up in foster care? Lot of kids do. Doesn't mean anything."

Lyllis narrowed her eyes. "Don't you get dismissive on me, Roland Edwards. You had one stop. You know how many she had? Like, ten.

Little skinny white girl, running like Flo-Jo. And every time they cornered her, she turned into you."

"The hell are you talking about?"

She grimaced. "Never mind. I don't break my promises. But I'm going to tell you two things: one, you hurt her, and I will tell the police everything I know about you. Not that they'll do anything, except maybe make your life nice and miserable for awhile. And two: you push her too far, and she's the one who's gonna make you sorry."

• • •

Gunderman saw the slight figure racing toward him and stopped his car. He glanced at the top of the hill, but the gray van was gone. Angrily he opened his door. "Where did he go with the eagle?" he demanded.

"I don't know what you're talking about!" shouted Luna defiantly. Her open aggression surprised him, even though his dozens of phone calls had unearthed a lot more about her than he anticipated. Don't take a chance, he thought, and reached for his handcuffs.

Sean, Bailey, and Cole hurried toward them. Luna recoiled at the rattle of the handcuffs, and Sean reached out protectively. "There's no need for that!" he protested.

"Stand back, sir!" Gunderman ordered. As he glanced at the trio he nearly missed Luna's fist, which flew out of nowhere at his face. He jerked his head back, spun her against the car, and pulled her arms behind her. "What are you doing?" he asked incredulously, as he snapped the handcuffs shut.

"Come on, man, leave her alone!" said Sean.

Gunderman glared at him. "You have been harboring a fugitive, which is a third degree felony!" he said. "You have jeopardized both your state and federal permits!"

"They had nothing to do with it!" said Luna furiously, turning to face him. "If you touch their permits or charge them with *anything* I swear to God I will contact every media outlet in the country and tell them you're a liar and a fool!"

Gunderman felt a surge of anger. "Get in the car!" he snapped. He opened the back door, covered her head with his hand, and pushed her inside. "I will be in touch with you," he told Sean. He slid into the driver's seat, made a quick three-point turn, and drove away.

There were no street lights on the small country road. Gunderman's solitary car cruised through the darkness, the windows up, the doors locked. The dashboard screen glowed a soft blue. Luna sat in the back seat, her hands pinned behind her, adrenaline flooding her system. Rivulets of sweat ran down her back.

"Why are you doing this?" Gunderman demanded, the intensity of his eyes visible in the rear view mirror. "Why are you breaking all these laws? The eagle's probably going to end up right back at Celia Jenkins' wildlife center, so what's the point?"

"Probably!" Luna shouted, her heart throbbing as the cold steel bit into her wrists. *"Probably* going to end up at Celia's? You mean unless Adam buys you off and takes him back to Florida? Or unless one of your stupid bureaucrats who knows nothing about eagles decides to send him to some random place in California? Did you look up his history? Do you have any idea what he's been through?"

The headlights illuminated an overpass scrawled with a single hieroglyphic. As they emerged from beneath it, a heavy thud shook the car. Gunderman swerved and jammed on the brakes, and a man in black slid off the roof, opened the door, and yanked him out.

"I'm a federal officer!" Gunderman grunted, as the masked figure slammed him face down on the road and closed a pair of handcuffs around his wrists. In quick succession he removed Gunderman's gun and keys, then pulled him into a sitting position and dragged him backwards into the woods. There was another heavy click, and a second set of handcuffs bound the officer to a slender tree.

"Let me out!" cried Luna from the back of the car, her voice rising in volume, her feet thudding against the door. "Get them off! Get them off me!"

Silently the figure returned to the car, pulled her out, and unlocked her handcuffs with one of Gunderman's keys. She rubbed her wrists, her face flushed, her breath coming in ragged gasps. "Get them off!" she whispered, brushing her wrists as if they were covered with hornets. The man crouched, pulled her down beside him, and removed his face mask.

"Look at me," said Warren, in his deep and lazy drawl.

Luna tried to concentrate but her trembling continued, her eyes on her hands as she rubbed them violently together. "Look at me!" he insisted, and grasped her chin. Breathless, she locked her eyes on his.

"Stop it," he said.

She struggled to breathe normally, blinking as he held her eyes. She took one last gulp, and with a final shudder she was still.

"You okay?" he asked.

"Yes. I'm okay."

Warren cocked his head and gave her a slow smile. "Don't make me ask you again." He replaced his mask, and disappeared.

Luna climbed into the passenger seat and wrapped her arms around her knees. Heat rose from her skin, leaving a chill behind. Warren emerged from the woods and slid behind the wheel. "You don't look so good," he said, eyeing her as he tossed his mask into the back. "You going to pass out on me?"

"No."

"All right." He pulled onto the road. "Well, this pretty much sucks," he added. "I just left one of my heroes cuffed to a tree."

"What?"

"That was Erik Gunderman. He works in the Loxahatchee. One of the kitties made it up there, I don't know how, and some prick winged her with a rifle. Gunderman collared the guy and netted the kitty, all's I had to do was pick her up and take her to surgery. Damned good man. This complicates things."

"If he's such a good man, why is he after me?"

Warren gave her an inquiring look. "Because you're an alleged felon?"

Luna rubbed the back of her neck with a shaky hand. "Right. How long do you think it'll take him to figure out it was you?"

"About two seconds. I left the keys near him, so we better get out of here."

"How did you find me?"

"Anna Lee called after you left Blue Moon. That is one hellacious woman."

"But..."

"I was heading for you when Gunderman showed up. Sean called me before you got to the end of the driveway."

"But how…?"

"Open your necklace. Just be careful."

Luna opened the silver bead hanging from the leather cord around her neck. Nestled on top of the downy eagle feather was a metal microchip.

"I tracked you. Now you're like one of my kitties. I put it in there the last time you spent the night, when you were sleeping. Don't lose it."

She threw her arms around his neck. "Thank you," she whispered. He kissed her forehead, pulled a phone from his pocket, and placed it on her lap.

"I can't see shit without my readers," he said, shifting the car into gear. "Find Jake."

"Who's Jake?"

"Just a homicidal old hippie. He doesn't bother anybody." He raised one eyebrow. "Long as you don't piss him off."

Luna tapped the phone, and handed it back.

"Jake! Yeah! Wassup, man. Listen, I got a hot van I need to swap out. What?" He peered around the dark country road, then sighed. "Oh, hell, I don't know. Some fucking place in Indiana."

• • •

Ned tilted the water bottle over his handful of dirt, made a muddy paste, and smeared it across the van's front license plate. He repeated the process with the back plate, the sound of crickets and tree frogs singing in his ears. The small dirt path where he was parked was deserted. The small country road he had pulled off was deserted as well.

He had driven through the hayfield, then taken a left. He had no idea where he was headed, let alone how to find Luna and free her from her arresting officer. He wanted to avoid the highways, but there were police on the back roads as well. Instead he had found this almost invisible path, and followed it into the woods.

He poured more water from the bottle onto his hands, rubbed most of the mud away, and dried them on his pants. The panic he felt while driving had subsided, but now threatened to re-emerge. A mosquito whined in his ear, and another bit his arm. Normally he would seek shelter in his car. But inside his car was Luna's meat-eating god of war bird, so he stayed where he was and slapped the back of his neck.

He scanned the list of rehabbers he had transferred from Luna's phone to his. He could call anyone, and the firewalls on his phone would protect him. But they wouldn't protect those he called, especially if they were surrounded by police and/or federal agents. He pressed his phone, a map popped up, and a small red arrow pointed to his exact location. This does me no good, he thought, as a swarm of mosquitos finally drove him into the car.

He pulled the door shut, turned around to check the crate, and froze. The cover had slipped. Mars stood on his perch, fully revealed, microseconds away from launching himself through the metal grate and seizing Ned with his bayonet feet.

Mars didn't move. Ned felt a pain in his chest, and remembered his body required oxygen. He took a breath and dropped his eyes, as Luna once told him wildlife consider a direct stare a sign of aggression. Quietly, he cleared his throat.

"So, like, here we are," he said, attempting a conversational tone, well aware that addressing this creature was further proof of his mental descent. "I'm good with you, if you're good with me."

The eagle watched him steadily, apparently unconcerned that Ned might consider it a sign of aggression. He still didn't move, though, which Ned took in a positive way. Long minutes ticked by, and Mars looked out the side of his crate. "Any thoughts?" asked Ned. "Because I'm coming up with nothing. I suppose I could call my parents, but...mmm...no."

He thought about a prospective conversation with his father, who usually answered the phone. "Would you like to hear a discussion between my dad and me?" he asked the eagle, whose gaze returned. But not in a hostile way, Ned thought, so he continued. "Ok, here's me: 'Hello, Dad?' And here's my father."

He extended his thumb and pinky as if he were holding a phone, and switched to a hearty but, he hoped, unaggressive voice. "'Why, hello there, Neddo! Glad you called! I want to talk to you about this theft and kidnapping business. You're dealing with some high-powered people, which is good, but it appears that none of them are on your team!'"

Mars shook his feathers, and Ned shifted in his seat and leaned back against the steering wheel. "You know what I'd say then?" he asked. "I'd say, 'But Dad — I was just punched in the face by Roland Edwards!'"

Theatrically he dropped his jaw. "And you know what he'd say?" he asked, and switched to an awestruck voice. "He'd say, *'Roland Edwards?* Heisman Trophy winner Roland Edwards? MVP thirty yard forty home run draft pick in the mile slam dunk twenty points off the Stanley Cup Kentucky Derby Day Roland Edwards? Why, Neddo, that's *sensational!* Shelley, come in here, *our Neddo* was just punched in the face by Roland Edwards! Aww, Neddo .... son! *Son!'*"

Ned stopped, afraid he'd used up the eagle's quota of patience. Languidly Mars extended his left wing and left foot, then emitted a soft exhalation. "You know something?" said Ned. "You're right."

Slowly he raised his arms, closed his eyes, and stretched, sighing deeply near the end. The tightness in his body began to disappear. He couldn't believe how much better he felt, even though he was still hiding in the woods, an accessory to a felony.

His new spiritual master gazed at him from an oversized animal crate. Ned wondered if eagles were categorized as soaring birds, whose feathers weighed more than their skeletons. "Listen," he said. "I'm going to get us both out of here, and I'm going to find your mistress. Or hostess, or whatever she is to you."

He brainstormed, analyzed, conceptualized, and free-associated, all to no avail. "Don't be afraid to jump in here," he said to Mars. He looked down at his phone, at the infuriating little red location arrow. Eventually he typed in **patron saint of bird thieves**.

There was no patron saint of bird thieves.

However, there was a patron saint of thieves in general: St. Dismas. Ned frowned. He hadn't actually stolen the bird himself, although he had driven the getaway car and was currently in possession. He re-typed "bird thieves," hoping for some kind of support group, and discovered a treasure trove of information: not about people who stole birds, but about birds who took things that didn't belong to them.

Bowerbirds stole each other's nest decorations. Steller's Jays took acorns from Clark's Nutcrackers. Cowbirds pilfered a single egg from a different species, then replaced it with one of their own. Gulls grabbed french fries and ice cream cones from tourists. Crows, the most larcenous birds on earth, made off with whatever they could get their beaks on. And Bald Eagles…Bald Eagles mugged hard-working Ospreys in midair, and took their fish.

"I can't believe this," said Ned, aggrieved. "Here I thought you were so noble, and your whole family is famous for your drive-bys! Or I guess it would be fly-bys." He gave a disheartened sigh. "Well, *that* bloom is off the rose."

He looked back on his life of a week ago, so normal and orderly; then he tried to picture himself at the fantastical haven of Hélène de la Croix, the Land of Oz for plunderous eagles. His phone rang and he jumped, sending it sailing onto the passenger side floor. He braced himself, afraid it might have triggered the eagle's slaughter reflex, but Mars remained on his perch. He retrieved the phone. **PRIVATE CALLER**, read the screen. "Hello?" he said.

"Ned!" came Luna's voice. "Are you okay?"

"Luna! Are you in jail?"

"No! Can you stay wherever you are for a little longer?"

"I guess…"

"Wait for me. I'll call you right back."

The line went dead. Ned slumped in his seat. Mars lowered his head, and began preening his feathers.

CHAPTER 14

Warren drove the blue Dodge Ram northwest. The back seats were folded down to accommodate the crate, and Luna curled before it on a blanket. Ned sat on the passenger seat, obsessively scanning the highway for police cars.

After they left him in the woods, Warren and Luna had taken Gunderman's car and driven the short distance to where Warren's borrowed sedan was parked. They switched cars, and left Gunderman's by the side of the road.

A half hour later, a man named Glenn greeted them in faded jeans, a jean vest, and a baseball cap emblazoned, "REPENT." Warren parked his car in an old garage, then all three climbed into Glenn's Dodge Ram and drove to the wooded path where Ned waited in the van. Well, look at you! Warren had said to Ned, taking in his short hair, taped glasses, and bruised face. Luna said you'd been feeling your oats lately!

Warren sipped coffee from a thermos as the highway signs flashed by. "Damned fine of Glenn to loan us his truck," he said.

Mars watched Luna from his perch. She tried to breathe slowly and deeply, knowing she was the reason he was not sleeping. People could master their own body language, and trick one another with a false smile or a casual pose. But animals could feel stress rise in burning waves from skin, fur and feathers, invisible but toxic, capable of causing sickness, pain, and death. Recognizing it was second nature to them, as well as to a select population of human beings.

Warren met her eyes in the rearview mirror. "Doing okay?" he asked.

"Sure am," she replied.

"Then call Sean and tell him." He gestured toward a battered leather knapsack on the floor. "Reach in there and get a phone for me, wouldja?" he asked Ned.

Ned rummaged through the knapsack. "Nah, the blue one," said Warren. The fourth phone was blue, and Warren returned Ned's look. "What?" he said. "You never know when you'll need an extra phone. Find Cole and put it on speaker."

"What are you doing with Cole's number?" asked Luna.

"I got everybody's number."

"Do you think Sean's line is bugged?" asked Ned.

"If Matheson has Celia's phone, then yeah."

"What about Gunderman?"

"Legally, he can't track a line that fast. You have to go through channels. And Jesus, I mean, it's not like this is a plot to blow up the White House."

"Hello?" said Cole.

"Cole, it's Luna!"

"Are you all right? Hold on, here's my dad!"

"Oh jeez, Luna, am I glad to hear from you," came Sean's voice, heavy with relief. "Where are you? Is this your one phone call?"

"No, I got away. I'm on the road with Ned."

"How could you get away?"

"Seaaaaan," said Warren. "Wassup, man."

"Warren?"

The kids' awed voices were audible in the background. "They're with the Panther Man!" said Bailey.

"We should stay off the phone," said Sean. "But Gunderman'll be back at me tomorrow. What should I say?"

Warren rubbed his head. "Tell you what. Act like you don't know shit, then when he threatens to take away your license tell him she's headed for…mmm…Nevada."

"Okay. But why Nevada?"

"Because she had a sudden urge to play the slots!" said Ned exasperatedly.

Warren's eyebrows shot up. "Aren't *you* a closet wiseass?" he asked.

"What happened to New Mexico?" asked Luna.

"Oh, right, I forgot about New Mexico," said Warren. "Okay, make it New Mexico."

"Sean," said Ned. "Can you keep the group list focused on New Mexico?"

"You got it," said Sean.

Ned hung up, gathered the phones, and dropped them back into the leather knapsack. Warren glanced into the rearview mirror, at Luna sitting silently with her knees drawn to her chest. "Hey," he said. "Why don't you tell Ned here another Hélène story?"

"I…I can't think of any right now."

"Tell him about when she took on the premier of Ontario."

"Oh, that's a good one. But I don't know if I can tell it right."

"'Course you can. Come on, quit making me do all the work."

Luna rubbed her eyes, and Warren gave an exaggerated sigh. "So after Hélène became the Canadian Bird Woman," he said, "people started sending her donations. She set up a nonprofit, and collected enough money to buy a house on a big piece of land. She built a clinic, put up a couple of flight cages, and called it the Port Clyde Eagle Sanctuary.

"Don't forget, by this time, she was a mythical figure. Anybody besides her volunteers showed up, she'd throw 'em the hell out. She hated the spotlight. Hated most people. Didn't matter. Just burnished her legend."

He paused, and Luna's voice drifted from the back of the Ram. "No one knew where she came from," she said. "She had black eyes and black hair to her waist. Her voice was a raspy little whisper. She could take an injured eagle and calm him down, heal him, and let him go. But if you crossed her …"

"She was like a dark, shimmery little fairy," Warren supplied. "Who wanted to kill you."

"Premier Barry Graham was running as an incumbent," said Luna, her voice stronger but still hushed. "He was no friend of the environment, but the movement was gaining strength so he had to pay it lip service. There was a developer who wanted to build an airport right near a wetland, close to prime eagle habitat. Graham promised Hélène that if she delivered the green vote, he'd turn down the airport.

156

So she put out the word. But just before the election she found out he double-crossed her, and the airport was a done deal."

Warren nodded, and Ned shifted in his seat to face her.

"They were scheduled to do a public photo op ten miles from her center," she continued. "Graham would stand in the middle of a field wearing a leather glove, and one of Hélène's volunteers would release a trained Golden Eagle from the top of a nearby hill. The eagle was supposed to fly a hundred yards and land on Graham's glove. But the day came and instead of standing by the premier's side, Hélène stood twenty feet behind him. Graham raised his glove, the volunteer released the eagle, and suddenly Hélène raised her own glove and whistled. The eagle shot through the crowd and passed Graham so closely he actually slapped him in the face with a wing."

"You can't plan something like that," said Warren. "Of course he'd fly straight to Hélène when she whistled, and she'd positioned herself so he'd fly close to Graham. But no way could you orchestrate the bird actually whacking him in the face. Birds know their space, they don't touch anything by mistake." He chuckled. "It was her magic."

Luna leaned forward. "She raised her fist in the air, and she held the huge eagle over her head," she said, keeping her voice low so as not to alarm Mars. "She shouted, 'Liar! Traitor! Did you actually think you could keep this from me?'"

Ned realized his mouth was open, as once again he was swept into the tumultuous past. "She'd told the camera people where to stand," said Warren. "Guy never held another office."

"And P.S.," added Luna. "No airport."

"How do you know all this?" asked Ned, as Luna settled back against the side of the truck.

"Awww, everybody knows it," drawled Warren.

The hours drifted by and Luna began to relax, her aching muscles to unclench. Mars slept on his perch, one head tucked beneath a wing. Ned and Warren's voices were low and convivial. "Okay, man, so here's your choice," said Warren. "A '71 Plymouth GTX 5.21, or a '70 Dodge Charger R/T 440 7.21?"

"Tough one!" replied Ned. "But I'd have to go with the GTX."

Warren held up his fist, and Ned bumped it. "Hey!" said Ned. "Why did that sign say Wisconsin?"

"Change of plan. Can't go to Dina Pontillo's with Gunderman on the trail."

Eventually the Ram slowed, turned, and started down a dirt road. "Red phone," said Warren. "Find Trish." Ned handed it to him. "Warren?" came a woman's voice.

"Incoming," he replied, and hung up.

Two women in their mid-forties waited outside a softly-lit house. "Hey there, honey," whispered the one in a yellow cotton dress, her straight hair long, as she gave Luna a hug.

"Long time, stranger," said the second, who wore shorts, an embroidered peasant shirt, and shoulder-length curls. She wrapped her arms around Warren, then turned and offered her hand to Ned. "I'm Trish," she said.

"Angelica," said the woman in yellow, disengaging from Luna.

Trish and Warren disappeared into the house, and Ned and Luna pulled the crate out of the Ram and followed Angelica into a low-slung building made of concrete blocks. "We call this 'the Bunker,'" she said as she flipped on a light switch, illuminating a wide hallway between two stalls. Angelica pulled one of the doors open, revealing a spacious enclosure. In one corner was a sturdy, Astroturf-covered perch, and in the other, a heavy folding table.

"We're bird-friendly enough to know you don't put one in a strange place in the middle of the night, and they don't like to be on the floor," said Angelica. "So we figured he could sleep in his crate on top of the table. I bought that perch at a conference ten years ago, figuring it'd come in handy someday."

"It's perfect," said Luna.

Angelica peered into the crate. "He's beautiful. Does he need anything else?"

"Thank you, but no," Luna replied. "Just sleep."

Angelica flicked off the lights, closed the door behind them, and led them toward a country cottage. The wheat-colored roof undulated across dormers, flowed past windows, and rolled over eaves like swells in a sea. "Trish used to work for a roofer," Angelica explained, "and he still gives her materials at cost. They're called steam bent shingles. Looks like the roof is melting, doesn't it?"

The inside was a cheerful hodgepodge of easy chairs, slipcovered couches, and area rugs covering wide, knotted floor planks. An ancient armoire with faded paint stood in one corner. Antique weathervanes hung from the walls. A colorful riot of wildflowers spilled over a blue glass vase. Trish and Warren lounged on two couches, wine glasses in hand.

"Sounds like you two could use a drink," said Trish, gesturing to a bottle and three waiting glasses.

By the time the recap reached Wisconsin, the wine bottle had been replaced twice. "Still not sure of the plan," said Warren, draining his glass. "In the morning I'll see if I can find out where Gunderman is. Not to mention Luna's so-called husband."

"Will you stop shooting at him?" said Luna.

"Why?" asked Warren.

"Ha ha! We knew that was you!" hooted Trish and Angelica, slouched together on one couch, slapping each other's hands in a high five.

Ned knitted his brows. Over the past three days he'd had a succession of texts from his normally uncommunicative business partner, who preferred leave any correspondence to the staff. **You never take time off!** was the first. **WTF?** came the second. **Did you kidnap Adam Matheson's wife?** demanded the third. It was hard to believe it had only been six days since he left Starfish Key.

"Guys around here still trying to change your minds?" asked Warren.

"Totally!" said Trish. "They never give up!"

Angelica grinned at Ned and Luna. "All the local menfolk want to turn us into good little heterosexuals," she said. "Or if that doesn't work, have a three-way with us. But they never drop by, because they're scared we'll let out the bears."

Luna laughed, then stopped and looked at Ned. He smiled tentatively. "The bears!" he said. "Is that what you call them?"

"That's what everybody calls them," said Angelica.

Ned's expression faded to weary disappointment. "They told me you do squirrels."

"Yeah, squirrels!" said Trish. "And bears."

"I'm sorry, Ned," said Luna.

"Yeah, sorry, man," added Warren, reaching for a wine bottle and pouring the rest into Ned's glass. "Here, have some more. We didn't want to tell you, 'cause you were already looking kinda raggedy."

"But think about it!" said Trish encouragingly. "What better place for you to hide out? Everybody thinks you're going to New Mexico, and that you're only staying where there's a flight cage." She held up her hands triumphantly. "And except for the volunteers, everyone's afraid to come here!"

"FYI, there's only one guy we'd have a three-way with," announced Angelica, leering at Warren. "And that's only when there's a full moon."

"There's always a full moon," replied Warren, returning her look. "Just sometimes you can't see all of it."

Ned frowned and regarded Luna, who smiled and shrugged like a fond mother.

"Come on," said Trish, rising. "It's late. Warren's in the front room, and you guys are in the guest house. It's all set up for you."

"Come here a minute," said Warren to Ned. At the other end of the room, Trish raised her hand and gently pushed a lock of hair away from Luna's eyes, while Angelica encircled her protectively with one arm.

"She won't sleep well tonight," said Warren, in an undertone.

"I wouldn't think so," said Ned.

"No. I mean she's gonna have trouble."

"What kind of trouble?"

"If she gets to sleep and you wake her up, she'll hurt you."

"What do you mean, she'll hurt me? And why would I wake her up?"

Luna approached. "Are you guys tired?" she asked. "I think we could all use some sleep."

The guest house was a single cozy room with a dresser, an easy chair, and a queen-size bed covered with a handmade quilt. Ned and

Luna tossed their bags onto the floor, and Luna disappeared into the bathroom. Ned heard a low chuffing sound outside. It seemed to be the kind of sound a bear would make if it was biding its time, waiting for a houseguest to blunder out into the dark.

Ned stared at the bed. Under normal circumstances it might have been rife with possibilities, but now it, too, seemed ominous. He heard the the shower, and thought about the day's events. The image of Luna handcuffed and hustled into a car by a uniformed officer flashed through his mind. He sat on the bed and rubbed his eyes with his hands. The bathroom door opened and Luna emerged, clad in a flowered nightshirt. "Are you okay?" she asked, looking concerned.

"Warren said you don't sleep well. He said not to wake you up."

She pulled a thick quilt from the chair. "Sometimes I have bad dreams. You know what? I can just take this blanket and pillow and sleep on the floor, then everything will be fine."

"Of course you're not going to sleep on the floor. We're both exhausted, and I sleep like a log. Why am I not supposed to wake you up?"

"I just… it's that… sometimes I wave my arms around. You don't want to get in the way."

"All right, I'll stay out of the way. What do you dream about?"

"I don't remember," she said vaguely. "Anyway, thank you. Go take a shower, you'll feel a lot better."

• • •

Gunderman emerged from the woods, canvassed the area, and spotted his car. He evaluated his performance as he walked, concluding his flaw had been his recovery time. There was the moment of impact, the swerve, and the brake; then he had a good five seconds to regroup and come out swinging before his assailant pulled him from the car. He had been trained to prepare for anything, and 'anything' included a black op-style ambush during the apprehension and transport of a solitary young woman. He would certainly not make that mistake again.

The keys were left just out of reach. He had contorted himself into a backward u-shape, untied a shoelace, pulled off the shoe and sock, then stretched out enough to snag them with his toes. It had taken nearly 20 minutes to unlock the two sets of handcuffs. At the edge of the woods was his pistol, propped against a yellow birch. The bullets were intact.

It was Warren, he thought.

Warren was only man who had both the skills and the motivation to pull it off, not to mention enough respect for a fellow environmentalist to make sure there would be no embarrassing rescue required. Gunderman let out a frustrated sigh. The man had been a SEAL! What happened to following the rules?

If anything, the encounter had strengthened his resolve to apprehend Luna Burke. But what if the cost was the arrest and prosecution of the man who had almost single-handedly saved the Florida panther from extinction? This really sucks, thought Gunderman. One of my heroes has just committed obstruction of justice, not to mention restriction of freedom of a federal officer.

He reached the car. He opened the door and scanned the interior, then lifted the driver side mat and retrieved the keys. Dammit! he thought. Obviously he's the one shooting at Matheson, as well.

• • •

Ned awakened and saw Luna asleep beside him, illuminated by a small night light. He searched his memory, hoping to recall they dove into bed and had wild sex before falling asleep. But instead he remembered bidding each other good night in a tame and civilized manner, a strip of space between them, then she turned her back and settled at the edge of the bed. Now she lay facing him, shuddering, a sheen of sweat on her skin.

He sat up carefully, recalling Warren's words. He hadn't put it all together before he fell asleep, which had been almost immediately. But now he remembered her solid punch to Roland's collarbone, and her similar attempt at Gunderman's face. He decided to remove himself from her line of fire and rose from the bed, turned on the bedside lamp, and crossed the room.

"Luna!" he called, but she didn't awaken. He called her again, and her breathing increased. Her hands twitched, her feet jerked, and her face contorted. It looked like torture, and he couldn't stand it. He spotted a small embroidered pillow. He picked it up, resumed his position by the door, and tossed it gently through the air.

• • •

Luna kept her eyes on the stars. She could see them through the apartment window as she heard the approaching storm. It rumbled, grew louder, and turned into a roar. Thunder had a physical presence, and once again it was crashing over the city. She felt it hard against her head. She crawled under the table, but it found her and slammed into her back. The room turned in a circle. The floor rose beneath her.

Roll away. Find the door.

The moon was full. Or maybe it was a lightbulb, she wasn't sure, but it turned people into silhouettes. Some of them were huge.

The stars vanished. The light was brilliant. The next crash hit her ribs and lifted her into the air. One side of the light raced to meet the other, then it disappeared altogether. Stay in there, you goddamn little bitch!

A blue house. The air was electric. You are a girl held fast by the devil, and we will cast him out! Grab something heavy. Shit! My eye! Hurry. Hurry. The window slid open with a screech and she was safe beneath the stars, her heart beating faster and faster until it kept time with her feet, thudding down a suburban street with her ponytail streaming behind her. There she is! Get her into the car!

A white house. Thunderclaps from all sides. The fucking little bitch threw boiling water at me!

A brick house. You liked those sneakers, didn't you? You think I gave them to you for free? Hit first. Roll away. Darkness and hunger and breaking glass. Grab something sharp. Run! The alley was lit by a streetlight and sliced by sirens. Whirling red lights and a dead end. Cornered. Jesus, she nailed me! Slammed to the concrete, pinned flat, arms pulled behind her, the stars were gone. Cold steel, a heavy click. Something soft hit her hip.

Luna ripped herself free and lashed out at her attackers, but her fists met only air. Frantically she scanned her surroundings and found herself in another unfamiliar room. At the door stood Ned, wearing a look of shock and pain. Her adrenaline ebbed, replaced by a flood of despair.

"Damn, Luna," said Ned, his voice unsteady.

Her body vibrated as she gasped for breath. He eased onto the bed and gingerly encircled her with his arms, and just as gingerly she leaned against him. He waited for her to break down, to start to sob; but she fought to control her resistant body, and with a trembling hand she curtly wiped her cheek.

Ned held her silently. He thought of his sleek and gleaming office in Key West, where emotions were conveyed through capital letters or exclamation points or flaming emojis. He searched the books he had read, the movies he had watched, trying to come up with a hero in his position who had been brilliant and tender and wise, but found no one who had been anywhere near his position. He heard a series of deep grunts and thought, at least I'm inside.

Eventually she lay against him, slumped and quiet, her breathing regular, her eyes closed. Ned moved and, in her sleep, Luna stretched out and settled onto her pillow. He pulled the blanket around her, and turned off the light.

CHAPTER 15

In a motel room in Indiana, Gunderman sipped his pre-dawn coffee as he stared at his laptop. **BILLIONAIRE BABE'S A BIRDNAPPER,** blared allthenews.com.

The previous night he had not given chase. He knew there was no way to track them, that Warren would find Harrelson, ditch the van, and head to a more secure location. Instead he checked into a motel, pulled his bags from the trunk, and spent the next two hours pacing his room. He couldn't prove it was Warren. And if he reported "ambushed by unknown assailant," he was sure Whittaker would immediately send more officers to back him up. He tried to decide whether he was simply embarrassed by his own failing, or truly believed that adding more officers would destroy any chance of solving the case.

It was the latter, he decided.

Gunderman filled out a report stating he had found evidence of Luna Burke, Ned Harrelson, and the missing eagle at a campsite in southern Indiana, knowing Sean Callahan and his kids would hardly contradict him. He brooded as he typed. He was going off-script, and he didn't like it.

At 7:30 he began calling every car rental company within 50 miles, asking if they had rented any large vehicles the previous day. After coming up empty he called Sean Callahan, whom he was sure knew Luna was free. He probably knew who freed her, too.

"I'm not trying to play hardball with you, Mr. Callahan, but it's an important case," he said, after the subject had denied any knowledge of Luna Burke's whereabouts. "I could have your rehabilitation license for this."

"And I could call Adam Matheson and tell him you used excessive force on his wife," Sean replied evenly.

"But you have no proof. And I'm not sure you want to let him know you were harboring her."

"Is there a reason for this call?"

"Where is she going?"

"No idea."

"Then unfortunately, I'm going to have to start the paperwork to suspend your license."

The line was silent.

"Let me get this straight," said Sean. "If I tell you what I know, I keep my license."

"Right."

"Fine. She's going to New Mexico."

"How do you know?"

"Because last night she called me from a burner phone. Our conversation lasted about 30 seconds, so that's all I can tell you. She *was* going to Pennsylvania, but not anymore. You know why? Because you scared the shit out of her. You proud of yourself?"

"You'd be willing to testify to this under oath?"

"Once you get me into a court of law."

Gunderman hung up and leaned back in his chair. His mission in life was to defend the natural world and its inhabitants, yet somehow an entire faction of those on his own side considered him the enemy. In actual numbers, there weren't that many wildlife rehabilitators; but at that particular moment, they seemed to be everywhere.

His mind drifted north, to Pennsylvania. He thought of Celia's fragile exterior, her iron resolve, her fair hair and warm eyes and slender, callused hands. He thought of Elias and Wizzie. He reached for his phone, wondering how far the news of last night's encounter had traveled.

"Western Pennsylvania Wildlife Center," Celia answered.

"Hello, Ms. Jenkins, this is Officer Gunderman."

There was a long silence. "Hello?" he said.

"What do you want?" she snapped.

Evidently, the news had reached Pennsylvania. "I just wanted to check in with you."

"I have nothing to say to you."

"Ms. Jenkins, she broke the law."

Unsurprisingly, Celia simply waited in stony silence. "Yesterday morning I spoke to my boss," he said. "He's the head of U.S. Fish and Wildlife's Law Enforcement Division. It turned out he'd just spoken with the director, who is head of the entire agency. The director said once we recover the male eagle, he might want to transfer it to a facility in Virginia."

He heard a soft intake of breath, then Celia's uncertain voice. "But…but why? Mars's mate is here with us."

"I know. It doesn't make a lot of sense to me, either. This is what we don't want — the eagle getting caught in any kind of departmental dispute."

"But…"

"I didn't mean for things to escalate the way they did last night. I really didn't. Please try to understand…what if Ms. Burke was just some random woman who stole an eagle? Wouldn't you be glad I was after her?"

He heard nothing, and plunged on. "My goal is to recover your eagle and return him to you. But the longer this goes on, the greater the chance that when we do find him, he'll end up caught in a bunch of agency infighting. And that's when he might end up in Virginia."

Gunderman felt a twinge of conscience. He had never given the whoppers he told during his performance of duty a second thought, as the ends always justified the means. But this time he pictured Celia, trembling in response to his words, her heart breaking at the thought of the permanent separation of the bonded pair of eagles. He realized he had just referred to the missing eagle as 'him' instead of 'it,' and 'your eagle' instead of 'the eagle.' He hadn't meant to do it. Still, it was probably helpful, so he said it again.

"All I'm asking is if you've heard or thought of anything — anything at all — that might help us recover your eagle and return him to you."

"No," she said.

"All right. If you do, you have my number. You know police and state conservation officers are looking for them, as well?"

"I know that," she said, the edge back in her voice. "And as far as checking wildlife centers? All of you are wasting your time. Eagles are scary birds. Most rehabbers don't even take them. And as of last night, the ones who do aren't going to risk losing their licenses. *Or* ending up in handcuffs."

Gunderman said goodbye and hung up. He knew perfectly well that fear played almost no part in the lives of most of these people, that you could drag an injured wolverine to a bunny rehabber and she'd set her jaw and get to work. And risk...they took risks like they breathed.

He looked out the window, seeing not a cluttered parking lot but the morning mist rising from the Loxahatchee. His laptop pinged, and his eyes widened in surprise. The new kid at the office had come through. He had called her last night, explained what he needed, and told her it was a rush job. Evidently she stayed up all night. He downloaded the program, and opened it.

Across his screen was a map of the United States, the country pale blue against a navy background. He moved his cursor to Indiana, clicked, and the state turned bright yellow. Another click, and a spray of black dots and stars appeared within its borders. Two lists appeared on the right side of the screen: State Licensed Wildlife Rehabilitators. Federal Licensed Wildlife Rehabilitators.

Gunderman explored the program. He slid his cursor to Key West and dragged it along Luna Burke's route, leaving a black trail. Florida. Georgia. Kentucky. Indiana. She had been traveling slightly northwest, covering approximately 300 miles per trip. And now?

If she continued on her slightly northwest pattern and went no further than her usual five-hour travel time, her next stop should be either northeastern Iowa, southern Wisconsin, or possibly just into Minnesota. If she was, in fact, going to New Mexico, her next stop should be southwestern Illinois or eastern Missouri. He moved his cursor in a circle, clicked, and the whole area lit up in yellow. Another click, and multicolored squares appeared within its border, accompanied by correspondingly-colored headings on the side of the screen.

Small Mammals. Large Mammals. Reptiles/Amphibians. Songbirds. Waterfowl. Game Birds. Raptors.

He clicked Raptors and scanned the list of names, addresses, and phone numbers. He frowned. Luna Burke wasn't an idiot; if she had just been apprehended at a raptor rehabber's, she wouldn't immediately flee to another. Gunderman began to suspect the new kid had stayed up all night for nothing.

He typed a quick email, thanking her and telling her he would contact her supervisor with a glowing report. Ten minutes later he was in the local coffee shop, digging into his eggs and musing about the players in the case. A billionaire. A former defensive lineman. A Chief of Law Enforcement. A former Navy SEAL. All formidable alpha males, whom very few would want to cross.

One of the few was Luna Burke, who had crossed three out of four of them.

Where would they go? If they went to a contact of Warren's, he had little chance of finding them. But both Warren and Luna were rehabbers, and foremost in their minds — beside outwitting their pursuers — would be the comfort of the animal in their care. In fact, the greater their own stress, the more they would seek to minimize that of the eagle. The bird needed rest and familiar surroundings, so the odds were high they would continue to seek enclosures meant for wildlife, not garages or basements.

Think like Warren, he thought. Find a place no one would want to look. Eagles are scary birds, Celia had said. Most rehabbers don't even take them.

Gunderman stopped, his fork in mid-air. He returned to his room and called up the new program. Once again he outlined his targeted area and scanned the tiny colored squares. He typed, clicked, and narrowed his search. Forty minutes later he had a list of five, and eventually his intuition went off like an air raid siren.

SMALL MAMMALS/LARGE MAMMALS. Tamarack Wildlife Center, 184 Rt 72, Rock Ridge, Wisconsin. Trish Delavan, Angelica Ruiz. Squirrels, bears.

Bears. Apex predators. A place no one would want to look. Rock Ridge, Wisconsin was on their way northwest.

It would take about four hours to drive from the motel to Rock Ridge. He was determined to keep it under wraps, to bring in only enough officers to cover the fact that Warren was with her. He would coordinate with the police sergeant and local conservation officers when he was an hour away, and wouldn't even tell them the nature of the operation until he arrived at the Rock Ridge Police Station.

And if he was wrong? No harm done. All law enforcement officers knew the value of hunches.

He would map the area and figure out how to set up a dragnet. If the three of them had arrived with the eagle last night, they'd probably rest today and take off after nightfall.

He glanced at the time. He'd aim for 4:00.

• • •

Ned appeared in the doorway of the kitchen, blinking and groggy. He scanned the busy floral wallpaper, the ruffled lace curtains, and the squirrel and bear knickknacks. He spotted a large coffeepot and a row of cups, chose the largest one, and sat alone at the table.

Trish entered the room, yawning and wearing a silk bathrobe. She smiled sleepily, picked up the coffeepot, and poured three cups. She took a sip from the first one and Angelica appeared, combing her long hair with her fingers, wearing pajama bottoms and a sleeveless shirt. She walked up behind Trish, kissed the back of her neck, and took the second cup. Warren sauntered in, wearing jeans and a rumpled t-shirt, and took the third one. They all exchanged smug expressions, then Warren settled into an easy chair with deep grunt.

Ned cocked his head at the sound. "That wasn't a bear I heard last night," he said, in an accusatory tone. "That was *you*."

"You'd have to be more specific," said Warren. "What time are we talking about? And where's Luna?"

"She's sleeping! She had a rough night!"

Warren looked at him intently, and Trish and Angelica's smirks disappeared. Ned glared at him. "Why didn't you warn me?"

"I did!"

"What happened to her?"

Warren shrugged. "She bounced around foster care. She doesn't like to talk about it."

"She had the mother of all nightmares! Does this happen all the time?"

"Did she cry?" asked Trish.

"No, she didn't cry! How can she have dreams like that and not cry?"

"We thought she might let go last night," said Trish. "That's why we sent her in with you."

"That's not the only reason," said Angelica, raising an eyebrow at Warren.

"Someday she'll crack," said Warren. "But until then, my job is to keep her together."

"Does that mean mine is to make her cry?"

"Not to make her cry," said Trish. "To let her."

Angelica noticed a flash of motion and looked out the window. "She's gone to see Mars," she said. "Ned, all I can tell you is it's really important that we get her to Hélène's."

"That's what everybody tells me!"

Warren rose. "We'll lay low today, then we're out of here tonight."

• • •

Elias sat on the office couch and watched the mist turn to rain. Heavy clouds obscured the top of the mountain. He loved the tenuous, transitory moment when the mist gained weight and mass and began to fall, sometimes delicately as snow, sometimes hard as hail. Eventually the rain would stop, leaving droplets hanging from leaves and rocks and blades of grass, and the world would be clean and fresh and ready to resume.

There were some things, though, the rain couldn't wash away.

Yesterday he had driven to Prattstown, bought a new cell phone, and placed it in Celia's hand. Don't put the group on here, he said firmly. You deal with the center, and I'll deal with Luna.

Thank you, Dad, she said, and gave him a hug.

When he alerted the group that Celia's phone had been lifted, they went silent on the subject of Luna. Instead they reverted to normal rehabber exchanges, avoiding all reference to her.

dorsalfin28@att.net Anyone tried that new skin glue from Weber & Tile?

rachelhopkins@santafewildlife.org Yes it's really good, much better than Dermaclose

withers@ndsanctuary.net They'll send you a sample if you write the rep Linda Davis ldavis@weberandtile.com

Late last night, things had changed. Elias was sleeping when Sean posted the news of Luna's arrest, escape, and flight to New Mexico. Elias pulled his eyes from the rain, reached for his phone, and read the replies once again.

bluestreak@juno.com WTF is going on in this country how dare that douchebag handcuff her like that!!!

reed@threehornedtoadsrescue.org C an't believe he cuffed her!

monarchs@cloud9.net Jesus H Christ Sean WTF? Assholes are drilling on protected habitat and F&W is after a rehabber?

annalee@bluemoonwildlife.org She's heading for New Mexico just like she planned, only reason she went to Sean's was because Matheson's goon tried to grab her

envirowacko@gmail.com What's that bastard doing being a goon when he won the Heisman Trophy

redfox@hotmail.com She just pulled in to Illinois

krangle@prairie.com Expecting her here in Missouri tomorrow

gary@newmexicorattlers.org We're ready and waiting in NM

Elias pocketed his phone. Sean hadn't specified how she escaped, but Elias assumed Warren was involved. Wizzie rushed into the room, damp and breathless, and sat beside him. "Where's your raincoat?" he asked.

"I lost it. Who are you texting?"

"No one. Just someone at the feed store."

"Is it Luna?"

"No," he sighed. "I haven't heard from her."

"Banshee's still not eating. How long before she starves herself?"

"She won't starve herself."

"It's not right, Pop. It's not right that someone can take Mars and make Banshee starve herself because she misses him so much. It's just not right!"

"I know."

"So what are we going to do about it?"

Elias made no reply. Through the window he could see Banshee on her perch, huddled alone in the rain. Her loud descending cry was silent. They had tried putting two different eagles in with her, and she had attacked them both. Risking everything for her and her missing mate was Luna, on the run. He frowned, and Wizzie broke into a grin.

"You're thinking, Pop! I can see you thinking! We're going to do something about it, aren't we?"

"Maybe."

Wizzie encircled his arm with hers. "You keep thinking, Pop. And if you need any help, you know where to find me."

CHAPTER 16

Luna opened her eyes and scanned the empty room. The bed was rumpled. She remembered her dream and its aftermath, and sat up.

Move on, she thought.

She followed the flagstones skirting the house. Mist sparkled on the needles of the Tamarack trees. The morning sky was a pale pink, and the air was filled with bird calls. She heard the high-pitched *plitseek* of an Acadian Flycatcher, and a Western Meadowlark burst into a series of whistles, warbles, and trills. They're in trouble, thought Luna. All the grassland birds. Farming. Pesticides. Development. Soon there will be nothing left to protect.

With an effort she pulled her eyes from the sky and continued toward the Bunker. She entered the concrete block building, pulled a large wrapped package from the refrigerator, and opened the stall where Mars had spent the night.

"Did you sleep well?" she asked. A moment later he stood on her arm and beat his wings gently, blowing her hair back from her face. Lightly she touched the feathers on his chest, then let him hop onto the floor. He lowered his head into the rubber tub, raised it, and let the water run down his throat.

"What a good bird," she said, once again grateful she was on the run with Mars, not Banshee. Nervous and suspicious, Banshee would never have survived this kind of trip. Luna pictured her in her flight cage, her eyes fixed on the horizon, waiting for the return of her mate. Mars turned, lifted off the ground, and landed on the Astro-turf covered perch. He peered out the window.

"It's okay," she said in a husky half-whisper. "It'll be all right. I'll get you both to Hélène's, and I'll never leave you until you're safe."

"Did you know half the time the power grid goes down, it's because of squirrels?" asked Trish, finishing her scrambled eggs. "People shouldn't be afraid of hackers, they should be afraid of *squirrels*. They shut down the NASDAQ in '87 *and* '94."

"It's not their fault," added Angelica. "You'd start chewing up the power grid too, if your teeth grew six inches a year."

After Warren disappeared, Trish and Angelica had made breakfast. Trish carried a plate heaped with food to Warren, who was on the phone in the den, then she leaned out the door and shouted for Luna. The meal passed uneventfully, with Trish and Angelica determinedly filling the silence with squirrel trivia.

"They're practically made of rubber," said Trish. "You see them fall out of a tree and you swear they've broken their necks, but they just get up like nothing happened."

"You want to see a cute squirrel?" said Angelica. *"Flying squirrels.* There's nothing cuter than a flying squirrel. We have three in the clinic. They're all asleep now, though, because it's daytime."

"Squirrels are scary," said Luna matter-of-factly. "Seriously, they'll take your hand off."

"Look!" said Trish, pointing out the window to the back yard. "Up there!"

An elongated contraption hovered between two mature trees, suspended by a 25-foot wire. At its finish line stood a platform filled with peanuts. A dozen feet away a gray squirrel sat on a tree branch, twitching, his eyes on the beginning section of wire. His luxuriant tail lashed like a whip.

"Crazy rodent!" said Angelica. "Sometimes I just want to give him a bunch of Valium and say, 'C'mon, baby, *relax.'*

The squirrel launched himself from the tree, hurtled through the air, and caught the wire with his two front feet. He spun in a circle, like a gymnast doing a Giant Swing, then braked with his tail and scrambled into a Plexiglas cube. Climbing out the top of the cube, he navigated through a spinning windmill, rolling PVC pipes, and a corrugated tube. He held the wire with all four feet and raced upside down toward a curtain of leather strips, seized one, and used it as a rope swing. At the critical moment he let go, sailed onto the final platform, and reached for a peanut.

"You guys clean up and we'll get dressed," said Angelica. "Then we'll show you the bears."

Luna stood beside Ned as they loaded the dishwasher. She gave him a detailed report on Mars and then fell silent, clearly not intending to discuss the previous night. After he placed the last spoon in the dishwasher basket, Ned planted his hands on the counter. "Are you all right?" he asked.

"I'm fine, thanks," she said, giving him a warm smile. "Let's go see the bears."

They followed Trish and Angelica into an office filled with filing cabinets, shelves, camera equipment, and monitors. Angelica flipped a switch and one of the monitors revealed three young black bears. It looked like a wild, wooded area, except for the 15-foot double fence visible on one side of the screen. On the ground, two young bears wrestled in the sun.

"Where's the third one?" asked Ned.

"Looking for trouble, no doubt," said Angelica. "She's the brat."

"We bottle fed them until they were five months old," said Trish. "Only the two of us, nobody else was even allowed in the room. The last thing you want is for a wild bear getting used to humans! We didn't even talk when we were feeding them. Mostly, we left them alone with each other. As soon as they learned to eat from a dish, they went outside."

"That enclosure is filled with stuff they'd eat in the wild," said Angelica. "Lots of berry bushes. Nuts, apples, vegetation, rotten logs with bugs. There's a shallow cement pool on the other side, eventually we'll start throwing fish in it. You know what we never feed them? Corn or honey. They start raiding cornfields or knocking over beehives, that'll get them shot."

She flicked another switch, and a sleeping bear appeared on the monitor. "Speaking of shot," said Angelica, scowling. "Here's a question for you. On one hand, you have an extremely stupid slob of a human being who leaves uncovered garbage outside his garage, even after being told by yours truly that he's laying out a wildlife cafeteria.

On the other hand, you have an intelligent young black bear who sees this windfall and decides to help herself. The stupid slob shoots the bear. Which one, in your opinion, needs rehabilitation and relocation?"

"So, we have this cool hospital set up at the end of the building," said Trish, pointing at the monitor. "Everything's concrete, of course. The rooms are long and in the middle there's a guillotine door. That way we can shift the bear from one end to the other when we need to clean it, and they don't see us providing the food. Cool, huh? Sometimes I have to put Angelica in there when she gets too homicidal."

"Oh, shut up," said Angelica. "You should have seen her cursing when that shot bear came in."

Angelica flipped on the last monitor. Another wooded area surrounded a small cinderblock building, partially submerged by earth. "Here's one of the dens. Big female in there, hit by car. She's way better now. Probably taking a nap."

The four of them left the barn and skirted the driveway. "There's the food truck," said Trish, pointing to a small camouflaged, motorized vehicle with tinted windows.

"It has a trap door, right?" said Ned. "So you can drive it into the pen and leave the food, and they don't associate it with people? Warren has one."

"We stole the idea from him!" said Trish.

"And there's the bear trap," said Angelica, pointing to a big aluminum tube mounted on a trailer frame. "If we need to relocate one, we bait it with a bunch of food, the bear goes in and steps on the pressure plate, and the door slams behind him. Nice, right? We can thank Saint Luna for both of those little items."

Luna waved her hand dismissively. "Come and see the pond," said Trish, leading them into the woods. "Bears are smart, and sometimes they won't go into those traps. We have this awesome heavy-duty net that has ropes at all four corners. You suspend the ropes from a tree limb, then you lay the net on the ground and cover it with leaves. It's spring-loaded, so you bait it, the bear steps on it, and suddenly he's hanging five feet off the ground. Really freaks them out, though, so you only do it as a last resort. Look out, Ned, we almost caught you!"

"Look how well it's camouflaged!" said Luna, admiring the dangling ropes that looked like vines.

"We put it up so we could make a video, we just haven't taken it down yet."

"Come on, we're not done with the tour yet," said Trish. "On the way back, we'll show you the flying squirrels."

• • •

Gunderman parked his car beside a brown SUV bearing a U.S. Fish & Wildlife Services logo. He walked into the Rock Ridge police station, and stopped at the front desk. Just visible through an open door, two Fish and Wildlife officers conversed with four uniformed policemen. One of the cops, thin and grey-haired, beckoned him Into the room and closed the door.

"Officer Gunderman," he said, offering his hand. "I'm Sergeant Nielsen." He introduced the three other cops, and the two Fish and Wildlife officers introduced themselves. "So, what's the big mystery?"

Gunderman described the situation, and watched the men's looks of surprise. "All right," said Sergeant Nielsen. "We can handle it."

"What's the address?" asked one of the men in blue.

"184 Route 72," said Gunderman. "Ruiz and Delavan."

"Aww, no!" groaned a second police officer. "You mean those bitches with the bears?"

The sergeant shot him a frown, and the officer cleared his throat. "Sorry," he said.

"Let's set it up," said Nielsen.

• • •

The afternoon sun slanted through the living room windows. Ned and Luna slouched on one couch, Angelica and Trish on the other, all eyes on the television. The front door opened. "Where've you been?" asked Trish.

"Around," said Warren.

"What's the plan?" asked Luna.

"Can't find Gunderman," said Warren. "He's probably not far behind us, so we'll head out after dark. No more rehabbers, he's figured that one out. And he knows we're heading north, so we should angle off. I got some buddies about three hours west, they'll put you up while I get Glenn's truck back to him. As for your fine husband, at the moment he's in San Francisco."

"Ned's going back to Florida," said Luna. "Trish will take him to the airport tomorrow morning."

Warren nodded at Ned. "You had a good run, man. You were a big help."

"Yeah," Ned replied, knowing it was the only sensible plan. He had tried to calculate the odds of making it to Canada with Luna and living happily ever, and come up with two hundred billion to one. *You only get one life, Neddo*, his father liked to say. *Don't screw it up.*

Warren sat on the couch beside Angelica. "When does the kitchen open around here?" he asked.

"Whenever you feel like opening it," she replied, then continued in an encouraging twang. "Get on in there, darlin', and whip us up a casserole! I betcha you'd look mighty cute in an apron!"

Trish's phone rang. She rose, pulled it from her pocket, and disappeared into the kitchen. "What time…" Ned began.

"Are you screwing with me, Charlie?" came Trish's agitated voice. She appeared in the doorway, eyes wide, as a male voice emanated from her phone. "Where are they? When? Thanks." She disconnected, her face ashen. "Gunderman."

"Where?" said Warren.

Trish gestured out the window. "Out there. Right now. He's here, and so are the police."

CHAPTER 17

Adam descended the stairs of his Gulfstream, greeted Roland, and they climbed into a waiting limousine. The hills of Pennsylvania slipped by as Adam stared moodily out the window.

The merger was sealed, the takeover completed. He had been distracted during a key meeting and nearly lost one, but he rallied and clinched them both. Even more satisfying than the deals themselves were the looks in the eyes of the men who asked about his bewitching young wife, as hungry for information as teenaged girls. All these captains of industry, Adam thought, with their safe, domesticated women, all living vicariously through me.

"I don't get this, Roland," he said.

Roland looked up. He had been reading his messages, the news, the sports columns, doing everything he could to distract himself from the fact that he was once again on his way to the same fucking animal place, on the same fucking mission: to find Adam's runaway wife. The wife who had become the thorn in his side, Lyllis's line in the sand. "What," said Roland.

"It doesn't make sense. I treated her like gold. I treat women like shit and they don't go anywhere."

"Then maybe you had it coming."

Adam frowned. "Before we were married I had people investigate her parents. You know, the ones in Pennsylvania who adopted her. The ones who were killed in the car crash. I didn't go any further, but I have people digging up her foster care records now."

"Juvenile records are sealed," said Roland.

"Oh, please," said Adam. "The cops have stepped up their game. I had the tech guys send Darcy the list of animal people from that phone you grabbed, and she's offering them incentives. She said they're pretty goddamned hostile. But all it takes is one." He paused. "You almost had her. You'll get her the next time."

Roland exhaled. According to the phone in his pocket, the guy in the Smokey the Bear hat had intercepted her in Indiana and taken her away in cuffs. How she escaped was a mystery, but it certainly wasn't something he wanted to discuss with Adam. "The last time I got her, she was kicking and screaming," he said. "Why do you think she's going to like it any better this time?"

"What she'll like better is to be alone with me without all this pressure. I just need to talk to her face to face. You know how good we are together!"

"Honestly? I don't. I'm telling you, she doesn't belong in your world."

"Then I'll adjust my world. You'll see. Have you ever seen Swan Lake?"

Roland gave him a weary look. "No, Adam, I never seen Swan Lake. But I know a couple of dancers, and you know what they told me about Swan Lake?"

"What?"

"The crazy-ass prince and the magic swan bitch both die in the end."

The car coasted to a stop. The driver opened the door. "That's because he was just a prince," said Adam, and slid out.

• • •

Celia and Elias stood by the office window, watching the limousine roll down their dirt driveway. "I still don't see why he had to come in person," said Celia.

"Because he wants to intimidate us," said Elias. "So don't let him."

"Where's Wizzie?"

"In her room. I told her if I even see her shadow, no animal care for a week."

After a knock on the screen door Adam appeared, Roland behind him. Adam extended his hand, and Elias shook it without returning his smile. Celia stood to the side, arms crossed tightly over her chest. Briefly she met Roland's unblinking stare, then quickly looked away.

"Beautiful land around here," said Adam.

"Yup," said Elias.

"I'll get right to the point," said Adam. "Luna's in trouble. Whatever difficulties we may have had were temporary. All I want to do is help her, but I don't know where she is."

"We don't, either," said Elias.

"I want both of you to know something," said Adam. "I love her very much. I laid the world at her feet."

Celia murmured something, her eyes on the floor. "Excuse me?" said Adam.

Celia felt her stomach churn. "I said, she doesn't want the world," said Celia, forcing her voice into something above a whisper. "And she doesn't want you, either."

Adam gazed at her. "You used to rent this land, didn't you?" he asked.

"We did," said Elias, trying to draw Adam's attention away from his daughter. "But thanks to your wife, now we own it. And nobody can take it away from us."

"That's true," said Adam, pulling a topographical map from his inner pocket. "But...may I?" He unfolded it and laid it on the desk. "Here you are," he said, pointing. "Here, north of you, is a 500-acre parcel. Over here are three houses. To the west is a 150-acre parcel, and here are twelve more houses. I'm thinking I might buy all of it. Some of the owners might not want to sell, but they'd probably change their minds if I offered them six or eight times what their properties are worth. Then I'd have a great big piece of contiguous land for Gladstone Oil and Gas, which I own. As you know, fracking is big around here."

Elias recovered first. "You can't build in there," he said, pointing. "*Those* are wetlands, and *that's* a protected wildlife area!"

Adam regarded him with a kindly expression. "Mr. Jenkins," he said. "Do you honestly think that under this administration, environmental regulations are even worth the paper they're printed on? It's a free-for-all. And if you've got local opposition?" He placed a finger on the map. "There's your wildlife area, and there's your little buffer zone. I can put the drill pad right next to it. You'll be able to see the lights from your driveway."

The room was still.

"Maybe you don't know where she is," said Adam. "But I'll bet you could find out in, say, two days. If you do, I'll donate $5 million to your wildlife center. You could save a lot of animals with that. Maybe buy some additional land so you can to protect yourselves a little more. If you don't?" He shrugged and began to fold the map.

Celia felt an unexpected surge of fury. She straightened her back and raised her chin. "Get out," she said.

Adam tucked the map into his pocket. "All I want to do is talk to my wife," he said, and Roland pulled the screen door shut behind them.

The limousine rolled back down the driveway. "I think that went fairly well," said Adam. "But what the hell is wrong with these animal people?"

Roland squinted at a patch of blue. Adam followed his gaze and saw a young girl sitting on a rock, her unruly red hair in a braid, her bare legs scraped and dirty below her shorts. As the car approached she scowled, and with a violent motion she lifted one arm and raised her middle finger.

"Jesus Christ," muttered Roland, and looked away.

• • •

"They're coming at four o'clock!" said Trish, as everyone scrambled to their feet.

"Shit!" said Warren. "I keep underestimating him!"

"We've got eight minutes," said Luna.

"What are we going to do with eight minutes?" demanded Ned.

Warren turned to Trish and Angelica. "Get her and the bird into the tunnel," he said.

"The tunnel!" said Angelica. "How do you know about the tunnel?"

Warren scowled.

"All right! Fine!"

Luna, Trish, and Angelica hastened from the room. Warren turned to Ned. "If they're already here, we can't use the truck. Listen — you're gonna have to stay here and slow 'em down."

"But how?"

"Figure it out!"

He started to leave, then turned back. "There's a tunnel that starts a hundred feet behind the Bunker and ends near the road. If there's any way you can get a vehicle out of here — go right out of the driveway, right again on Pine Lane. The tunnel comes out halfway down." He clapped him on the shoulder. "Do your best, man," he said, and disappeared.

Ned glanced out the window to where Angelica hurried toward the woods, Trish and Luna behind her carrying Mars's crate. He spotted something glinting on the floor, so he crossed the room and bent down. It was Luna's necklace.

"Oh, no," he breathed, staring at the broken clasp. He looked past the front door to the parking area, where the Ram, Trish's Honda, and Angelica's Jeep all waited side by side. It was eerily quiet. In the distance, he could see a flashing red light. He slipped Luna's necklace into his pocket.

The driveway was narrow, flanked by cedars and dense under-brush. Two squad cars made their way briskly toward the house, stopping just shy of where the driveway fanned into the parking area. The first squad car braked, backed up, and stopped sideways, blocking the parked cars. The second one pulled up behind it.

Gunderman, a police sergeant, and an officer emerged from the first car and walked toward the house. Two more officers climbed from the second car and headed toward the Bunker. The red light continued to flash at the end of the driveway.

Five of them here, thought Ned, an unknown number out on the road. There was no way to get the Ram out of the driveway. Even if Luna managed to make it to the road, she could hardly hitch a ride accompanied by a giant eagle crate. His gamer's mind searched for possibilities, and came up empty. There was a heavy knock on the door. "Rock Ridge Police Department!" came a voice. "Open up!"

"Coming," called Ned, moving slowly. He swung the door open, and Gunderman and the police officers eyed him steadily.

"Where are they?" asked Gunderman.

Ned was silent. A police officer reached for his handcuffs. "Wait!" said Ned, raising his hands. "I want immunity!"

"What do I get?" asked Gunderman.

Ned took a deep breath. "They're still on the property, but they've split up," he said. "I'm reaching into my pocket, okay?" They nodded, and he pulled out Luna's necklace. He opened the bead, and showed them the tracking device.

"It's how the guy helping her knows where she is," said Ned. "The clasp is broken, so they probably don't know she dropped it. She can't get far without him, and it will lead him straight to me."

• • •

Mars waved his wings in protest only briefly before settling down, hopping into the crate, and settling onto his perch. Luna took one side, Trish the other, and they followed Angelica through the woods to an old stone shed built into the side of a hill. "It came with the house," panted Trish. "I don't know what they used it for."

"We forgot about it," said Angelica, struggling to open the rusted iron door. "Give me some room, here." Gripping the door's heavy handle, she pulled it with all her weight. The door opened with a screech.

The room was circular, windowless, and cluttered with old metal furniture and gardening equipment. Luna and Trish lowered the crate to the floor. "We haven't been back here in years," said Angelica, pulling a stack of chairs aside and revealing a small inner door. Trish yanked it open. There was nothing but darkness.

"Do you think it's caved in?" asked Angelica. She pulled out her phone and flipped on the flashlight. The silent tunnel was bedecked with cobwebs.

"Assuming we can get through it," said Trish, "what are we going to do once we get to the end?"

"We'll figure it out when we get there," said Luna.

"Follow me," said Angelica.

• • •

Warren stopped next to a hickory tree and caught his breath. He had jogged through Trish and Angelica's densely wooded property, hidden by the forest as he scanned Route 72 and Pine Lane for squad cars. There was a cruiser parked on 72, blocking the bottom of the driveway as two officers patrolled on foot. A Fish and Wildlife SUV glided down Pine Lane, but then it disappeared.

He approached a stream, scooped up a handful of mud, and wiped it over his face and arms. He kept moving until he spotted a pile of boulders leaning haphazardly together. The landform was unremarkable, except to the naturalist or outdoorsman who might suspect the boulders concealed a cave. When Warren happened upon it six years earlier he had entered it, found the tunnel, discovered the shed, and filed it away for future need. The need had arisen the previous evening, hence their flight into Wisconsin.

He pulled out his tracking device and his face fell. "The hell is she doing?" he muttered, as the blinking red dot placed her at least 30 yards from the tunnel. Pocketing the device he jogged through the woods, all senses on alert. He passed a section of bear fencing, and saw Ned standing alone.

Ned turned, and when Warren saw his expression he stopped in his tracks. In a split second, Gunderman and three police officers appeared from behind the trees. Warren spun and sprinted away, but four steps later the ground hurled him upward, rustling and blurring and surrounding him with patterns of dark and light. He fell, bounced, and as the patterns swam into focus he realized he was hanging from Trish and Angelica's bear net. He raised a hand to cover his face.

"You want to finish this up?" shouted Ned. "There's no way he can get out of there, so come on and I'll show you where she's hiding!"

I'm going to kill that guy, thought Warren.

"All right," said Gunderman.

"Stay with the suspect," said Sergeant Nielsen to one of the men.

Gunderman glanced at Warren. "The suspect is secured, Sergeant," he said. "We're going to need all your men. I'll take responsibility."

The three officers hesitated, and a snuffling sigh emanated from the far side of the double fence. Just visible over the crest of a hill were the head and shoulders of a very large black bear.

"Right!" said one of the cops, and they all hurried toward the house.

Warren watched them go. He reached into a pocket, flipped open his trusty Border Guard, and began to saw.

• • •

The fourth officer was waiting by the Bunker. "She and the bird are in the basement," said Ned as he, Gunderman, and the three officers reached the house. He pointed at the guest house. "There's another guy in there. "

"Why are you cooperating now?" asked Gunderman.

"I didn't think it would go this far," said Ned. "I just want to get out of here."

The sergeant and one of the men peeled off toward the guest house. Ned opened the front door and led Gunderman and two officers to the kitchen. "I'm not going down there," said Ned, gesturing to a red door. "There's a bear. It's in a cage, but it's still a bear."

Gunderman and the two cops stared at him suspiciously. Ned crossed his arms and leaned against the counter, feeling the throb of his heart, his only plan to stall them as long as possible. "I'll go down with you," said one of the officers to Gunderman. "You go first."

"Keep an eye on him," said Gunderman to the second officer, nodding toward Ned, as he led the first officer down the stairs. Ned slumped as the uniformed man stood in the basement doorway, his hand resting on his gun. On his belt hung a radio, a baton, a Taser, a flashlight, a set of keys, and a pair of handcuffs.

Ned felt a surge of adrenaline. He pictured the three policemen herding Warren toward the net. He stared at the handcuffs, soon to be clasped around Luna's slender wrists. Last night she had curled against him, trembling and gasping for air.

Right out of the driveway, said Warren. Right again on Pine Lane.

Ned launched himself forward and caught the waiting officer off guard. As the man reached for the railing, Ned slammed the door shut and slid the deadbolt home. He stopped, horrified at what he'd done, then he rushed from the room.

Ned burst through the front door, ran to the Ram, and climbed into the driver seat. As he turned the ignition, he saw the two officers in the doorway of the guest house. The sergeant looked up and spotted him.

You're just not a team player, Neddo, said a voice in his head.

"Yes, I am," he muttered aloud, slamming it into gear. "I just hadn't found the right team."

The big blue truck roared forward. It caught the first police car dead on, spun it in a half-circle, crunched it into the second one, and shoved them both into the woods. Ned stomped on the gas, aiming for the cruiser blocking the end of the driveway. The two officers patrolling on foot looked up in astonishment, then threw themselves into the ditch as the Ram burst onto the paved road and crashed into the cruiser. Ned yanked the wheel to the right and a shot rang out. Glass shattered and tires screamed as he floored it down Route 72.

In a hundred yards was the small sign for Pine Lane. He skidded around another turn and there was Trish, waving frantically. Behind her were Luna and Angelica, holding Mars's crate between them. Ned braked, Trish opened the back door, and they slid the crate into the truck.

"Will you guys be all right?" cried Luna, as she yanked the passenger door open and jumped in.

"Go! Go!" barked Trish, waving them on like an air-traffic controller.

"Easy!" gasped Luna, as the truck lurched forward. "This is too much stress for him!"

"For *him?*" shouted Ned.

"Look!" she said, pointing ahead to where Warren was running out of the woods. "Don't stop, just slow down!"

She swung the door open, climbed into the back, and Warren lunged into passenger seat as the Ram passed him. He pulled the door shut, then turned to Ned.

"Good man!" he boomed, and clapped him on the back.

CHAPTER 18

Ropes of bittersweet and Virginia creeper wound around the abandoned gas station, encircling rusted pumps and pushing their way through the roof of the rotting garage. Shepherd's purse and wild radish adorned three junked sedans. Pigweed rose from a pile of old tires like masts on a beached schooner.

There were no cars on the small country road. Luna, Ned and Warren stood behind the garage, all regarding the Ram. Both headlights were shattered, the grill smashed, the sides scratched, gouged, and dented; there was a small oval hole in the rear window, surrounded by a series of radial cracks.

"Thank you!" gasped Luna, incandescent with exhilaration. "Thank you both for being so incredibly awesome!" She threw her arms around Ned and gave him a kiss on the cheek, then planted one on Warren's. "They'll *never* get us!"

Ned regarded her, baffled. "Pay no attention to her," said Warren. "It's the adrenaline."

"Do you know what I just did?" Ned demanded, enunciating exaggeratedly as his composure teetered. "I just pushed a police officer down a flight of stairs! I locked him, Gunderman, and another cop in the basement, and then I destroyed three of their cars! I assaulted a police officer, and another one *shot his gun at me!*"

"Wow!" cried Luna, and gave him a blinding grin. "Good thing he was a lousy shot!"

Ned turned on her, eyes blazing. "'Good thing he was a lousy shot?'" he shouted. "Are you nuts? You're endangering the lives of all of us, just for that stupid bird?"

Luna stopped, her eyes wide, then she rushed toward him and thumped him heavily on the chest. "'Stupid bird?'" she shouted back. "So *that's* what you really think? You were supposed to be gone at the Florida border! Why are you still here?"

"I was *supposed* to be gone at Warren's! And I'm still here because — according to you — *you're my tar pit!*"

"All right, break it up!" said Warren, stepping in and pushing them apart. "And would you keep it down?"

Warren sat in the driver seat, cleaning the mud off his face and arms with a rag and a bottle of water he found under the back seat. Ned slouched on the passenger side, staring angrily into space. Luna pulled the cover from the crate and addressed the eagle in a husky half-whisper. "It's okay," she said, sending an unwanted pang through Ned's heart. "It'll be all right." Mars rattled his feathers, the soft slaps audible through the car.

"So," said Warren. "One thing we're not gonna do is drive around town in a hot truck. Forget the next stop — it's three hours away, we'll never get there. Gotta figure out a new game plan."

Luna rummaged beneath her seat and retrieved a stack of license plates. "We've got Missouri, Nebraska, and Michigan," she read.

"Oh, make it Michigan!" said Ned. "Then they *won't even notice* the rest of the truck!"

"Warren!" snapped Luna. "Can we just drop this guy off in …"

"Knock it off!" Warren growled, a threatening rumble that made all sound in the truck cease. "That's better," he continued pleasantly. "I should call Glenn. Maybe he's got some guys in the area. Blue phone. Grab my readers, too."

Luna reached into Warren's knapsack and retrieved his phone and glasses. "I left my stuff at Trish and Angelica's," she muttered, looking pained.

"Glenn! Wassup, man. Listen — I know I was going to return your truck tonight, but there's been a snag."

"Where's my truck?" came Glenn's voice.

"I'm sitting in it. It just needs a little TLC, which I will give it as fast as humanly possible. Meantime, you know anyone around Rock Ridge, Wisconsin?"

"You better watch your back," said Glenn, then there was a heavy click.

"Huh!" said Warren. "That could've gone better." He rubbed his beard. "Let me give this one a shot." He scrolled through his phone, pressed a number, and waited. After a few moments, he disconnected and tried again. When there was no answer, he tried another number.

"Hello?" came a woman's voice.

"Hey Ruby, it's Warren! How you doing? Sal around?"

"No."

"When's he coming back?"

"You tell me!" she said belligerently.

After he hung up, Warren turned to Luna. "What about you?"

Luna shook her head. Warren turned to Ned. "You?"

"Oh, sure!" said Ned, roused from his vision of a furious judge pounding a gavel. "All my best friends live in the backwoods of Wisconsin!"

"I'm not feeling the love in here," said Warren, peering over his readers.

"Wait a minute!" said Luna. "What about Stanley?"

"Who's Stanley?" asked Ned suspiciously.

"He's the turtle guy!" said Luna.

Ned turned to Warren. "Didn't you just finish saying no more rehabbers? Gunderman *knows* we're going to rehabbers! What about Stanley's license?"

"That's the beauty of Stanley!" said Warren, scrolling. "He hasn't got one."

"As deeper we sink," Ned muttered, and leaned his head against the window.

"Stanley! Wassup, man?"

A surprised voice emerged from the phone. "Warren? How are you? *Where* are you?"

"I am in an undisclosed location with two people who would probably prefer to remain anonymous. Except for one is Luna."

"Luna! No joke?"

"Hi, Stanley!" called Luna, as Warren pressed speaker.

"Luna! This is crazy! You know you're all over the police scanners?"

"Oh, yeah. I guess."

"So, are you with that guy Ned Harrelson? Is he the other person?"

"Ugh," said Ned.

"Is that him?" asked Stanley. "Is that Ned Harrelson groaning in the background?"

"What about me?" asked Warren. "Aren't I all over the police scanners?"

"Sort of. You must be the 'Unidentified White Male.' Evidently, they don't have your name."

"Gunderman didn't give you up!" said Luna, slapping him on the shoulder.

"Aww," said Warren, smiling affectionately. "That sonofabitch."

"Stanley, where are you?" asked Luna. "Didn't you move?"

"I did," said Stanley. "I'm in northeast Iowa. Hang on a minute, here. You can't be far from Trish and Angelica's, which is Rock Ridge, so I am… 87 minutes from you."

"They won't be expecting us to go south!" said Luna encouragingly.

"Can you put us up in your fine hotel?" asked Warren. "Like, tonight?"

"Of course! Absolutely! Are you still in the trashed blue Ram? Indiana plates?"

Ned snorted.

"Yes!" called Luna.

"Want me to pick you up?"

"No way can we ditch the truck," said Warren. "Trust me on this."

"Then I'll direct you. I've got scanners on five precincts, so I know where the cops are. I'll get you around them. Good?"

"Fabulous!" said Luna.

"Let me get set up. Give me ten minutes." He hung up, and Warren turned to Ned.

"No sweat," he said. "Stanley's good with legal issues."

Ned swallowed. "What do you think they'll charge me with?"

"Don't know yet," drawled Warren. "The night's still young."

• • •

Trish and Angelica's driveway was jammed with vehicles. Gunderman stood in front of the house, grim-faced, as two men hoisted one of the police cruisers onto a flatbed truck. Two additional squad cars had arrived, as well as the Fish and Wildlife SUV. The ground was littered with glass and metal.

As soon as he heard the scramble and the slammed door, Gunderman knew he had made another serious mistake. He had predicted that Warren would be out of the net in two minutes; he hadn't predicted that Harrelson would catapult a police officer down a flight of stairs, lock the door, and wreck three cruisers. He had paid no real price for losing Luna after he'd captured her at Sean Callahan's. Obviously, this would be different.

Gunderman stood beside Sergeant Nielsen, who regretted his decision not to call for backup as much as Gunderman regretted his decision not to make Ned lead him down the basement stairs. Trish and Angelica waited nearby, wearing looks of surly contempt. A police officer approached them, unbuckling his handcuffs. "Sergeant, do you want me to…" he began.

"You must be kidding, *Sammy*," snapped Angelica, and raised her hands to her hips. The cop stopped, and Trish turned a poisonous gaze on the sergeant. "We already told you, *Gavin*," she said. "She's on her way to *New Mexico*."

Sergeant Neilson gave an irritated grunt and waved toward a squad car. "Take them in," he growled. "Book them, get statements, then release them."

The officer Ned had knocked down the stairs spoke up. "I'll fill out a report, Sergeant," he said. "Losing the suspect was my fault."

"Thank you, Officer," said Gunderman. "But I take full responsibility for the entire operation."

"I don't need any of this," muttered Nielsen, as his radio crackled to life. "Yeah," he said. "Anything?"

"Negative, Sergeant. So far, no trace of them."

• • •

The Ram slowed to a crawl. They had driven the last mile and a half in darkness, the only light coming from the dashboard, the headlights, and a spray of stars in the sky. "Look on the left," came Stanley's voice. "Another ten yards. See the tree limb on the ground? Okay, edge in and drive over it. Can you see the trail?"

A neatly-dressed man of medium height stood before a cozy house surrounded by woods. He was slightly round and had a shock of white hair. "Fugitives!" he said cheerfully, and grasped Warren's hand. "Warren," he said warmly, and turned to the others. "Luna! Ned! Welcome! This is great. I feel like I'm on an episode of 'America's Most Wanted!'"

After they settled Mars in the clinic, Stanley supplied them with grilled steak, potatoes, assorted vegetables, and several bottles of wine. He listened appreciatively to their travelogues and stories of mutual rehabber friends, wore a look of concern during the recounting of the raid at Trish and Angelica's, and raised his eyebrows whenever the tension between Luna and Ned spiked.

"Ned thinks Mars is *'a stupid bird,'*" Luna explained, giving Ned a dagger look.

"People say the darnedest things *after they've been shot at,*" Ned retorted.

"Settle down, kids," said Warren, "or no dessert."

After dinner Stanley led them into his study, which was spacious and wood-paneled and home to a large foldout couch. Three telephones and a half dozen radios rested on an old oak table, one bookshelf was stacked with screens and transmitters, and another overflowed with manuals and textbooks. "This is how I keep track of everybody," he explained.

Eventually Warren concluded they were set for the night, claimed the couch, and ordered Ned and Luna not do anything dumb. Stanley refused offers of help with the dishes, and directed them to supplies in the bathroom cabinet. When Luna started down the hallway toward the guest room, Ned held back. He waited until the door shut with an audible click, then he turned to Warren and Stanley.

"*She's* got mental problems!" he hissed, pointing dramatically toward the hallway. "She's a landmine! Shouldn't she be in a place?"

One second Warren was by the couch, and the next he materialized in front of Ned and grabbed him by the shirt. "A place?" he repeated, teeth clenched. "What kind of place?"

Stanley quickly inserted himself between them. Warren retreated a few steps, rubbed the back of his neck, then returned to Ned. "Listen," he said, smoothing Ned's crumpled shirt. "We just need to get her to Hélène's."

Ned trudged toward the guest room, still rattled by the look on Warren's face. Talk about nightmares, he thought.

The guest room was similar to the rest of the house, neat and orderly and furnished in earth tones. There was a queen-sized bed, a stained glass lamp, and vintage prints of assorted reptiles. Ned heard the sound of the shower. He closed the bedroom door and yanked one of the curtains shut. Luna emerged wearing what appeared to be one of Stanley's button-down shirts, and grimaced when she saw him. "Stanley will have you out of here tomorrow morning," she said frostily.

"Good!"

"And I'll get my own stupid bird to Canada!"

"Fine! Bon voyage! As for tonight, I'll sleep in the living room!"

He held her simmering stare as he headed for the door. Just as his hand shot past the doorknob and encircled her shoulders, she flung both her arms up and around his neck. Their kiss was long and fiery.

Suddenly Ned pulled back. "What's wrong?" she whispered.

He hesitated, torn between lust and fear. "I'm not sure this is a good idea."

"Why?" she asked. "Is it because you think I'm nuts?"

Ned was determined to play it cool after his encounter with Warren, but the stress of the past week got the better of him. "Yeah, I think you're nuts!" he blurted out. "You, and everyone you know!"

She stood straight and square and nodded, as if acknowledging the validity of his opinion. Her eyes held his. "I'm not crazy, Ned," she said finally. "I just have a few issues."

Ned factored this into his critical thinking, a process which took about three-fifths of a second, then he pulled her toward him and pressed his lips against hers. He stopped, removed his glasses, and tossed them onto the dresser. In one fluid movement, picked her up and carried her to the bed.

Luna rolled, straddled him, and removed Stanley's shirt. She flung it into the air, it slid off the windowsill, and came to rest on the floor. Ned stopped, staggered by her abruptly revealed body. She pulled off his pants and seized him with a proprietary grip, and with a sharp intake of breath he sat up, flipped her beneath him, and plunged inside her.

Ned felt like a finely tuned engine. The motion was constant, fluid, and deep; the sensations overwhelming, the visuals beyond his imagination. She was everywhere, silky and slippery, wrapping him in a breathtaking swirl of erotica, his unattainable dream woman come to life.

Luna felt like a bird on the wing. She dove, spiraled, and rode the wind, anchored only by Ned's awestruck gaze. He was everywhere, hard and demanding, gentle and tireless, taking her to greater heights; to where the sky was wide, the air was clear, and no one could find her.

Eventually they collapsed, exhausted. Ned lay on his back, breathless, Luna beside him. The blue sheets eddied around them like a late summer stream.

Ned gazed at the cream-colored ceiling, at the white molding around its periphery. He couldn't see any of it clearly, of course, as his battered glasses were on the dresser. He wondered if there was a Richter scale of human pleasure, if titanic sex could alter one's brain chemistry in any permanent way, and how much time they had before a squadron of law enforcement officers burst into the room and arrested them both.

Luna rolled over and rested her head on his chest. Ned was so floored by this epic act of voluntary intimacy that he couldn't disguise his astonishment. Cautiously, he folded one arm around her. This is all I need, he thought. For the rest of my life, this is all I need.

After a minute or two, though, he found himself waiting for her to follow her monumental act with words. After that kind of afternoon, shouldn't she want to talk about it? After that kind of sex, shouldn't she be wide awake? He waited for the dam to burst, for a torrent of emotions, memories, comparisons, strategies, declarations, and questions to gush forth.

The room remained soundless. He glanced down, wondering if she were even conscious. Her eyes were closed. "Luna?" he said.

Luna stirred, poised at the edge of sleep, and felt Ned's arm around her. The silence was so beautiful, so calm, so comforting. It was like dawn, she thought dreamily, fragile and perfect, when not even the birds had awakened; after she had survived the night, but not yet faced the day. She held him and kept her eyes closed, trying to preserve their rumpled blue bed and transient safe house in her mind. She would remember them, she thought, after time had passed, and things had changed, and he was gone.

"They didn't catch us, Ned," she said, in the husky half-whisper she used for no one but Mars.

The pang in his heart grew warm, took root, and bloomed like a wildflower. He rested his cheek against her head. "Don't worry," he said quietly. "They won't catch us."

CHAPTER 19

Ned awoke with the sun in his eyes. One set of curtains was closed, the other open. The bedsheets were bunched haphazardly. A pillow rested on the floor. He was alone.

Thankfully, there was a pot of hot coffee in the kitchen. He sipped his cup, unable to stop a continual loop of the previous night's activities from playing in his head. As far as he knew, Luna had suffered no nightmares, and he was fully prepared to take the credit. He poured himself another cup and carried it out the front door.

Ned sat on the top step of the porch. From what he could see, Stanley's compound consisted of the house, an outbuilding, and a single small flight cage. Luna appeared with a bucket, various cleaning tools, and a sheaf of crumpled fish wrapping in a clear plastic bag. "Morning," she said, and she put it all down, climbed the stairs, and settled beside him.

Ned hesitated, unsure how to proceed. He steeled himself, touched her lightly beneath the chin, and kissed her. He waited, trying not to look apprehensive. Luna smiled and squeezed his hand. "It's a new day, Ned," she said. "Let's go find Stanley."

Ned opened the screen door to the outbuilding. "Stanley?" Luna called.

"Back here," came his voice.

The sound of cricket song filled the air. To the right was an orderly office, to the left, a room filled with fish tanks and several tubs. In a third room stood Stanley, leaning over a steel table half-covered by a white sheet. "You two look pleased with yourselves," he said, with an amused expression.

On the table lay a groggy turtle, the edges of her shell held together by a lightweight clamp. "Early delivery," announced Stanley. "Luna, my dear, can I press you into service?" He nodded to a plastic bottle. "Would you take that saline, point it into this break, and squeeze a steady stream? There, that's right. How often have I said to myself, 'Why can't I grow a second pair of hands?'"

He addressed Ned without taking his eyes off the turtle. "So, Ned! This is a Western Painted Box Turtle. Isn't she gorgeous? I mean, besides the fact that she's been used as a chew toy by a damned Bernese Mountain dog? Look at those yellows and oranges! I'm going to tilt her *verrrry* slightly so you can look at her plastron, that's the underside of her shell. It's art! It's a Rembrandt crossed with a Rorschach test."

"I've never seen one close up," said Ned. "Can you save her?"

"Look here. If I lift this section of shell, you can see right inside her. You don't get queasy, do you? As long as her internal organs haven't been damaged, I can actually glue her shell back together. A little more here, please? The saline will flush any dirt or bacteria from her organs and surrounding muscle and tissue, then we can put her back together like a puzzle. You have to use this special medical glue or she'll get an infection, and she'll need to be on antibiotics and pain meds for a while. Turtles' metabolisms are slow, and they take a long time to heal. But I'm pretty sure she'll be all right. According to her abdominal rings, she's about twelve years old. If she heals and I let her go, she could live to 55."

Stanley straightened. He gently lifted the turtle from the table, carried her to a tank lined with paper towels, and positioned a heat lamp above it. "Thanks for your assistance," he said, washing his hands in the sink. "Come and I'll show you around."

He led them into a room filled with terrariums and heat lamps. "There's a Spiny Softshell, that one's a Musk, there's a Midland Painted, and over here is a Hieroglyphic River Cooter. Don't you love that name? She's an endangered species, and some bonehead was keeping her as a pet. Not feeding her right, of course, so she had metabolic bone disease. Not enough protein, not enough calcium. The guy had metabolic *bonehead* disease, which is not enough brain cells. Idiot!

"Here's an Eastern Mud Turtle, also endangered. You take a beautiful piece of land filled with ponds and streams and turn it into another cheesy subdivision, and where do the turtles go? It's not like they can gallop away in a thundering herd and find another home."

They followed him into a room lined with fish tanks. Half were carpeted with dry dog food, apples, and carrots, and swarmed with small worms, crickets, or slugs. The other half were filled with water, home to smalll crustaceans and medium-sized fish. A refrigerator stood in the corner. Jars of vitamins and supplements crowded the shelves.

"This is the cafeteria," said Stanley. "What do people think of when they picture a hungry wild turtle? Do they envision him searching everywhere for a little jar that says "Turtle Food," filled with grubby little dried-out chunks of God knows what? Do they imagine him combing the countryside for the perfect head of iceberg lettuce?" He turned to Ned. "Am I ranting?" he asked. "Tell me if I'm ranting. I probably won't stop, but you can tell me."

"You're ranting," said Luna.

Stanley sighed. "Rehabbers rant," he said ruefully. "It's our lot in life. Come on, you want to see my monster?"

"Your monster *turtle?*" said Ned. "Please. We just left the bears."

Luna gave him an arch smile as they followed Stanley to the last room. In the corner was a concrete pool with four-foot sides, half-filled with water. Resting firmly in the center was a snapping turtle so enormous that for a moment, Ned thought it was a prop. Dark, spangle-eyed, its shell rising into three rows of dorsal spikes, it looked like a cross between a medieval weapon, a dinosaur, and a Sherman tank. Its heavy beak was short, curved, and sharp. It turned its head, and stared directly at them.

"Whoa, Stanley!" cried Luna.

I've been shot at, thought Ned, so I'm not about to get rattled by a freaking turtle. He addressed Stanley nonchalantly. "Can it get out?"

"So far — no," said Stanley, and continued enthusiastically. "Aren't snappers cool? They stick out their tongues, and fish think they're worms, and usually that's the fish's last thought. You know, the earliest turtle existed about 157 million years ago. Earliest man — maybe a million and a half. Think about it! Turtles are a link with a past we had no part of. They're like time travelers! Doesn't that blow your mind?"

"Where'd you get him?" asked Luna.

"He came from a traveling animal show. The guy bought him when he was a hatchling, and didn't count on him growing up to be 250 pounds. The guy's one of those macho jerks who are too busy showing off to take decent care of their animals. Alligator Snappers, like that one, get pretty grouchy when they're hungry. Apparently it was three days past dinner time, so the snapper helped himself to two of the guy's fingers."

Luna burst out laughing. Stanley joined in, both wearing aghast expressions as they each waved a hand with two fingers curled down. Ned regarded them with dismay.

"Oh, Ned," Stanley sighed, wiping his eyes as Luna tried to control herself. "I'm sure you think we're terrible people. But there's this thing called payback." He turned to Luna. "Thanks again for the pool," he said. "So that's it, except for the copperhead. You want to see a copperhead?"

"You mean the poisonous snake copperhead?" asked Ned.

Stanley led them to his office, where the thick, four-foot serpent lay coiled beneath a heat lamp in a plant-filled terrarium. Coppery red, with a sand-colored, dark-edged hourglass pattern that ran the length of its body, it flicked its tongue but otherwise remained motionless.

"Beautiful!" breathed Luna, bending down for a better look. "And where did he come from?"

"Guy found him in his basement. Local people find snakes, they call my friend Ted. Ted's my front man, because I'm under the radar. Honestly, people are so stupid about snakes! It's one thing to be afraid of poisonous snakes, okay, maybe understandable, but they see a little garter snake and immediately want to kill it. Idiots!"

"What will you do with him?" asked Luna.

"Northern copperheads are very social. Sometimes they even share dens with timber rattlers or rat snakes! I know of a den about an hour from here, I'll take him up next week. They're not aggressive, you know. They'll defend themselves, of course, but generally they're pretty laid back. They're not like water snakes, who can be really pissy."

Ned wondered if Luna already knew the personality traits of snakes, or if this was all news to her. "You know what?" said Stanley. "Sometimes if you pick a copperhead up, he'll release a musk that smells like cucumbers!"

Ned headed for the door. "How about breakfast?" Stanley called after him.

The kitchen table was laden with brightly colored pottery bowls, each filled with an assortment of fruits, berries, and cereals. Stanley poured coffee into matching mugs and set down a plate of wheat toast. "Warren left early," he said. "A friend of mine's going to fix the Ram. Or try to, anyway. So tell me — are you set with Hélène?"

"Yes," answered Luna. "We just need to get to the border."

"What a woman! She's probably readying her army. Well, you're welcome to lay low here as long as you like. I'm sure all of you could use the rest."

"Why aren't you licensed?" asked Ned, fortified by coffee.

"I was a model rehabber for 30 years. Everything by the book. Then I got involved in a bunch of bureaucratic bullshit, and I thought...this stinks! There are *way* too many people pissing me off. So here I am, the hermit in the woods. The only people who know where I am are two wildlife centers. They sneak me all their turtles, plus the occasional raptor if they have no room. And there's Ted, who calls when he has a snake. And by the way, nothing's changed — I *still* do everything by the book."

"Stanley wrote the definitive manual on turtle rehab," said Luna. "As well as four field guides!"

Stanley smiled, embarrassed. "There are three reasons you don't have to worry about staying with me," he said. "One, I've set up a program so if any squad cars come within five miles, I'll get an alert on my phone. Two, Adam is in Texas for a some big meetings, according to *The Financial Times* and *IBD*. And three, I have a friend at the Fish and Wildlife office in Titonka, and one at Department of Natural Resources in Des Moines, so that means I know where Gunderman is. Right about now he's heading for the Fish and Wildlife office for a 10:00."

"Gunderman," said Ned disapprovingly.

202

Stanley looked surprised. "He's one of the best we have."

"That's what Warren says," sighed Luna.

"It's true. You of all people should know that, and not take it personally." Stanley turned to Ned. "There are two kinds of government conservation officers. One loves the natural world for what it is, and they do their darnedest to protect it. The other loves the natural world for what they can get out of it. That type of 'conservation officer' doesn't give a shit about wildlife unless it's mounted on a wall or dangling from a hook.

"Don't get me wrong. I'm not anti-hunting or -fishing per se, as long as you eat what you take. Hunting and fishing licenses pay to keep a lot of land open that might otherwise be developed. But a good number of these department guys actively work against licensed rehabbers for no other reason than they're old school, macho assholes. As opposed to someone like Gunderman."

He reached for the strawberries and regarded Luna. "He's after you for all the right reasons. I'll do my best to make sure he doesn't catch you, but I'll go to the mat defending his right to try."

Ned puzzled over this. "We live in a moral minefield, my friend," said Stanley, and handed him the coffee pot.

• • •

The afternoon sun shone on the weedy grass, then vanished behind another cloud. Mars surveyed his latest domain from a perch. Luna sat on the ground, fiddling with the silver bead on her necklace. Stanley had given it back to her after breakfast, the broken clasp repaired.

Ned appeared at the door. "Come in," said Luna.

"No way."

"Really. Ever since you were stuck in the van together, he's been all right with you. I can tell."

Hesitantly he entered, and closed the door behind him. He hugged the slats and sat on the other side of Luna, his eyes on Mars.

"What time is the match?" he asked.

Luna smiled. She kicked the tennis ball by her foot, and it came to rest several inches away. "Stanley was nice enough to find a ball for him, but he doesn't seem to want to play. I think he's getting tired."

"Where is everyone?"

"Stanley's with the turtles. Warren's waiting for the Ram, then he'll take it back to Glenn. He said we could sit tight for a few days."

"Luna? I'm wondering if we should call it quits before it gets any worse."

She lifted her eyes to his. "I can't, Ned," she said. "But you can."

The perch groaned, and out of the corner of his eye Ned saw the huge bird fly toward him. He tried to scuttle backward but the slats of the flight cage held him fast, so he gritted his teeth and waited for his last moment on earth. He felt a billow of air and heard a thump, like a gust of wind on a heavy sail. He saw a rush of feathers, fierce yellow eyes, and a great hooked beak. The eagle landed next to Luna, reached out a huge, nightmarish foot, and snatched the tennis ball. Hypnotized, Ned watched as two black talons sliced through the small sphere like chefs' knives through butter.

"Ha ha, you goofball!" cried Luna, rocking back and forth with delight. "*Now* what are you going to do, with a tennis ball stuck on your foot?"

The eagle stomped the ground, knocked the ball off, and grabbed it again. "You're so funny!" she chortled, then turned her wide grin on Ned. "Remember when you used to be afraid of him?"

Ned sagged against the flight cage, heart pounding, unwilling to let Luna know he had been sure death was upon him. "Batshit crazy" is what Earl would have called her, after wiping his oil-stained hand on a rag and spiraling a forefinger next to his head.

Ned pretended to join in on the jocularity, hoping his heart would slow before it gave out. He realized "batshit" was now irrevocably linked with Esther, hard at work in her Southern plantation house, and he could no longer toss off phrases like eagle-eyed, bear-like, squirrely, or turned turtle. He thought of his empty apartment, of his *Gamer's World* magazines, and of his neighbor's shrieking chihuahuas, which, long ago, he had considered the local wildlife.

I can't call it quits, he thought to himself. Once this is over, how do I go home?

• • •

Roland sat at a bar overlooking Chicago, glaring at Celia's phone. Adam had climbed aboard the Gulfstream with Paszkiewicz and Ortega, his backup security men, and flown to Houston. I want you to stay in Chicago, he told Roland. She's heading north. The second a real tip comes in, I want you on it.

For fourteen years Adam had factored him into his travel schedule. Fourteen years of mutual respect and camaraderie, working around each other's idiosyncrasies. Then a year ago Luna had appeared, and everything began to change. Roland's eyes returned to Celia's phone.

annie@friendsofsaltmarsh.org Where is everybody? Can't find Gunderman or the goon

reticulatedpython@juno.com How the heck do you lose track of a goon that big

dorsalfin28@att.net Somebody better tell David Sibley he should write A Field Guide to Goons

gduncan@bobcathollow.org Somebody better tell the goon the Maltese Falcon is in New Mexico

Roland did a slow burn. The animal freaks wouldn't let up, relentlessly going out of their way to insult him, obviously not caring that their personal email addresses were right there in his full view. They bullshitted on about New Mexico, despite the fact that two nights ago local news stations had reported police activity at the compound of a pair of bear rehabilitors outside Madison, Wisconsin. A few phone calls revealed that agents from Fish and Wildlife had been there, too.

Bear rehabilitators. Roland gave a disgusted sigh.

He scrolled backward, knowing he should turn the phone off, searching for a particular message like a fingernail searching for a scab.

envirowacko@gmail.com What's that bastard doing being a goon when he won the Heisman Trophy

Roland bit his lip, fury flickering through his veins. His own phone rang, and he pulled it from his pocket and glanced at the screen. "Yeah," he said.

"There's a guy trying to get a hold of you, Mr. Edwards," said a voice. "His name is Dennis Fields. He says he knew you from high school, and has some information for you. Put him through?"

"Go ahead."

After a soft click, a clear voice came through the phone. "Roland," it said. "It's Dennis Fields. Do you remember me? I played football with you at Calvin Buckner."

"Yeah," said Roland. "I remember you. Kind of blond. Tall. Skinny through junior year, then you busted out. Played halfback."

"That's right," said the voice. "I thought I had a shot at the big time, but it didn't work out. So, I'm a CPA. I do people's taxes. Y'know, I used to watch you play when you went pro."

The voice paused. When there was no reply, it continued.

"Look, I know your boss is looking for his wife. Normally, I wouldn't get involved. Especially...I mean, I just wouldn't do it. But my son's had four surgeries, and the insurance company's not paying up. My mother's got Alzheimer's, she needs special care. Our savings are almost gone. I know where Matheson's wife is, but..."

"I'll make it worth your while," said Roland.

"I hate to rat out the guy she's staying with, Stanley's a good guy. He's got some kind of wild animal hospital back in the woods. Only reason I know is sometimes my cousin helps him out. She was supposed to go this week, but he told her he had guests. And he never has guests."

"You get a visual?"

"Yeah. I had to hike in, but last night I took a picture through the window. It's her. That guy Harrelson is with her. Here's the thing. My condition is that Stanley doesn't get in any trouble."

"No trouble. I just want to relieve him of one of his guests. He can keep the other one."

"All right."

"I'll call you back."

Roland hung up. He looked over the skyline, finished his drink, and tapped his phone.

• • •

The boardroom was at the top floor of one of the tallest buildings in Houston. Natural light poured through the panoramic windows. Small, discrete spotlights added just enough to showcase the documents resting on the mahogany table. Twelve men sat in leather chairs.

"We don't want to do that," said Adam, sitting at the head of the table. "Not when there's another option. If you'll take a look at page 62…"

The phone in his pocket gave three quick buzzes. "Gentlemen," he said, rising. "Will you excuse me for a minute?"

The adjoining room was empty. He raised his phone. "What have you got?" he asked.

"She's not far."

"Can you get her tonight?"

"Yup."

"Great job, Roland! I'll fly up as soon as I finish. Now listen to me, don't go in there busting heads. Just get her, and bring her to the house. Clear? I'll call you in an hour."

He hung up, then scrolled down and pressed another number. "Mr. Matheson!" said a female voice. "How nice to hear from you!"

"Hello, Gisele. I have to make this quick. I need something stunning in Luna's size. Silk. Lavender. Floor length. Elegant, lots of lace. Matching robe. Deliver it today to the Chicago house. Okay? Thanks."

He smiled briefly to himself, pocketed his phone, and returned to the boardroom.

• • •

Roland stood behind a cluster of trees, watching the house. In the living room sat Luna, Harrelson, and Stanley Paxton, all drinking wine after dinner. He had checked out Paxton: the guy wrote books about turtles.

Another clusterfuck, thought Roland.

He envisioned how easy it would be to kick in the door, knock both guys out, and grab her. He sure as hell wouldn't have to hang around in the woods with bugs everywhere, playing this stupid waiting game. But no, because his boss was losing it.

He watched her through the window. She seemed content, so it could be a haul. But sooner or later she'd get antsy, leave the house, and wander around in the dark, like she used to do in Florida. He remembered spotting her at two in the morning, high on a limb of one of the trees Adam planted in order to impress her. What the hell are you doing? he had called, irritated.

I'm looking at the ocean! she retorted defensively. Do you mind?

A half hour later, she rose from Paxton's couch. Harrelson rose too, but she shook her head and gestured for him to stay seated. Roland watched her leave the house alone, unable to believe his luck.

482-673-2593 Back up he texted, and a black SUV rolled silently toward him.

He waited in the shadows. She stood in the moonlight beside the slatted cage, her face tilted upward.

Little skinny white girl, Lyllis had said, running like Flo-Jo. And every time they cornered her, she turned into you.

Roland hated when women talked in riddles. You push her too far, Lyllis had added, and she's going to make you sorry. None of it made sense. Still, better to take no chances, so he made neither a sound nor a move until Luna shut the door behind her and started back toward the house.

She started flailing the second his arms closed around her. He lifted her off her feet. When she jackhammered an elbow into his stomach and slammed her heels into his shins, he grunted and swung her sideways under one arm. Thrashing wildly, she sank her teeth into the heavy glove he had clamped across her mouth.

The SUV rolled to a stop. A man slid from the driver seat and opened the back door. As Roland shoved Luna into the car, he glimpsed Harrelson and Paxton rushing from the house. "Move!" Roland shouted, and the SUV rocketed down the dirt road and sped away.

CHAPTER 20

In an anonymous motel room outside Rock Ridge, Wisconsin, Gunderman sat before his computer. The screen framed the scowling face of Daniel Whittaker, Chief of the Law Enforcement Division of U.S. Fish and Wildlife Service.

"I gave you this assignment because you were a perfect fit!" said Whittaker, his crew cut seeming to bristle with outrage. "A uniformed officer with the instincts of an undercover agent! Exemplary record — until now! Do you mind telling me what the hell happened?"

Gunderman swallowed. "I'm sorry, sir. I take full responsibility…"

"No shit, you take full responsibility! That's not telling me how you, two department officers, and half a dozen uniformed cops managed to lose two suspects and an adult Bald Eagle *after you had them surrounded!*"

"Sir, I…"

"And then we have this Unidentified White Male, who, according to both the police and your own report, *you left hanging in a bear net.* I don't know, but somehow my law enforcement intuition tells me that he should have been considered a person of interest — if not a suspect — *and not left alone!*"

Gunderman cleared his throat and met Whittaker's unblinking stare. "Gunderman," said Whittaker evenly. "Do you know something you're not reporting?"

"No, sir."

"I ought to fire you! I've got a dozen men arriving in Rock Ridge tomorrow morning, and I want *you* back in Pennsylvania! It's bad enough with one missing eagle, I don't want two! If this crazy goddamned Luna Burke thinks she's going to grab that female eagle and stash it with another one of her buddies somewhere, she's got another think coming! Are you listening to me? *Do not lose that second eagle.* We're already getting hammered in the press!"

"Yes, sir."

"This investigation is doing a nose dive. Pull it up!"

Gunderman locked his motel room door and walked to a corner bar he noticed earlier in the day. The bartender poured him a shot of Jim Beam, and he downed it in a gulp. He took a breath and closed his eyes. "Another?" asked the bartender.

"Yeah," he nodded.

From his barstool outside Rock Ridge, Gunderman could see miles of gently rippling sawgrass and in the distance, a tree island. The trail ahead of him skirted a swamp. He stopped and squinted, as hovering in the sky was what looked like a Snail Kite. They're endangered, he thought, and reached for the binoculars in his backpack.

Gator on your right, came a lazy drawl.

Gunderman flinched in surprise. He looked down at the alligator's eyes and nostrils, just visible above the waterline. He backed up a few steps, then regarded the dark-haired man who sat on the ground, leaning against a cypress tree. He's not big enough to eat you, said the man.

I know, said Gunderman. But usually I'm better at spotting them.

Soon he sat cross-legged, engrossed in the mechanics of a tracking device that could follow the route of a collared panther. Young male, said the man. He shouldn't be this far north, but they don't always do what you tell 'em.

Gunderman rose and followed him through the swamp, until the man stopped abruptly and cocked his head to the left. Draped across a fallen tree was the panther, regarding them with pale and curious eyes. His slender, cream-colored body looked almost boneless. Gunderman gasped and looked up at his new companion. When his eyes returned to the tree, the panther was gone.

Now you see 'em, now you don't, said the man.

They parted company at the end of the day, Gunderman to return home, the man to venture deeper into the swamp. How old are you? he asked.

Ten, said Gunderman.

They need help, he said, nodding toward the sloughs and the mudflats.

I'm going to help them, said Gunderman.

Find a way. And when you do, don't let anyone talk you out of it.

The bartender appeared, holding a bottle and wearing an inquiring look. "Thanks," said Gunderman, and shook his head. He pulled a bill out of his wallet, slipped it under the glass, and left the bar.

• • •

Luna opened her eyes. Blocks of color throbbed and shifted. Her head hurt. She squinted, and the colors tightened into images. She was in a room.

She moved her fingers, and the material beneath them was soft. She looked to the side, and when the dizziness passed she saw a row of pillows. She was in a bed.

She sat up slowly and groggily, fighting waves of nausea. She recognized the massive bed, the Art Deco furniture, the original Klimts and Toulouse-Lautrecs. She was in Adam's bedroom in Chicago.

The curtains were drawn, the music low. A half-dozen candles burned in ornate silver candlesticks. An ice bucket held a bottle of champagne. Luna swallowed, her throat dry, and briefly rubbed her eyes. She looked down at herself, clad in lavender silk delicately trimmed with lace.

The door opened and Adam entered, wearing a dark blue suit and carrying an oversized crystal glass. He closed the door, his smile contrite. "Luna," he said. "I'm sorry about these circumstances. I really am."

He sat on the edge of the bed. "Here," he said, a look of concern on his handsome, craggy face. "It's water. You should drink a lot of it."

She drained the glass while Adam solicitously plumped her pillows. "Remember when you used to get overwhelmed?" he asked. "You'd say you couldn't take it anymore, that you just wanted everyone to leave you alone. And then we'd go away, just the two of us, and it would be great again. Do you remember?"

Luna's mind moved lazily. Which was real? she wondered. Adam's solid presence, or the blur of road signs and guest rooms? He brushed a lock of hair from her forehead and smiled encouragingly. "You know, I was afraid you'd forgotten what we have together."

Luna looked down at her silk negligee, at the glint of diamonds around her neck.

"Do you like them?" he asked. "There's a matching robe on the chair. Keisha and Violet helped you. You were a little under the weather."

He leaned forward and touched her cheek. "I love you, Luna," he said, his dark eyes on hers. "Never in my life have I loved a woman the way I love you. Don't you see how epic we are together? Come home."

Home. She tilted further off balance, once again wrapped in his aura of invincibility, the shimmering ghosts of spectacular houses and penthouse apartments lined up behind him. "You'll always have a home when you're with me," he said, and kissed her deeply. She began to respond. She closed her eyes, and leaned into the swell of the ocean.

There's some endangered birds nesting over there, he said, both of them standing on the foredeck of the *Luna-sea* in the blazing sun off Majorca. World Wildlife Fund wants to talk to you about them.

Why? she asked.

Because I just bought the island for you. Merry Christmas.

She opened her eyes, expecting the sun and the sea, but instead she saw a black SUV barreling through the night. Would you shut up? Roland demanded, stopping her torrent of insults with a gag, her flailing arms with some kind of straitjacket. He removed the gag, and held an evil-smelling cloth to her face.

She flinched, shook her head, and once again she was in Adam's bedroom. "Are you okay?" he asked.

"No!" she said. "You kidnapped me!"

He gave her a rueful look. "I would have taken you out to dinner, but you wouldn't answer your phone."

Her expression of disbelief darkened. She pulled further away, and gathered her legs beneath her.

"I have a deal for you," said Adam encouragingly. "Let's go away for a couple of days. If you tell me where Mars is, I'll have him delivered right back to your friends in Pennsylvania. We'll spend the weekend together, and then if you still want to leave, I won't stop you. How does that sound? Don't worry about the legal stuff, it's not an issue."

Luna winced, unable to connect his kindly expression and congenial tone with her gagged and straitjacketed ride with Roland. She looked down at herself, resplendent in silk and diamonds.

"Come here," he said, his voice soothing, his touch gentle. "I know all this has been too much. I'm sorry." He took her hand. "I did something to show how much I care about you. I know you had a rough time when you were a kid. I thought maybe if you came to terms with it, you'd feel better. Maybe it's what gives you those nightmares. I thought maybe I could make them stop."

Her eyes widened, and he continued.

"I have the contact information of your foster parents. I had no idea there were so many. I can deal with these people any way you'd like me to, if it would give you some closure."

Luna gasped. She yanked her hand away and stood abruptly. The look on her face made Adam recoil. "You had no right!" she said in a furious undertone.

"But I was trying to help you!"

Her voice rose. "I don't need your help! I don't need you spying on me and putting bugs in my phone and digging up things that are none of your business!Where are my clothes?"

"You need me more than you think!"

He stood, and an edge crept into his voice. "You and I are great together, and you know it! You want to set up an environmental foundation? I'll fund it! I told you I'd build some green companies, and I will! We've only been married six months!" His eyes darkened. "And what the hell are you doing with that kid?"

When she stiffened, Adam checked himself and softened his tone. "I'll do anything you want. But without me, you're going to have a hard time."

Luna locked her eyes on his. "I can survive just fine without you. And that's exactly what I'm going to do, unless you tell me why I can't."

Neither of them moved. Adam held her gaze. "Because it might get out that you stabbed a cop when you were twelve," he said, and paused. "Twice."

Luna's expression turned to ice. "Let it get out," she said, and started toward the door.

"You won't get past Roland," called Adam.

She scanned the room, her eyes pausing on the windows and the balcony doors. He stepped forward and closed his arms around her. "You belong to me," he whispered, and kissed her.

For the smallest of moments he believed he had won her back, so the knee that slammed into his groin came as a complete surprise. At first it didn't hurt, but then a wall of pain struck him with such force he doubled over, feeling as if he were about to vomit. Luna reached for the dresser, seized a heavy silver candlestick, and swung it against his head.

Adam heard a thud. He felt another blaze of pain, and the deep wool rug rushed toward him. Through blurred vision he saw an auburn curl and a sliver of blue. "I don't belong to anyone," Luna whispered, her face inches from his, then everything went black.

She crossed to the door and opened it a crack. The hallway was empty and silent, so she crept forward. Four flights down the grand staircase was the front door. "Not now," came Roland's voice, accompanied by his footsteps. "He'll have to call you back."

Luna returned to the bedroom, saw Adam lying motionless, and locked the door. She pulled the curtains away from the south windows, revealing a dark balcony bedecked with iron furniture and flowering plants. Rain fell heavily, spattering the garden beyond. Luna eyed the luxurious white swags undulating along the curtains, yanked two of them down, and tied them together using a foolproof knot Harry had taught her.

She froze at the sound of the knock. "Adam," came Roland's voice. "It's important. You gotta take this call." A few moments went by. "Adam. Adam?"

A key slid into the lock.

Luna steeled herself. "Dammit, Roland!" she called, making her voice sound lazy and sleepy. "Will you give us ten minutes? He's asleep."

The key slid from the lock. "All right," came the voice, along with the sound of retreating footsteps.

She exhaled with relief. As she grabbed the swags and headed for the balcony, she glanced down at herself. She reached for the floor length hem, pulled it up, and knotted it mid-thigh. Quickly she slipped into the robe, repeated the process, and reinforced it with the silk belt. On her way to the balcony, she stopped. Her hand went to her throat.

Frantically she searched the tops of the dressers and the shelves. She yanked open the drawers of the bedside tables, leaving them jutting haphazardly, and rushed into the bathroom. Her eyes raced over glass and marble and there it was, curled into a crystal bowl next to one of the sinks.

Once again, she felt a wave of relief as she fastened the leather cord with its silver bead around her neck. She crossed the bedroom and stepped out onto the balcony, her gown quickly soaked by rain. As she double-knotted one end of the swag to the balcony railing, she felt a spin of vertigo: four floors up was very, very high. Spurred by the thought of Roland's key in the lock, she gave the knot a final tug and climbed over the railing.

Luna grasped the swag in a death grip and lowered herself as fast as she dared, second by second, inch by inch, until her feet hit the flagstone walkway. She sprinted barefoot down the quiet residential street toward LaSalle, her drenched silk robe loosened and trailing behind her. When she reached the corner she peered through the downpour at the oncoming headlights, and raised her arm.

Three cabs screeched to a halt, and a crash of metal sent a taillight spinning past her feet. Nearly blinded by rain, she ran from the commotion. Half a block later she raised her arm again, and a single cab stopped beside her. She opened the door, climbed in, and the cab pulled away.

"And where are we going on this dark night, my lady?" asked the driver, in a musical Caribbean accent. He regarded her in the rear view mirror, frowning in concern. "Do you need help?" he asked.

"No," she said. "But thank you."

"Where should I take you?"

"I hadn't gotten that far."

"A friend," he replied. "Your best friend. Where does she live?"

Luna hugged herself. "I have only one friend in Chicago, and I don't know if she's still my friend."

"Let's try. If she doesn't let you in, we will come up with another plan."

"Thank you so much," said Luna, then let out a soft groan. "I don't have any money!"

"This is no surprise to me," said the driver, his smile returning. "I could see when I picked you up that you had no pockets. It is no problem, I will win the Story Slam on Saturday and drink all night for free."

"Wait," she said, raising her hands and finding a large stud in each ear. "Here," she said, unscrewing a diamond and handing it through the divider. "It's real. And here," she added, removing the other. "Take this one, too. And thank you for being a kind man."

They pulled up to a wide brick building. "I will wait until you are inside, my lady!" he called as she slid out of the car and hurried through the rain. In the vestibule she leaned on a buzzer, waited, then buzzed again. "Goddammit, who is it?" came a voice.

"Lyllis?"

There was a pause. "Luna?"

"Yes!"

The door buzzed. Luna waved at the cabdriver, glanced at the elevator, then took the stairs to the fifth floor. She opened the stairwell door. Waiting for her was Lyllis, wearing a multicolored kaftan and an expression of astonishment. Luna hesitated in the doorway, ready to bolt back down the stairs.

Lyllis scowled. "Those sonsabitches," she snapped. She held out her arms, and Luna rushed into her wide embrace.

"Damn!" said Lyllis, holding her at arm's length. "You look like a porn star who fell overboard." Her eyebrows rose at the sight of the diamond necklace. "A rich one."

"Can I use your phone?"

"Get in here," Lyllis replied, and towed her into the apartment.

• • •

Roland unlocked the bedroom door and found Adam on the floor, slowly regaining consciousness as rain pelted sideways through an open window. He called Seth Connolly, Adam's personal physician, who arrived halfway through the seismic event that followed. Roland thought he had seen his employer's emotional range, but he was wrong.

Adam erupted into volcanic fury. He roared expletives while clutching his crotch, swaying dizzily, and bleeding from a good-sized head wound, all while fending Seth off and refusing to go to the hospital. Roland called an ambulance and then the police, reporting that two men had climbed through a window, attacked Adam Matheson, and fled with a wallet full of cash. When Seth went to signal the arriving EMTs, Adam sank onto a chair.

"Roland," he said, with seething malevolence. "Get her."

Roland followed the stretcher as they rolled it toward the ambulance. "She's got to be at Lyllis's," Adam hissed. "You get her, and you contain her. We're going to the island!"

For the first time in fourteen years, Roland lost control of his expression. He didn't know what his face displayed, but whatever it was infuriated Adam still further. "Don't you fail me!" he snapped, as the medics lifted his stretcher.

Seth followed the ambulance in his Lexus. Roland climbed into his BMW and headed, slowly, for Lyllis's. It's the concussion, he thought, remembering a half dozen of his teammates talking like lunatics after they'd been knocked cold on the field. But he knew it was wishful thinking, and Adam meant every word.

The island was off the coast of Spain, a sunny paradise of blue water and white beaches. Adam had bought the whole damned thing for her. On one end he'd built a small — for him — eco-friendly villa.

On the other, fenced and off limits, was some kind of endangered bird group home. Twice Adam had whisked her there, and she'd returned rested and better able to cope. Apparently he planned to do it again, even though Luna obviously had no intention of climbing aboard the Gulfstream herself.

Jesus Christ, he thought, trying to consider the ramifications of what had the makings of an international crime. Officials at both airports knew Adam Matheson, and would be sympathetic if they saw his young wife out like a light. Bad case of the flu, he could hear Adam say.

But what would happen when she woke up? He tried to imagine Luna transforming into a halfway decent Matheson wife: lunching, shopping, decorating, gossiping about whose husband was screwing whose nanny. Failing, he pictured her bashing him on the head and hijacking the aptly-named *Luna-sea*, which was what this whole damned thing had been from the start.

She was a pain in the ass. A freak. An orphan. Who would miss her if she disappeared? Okay: who would miss her who could affect him directly?

Lyllis.

You are one-half of a fucked-up bromance, she shouted at him years ago, after a cellphone captured him beating two men long after they quit fighting. She stopped referring to Adam by name, and instead asked questions like: are you still going to London with that arrogant motherfucker, or can we finally go to the lake?

She had come to the hospital every day after the tackle. She stuck with him when the doctors delivered the news, when he was drunk for what seemed like six months straight. She was supportive of his new job, until it became clear that turning his back on the sport he loved was not a positive choice. Why can't you spend an hour and talk to his team? she demanded, back when Michael was in middle school. He's your nephew! Who has the chance to make a difference in those kids' lives — one of the best defensive linemen who ever lived, or Adam Matheson's enforcer?

He pulled up in front of a wide brick building, and glanced at the clock. 2:04 a.m. He didn't even have her keys anymore. Roland paused, watching the rain, then looked up at Lyllis's window. The light was on. She'd be expecting him, so there was no point in trying to surprise her. He hadn't brought his kidnapping equipment, he thought disgustedly, so why was he even here? He remembered the red-haired brat in her blue t-shirt, raising her middle finger at Florida's wealthiest financier.

He tried to figure out how he could play the middle. That finger was nothing compared to how Lyllis would react when she found out what he had done to Luna. She would probably take Luna wherever she was going herself, knowing he'd think twice before trying to stop her.

Which was true.

He glanced back up at the apartment. If the two of them were in there, they wouldn't be for long. He had a small window: Adam was probably getting CT scanned, and Roland knew from experience that doctors wouldn't let you shout into your cell phone while you were inside the machine. Maybe they'd get fed up and sedate him, and give everyone a break.

Roland came up with a strategy. Lyllis wouldn't go anywhere near her car, since he knew the make, plate number, and where she kept it. He'd wait an hour, then call the security company and tell them to watch her apartment and her garage. He would tell Adam she hadn't been home, and that he checked her garage and her friends' apartments. He would do enough busy coordinating that Adam would think he was doing his job instead of avoiding it.

Roland stepped on the gas. There was a chance getting whacked upside the head would knock some sense into the man, but the odds were not good.

• • •

Lyllis wrapped Luna in a towel, listened to her brief summary, then handed her a cell phone. Luna called Warren. She had never heard him sound so angry.

"I'm going to kill both those bastards," he said. "Stanley called me, I got some guys heading for Chicago right now."

"No! It'll just make things worse! Besides, I don't know what I've done to Adam, when I left he was out cold."

"What happened?"

"I, um…y'know. Hit him."

Warren sighed. "Look, my guys are going to get you to Minnesota. I got buddies there with a cabin, that sonofabitch could hire an army and he wouldn't get through 'em. Where are you?"

"At a friend's."

"What friend?"

"Uh…Lyllis. You don't know her."

"Lyllis! Wait a minute — she's not Roland Edwards's girlfriend, is she?"

"Where else was I supposed to go?"

"Will you get out of there?"

Luna took a quick hot shower, emerged in Lyllis's pink and turquoise robe, and found Lyllis hanging up her phone. "My cousin works the night shift at the hospital, and she said Adam came in with a bloody head a half hour ago. So you didn't kill him, but let's just say he wasn't a happy man. Follow me."

Lyllis bustled into the bedroom and begin pulling clothes out of her closet. "Here," she said, tossing her a navy button-down shirt and a striped scarf. "On you, it'll be a dress with a belt. Think Garbo," she added, tossing her a hat and a pair of sunglasses. "And take off that bling. Give it here, I'm gonna hide it."

Luna unfastened the diamond necklace. "We need to go right now," said Lyllis. "There's only one fight in the world Roland Edwards will back away from, and that's with me. But let's not push our luck."

CHAPTER 21

E lias poured himself a second cup of coffee and glanced out at the misty morning. His laptop lay open on the kitchen table, flanked by two phones. One was his regular cell phone, the second he had purchased yesterday. The banner on his computer screen read **Ten Frequently Asked Questions About Your New Burner Phone.**

He had bought it on impulse. He wasn't clear about this hacking business; he knew at one point Luna had one so her husband couldn't track her, and considering the way things were going, he thought he should have one, too. After one of the volunteers showed him how to transfer the numbers of the 119 rehabbers in Luna's group onto his new phone, he sent out a message.

> 529-628-4720 Rehabbers: this is my new untraceable burner phone so I'm not going to ID myself except you know me from the West Nile Virus conference last year. Be careful. Don't write anything someone could hack.
>
> amphibious632@hotmail.com Gotcha
>
> bluestreak@juno.com Yokay
>
> sunny@capedaviswildlife.org Affirmative
>
> rackocoons@hotmail.com Where's Esther? Our potential Wikileak?
>
> chiroptera@gmail.com Right here, Bob! Why don't you fuck off?

Ten minutes later, as he continued to investigate the capabilities of his new device, it sprang to life. Elias jumped, assuming it was the police. "Hello?" he answered hesitantly.

"Yo, Elias," said Warren. His tone was determinedly casual, though tightly harnessed anger clearly seeped around the edges. "Good job, getting a burner. Listen. Can you get Banshee to a location outside Lake Arrow, Minnesota by tomorrow afternoon?"

"What?" said Elias.

Warren explained this would be the meeting point for Stanley, Ned, and Mars, who would be coming from Northeast Iowa; Luna, who would be coming from Chicago; and Warren himself, who would be coming from Indiana. Elias needed to bring a vehicle large enough to accommodate two eagle crates and three people, because from there Elias, Warren, Luna, and the two eagles would head for Hélène's.

"But…Luna's in Chicago?" asked Elias. "What's she doing in Chicago?"

"Long story," said Warren. "One more thing," he added, as if he were asking Elias to grab him a beer from the refrigerator. "Can you throw together enough paperwork to get the birds across the border?"

"Uh, maybe," said Elias, knowing the paperwork to get American wildlife into Canada took weeks, if not longer.

"Good!" said Warren. "I'll call you back."

Elias felt a sizzle as he hung up. He and Warren were two cool guys working under the radar, planning a special op on their burner phones. It only lasted a moment, though. Don't be ridiculous, he told himself. It wasn't like Banshee could just vanish, especially with Gunderman nosing around. And even if Elias managed to smuggle her out, it would take about five minutes for Gunderman to put it together and issue an APB on the center's SUV. Elias pictured himself flooring it toward Minnesota, a platoon of screaming police cars in his wake.

He closed his computer and pocketed his new phone. He left the kitchen, crossed the field, and hiked to the top of ridge, puzzling over why Luna had decamped to Chicago, and how he could get Banshee to Minnesota. He sat on a boulder, caught his breath, and looked over the lush Pennsylvania landscape. He and his fellow rehabbers spent their lives fighting ignorance, indifference and greed, struggling to help those who had no voice. It was clearly a one-sided battle. How much difference did the life of a bluebird, a badger, or an eagle really make?

A lot.

Elias clung stubbornly to his belief. He could take a wild creature on the brink of death, bring her back to life, and set her free. Not every time, of course. But when the magical, mystical, odds-defying sequence worked, it was enough to prevent him from laying down his arms, despite his weariness. And if he and his compatriots could perform these little miracles, year after year, they could certainly make an eagle disappear from Pennsylvania and reappear in Ontario.

He pulled out his phone.

529-628-4720 Everyone: Need unrl f BAEA 5.7 k no records. Right now.

Elias thought of Adam Matheson's hackers scratching their heads over the animal nut gobbledygook, unable to recognize BAEA as the American Ornithological Union's abbreviation for Bald Eagle. They wouldn't realize he was asking if anyone had taken in a female weighing about five and a half kilograms, whose injuries had rendered her unreleasable, and whose statistics had not yet been logged into the exhaustive records the state and federal government required rehabbers to keep. It might not stump hackers for long, but it would certainly slow them down. After a moment, his phone chimed.

pacificawild@outlook.com Sorry

gduncan@bobcathollow.org None

envirowacko@gmail.com Will ask around off-line

bluestreak@juno.com Checking.

ben@coldcreekpreserve.org Just got one in! Roadside zoo confiscation.

529-628-4720 Can you make her disappear?

ben@coldcreekpreserve.org No. Conservation Police brought her in, there's a paper trail.

kelly@muscongusbaywildlife.org Wish I could raise the dead. BAEA intake this morning, DOA. Power line.

Elias paused, thinking furiously. He raised his phone.

529-628-4720 Paper trail?

kelly@muscongusbaywildlife.org Not yet. In the freezer.

529-628-4720 Princess and the Pauper. Right angle to NER. Are you both following?

Elias's phone was silent. He waited, praying the two rehabbers knew enough of Luna's plans to decipher his shorthand. Finally, his phone chimed twice.

<u>kelly@muscongusbaywildlife.org</u> Overnighting.
<u>ben@coldcreekpreserve.org</u> Will deliver. Send me time and place.

Elias sent Ben a private message.

529-628-4720 6:15 tonight?
<u>ben@coldcreekpreserve.org</u> You got it.

Elias snapped his phone shut.

Kelly, from Muscongus Bay Wildlife in Maine, had been a friend for years. So had Ben, who was from Cold Creek Preserve near Buffalo, New York. Both were longtime rehabbers who conscientiously followed the rules. That is, until it was clearly time to circumvent them.

Elias went over his plan, looking for holes. Earlier this morning Kelly had taken in a female Bald Eagle, dead on arrival after hitting a power line in Maine. Kelly had put her in the freezer, and not yet filled out the paperwork required for eagles. Normally she would complete the forms, pack the dead eagle in ice, and overnight her to the National Eagle Repository, the federal agency which collects protected but deceased eagles and distributes their feathers to Native American tribes.

But now, instead, she would overnight the dead eagle to Ben. Ben's female eagle, confiscated from a roadside zoo in Buffalo by the state's Conservation Police, was very much alive. But today Ben would record that she suddenly collapsed and died, probably due to stress and age. Tomorrow Ben would receive Kelly's record-less eagle, repack her, insert a copy of his own records, and send her on to NER. This afternoon he would take his confiscated eagle and drive her to the Western Pennsylvania Wildlife Center. The Pauper and the Princess would switch places, the confiscated eagle would move from a dirty little zoo in upstate New York to a palace of a flight cage in

Pennsylvania, and Banshee would reunite with her mate and roll on up to Ontario.

And the plan would work because of the general blindness of humanity. Elias pictured Banshee: the slight droop of her left wing, the crooked third toe on her right foot, the unusually loud, rapidly descending notes of her cry; the way she cocked her head to compensate for her blind left eye, visible only by its slight sheen when she looked toward the sun.

He could pick her out of a flight cage filled with eagles. But then, he knew her.

He would have to borrow a car, call Hélène, expedite the paperwork, and find a way to get rid of Gunderman for a couple of hours. The plan would work, and no one but Elias, Celia, Stanley, Warren, Luna, Ned, and 119 rehabbers scattered across the country would know.

Elias stood up and gazed over the hills and valleys, home to wild creatures determinedly living their lives. He raised his fist in tribute to the resistance, then he followed the trail down the mountain. Halfway through the field he noticed the hammock was swaying, and he slowed to a stop.

It was covered with a colorful quilt. Celia swung gently, radiant, a six-month-old Wizzie beside her. On Wizzie's other side was Luna, just turned seventeen. She had been living with Harry and Rose for almost two years. She was still quiet and guarded, but her transformation had been a thing to behold. The three of them swung in the summer shade. Dad! Join us! Celia beckoned.

Come on, Elias, called Luna, smiling. There's always room for you.

He blinked, and the hammock was empty. Life is filled with miracles, he thought. Let's see how many we can find now.

• • •

"Who do you think Warren's going to kill first?" asked Stanley, his eyes bleary above his steaming coffee cup. "Matheson or Edwards?"

Ned sat beside him. Neither of them had slept much, even after Warren had phoned to say Luna was safe. "I still can't figure out how she got away," said Ned, "unless another mob of rehabbers with guns showed up at his house."

Stanley regarded him sympathetically. "I'm glad I'm not you," he said.

"Why don't I go home?" asked Ned. "She's married! And she's not just married, she's married to *Adam Matheson*. Plus, she's a felon. I could go on."

"You could."

"I don't even like birds. I thought they'd grow on me, but no. Not at all. That one out there? It still scares the shit out of me. You know something? The first time I met her she had fish puke all over her." He leaned his head on one hand. "What's going to happen when she gets to Canada? Notice I'm saying *when*."

"That's what we're all waiting to see."

Something in his tone made Ned squint. "What do you mean?"

"Nothing. It's a rehabber thing."

Ned snorted. "I'm either one step above or one step below a rehabber, depending on how you look at it."

Stanley put his cup down. "Have you noticed the Greed Is Good crowd is back in charge of this country? Every day they rip another environmental regulation to shreds."

"And?"

"And we need our own Hélène."

Ned regarded him blankly.

"You don't know what it's like, Ned. The destruction. The suffering. You work for decades to change the laws and finally you win, but only for a minute. You feel triumph and hope, and then another sleazy politician takes it all away. You get tired. You need someone to inspire you not to give up."

"Are you saying it's *Luna?*"

Stanley looked back at him with a mixture of embarrassment and defiance. "I know, I know! I know how it sounds! But she's already mythical. When Harry and Rose took her to Ontario for her sixteenth birthday, Hélène spent *ten minutes* with her, then handed her a Golden Eagle. You know what Golden Eagles are like? They're like Mars on steroids. Luna handled that bird as if she'd done it her whole life.

Everyone could see it. After they left, Hélène said Luna was the one. And we've been waiting ever since."

A two-toned whistle emerged from Ned's phone. It was Carlene, texting from her painted bird room in Florida.

bluestreak@juno.com Goddamn cops were at the panther refuge and F&W just released this photo

He clicked on the attachment. Beneath the U.S. Fish and Wildlife Services logo was a photo of Warren, eyes on the distance, holding a pair of binoculars beneath his chin.

"What is it?" asked Stanley

"Warren's officially a Person of Interest," said Ned, tilting the phone toward him. "They're tightening the net." He put the phone down. "Does Luna know who…what…she's supposed to be?"

"No," said Stanley. "We don't think she could take it."

• • •

Celia stood by her office window, her eyes on the flight cage where Banshee stood, stubbornly motionless, on her perch. The volunteers' morale was down. They tried not to question her directly, knowing she had no answers, but Celia could see the concern in their eyes. Even worse, she could feel it: anxiousness hung like a fog, emanating from people who knew its effect on wildlife and tried to suppress it. She saw a flash of motion, and watched her father cross the field.

"Dad, what is going on?" she asked, as Elias entered the room. "No one knows what happened after Trish and Angelica's! Do you?"

"I know they're okay," said Elias, "but that's all I can tell you. Just hang in there a little longer. Can you do that?"

"But when is it going to end? Banshee's still not eating! Are we all supposed to just sit and watch? And Officer Gunderman — why does he have to come back here?"

"It's not our decision, Celia! And don't forget what he did for Warren!"

Celia turned toward the screen door. Standing outside was Gunderman, lowering his hand as if he had changed his mind about knocking.

"Officer Gunderman!" said Elias. "Come in."

Celia watched him enter the room. As usual he stood straight and tall, his uniform neatly pressed, his eyes level. But there was something defensive and guarded about him, an inner cloud which had not been there before. The first time she met him she noticed his face was handsome and kind, but she dismissed it. Now, she noticed it again.

"Good morning," he said politely, and she wanted to sit him down and ask, what happened? Are you in trouble because of what you did for Warren?

"I just wanted to let you know I'm back in town," he said. "I won't disturb you for long, but we believe Luna Burke may try to take the missing eagle's mate. I still hope her plan is to cooperate with us, and to return the missing eagle. If so, I will do everything possible to help her."

Celia and Elias exchanged glances.

"But if her plan is to take that second eagle, it's my job to stop her." He regarded each of them in turn, and sighed. "Basically, right now I'm a bird guard." He paused, then backed toward the door. "Thanks for your time. I'll swing by again this afternoon."

He left the room, and Elias turned to Celia. "Just keep the faith," he said. "I'll be back in a little while."

• • •

The apartment was small and neat. It had been empty when they arrived, its owner in Springfield visiting her mother. Lyllis insisted Luna take the bedroom, then she busied herself with the foldout couch. This is why friends need to keep copies of each other's house keys, Lyllis said.

A half hour later Luna turned out the light on her bedside table. She expected the worst, but almost immediately she fell into a dreamless sleep. Eventually she awakened with a start, rose, and pulled on Lyllis's shirt. She padded barefoot into the living room, now flooded with daylight, but the apartment was empty. On the dining room table was a note in loopy script: BACK SOON. The sky was overcast. The kitchen clock read 11:13 a.m.

"It's me!" came a voice from the hallway, accompanied by the click of a lock. "Don't freak out."

228

Lyllis entered, followed by a tall, broad-shouldered young man with long braids and more than a passing resemblance to Roland. He saw Luna's look of apprehension, and smiled apologetically. "You don't have to worry," he said. "Kidnapping doesn't run in the family."

"This is Michael," announced Lyllis, placing a shopping bag on the table. "Roland's nephew. *My* nephew too, though maybe not officially."

Michael shook her hand, then reached into a bag and offered her a cup of coffee. "I had a big fight with your friend Warren this morning," said Lyllis. "I don't know how he got my number, but he called me and said two of his friends were going to pick you up. I said hell, no."

Lyllis put her hands on her hips. "Warren said your next stop is a cabin outside Arrow Lake, Minnesota. We're going to get you there tonight. And if Roland thinks he's going to grab you again, he's going to have to get past his own family. Michael and I are the best bodyguards you've got."

"Thank you, but it's too dangerous," said Luna, shaking her head. "Where are Warren's guys?"

"I just don't know," said Lyllis, exaggeratedly baffled. "And I can't find out from Warren, because I turned my phone off."

"There's no point in arguing with Lyllis when she gets like this," said Michael. "Uncle Roland'll be watching her garage, so we rented a car. Warren promised to let us get you to his friends' place in Minnesota, and Lyllis promised to not smash his tracker." He gestured to Luna's necklace, and she touched the silver bead.

"But what about your phones?" she asked. "Did you make any calls they could hack?"

"Michael's girlfriend rented the car for us fifteen minutes ago, and we're getting out of here right now," said Lyllis. "They won't have time to put it together. I bought you some clothes," she added, pointing to the shopping bag. "Underwear, pair of pants, shirt, sweater, and socks. 'Course I know your sizes. Look underneath, 'cause the most important items are at the bottom. Size 8, regular width."

Luna pulled out a box.

"Running shoes," said Michael.

• • •

Gunderman drove through town with both hands balanced on the wheel of his car, still shaken by the sight of Warren's face on the Fish and Wildlife release. A call from Whittaker was imminent, and it would not be pleasant.

He pulled into a space close to the police department. He slid out and spotted Elias, sitting in his parked truck. "Officer Gunderman!" said Elias through his open window. "Can I talk to you a minute?"

The men met on the sidewalk. "I have a favor to ask you," said Elias. "Today is the anniversary of my daughter's husband's death. Sometimes she gets a little sad. Would you consider taking her out to dinner tonight?"

Gunderman pictured the photograph of Celia, blonde hair gleaming in the sunlight, gleefully hugging her husband's killer.

"What do you think?" pressed Elias.

"Oh. Yes. I'm sorry to hear that. Certainly, whatever I can do to help."

"That's very kind of you," Elias said smoothly, as if these were arrangements he made all the time. "There's a great little Italian place on Maple. How about six o'clock?"

"All right."

"I realize we have our differences, but you're a good man," said Elias. "I'm sure I don't need to tell you this, but Celia's awfully sensitive. Best not to bring this up."

"Understood."

Elias smiled, clapped Gunderman on the shoulder, and headed down the street. Does he really think I'm going to fall for this? thought Gunderman. Is Warren involved?

• • •

The smell of bacon filled the kitchen. The windows framed a cloudy afternoon. Elias was spreading mayonnaise on six pieces of toast when Celia dropped the skillet onto the burner with a crash.

"A date?" she gasped.

"You want to help Luna?" asked Elias, glancing behind him and keeping his voice down. "You want to get Banshee back with Mars? Then go out to dinner and don't ask any questions."

"But...did you already ask him?"

"I just set it up. Go along with it, have a nice dinner, and do your part."

"But I don't want to go on a date!"

"Suck it up, Celia! This is the only ..."

Elias stopped abruptly as Wizzie walked into the room. "Who's going on a date? Not Mom."

"Yes, Mom," said Elias.

"With who?"

"Never mind," said Elias. "You don't need to know everything that goes on around here."

Wizzie peered at Celia. "But who would *you* ever go on a ..." Her jaw dropped. "Is it Officer Gunderman? Are you going on a date with Officer Gunderman?"

Celia threw Elias an irritated look.

"When did this happen?" cried Wizzie. "Can I come?"

"Of course you can't," said Elias. "Don't be ridiculous. And it's not a date, it's a business dinner."

"But I heard Mom say a date!"

"It's a date for a business dinner!"

Wizzie looked imploringly at Celia, who was busily making sandwiches. "Mom! I can go with you, right?"

"No," said Celia, determinedly avoiding eye contact with her daughter.

"But he doesn't even *have* a business! He works for the government! Are you allowed to do this? Isn't it like dating your parole officer?"

"You're not going," said Elias. "You're going to Anna's for a sleepover!" He glanced at his watch. "Aren't you getting picked up soon?"

"But it wasn't even Anna's idea! She said all of a sudden her dad told her she was having a sleepover, and..."

"...and that's all she wrote, Wizzie!" finished Elias, grabbing a sandwich. "You're going to Anna's, Mom's going out to dinner, and

I'm holding down the fort! You ladies have lunch, and I'll go check on the beavers!"

Pulling a baseball cap off a hook, he hurried out the door toward the clinic and went over his mental checklist. Wizzie, done. Celia, done. Well, basically done; Celia couldn't admit to something she didn't know. The only potentially awkward moment would be if Gunderman brought up the supposed death anniversary, but Elias was sure he was too polite to do it. Even if he did, Celia would be too shy to correct him.

Gunderman would assume there was an eagle heist in the works, but if he didn't go along with the dinner, he could derail what might be his only chance to apprehend Luna. He would probably post a cop on the road, which was why Elias needed to borrow Owen's car.

He finished his sandwich. The Princess and the Pauper plan will go down in rehabber history, he thought. He almost wished he could explain it to Gunderman, just so Gunderman could more fully understand the importance of keeping a bonded pair of Bald Eagles together. He'll learn, he thought.

• • •

Gunderman watched Elias stride away, then he turned and entered the Prattstown Police Department. The day before he had met the chief, a genial man in his fifties who hadn't let on, if he knew, that Gunderman had arrived from Rock Ridge in disgrace. The chief had shaken Gunderman's hand, pledged his support, and encouraged him to use their database.

Today the station was quiet. Right now I'm a bird guard, he had said to Celia and Elias, deliberately trying to rouse Celia's sympathy and prod her into revealing a plan. But it was true, he *was* a bird guard. And now it was clear Elias had a plan, but whether Celia was in on it was anyone's guess. Gunderman nodded at an officer, and sat at an empty desk in the corner. His cell phone rang, and he pulled his eyes from the computer.

"Get onscreen," ordered Whittaker.

Gunderman tapped the keyboard, feeling a chill at his boss's tone. Whittaker appeared at his desk, his eyes hard. He slapped a folder down, removed a photograph, and turned it toward his computer screen.

The old black and white shot showed a dozen fit, muscled young men clustered on a beach. They were short-haired, clean-shaven, and shirtless, all wearing shorts and the occasional brimmed cap. Gunderman squinted at the man beside Whittaker's pointed finger: a young Warren, grinning rakishly at the camera.

"Warren Trask," said Whittaker, snapping off the syllables. "Naval Special Warfare Group Three, SEAL Team One."

He picked up a second photograph and slid it in front of the first. Another old black and white shot showed a group of men in full camouflage, bullet belts crossed across their chests. Warren stood beside Whittaker's pointed finger, staring steadily at the camera, an M-14 balanced casually on one shoulder.

"Warren Trask," he said. "Rung Sat — 'The Forest of Assassins.' I'll spare you the medals and citations."

Whittaker picked up a third photo. "Warren Trask," he said. "Founder of The Florida Panther Recovery Unit."

The recent color photo showed Warren, grey-haired, bearded, sitting on the hood of a battered jeep. His eyes were fixed on the distance, and he held a pair of binoculars just beneath his chin.

"And you know what?" continued Whittaker, his voice rising. "There isn't *one shred of evidence* linking a trained combat vet, decorated sniper, and defender of the environment to *any of this Matheson bullshit.* None of the police officers involved in the capture of the Unidentified White Male will give a positive ID because one, they tackled him from behind, two, his face was camouflaged, and three, he kept it hidden when he was *in the fucking bear net.*"

"Yes, sir," said Gunderman.

Whittaker lowered the photographs. "This information should have come from you. Can you make a positive ID of this man?"

Gunderman held Whittaker's gaze. He swallowed. When he finally spoke, his voice was harder than he meant it to be.

"No, sir."

Whittaker gave a grunt of disgust. "Your regional supervisor has been my best friend for 40 years."

He slammed his hands down on the desk and shoved the file aside. "You listen to me, Gunderman," he said. "I want both those eagles, I want this case wrapped up, and I want Luna Burke headed for court. You've got 48 hours. If I don't get all of it, you're out."

He reached forward and severed the connection.

CHAPTER 22

At 5:45 on the dot Gunderman stopped his car in front of Elias's house. He knocked on the door, wearing a neatly pressed shirt, slacks, and a navy jacket. Celia emerged in a flowered summer dress and gave him a reluctant smile. The hem brushed her legs as she walked to the car, unsteady in low heels. Elias appeared in the doorway of the clinic, waved, and went back inside.

Gunderman stopped the car at the end of the driveway. A police car was parked across the road. As they passed, the officer raised a hand through his open window. "Hello, Celia!" called the officer. "Hello, Erik!"

"Hi, Larry," Celia called back, then turned an accusatory stare on Gunderman.

"Did you really expect me to just leave?" asked Gunderman. "This is a chess match. You can't say you didn't know that."

Celia frowned and looked out the window. "I'm not your enemy," said Gunderman.

Celia gazed back at him. "I know you're not," she said. "You're Luna's."

Gunderman bowed his head slightly, unwilling to let her see how much this pained him. He could talk about the big picture until he was hoarse and it would make no difference to her. His was a world of absolutes, and hers was filled with exceptions. They rode to town in silence.

• • •

The covered eagle crate rested on the grass near the driveway. There was no sound, which meant Banshee was perching calmly. Elias stood beside her, scanning the edge of the woods. Two people emerged, carrying an identical crate.

"Ben!" called Elias, and waved. Ben was lean and grey-haired, his companion small and stocky. Carefully they crossed the field and put the crate down in front of the flight cage. Ben and Elias hugged and clapped each other on the back. "Long time no see!" said Ben. "Meet Melody!"

Elias shook her hand. "And here..." finished Ben, pulling the cover from the crate, "...we have Confiscated Eagle Number Four, from now on known as Banshee!"

"Fantastic," said Elias. "How was the trip? Any trouble?"

"Good trip," said Ben. "No trouble."

"There's a police car at the end of your road," said Melody. "Can't you just carry your eagle through the woods?"

"We can't, she's too nervous. She's okay in a car, but if her crate is unsteady she panics and starts thrashing. She'd break a wing."

"Then how are you going to get past the police?"

Elias glanced anxiously at his watch. "If Owen doesn't get here soon, that'll be a good question."

"Look!" said Ben, and pointed to the black car rolling toward them. It stopped outside the office, executed a three-point turn, and backed up to the grass.

"You're taking Banshee in a hearse?" asked Melody.

Owen was round and serene, with a soft voice and sandy hair just going grey at the temples. "Hello there, people," he said warmly, as introductions were made. "Hello, birds," he added, addressing both crates.

"I need to get out of here," said Elias. "Owen, will you help me put this crate in your car? Ben, you can get your eagle settled — food and water's already in there. You sure I can't offer you beds?"

"Thanks, but we need to get back."

Owen and Elias slid Banshee's crate into the empty hearse and shut the door. Ben and Melody started toward the flight cage, but paused at the sound of an engine. Another car was making its way down the driveway.

"Oh, dear," said Owen.

236

Elias watched, his heart thudding. Gunderman, he thought. What happened?

The car reached the office, stopped a few yards from the hearse, and two small faces peered through the backseat window. A door opened, and Wizzie slid out.

"Pop!" she called. "What the heck are you doing?"

A man emerged from behind the wheel. "Hey, Elias!" he exclaimed. "Hey, Owen! Is everything okay? Why is Officer Davis parked across the road?"

"He's taking a rest!" replied Elias. "And Owen is paying a social call!"

"Okay, then catch you later. Anna's come down with the stomach flu, so I'm dropping the girls off and running to the drugstore."

He waved goodbye and drove away. Wizzie dropped her overnight bag on the ground, looked pointedly at the hearse, and walked toward the group. She stopped in front of Elias.

"Is there anything you want to tell me?" she asked.

• • •

The cozy Italian restaurant was at the corner of Maple and Baker. Celia and Gunderman sat a table beneath a trellis covered with roses, half-finished glasses of wine before them, each intently studying the decor.

"I'm sorry if this is a difficult day for you," said Gunderman, attempting at least a passable conversation. "Being the anniversary of your husband's death, and all."

"This isn't the anniversary," said Celia. "It was in March."

Silence fell while they held each other's gaze, each waiting for the other to speak. Just get through the dinner, Celia thought. Just give Dad time to do whatever he's doing.

"The actual day was in March," she said, "but today's the day we observe it."

Gunderman glanced at the other diners. When was the last time he'd been on a date? Or even hung out with friends? He remembered an outdoor bar in West Virginia where he and his fellow wildlife officers, newly graduated, were celebrating before splitting up into ten weeks of field training. He had lost touch with them over the years. His fault, not theirs.

Too busy. He'd get to it later. He'd see them at the reunion, or maybe the next one. Since his daily routine brought him into contact with so many people, it became increasingly easy to spend his free time alone in the Loxahatchee. Surrounded by cattails and wading birds, reveling in the beauty of nature, he felt more and more connected to other species, and less and less to his own.

A heart-shaped locket hung from Celia's neck by a delicate gold chain. His eyes dropped to her slim hands, with their short nails, scrapes, and callouses, a band-aid wrapped around one finger. I'd want her on my side if war broke out, he thought, and drained his glass. "Would you like another?" he asked.

"Yes, please," she said.

• • •

Owen drove the hearse slowly and carefully down the driveway. Elias sat on the passenger side of the bench seat, Wizzie between them. "You're not coming with me," said Elias firmly. "We'll drop Mr. Trumbull off at his house, then you can stay with him until Mom gets home."

"But Pop!" cried Wizzie. "You can't do this by yourself! You need me!"

"You're not coming!"

"I'll be your road dog!"

"My what?"

"Elias?" said Owen. "Don't forget, Officer Davis is parked on the other side of the road."

"Oh, Christmas," said Elias.

Owen's serene smile began to fade. "He's going to see you," said Owen. "Will he stop us if he spots you?"

"He won't see us," said Wizzie. "Hurry up, Pop, you get down on the floor there, and I'll lie flat on the seat. See? It'll look like Mr. Trumbull is driving all by himself."

The hearse stopped, accelerated slowly, and turned left. "You see?" whispered Wizzie. "You *do* need me."

"Have a good night, Owen!" called a voice from outside.

"You too, Larry!" returned Owen, and waved his hand.

• • •

The light was fading as Celia and Gunderman finished their dinners. "What does the average American care about?" asked Celia, in her soft voice. "Reality shows and gadgets. They have no connection to wild things at all. They're afraid, or they can't be bothered, or they don't see why they should care about the life of an otter. They don't go out and look at the night sky. They've never been in a meadow in the springtime."

She paused. "You know something?" she asked. "Sometimes when I'm hiking, I stop and look at the sun through the pines. I watch the snow fall from the sky, or the rain sweep over the valley, and I think, I'm alone. I'm alone all the way out here in the woods, and it's so beautiful that I'm never coming out."

Just don't move, Gunderman's grandmother used to say, and they'll decide whether or not to trust you. Each afternoon at dusk he bundled into his coat and boots and sat on the snow, waiting for the deer to glide silently from the forest. He stayed immobile, grasping a handful of hay, his arm resting on his knee. Each time they came closer and closer, until one evening the most beautiful doe he'd ever seen stretched her neck and pulled the hay from his hand. Reflexively he pulled away, and the doe flinched and disappeared.

He hesitated. "But...you do," he forced himself to reply, before he lost his nerve. "You come out."

"Because of Wizzie," said Celia. "And my dad. And the volunteers, and the animals. And because it's so important to keep the wildlife and the wild places safe. Especially now. It's a scary time."

He didn't even hear the ring of his phone. Celia looked at him inquiringly. "Would you like to get that?" she asked.

He pulled it from his jacket pocket. It was Officer Davis, saying his shift was ending. "Thank you," said Gunderman. "I'll be there in fifteen minutes." His eyes returned to hers.

Celia's pale hair framed her delicate features. The lights entwining the trellis around her sparkled. "It's all right," she said, raising her hand for the waiter. "You're just doing your job."

They approached the driveway and waved at Officer Davis. The center was deserted. Celia glanced at the flight, to Banshee's solitary silhouette. "There she is," she said, wondering what had happened. "Do you want to see her?"

They walked up the hill to the flight cage. Banshee faced the mountain, her back to them. Gunderman squinted, feeling a tingle of alarm. The eagle turned around, and he and Celia both took a breath.

"That's not Banshee," said Gunderman. "Call your dad."

Celia pulled her phone out of her bag and tapped it. "It's gone straight to voice mail," she said.

Gunderman turned and strode toward his car. "Erik?" she called, but he slammed the door and drove away.

• • •

The rented Honda rolled steadily through the twilight, heading northwest on a sparsely traveled highway. Lyllis kept the speedometer at a careful 65, supplying a running commentary as Michael searched for radio stations and rummaged through the glove compartment. "Look!" he said, pulling out a paper map. "An antique!"

Luna sat in the back. She tried to picture only Mars and Banshee, but a kaleidoscope of human faces whirled around her. Adam. Roland. Ned. Warren. Lyllis. Michael. Her rehabber friends. Spinning beyond them were others, the ones she had almost succeeded in blocking from her memory. In the middle were Harry and Rose. Above them all, almost invisible, was Hélène.

Lyllis cruised along the right lane as twilight faded to darkness. A pair of headlights appeared behind them, illuminating the inside of their car. Lyllis glanced in her rearview mirror, then the dark SUV accelerated and hovered beside them.

"What's the matter with that guy?" asked Lyllis, unable to see through the SUV's darkened windows. It sped up and pulled into their lane, and a second set of headlights shone behind them. An identical SUV accelerated and hovered, matching their speed. "What the…"

said Michael, as both SUVs began to slow down. Blocked, Lyllis slowed with them.

"How did they find us?" cried Luna.

"That sonofabitch," growled Lyllis, peering into her rear view mirror and searching the dark highway behind her. "I am not giving you up!"

"Please, just stop!" Luna pleaded.

The speedometer dropped to 40. "There's nobody behind us," snapped Lyllis. "You two hang on, because when we hit 20 I'm going to jam on my brakes, then I'll cross the divider and go the other way!"

"Don't!" Luna cried, as the highway curved to the right. "Somebody's going to get hurt!"

"Look out!" shouted Michael. Stopped on the side of the road was a car, tail lights flashing, parked too close to the right lane. Lyllis jerked the steering wheel to the left to avoid it, and slammed against the SUV beside them. The Honda shuddered, serpentined, and clipped the SUV ahead, then rocked and became airborne as it left the road. It sailed down the embankment, landed on two wheels, and rolled. It came to rest upside down, and its tires squeaked as they spun.

CHAPTER 23

Owen stood next to his garage and waved goodbye, wearing a worried smile. "Be careful!" he called. "Call me!" Elias and Wizzie each waved from their window as they drove away.

"So, Pop," said Wizzie. "Mom really doesn't know about any of this?"

"No," said Elias. "And if Anna hadn't gotten the stomach flu you wouldn't, either."

"But aren't you glad I'm here? We're a team! You don't want to drive to Minnesota all by yourself."

"Of course we're a team. But you shouldn't be involved, because you're not an adult. And it's…"

"Illegal?"

"Well…yes."

"But it's the right thing to do?"

"It's the right thing to do."

"Then that's good enough for me. Maybe I could do a report on it for school and get extra credit."

"Oh, stop it."

"Just kidding, Pop. It'll be our family secret. I mean, unless we get arrested, then I suppose everyone will know. Am I too young to go to jail?"

"We'll find out, won't we?"

Wizzie gave him a disapproving look. "How do you think Mom's business dinner went with Officer Gunderman?"

"No idea."

"Has she called?"

"Not sure."

"Because you turned your phone off?"

"Yup, but first I texted her that you're with me, so she wouldn't worry."

"But why isn't she involved? She's a grown-up! I'd think…" Her jaw dropped. "Wait a minute! Did you set up their dinner so they wouldn't be around when you switched eagles?"

"Can you leave me alone for five minutes?"

"Wow, Pop! You're…wow! You're amazing! Where did you learn how to do this stuff?"

"Oh, I don't know," said Elias, trying not to look pleased.

"Huh! Well! How far is it to Minnesota?"

"Far. But we're stopping in Indiana."

"Why?"

"We're picking up Sean Callahan, because you're no help with the driving."

"Sean Callahan! You mean Cole and Bailey's dad? Cole, who trains the hawks? And Bailey, who makes medicine out of plants?"

"That's the one!"

"Aww, this is awesome! I'm so glad Anna got sick!" She beamed and crossed her legs. "So Pop, where do you think Luna is right now? I can't wait to see her, it's been so long."

"Me, too. And I think she's in a car on her way to Minnesota. I'll bet she's feeling pretty lucky right about now."

• • •

The darkness was soft and gentle. So quiet after the wail of metal and the crash of glass, so still after the world had turned cartwheels, then come to rest.

Luna felt a sharp pain in her left arm and a dull throb in her head. When she opened her eyes she found herself upside down, held firmly by her seat belt.

"Lyllis!" she cried. "Michael!"

From one side of the car she heard an exhalation. From the other, a groan. "Ohhh," whispered Lyllis. "They're back," said Michael, as headlights illuminated the interior of the car.

"Please tell me you're all right!" Luna pleaded, struggling to unfasten her seat belt.

There were voices, then footsteps. "Hello?" called a voice, young and female. "We called 911!" added another, deep and male.

Luna's buckle opened and she dropped downward, landed on her shoulder, and felt another bright blast of pain. There were more footsteps, and more voices. "How many of you are there?" asked one. "Can you talk?"

"Three," said Michael weakly.

"Don't fall asleep!" ordered a voice, and two young men crouched by Michael's window. "Hey, are you with me? We're all from the University, taking a road trip to New Orleans. Where were you going?"

"Never mind!" murmured Lyllis, her eyes narrowed against the pain.

"I'm sorry!" Luna whispered. "How badly are you hurt?"

"It's not on you, baby," said Lyllis.

"Lyllis," said Michael. "You're a shitty driver."

Luna tried to pull herself toward the open window. Her hand touched the ground beneath the Honda's roof as sirens called in the distance. There were new voices, louder and more authoritative. Metal creaked and squealed as the doors were forced open. Hands reached into the car, and Luna pulled away. "Take care of them first!" she said.

"Relax," said a paramedic. "We'll take care of all of you."

They eased her onto a stretcher and carried her up the embankment. Luna scanned the area and found two ambulances, a fire truck, a police car, and a dozen college kids clustered beside two blue vans. Behind her was the overturned Honda and beyond it, a stretch of woods. The SUVs were nowhere in sight. "Are they all right?" asked Luna.

"They're awake. They're injured but conscious. Can you look at this light?"

Luna tried to process the swirling mix of sight and sound as the EMTs placed her stretcher in the ambulance. A paramedic cleaned the blood from the side of her head with damp gauze and applied a bandage. "Your friends are right behind you, he said." He cleaned her blood-soaked arm, applied a line of butterfly closures, and wrapped it tightly. Two more EMTs placed Lyllis's stretcher beside her.

"They're putting Michael in the other ambulance," said Lyllis.

"He's stable," said an EMT. "You're all very lucky."

"You okay, baby?" asked Lyllis.

"Yes, are you?"

"Broke my damned leg. Feels like I busted some ribs."

An EMT conferred with the paramedic, both bent over the splint on her lower leg.

"Lyllis," Luna whispered, leaning toward her. "They're out there somewhere. I can't go to the hospital, they'll follow me."

"But the hospital will protect us!" Lyllis whispered back. "They have security!"

"They'll call the cops, and the cops are after me, too. There's already one out there now."

"Then you're gonna have to run," said Lyllis. "Can you?"

"Yeah."

"Go *now.*" Lyllis fluttered her hands by her neck. "I can't breathe!" she announced.

Luna regarded her with alarm, and Lyllis frowned and gave her a surreptitious wave of dismissal. The two medics reached for the monitors, and Luna slipped out the back door. She angled away from the light, and into the safe and darkened woods.

• • •

Cicadas. Tree frogs. A Barred Owl. The occasional rush of a passing car. Gunderman drove in silence, his windows open, surrounded by the sounds of the night; hearing, instead, a crack, a snap, and a roar as his entire career went up in flames.

What was wrong with this case? He kept making rookie mistakes. He needed to get back to the Loxahatchee, but thanks to the mad quest of Luna Burke, there was a good chance soon he might no longer work there.

He dialed a number. "Evening," he said. "This is Officer Erik Gunderman, U.S. Fish and Wildlife Service. Could I leave a message for Officer Davis, please? Could you tell him I need a list of every car that entered or exited the Western Pennsylvania Wildlife Center tonight? He has my number. Yes, thank you."

Get into their heads, his criminal psychology professor used to say. He had tried to profile Luna Burke, the defensive, violent, lawbreaking young woman with a troubled past who had somehow become a symbol of…what? A lone figure on a doomed, misguided mission.

He remembered her in Sean Callahan's driveway, eyes ablaze, spitting insults at him as she defended Callahan and his kids. He could hear her shouting as he drove her, handcuffed, into the night. Aggressive. Furious. Defiant. He had met her eyes in his rearview mirror, and seen all of it.

But then, just for a second, he had seen a flash of something else. Fear.

Black and bottomless, then it was gone. It disappeared so fast it had also vanished from his memory. He pulled his car to the shoulder of the road.

Part of her was still a girl, he realized, and she was afraid. He reached for his laptop. It was more than a long shot; odds were she wasn't anywhere near Pennsylvania. He hadn't bothered to go to Rose and Harry Burke's farm, as local officers told him it had been deserted since their death. Another mistake. He called up a file, and eased back onto the road.

Twenty minutes later he turned onto a dirt driveway. At the top of a hill in the distance stood a farmhouse. As he drove closer he saw a barn behind it, both illuminated by the rising moon. There were no signs of life, and he felt a twinge of disappointment. Luna Burke had not returned to the only real home she had ever known.

The front door was covered with graffiti. Three windows on the second floor were broken. The barn's sliding door hung haphazardly from its hinges, held in place by a padlock. He pulled on a pair of latex gloves, grabbed a flashlight, and slid from the car. He climbed the front porch stairs and turned the knob, but the door was locked. The first floor windows were locked, as well.

He lifted the mat, searched under a flower pot, and slid his fingers around the doorframe. He walked back down the stairs, ran his hand beneath the top step, and pulled out a key. He slid the key into the lock, and opened the door.

The house was dark and silent. Gunderman's flashlight illuminated the dishes still piled in the sink, the mail unopened on a counter. The sun-bleached chairs, faded magazines, and neat line of hiking boots were all layered with dust. On a table by the stairs was a large framed photograph of a grey-haired couple, beaming, both wearing hats, gloves, and heavy coats. Between them, holding a Golden Eagle, was Luna. She was thin and pale, too small for her coat and dwarfed by the massive bird cradled in her arms, but her smile shone like a searchlight.

She's so young, thought Gunderman, mystified. She couldn't have been with the Burkes that long, yet she was handling a Golden Eagle. There weren't many strong, experienced wildlife people who would go near a golden. He peered at the enormous slatted flight cage looming behind them. Where had the photo been taken? There was no flight cage anywhere near that size at the Western Pennsylvania Wildlife Center.

He climbed the stairs and paused in the doorway of a room with a king-sized bed and matching oak dressers. A few steps farther down, two single beds flanked a bedside table. He continued to the last bedroom, and shone his flashlight inside.

A colorful quilt covered a queen-sized bed. Flowered pillows adorned a comfortable chair. A few glittering silver stars hung from the ceiling by delicate threads, while a dozen more lay ripped and shredded across the the floor. Gunderman stepped carefully around the jagged edges of a cup, across the shards of a shattered mirror.

The top of the dresser was crowded with framed photographs. Luna and Celia feeding baby opossums, Luna and Elias releasing a songbird, Luna, Harry, and Rose standing before a Christmas tree. Gunderman raised his flashlight to a bulletin board hanging from wall near the bed. In the center Harry and Rose smiled at the camera, their arms around each other. Like planets around the sun, a dozen pictures of the rescued eagle revolved around them.

Don't get sidetracked, thought Gunderman. She broke the law.

His gaze traveled over the scattered clothing, the open drawers, the closet door ajar. An envelope lay ripped and crumpled in a corner.

Dust swirled as he removed the letter and pieced it together. Dear Ms. Burke, it read. Congratulations on your admission to the Cornell University College of Veterinary Medicine.

He tucked the letter back into the envelope. I'm sorry, son, his father had said, his voice unsteady, calling in the spring of Gunderman's junior year. She just didn't wake up. She had a good long life. Your mother's making the funeral plans, she wants to know your schedule. You know your grandmother would be mad as a wet hen if you missed an exam for this.

Gunderman felt a forgotten pang of grief, a memory of his sunlit life abruptly rendered dark and unrecognizable. Is Warren still with her? he thought. Is she alone?

He turned and shone his flashlight behind him. On the strip of wall between the doorway and the closet was a framed photograph. Luna stood before an enormous slatted flight cage, smiling, protectively embraced by a diminutive woman with upswept white hair. Gunderman stared at the woman's fierce dark gaze, and felt a jolt.

It was Hélène de la Croix. The Canadian Bird Woman. The radical, reclusive face of the environmental protest movement, heroine to all those who felt the damage beneath their hands: the broken spines, the crumpled wings, the fur and feathers covered with oil and washed up on the sand. In a war too big to win, where angels worked anonymously and villains were profiled in *Forbes*, she was their warrior queen.

And whether or not she wanted to be, he realized, Luna was her heir. He had been wrong. Hers was not a misguided mission; it was a journey of wild and heedless love, unencumbered by rules or logic or any thought of the future. And the entire scattered, bonded, fervent adopted family of the orphaned girl and the rescued bird were risking what they held so dear — their licenses — in order to help her.

She's going to the Port Clyde Eagle Sanctuary, he thought.

He left the room, locked the front door behind him, and slipped the key back under the porch stairs. He slid into his car, pulled off his gloves, and tapped his voicemail. "Hello Erik," came a voice. "This is Officer Larry Davis. You wanted a list of the cars that entered and exited the wildlife center tonight. There were two. One was a blue

Hyundai, belongs to Peter Kellogg, Pennsylvania plate GRW-6021. I could see it was full of kids, no room for an eagle crate. The only other one was Owen Trumbull's hearse, and Owen was the only occupant of the vehicle. Pennsylvania plate number HJL-3578. If you need anything else, please call me. Have a good night."

Gunderman closed his eyes. Elias had smuggled the eagle out in a borrowed hearse.

He tapped his phone again. Celia said Banshee panicked if you rocked her crate, so they couldn't park in a remote area and carry her over the border. They would need to cross in a vehicle, and the closest border crossing to the Port Clyde Eagle Sanctuary was Fort Frances, on the Canadian side of the bridge at International Falls, Minnesota. Luna had last been seen — or almost seen — in Wisconsin. It was close to a straight shot north.

Did she have any identification? She would need paperwork to get the birds across: a 3-177, a 50 CFR 21. Attempting any of it was crazy, the odds stacked against her. And that was why Hélène de la Croix would help her, even if Luna were a stranger. The odds were beginning to even out.

Elias would have to break up the trip, as it was a 17-hour drive from his wildlife center to International Falls. Would he meet her in the hearse and drive her and the birds to the border, or would he simply hand off the eagle and return to Pennsylvania? Either way she would cross at night, when there were fewer officers on duty. Her husband was blanketing police departments with donations. Where was he?

Gunderman pulled out his laptop and typed **flights Pittsburgh to International Falls**. He would rest up this evening and fly to Minnesota in the morning. He would be there when they arrived. If he was right it would save his job in the Loxahatchee, where he lived in a world of absolutes. Not like Celia, who lived in a world of exceptions.

Thunderclouds, slashing rain. A woman with outstretched wings chained to a wooden cross, the wind whipping ropes of drenched hair across her high cheekbones, her feral eyes, and her expression of wild fury. As she struggled to burst from her chains, a perfect bolt of lightning bisected the roiling sky.

He forced the image away. Do your job, he told himself. Just do your damned job, then you can go home.

• • •

The woods were fairly sparse. By day they wouldn't have offered much of a screen, but by night they provided a protective cloak. Luna moved silently in her running shoes, her pain and lightheadedness receding as she angled away from the highway and toward a soft glow in the distance. Eventually she emerged onto a small county road.

A car approached, and she stuck out her thumb. It stopped beside her, and the passenger window eased down. "Where you going, little lady?" asked the man. He was middle-aged and sharp-featured, his hair slicked back.

"Thanks anyway," said Luna, retreating a step. "I changed my mind."

"Come on," he said, reaching toward her and opening the passenger door. "I'm a real nice guy."

Luna's hand slid down the side of her cargo pants to the deep pocket along her thigh, to the straight-edged knife she took from Lyllis's friend's kitchen drawer. She had wrapped the blade in a small towel, then encased it in layers of packing tape she found on a shelf. "I said, 'thanks anyway,'" she said, slipping it from its makeshift case and holding it up.

The man pulled the door shut. "Bitch!" he snapped, and drove away.

A few minutes later Luna stuck out her thumb again, and a pickup truck coasted to a stop. She looked in the window and found a sandy-haired young man. "Hey!" he said, giving her a wide smile. "Need a ride?"

She climbed in and closed the door. "Where you going?" he asked, pulling back onto the road. "Because I'm…"

He paused, his face clouding. "Your head is bleeding," he said. He drove slowly, taking in her heavily bandaged arm, her torn pant leg, the dirt still clinging to her shirt. "Here," he said, reaching for his phone. "Let me find the nearest hospital, and I'll drive you."

"Thank you," said Luna. "But I have to get to Minnesota. If you don't mind, I'll just ride with you as far as you're going."

"Are you sure?" he asked doubtfully. "There's a first aid kit in the glove box. My name's Jesse, by the way."

"I'm L…Lisa. And thank you."

Jesse drove into the night. When he found Luna reticent, he chatted about his family's farm, his community college courses, and his unrequited love for his biology lab partner. Luna tried to listen, her mind straying to Lyllis and Michael, her eyes searching for black SUVs. There were no other cars on the dark county road, until she saw a pair of headlights a mile or so behind them.

"Then what did she say?" asked Luna, trying to sound casual. When she glanced back, the headlights were closer. They gleamed, then a curve hid them from view. "Could you drive faster?" she asked.

"Sure," said Jesse agreeably, and the speedometer rose a notch.

The lights appeared again. "I mean," she said urgently, "can you drive a lot faster?"

He saw her look of alarm. "What's wrong?" he asked, and glanced at the rearview mirror. "Is someone after you?"

The road curved again. When it straightened, a red traffic light appeared and Jesse took his foot off the accelerator. Beyond the light, three cars sped by on a well-lit road. Behind the cars was a huge semi, the sound of its engine growing louder as it approached. Luna turned around and was blinded by headlights.

"Run it!" she screamed.

Jesse gave her a panicked glance as the semi's horn let out a deafening blast. He jammed his foot on the brake, and the pickup screeched to a halt beneath the stoplight. The semi blazed by, pelting them with gravel. The car behind them stopped, and the door opened.

Luna fumbled with the button of her cargo pants, and seized the handle of her knife. Jesse gasped as a gun was shoved against his head. Luna lunged past him, thrust the knife through his window, and slashed at a grey-haired man with a flat, malevolent gaze. The man leaped backward, fast as a dancer.

"What the fuck, Luna!" he bellowed.

She froze as his features swam into focus. "Warren!" she cried, and dropped the knife.

Warren slid the Glock's safety on as Jesse raised a trembling hand to his mouth. "I think I'm going to be sick," he whispered, and Warren opened the door and stepped aside.

CHAPTER 24

T he two men sat on folding chairs beside a campfire, drinking beer as the crickets sang. They were in their late 60s, fit, and tattooed. They wore t-shirts, cotton camo pants, and heavy pistols in their shoulder holsters. Six semi-automatic rifles leaned against a nearby Jeep.

Beck was bald and wore a gold hoop in one ear. Flagler wore a bandana around his thick grey curls. Their conversation was interrupted by a three-toned ring, and Flagler pulled a phone out of his pocket. "You here?" He pocketed the phone. "He said 'don't shoot.'"

"We'll see," said Beck.

A silver Mercedes coupe pulled up on the dirt path beside them, and the driver side window slid down. "Good evening, gentlemen," said Warren.

"Nice ride," said Flagler.

"I don't know why people leave their valuable possessions unattended," said Warren. "That can be a mistake."

"Good thing they do, 'cause nobody's loaning you their car anymore," called Beck. "We know what you did to Glenn's Ram."

"*That* was a mistake," said Warren.

"How is she?" asked Flagler.

"Sleeping," said Warren, glancing at Luna. "But she appreciates your hospitality."

"Maybe we'll come up later," said Beck, and turned back to the fire.

• • •

Adam lay in his hospital bed, staring out the window into the darkness. The previous night the doctors had run a battery of tests. He agreed to stay an additional night so they could run more tests and the Chicago police could search for the two men who had assaulted and robbed him. He hadn't admitted to the groin injury, and his balls still ached. There were seven staples in his head.

Lyllis's apartment had been empty, Roland said, so he had gone to her garage and to her friends' places. Nothing. Roland had been edgy and short-tempered, and for the first time in fourteen years Adam hadn't trusted him to get the job done. He called one of his tech guys and told him to hack Lyllis's phone. She had turned it off, but not before she texted someone to meet her at a rental car company.

Adam shifted his gaze to the black screen of the television. His thoughts slid to a party in Miami a month ago, Luna walking beside him in a shimmering column of silver. She had nearly refused to go, only capitulating at the last minute. And naturally, inevitably, they passed a semicircle of guests clustered around a stout man and his overly made-up wife.

… best game ranch in Texas! boomed the man. Have you ever heard of Greater Kudu? Magnificent animals, and both of us bagged one! $35,000 each! Any of you know what it's like to bring one of those things down?

Adam remembered the silence that fell just before Luna spoke. I do, she said. It's like shooting a cow in a field. That's why they call them game ranches.

The woman let out a high-pitched laugh. Oh, you! The zoo-keeper! You must be one of those animal rights nuts!

And you, said Luna. The desperado. Once you've failed at being a woman, you might as well try being one of the boys.

The woman's jaw dropped. I don't think much of your new wife, Adam, snapped the man, and you can forget about that deal!

Adam followed Luna to the outdoor bar, where the night was warm and the harbor lights glowed. Away from the crowd, she turned toward him.

Looks like I wrecked your deal, she said, not appearing even slightly apologetic. Instead she looked at him with hard appraisal, as if she were sizing up a potential adversary and concluding she could take him. Her expression flooded him with a combination of apprehension, exhilaration, and nearly unbearable desire. I don't care if you wrecked my deal, he said, and for a moment they faced each other like gladiators, each waiting for the other to make the first move.

His phone rang. "Yeah," he said deliberately, waiting to hear his security man say they had followed Lyllis's car out of Chicago, discreetly pulled it over, and were on their way back with Luna. Instead he listened, then flushed scarlet. "What have you done?" he shouted. "What do you mean, she wasn't in the ambulance? You find her, and if you've hurt her I'm going to kill all of you myself!"

He threw the phone across the room, ripped out his IV, and swung out of bed.

• • •

Ned and Stanley watched the silver coupe pull up to the cabin, both wearing looks of relief. Warren opened the passenger side door and Luna emerged, a cotton jacket draped around her shoulders. Luna returned Ned's embrace, then winced and shrank back. When Ned spotted the dark patch on her sleeve, he grasped the front of the jacket and pulled it aside.

"Goddammit, Luna!" said Warren, scowling at Luna's blood-soaked bandage. "Why didn't you tell me it was bleeding again?"

"It's fine," she said. "Really, I'm fine. Are you two all right? Is Mars okay?"

"He's..." Stanley began, as Luna turned pale and swayed. "Let's get her inside," said Ned, supporting her.

The cabin was old and rustic. Luna and Stanley sat beneath a hanging lamp in the kitchen. Stanley unwrapped her bandage as Ned and Warren leaned against the peeling Formica counter, arms crossed and faces set.

"What about the head?" asked Stanley, peering at the gauze and adhesive. "Do you have a concussion?"

"No," said Luna.

"Don't believe anything she tells you," said Warren.

"Can you call the hospital again?" she asked.

"You talked to Lyllis two hours ago. They're both asleep."

Stanley removed the bandage from Luna's bicep. He peeled away the soaked butterfly strips, stared at the jagged gash, and let out a soft sigh.

"Christ," breathed Ned.

"Get up," Warren ordered. "I'm taking you to a doctor."

"No, you're not," said Luna. "Don't be absurd."

"It needs to be stitched," said Stanley.

"You can do it, can't you?" she asked. "You have a kit, right?"

"Only the one that stays in the car. I have suture material, but I don't have any lidocaine."

Luna gave Stanley a small, rueful smile. "Okay, then," she said. "We'll do without."

"Wait a minute," said Ned. "You mean the stuff that numbs it?"

"Stop it!" said Warren tightly, pushing himself away from the counter. "I'll go to a hospital and get you some."

"And what will you say?" asked Luna. "'Excuse me, but can I have some lidocaine? Because my friend needs stitches, but she's a wanted felon so she can't come here herself?'"

"How many times did I ask you if you were bleeding?" Warren demanded. "I even woke you up once, and you..."

"Why don't you go to the hospital and help yourself? Then you can get arrested for stealing a bottle of lidocaine as well as for Grand Theft Auto and Attempted..."

"I don't know even know why I..."

"Can we dial this back?" Ned asked loudly. He straightened his duct-taped glasses, and regarded Luna. "It's up to you, isn't it?"

"Yes." She turned to Stanley. "Can you get your kit?"

Stanley rose. Luna regarded Warren, with his clenched hands and distressed expression, and gave him a look of such tenderness that Ned blinked. I didn't know she could look that way at a human, he thought.

"You really piss me off sometimes," said Warren. "I'm going to get you some alcohol," he added, and followed Stanley out of the room.

Ned sat on the chair beside her. He glanced at her bloody wound, then quickly looked away. For just a moment, she looked small and frail. "Would you…" she began, hopefully, then her impassive expression slid into place.

"What?"

"Nothing. Never mind."

"Do you want me to stay with you when Stanley stitches you up?"

"No. I know you don't like this kind of stuff. You don't have to."

"I know I don't have to," he said, and reached for her hand.

• • •

Warren, Beck, and Flagler leaned against the Formica counter, watching Stanley clean Luna's wound with gauze. The contents of a medical emergency kit were arranged neatly on the table. Ned poured shots from a bottle of Jack Daniels into two waiting glasses, then he and Luna tapped them together and threw them back.

"Give her some more," ordered Warren. "Don't give any to Stanley."

Stanley rolled his eyes, and pulled apart the plastic sleeve containing the sterilized needle and thread. Ned poured another round.

"You ready?" asked Stanley.

"Yup," said Luna, after downing her shot. "I'm good."

The color drained from Warren's face. Luna fastened her eyes on an ancient coffeepot. When the needle pierced her skin, she gasped and clenched her jaw.

"You okay?" asked Ned.

"Fine," she managed. A second later, she flinched and gasped again.

"Done," said Stanley, after he'd tied the knot and snipped the thread. "That's one."

"How many you think she'll need?" asked Ned.

"Maybe fifteen," said Stanley.

Luna regarded the three men standing by the counter. Beck rubbed his bald head, Flagler pulled at his grey curls, and Warren wore a look of utter torment. "Come on, guys, man up," she said. "If I can take it, so can you."

Ned rose from his chair. "Why don't you all wait outside?" he said.

"Don't forget your arsenal," said Stanley.

They shouldered their rifles and filed out. "I wish we had a TV," mused Stanley. "Just for distraction."

"Hey," said Ned to Luna. "Remember when we were heading for Trish and Angelica's, and you told me the story of Hélène and the premier? Why don't you tell me another one?" He poured more whiskey. "But drink this first."

"Tell him about Hélène and Chem-Dust!" said Stanley.

"Okay," she said, when the shot was gone. "So: Canada in the early- to mid-1980s. The environmental movement had taken hold, but the system was still rigged. There were some environmental laws on the books, but enforcement was a joke. Like ...ah!"

"Okay?"

"Yeah. As in America, more Canadians were jailed for trying to protect the environment than for damaging it. And...oh!...pesticides were a huge battleground. Terrible toxicity levels, and almost no regulation. Ontario banned 2,4,5-T in 1980, but there were dozens just as toxic still on the market."

Stanley snipped the thread. "That's two," she said with relief. "So, do you know why 2,4,5-T was famous?"

"Why?" asked Ned

"If you combine it with 2,4-D, you get Agent Orange. So. Hélène had been running her sanctuary and fighting...ah...fighting environmental battles for years when she found out Chem-Dust was moving into Canada. It was an American company that sprayed pesticides on farms. The...uh!...the chemicals were legal, but they killed wildlife, destroyed native plants, and caused birth defects. The company used chemicals like chlorpyrifos and diazinon, which are organophosphates. Do you know why organophosphates are famous?"

Ned shook his head.

"They used them in gas chambers," she said, and braced herself for Stanley's needle. "Hélène and her activists fought Chem-Dust from the beginning. Legal protests did almost nothing. Ow! Can I have some more?"

"Absolutely," said Ned. "I'll join you."

"Leave some for me," said Stanley.

"The owner just paid people off until he got the green light," said Luna. "Then he decided to show everyone just how hard he was trying to appease the environmentalists, so he invited Hélène to a public forum. A town hall-type meeting. But as you know…mm… meeting Hélène in public is never a good idea.

"There was a huge — ah — crowd, with police and press. There were two podiums. The owner said the aim of his company was to provide food for people, and that since the poisons he used were legal, they were all perfectly safe. Hélène leaned into her microphone, and spoke one word. Ouch!"

She frowned. "Stanley, you're wrecking my story! Now, where was I? She said…" Luna dropped her voice to a hoarse whisper. "'Bullshit!'"

"Here comes another one," said Stanley.

"Aye! And then she pulled a rotten egg out of her pocket, and she nailed him! Right under the chin!"

"No joke!" said Ned. "She egged him?"

"Totally!" she exclaimed, and pointed to her glass. "Bartender!"

Ned poured. "They arrested her immediately, which was her goal all along. The district judge was notorious. If he couldn't find a way to let major polluters off completely, he'd fine them a dollar. He and Hélène…ah!…were bitter enemies.

"The judge ordered an open court, because he wanted everyone to witness him being lenient with an environmentalist. The court was packed. He told Hélène if she paid a fine, did community service, and apologized, he wouldn't…yowch!…send her to jail. She wouldn't go to jail for assault with a deadly egg!"

She snorted contemptuously. "The owner was standing across the courtroom. She said to him, 'In order for me to apologize …. *don't I have to be sorry?*'"

"Hold still!" ordered Stanley.

"Ow! Then she turned on the judge, and said in her sandpaper voice: 'How dare you tell me to apologize! You think I'd apologize to those who would destroy us? You've spent your entire career sucking up to rich and powerful Canadians, now you're going to suck up to rich and powerful Americans, as well?'"

Ned and Stanley exchanged grins and Luna continued, her words beginning to slur.

"The audience went nuts! And as the bailiffs towed her out of the courtroom, she shouted at the judge, 'You're poisoning your own country, you Judas bastard! You should be dragged from your bench and hanged!'"

Stanley chortled. "One of her friends smuggled a tape recorder into the courtroom," he said. "He ran out of the building and drove to the local radio station, and the whole thing was broadcast that afternoon!"

"Let me guess!" said Ned. "No Chem-Dust!"

"Thass right!" said Luna triumphantly. "An' then the op-ed pieces on the judge began! He was gone in ten months!"

When Warren, Beck, and Flagler returned she was slumped in her chair, smiling drunkenly, her jagged gash neatly sewn and bristling with black thread. "*You* are an artist," she said, pointing her finger at Stanley like a conductor waving a baton. "As for *you*," she added, shifting her finger dramatically to Ned, "I like you in that special way." Ned's heart leaped, and the three armed men entered the room.

"Comrades!" she greeted them, saluting. "Stanley embroidered me! Don't you think it looks like a hibiscus?"

"No more for you," said Ned, sliding the whiskey out of her reach.

"No more for you, either," said Stanley, sliding it away from Ned. "I'm going to bandage this up, then the rest of that bottle belongs to me."

Warren crossed the kitchen and stopped beside her. "You all right?" he asked.

"Wern," she said, peering at him and mangling his name, her voice soft with concern. "You look so upset! What's wrong?"

Warren touched her cheek and then straightened, blinking rapidly. He put a hand on Stanley's shoulder, patted Ned twice on the back, and left the room.

"Give me that whiskey," said Stanley.

CHAPTER 25

"Morning," said Roland, greeting one of the housekeepers. He walked through Adam's townhouse, entered the office, and found Adam's two long-time security men standing on either side of the desk. Paszkiewicz and Ortega nodded at him, and Roland gave Adam an inquiring look.

"You guys can go," said Adam.

"Anything?" Roland asked.

"No."

Adam worked on his computer, Roland on a laptop. A half hour went by. Adam's phone stayed silent, but eventually Roland's rang.

"Yeah, baby," said Roland, as if the call surprised him. He looked confused. His voice lowered. "Was I in what car?"

He raised his eyes to Adam's, wearing a terrible look of betrayal. "I'll be there," he said, as Adam pressed a small black device on his desk. Roland slipped his phone into his pocket, and his expression turned murderous. As he began to rise from his chair and Paszkiewicz and Ortega burst into the room, their handguns aimed at his face.

"Come on, Roland," said Paszkiewicz quietly. "Let's go."

Roland hesitated, measuring the distance between his chair and the desk, weighing the odds of reaching Adam and breaking his neck before Paszkiewicz and Ortega brought him down. But then he thought of Lyllis and Michael, lying in their hospital beds.

Adam held his gaze. "They were supposed to pull them over," he said. "I swear to God, they weren't supposed to crash."

"You and I are done," said Roland, and left the room.

• • •

Ned opened the door, balancing a hot cup and a cold glass, and found Luna lying in one of the single beds, staring out the window. She rose to a sitting position, wearing the large frayed T-shirt they had found in a closet. Her shirt and pants hung from wire hangers, the bloodstains washed out, the rips sewn together. Resting on the dresser was the kitchen knife in its makeshift case.

Ned had helped her into the bedroom after Stanley bandaged her arm. He peeled off her clothing, settled her between the sheets, and covered her with a wool blanket. She fell asleep immediately. He picked up her shirt and pants, wondering why they were so heavy. He returned to the living room, where Stanley was slouched with the whiskey on his lap.

And miles to go before I sleep, Stanley had said, eyeing Ned, the shirt, the pants, and the knife. Tell you what, he continued. You wash, I'll sew. I like sewing things that don't say ouch. As for that last item, let's ask Warren.

"Morning," said Luna, sitting up.

"How do you feel?" he asked, handing her the glass. "Here. Gatorade. Stanley wants you hydrated."

"Thank you. I've had better mornings."

"Me, too." He pulled a bottle of aspirin out of his pocket and sat on the edge of the bed. "Best I can do for now."

She popped two aspirin and drained the contents of the glass. He put it on the nightstand, and offered her the cup of coffee.

"Thank you," she said, moving over. Ned inched carefully onto the bed, propped the pillow behind her, and stretched his legs.

"Have you heard from Lyllis and Michael? Is Mars okay? What time is it?"

"Lyllis called Warren. They're okay. And no one's found the guys who were after you."

"They won't find them."

"It's almost one o'clock. Mars is fine, Warren and Stanley are outside with the guys, and Elias and Wizzie and Banshee are less than an hour away."

She looked at him in disbelief. "What? They're coming here?"

"Road trip from Pennsylvania. They picked up Sean Callahan to help with the driving. They'll get a few hours rest when they get here, then tonight we're heading for International Falls."

She closed her eyes. "I don't know how to thank all of you," she said, taking his hand and leaning her head against his shoulder.

"I need to ask you something," he said.

"Sure."

"Why did you marry him?"

Luna was silent. She raised her head and her eyes returned to the window. "I used to wish for things when I was a kid," she said. "A bike. A sparkly dress. A puppy. One night, I wished I could turn into a bird. After that, it was the only thing I ever wished for." She sighed. "Then I met Harry and Rose, and I didn't have to wish for anything anymore."

She put her coffee on the nightstand and pulled her knees to her chest. "Then Harry and Rose were gone. They left me the house, but I couldn't live in it. I didn't know where to go, so I applied for the job with Adam." She paused. "He was different then. Or maybe I only thought he was."

Ned reminded himself not to stare at her. He stayed immobile, afraid she might stop.

"I said I'd never marry him, but he wouldn't give up. He said, 'Tell me what you want more than anything in the world. Tell me your wish, and I'll make it come true.'

"I said, 'I wish I could turn into a bird. That's all I want.'"

She paused again. "I love Cape Vultures. They're endangered. He said for my birthday he wanted to take me to South Africa, and maybe I'd see one. I couldn't resist. I thought we'd be driving around in a Land Rover, but he hired a paraglider to take me up in a tandem harness.

"It was just before sunset. We flew above these enormous towering cliffs, and the sky was pink and orange and purple. There was almost no sound. I was flying. I was flying! In the distance, I saw a Cape Vulture. I was so excited. She flew toward us and looked us over, and then she flew away. A minute later, I saw another one. And then another, and another. And then the sky was filled with them."

Her face was rapt. "I could feel the wind, and hear their wings. I was one of them. And all of us were free."

Her look of joy faded. "I married him that night."

Ned felt an ache in his throat. "But…" he began. "Was it because you'd made a deal? Did you *want* to marry him?"

"More than anything in the world," she said.

• • •

Roland parked his car, entered the hospital, and took the elevator to the third floor. The corridors were busy. He stopped at the front desk.

"Excuse me," he said. "I'm looking for Amaryllis Hart and Michael Edwards. They came in last night."

He glanced down the hallway, where a security guard talked to a nurse. The woman behind the desk checked her computer. "Roland Edwards?" she asked.

"I'm sorry. No visitation. Request of the patients."

Roland blinked. "Excuse me?" he asked, as the woman caught the eye of the security guard.

"Backup, third floor," said the security guard into his device.

"What are you talking about?" Roland demanded. "They're my family!"

"I'm sorry, sir," said the woman. "It's patient request."

"Then it's a mistake!"

Her co-workers looked up. The door to the stairwell opened, and another security guard emerged. He spotted Roland, and his face fell.

"Get one of them on the phone!" said Roland, his voice rising. "Right now!"

"Goddamn it, Roland!" Lyllis's voice cut through the silent hallway. "We're in 406!"

Roland hurried into the room and stopped at the sight of Lyllis and Michael, the curtain between them drawn back. Michael lay in the second bed, his head bandaged, his arm in a sling. Lyllis lay in the bed by the door, her leg resting on a stack of pillows and encased in a cast. "What do you want?" she snapped.

"I…I want to see you're both all right."

"Do we look all right?"

"I swear I didn't know he would do this!"

"You knew he was capable of it! You've known it for years!"

He shifted his gaze. Michael's cheerful, open demeanor was gone, replaced by one of sadness and disillusionment. "Your damned boss nearly killed me, that's one thing," said Lyllis. "But he nearly killed Michael, and he's your blood! How are you going to explain this to your sister?"

"I'm not with Adam anymore! I just quit!"

"How long will *that* last? Until tonight?"

"Lyllis…"

"It's too late. You want to talk to Michael? Go ahead. I got nothing more to say to you."

She closed her eyes. Michael stared at him, his lip trembling. "Michael?" said Roland. "You really thought I'd watch you crash, and then leave you there?"

Michael's voice was barely audible. "Leave me alone," he said, and turned his face away.

Roland crossed the hallway and took the stairs, then slammed through the heavy door to the parking lot. He had quit Adam over the two people he cared most about in the world, and they had abandoned him. They believed the worst about him. He should have known. Why had he ever trusted them?

Adam would take him back.

He squeezed his key, and a pair of headlights flashed in response. Roland reached for the door handle, but instead he slammed his fist into the side of the dark blue BMW with such force the metal gave way. The pain in his hand snaked up his arm. He leaned against the car, his head spinning with loss and regret. He raised his to his eyes, and his fingers came away wet.

There's only one way to set this straight, he thought. He opened his door, slid into the car, and tapped his phone.

"Roland?" came a voice.

"Justin. You gotta do something for me."

"What?"

"I need some info from Adam's phone."

"What happened?" Justin asked. "You're locked out. They shut you down."

Roland clenched his teeth. "I got you that job! You wouldn't be working for Adam if it wasn't for me!"

"I know! It's not like I haven't said how grateful…"

"I don't want your gratitude! I want you to monitor Adam's phone and tell me if anyone finds his wife!"

"Come on, man, you're putting me in a really bad position!"

"You have my word it'll never come back at you!"

Justin sighed heavily. "All right. All right. Just please…be careful. I'm never gonna get another job like this one."

Roland dropped his phone on the seat beside him, and drove out of the lot.

• • •

Luna pulled on her clothes and slipped the knife back into the side pocket of her cargo pants. Ned hadn't asked about it. She wondered how much Warren had told him.

Just for a moment she recalled the past weeks, something she had trained herself not to do. You ever start losing your way, Warren always said, concentrate on completing the mission. She was so close. Once she completed the mission she could assess the damage, which was growing by the day.

She left the bedroom. She found Ned waiting for her in the living room, and Warren walking in the front door. "Come here," said Warren, sitting on the battered couch and gesturing to the coffee table. "Right leg."

Complete the mission, thought Luna, as she rested her foot on the table and rolled up her pant leg. "Hold this," said Warren. He handed her a small black Ruger, then fastened the velcro straps of a holster snugly around her calf.

"Wait a minute!" said Ned. "What are you doing?"

They heard the sound of a car. "That'll be Elias," said Warren, without looking up. Eagerly Luna looked out the window, and saw a gleaming hearse coast to a stop. A wave of dread and confusion hit her with such force she swayed, pulling her leg from the table so she didn't fall, time and place spinning away as grief burned her like a hot stove. A faceless crowd gathered, and the predatory black car turned toward her. She dropped the gun, and Warren snatched it before it hit the floor.

Ned reached out to steady her. Warren looked at her ashen face and followed her gaze. "The hell is that?" he snapped.

"It's the car Elias borrowed so he could get past Gunderman," said Ned. "I thought you knew."

"Shit!" said Warren.

The sky was pink and orange and purple. Luna felt the rush of the wind and the warmth of the fading sun, the peace of belonging to a silent and boundless world. She heard her name, but didn't respond. The sky was filled with birds.

"Where is she?"

The excited young voice startled her. Once again Luna focused on the window, and this time spotted a small figure with a long red braid. "Wizzie's here!" she gasped. "And Elias and Sean!"

"It's all good," said Warren. "You can see them just as soon as we finish this up. Okay?"

"Okay," she said, nodding.

"You can't give her a gun!" Ned sputtered. "The knife is bad enough!"

"Listen, man," said Warren. "Edwards lost her twice. You know how pissed he is right now? She knows how to handle things. Right, Luna? What are the rules?"

"No body shots," she replied. "No one wearing a uniform."

Warren raised his eyebrows at Ned. "Satisfied?"

"No, I'm not satisfied!"

Warren held out the Ruger. Wordlessly Luna took it, pressed the release button, removed the magazine, and checked the seven bullets. There was a solid click as she replaced the magazine. She pulled the slide, peered through the empty chamber, then snapped it back into place. Lifting her foot to the table, she slid the pistol into its holster and rolled down her pant leg.

"Good girl," said Warren. "Your professor gives you an A."

"How do I get off this train?" Ned demanded, glaring at Warren. "Don't they have metal detectors at the border?"

"Probably, so I'm giving this job to you," he replied. "Knife?" he asked Luna.

"Right here," she answered, patting the pocket of her cargo pants.

"Normally they don't put eagles through metal detectors," Warren said to Ned, "so before we leave here, I'm going to wrap the weapons in a towel and put them under the perch in Mars's crate. I need you to make sure that once you're out of the border station and into Hélène's vehicle, you put them back in the pocket and the holster before you leave the parking lot. This is very important. Are we clear?"

"But where will you be?"

"Around."

Luna felt waves of stress rolling off Ned, who seemed to be upset about the knife and the gun. "Don't worry, Ned," she said, as if she were talking to Mars. "It's okay. It'll be all right."

Warren thumped him on the shoulder. "Let's go," he said, and led them out of the house.

"Luna!" cried Wizzie, and raced toward her. "Watch her arm!" ordered Stanley.

Luna hugged Wizzie tightly. "I've missed you all," Luna whispered, then turned to embrace Elias and Sean.

Luna tried not to look at the hearse as Elias opened the back door. In place of a coffin was a covered eagle crate, wedged in place with blankets, duffel bags, and a large cooler. Luna lifted the cover, and Banshee returned her gaze.

"Time for a reunion," said Elias.

Elias and Stanley carried the crate to a small cabin a hundred feet away. Luna opened the front door and found a single room, devoid of furniture, and Mars on his collapsible perch in the corner. Elias and Stanley slid the crate inside the door and retreated. "Can I come in with you?" asked Wizzie. "Don't forget, Mars likes me!"

Ned, Stanley, and Elias stood outside one of the windows, and Warren, Beck, and Flagler outside the other. Luna closed the door behind Wizzie, and opened the crate.

Banshee hopped off her perch, her eyes focused on the eagle in a dominant position on the other side of the room. The feathers on her head rose aggressively. She let out a combative call. She stepped from the crate, and Mars landed with a thud before her.

Her snowy feathers relaxed. His beak touched hers with a heavy click. "Awww!" came a sigh from each window, and Luna felt a sob rise in her throat.

"What is it, Luna?" asked Wizzie, and hugged her unbandaged arm. "Look! They're back together again!"

CHAPTER 26

The metallic blue Alpha Romeo inched down a rutted driveway, and Darcy pushed back a lock of black hair. She fixed her eyes on the road, picturing the look on Adam's face when she dropped her dress in the hotel in Charleston. One wheel hit a pothole. Neither of us were made for this, she thought, feeling solidarity with her car.

She had been at it for five days. She had dressed to impress at the first place, a well-funded wildlife center near Miami: a slim Dior skirt and blouse, Louboutin heels, Cartier at her ears, neck, and wrists. She had walked in wearing her brightest smile, expecting looks of envy from the women dressed in either medical scrubs or those stupid khaki hobo outfits Luna wore. Instead she received nothing but indifferent stares and one polite, Can I help you?

She had been ushered into an office. A man and two women listened to her story, which she had practiced until it flowed smoothly from her lips. Adam Matheson only took the eagle from the Western Pennsylvania Wildlife Center to make his wife happy, she said. He didn't know it was illegal, or the problems it would cause. He willingly paid the fine, but Luna was still in legal jeopardy. He was pouring money into green technology, and wanted to make further amends by donating $5 million to any wildlife center that helped him reach her.

Darcy sighed. Her audience of three had listened, their expressions bland, then all but rolled their eyes at each other. What's the wife's name, again? asked the man.

And that had been the high point. She tried dressing down, but it didn't work. She had been to big centers, to small centers, to backyard operations, and the results were the same: no dice. She could see their astonishment, even when they tried to hide it, when she said, 'five million dollars.' But then they either nodded vaguely and said they'd be in touch, or they lectured her about her evil boss and the fossil fuel industry, or they cursed at her and threw her out.

On the seat beside her was a dedicated phone. Each time she talked to a rehabber she added their name, town, phone number, and the order in which she had visited them. At this point they were all blending together, and the phone hadn't rung once. She couldn't believe these scruffy, smelly people would turn down five million dollars, no matter what they had to do for it.

Darcy stopped at the end of the driveway, debating whether to break for lunch. She believed with absolute certainty that Adam would soon grow tired of this crazy zoo girl, who had no business being with him and obviously did not appreciate anything he gave her. The sound of the phone startled her.

(3) Mary Taggert, Kendall, FL, 352-888-2827

Darcy stared at the screen, surprised, and immediately pictured the caller. She was a solo rehabber working out of her house, a run-down ranch with a shed behind it. Practically a trailer home. She was middle-aged, visibly exhausted, and vicious. Darcy had kept her smile firmly in place when she stepped into the house, which was so old it didn't matter that it was clean. Nice kitchen, thought Darcy, circa 1957! How did people live like this?

The woman was quiet, contained, and had an unblinking stare. Like a snake, thought Darcy, as she gave her speech. When Mary Taggert finally responded, Darcy felt calmed by her voice but stung by her words.

I have no idea where Luna Burke is, the rehabber said. But I have a question for you. What do you do for Adam Matheson when you're not running down his wives? You keep him company? Keep his bed warm? Stick around, hoping someday he'll see the gold right under his nose and make you the next Mrs. Matheson?

Darcy's bright smile had faded, then she regrouped and pulled a card from her purse. You call me if you change your mind, now, all right? she said, then she rose and let herself out.

The voice on the phone was hoarse and strained. "This is Mary Taggert. You came to my house five days ago."

"Yes, hello, Mrs. Taggert," said Darcy. "I remember you."

"Is the offer still on the table?"

"Yes, it is."

Darcy heard the sound of a tissue being pulled from a box. "I'm not going to tell you where she's going until the money is here in front of me," Mary Taggert said. "And I'm only doing this because I love my grandson more than I hate you and your boss."

Darcy paused at the grief in the woman's voice. "Could you give me a minute, Mrs. Taggert?" she asked. "I'll call you right back."

. . .

Adam stared at the empty seat in the corner, at the abandoned coffee cup on the table. Roland was gone.

My closest friend, he thought. All because of Luna.

Adam, he heard her whisper. Lilac-colored silk. Stars in a summer sky. He remembered her standing alone on a balcony, leaning toward the sea, as if there were some kind of salvation in the empty blue horizon. His phone chimed.

He glanced at it and hesitated. The last time he talked to Jay Sheinkopf was at the beach house party, the night Luna crashed through the garden room door like a comet. "Jay!" he answered heartily.

"Adam!" came the grating voice. "Just checking in. Heard the criminal element broke into your house. You good?"

"Of course I'm good. I'm a black belt! When they left, they looked worse than me."

"Fine, fine. Speaking of the criminal element, how's your wife? And what's the actual market value of an eagle?"

"All under control, you bastard. Goddamn media blows these things completely out of proportion."

"You can tell me. What's the story? Who's this guy she's with?"

"Her cousin! And she's just having fun. You know Luna!"

"I'd certainly like to!"

"Don't hold your breath!"

Jay immediately picked up on his change in tone. "I'm telling you this as a friend, Adam," he said. "You ever need help? Call me. Fresh lawyers, a dependable judge, you name it. Yours. Or, who knows? You ever decide she's too hot to handle? Send her over."

Adam's head began to throb. "Sorry, Jay, but you know women! They don't like going from the major to the minor leagues!"

"You keep me in mind, Adam!"

"You bet!"

He hung up, willing himself not to hurl his phone against a wall. He could almost feel the staples erupting from his skull. He could almost feel her throat beneath his hands.

And then, suddenly, he could feel all of it. He could feel the metal clips rocketing out of his scalp like tiny missiles. He could feel the the softness of her throat, the delicacy of her neck.

His hands were alive with sensation. He squeezed and her pulse quickened, keeping time with his own, the two of them entwined. They beat together, faster and louder, the tension growing and racing toward all that bursting joy; the joy she had stolen away from him, turned black and bitter, the joy he could resurrect only if he if he tightened his hands so hard she melted between his fingers, like clay.

He stopped, horrified at himself. What was he thinking?

She was his forever, and once they reached the island she would see it as clearly as he did. The island had solved their problems before, it would do it again. And if the process took longer than he anticipated, well, he'd just leave her there to think about it. He pondered possible timeframes, and a thought exploded into his mind. It was a mind-boggling, life-changing thought.

They could move there together.

He had enough money for a dozen lifetimes. He could downsize. Restructure. Get out of the industries Luna despised. Well…some of them, anyway. He could leave for important meetings and conferences, and the rest of the time live in paradise with his beautiful wife. His spellbinding wife. The woman who could soon be separated from all the men who coveted her by five thousand miles of ocean.

Maybe Roland was right, she wasn't cut out for his life. His *former* life. But she would fit just perfectly into his new one. No more crowds, no more parties, no more glare of the spotlight. Minimal staff, with strict instructions not to bother her. She would take solitary walks on the beach, and he would build her an eagle palace. He had sworn to cherish her, to guard her, to protect her from harm, and this was how he would do it.

He grinned. It would work. She would find her salvation not in the empty blue horizon, but in him. All that was missing was Luna herself. He pictured the prince and the swan maiden, center stage. It was about to happen.

Six notes of a ring tone emerged from his phone, the eponymous refrain of the old Sinatra song, "The Best Is Yet To Come." It had been programmed by Darcy herself, probably during a moment when he was too spent to protest. "Yeah," he said.

"Adam!" came her voice. "I've got one!"

• • •

Roland prowled his spacious apartment, still angry. He had returned from the hospital, stripped off his suit, and thrown on sweats. He ran for an hour, then went thirty minutes with his punching bag. It hadn't helped.

He drained a tall glass of water, sweat dripping from his forehead, and looked out the window at the city of Chicago. He hadn't felt like this since the day the doctors told him his knee was jacked.

His phone rang. He glanced at the screen, then answered it quickly. "Justin."

"Got the info for you."

"Go ahead."

"Darcy called Mr. Matheson. One of those animal people told her Mrs. Matheson is going to the Port Clyde Eagle Sanctuary in Ontario. She's crossing at International Falls tonight, and he's heading there in the Gulfstream."

Roland closed his eyes. "Thanks, man. This is the last you'll ever hear about it. You got my word."

It was time to rectify what had gone wrong. He placed his phone on the table, opened his desktop, and typed **Chicago to International Falls, MN.**

• • •

Gunderman sat in a window seat. "We are beginning our descent to International Falls, Minnesota!" said a cheerful voice. He took a last look at his computer screen, at the photograph of Hélène de la Croix holding an eagle on her raised fist. The banner read **Port Clyde Eagle Sanctuary.**

He had made a long list of possibilities, a smaller list of probabilities, and factored in the odds of Warren being with Luna, which he put at 100%. He had considered issuing a multistate APB on the hearse, but dismissed the idea. Catching Elias and the female eagle in a hearse, but losing Luna and the male eagle at the border, would only inflame an already infuriated Whittaker. Better to play his cards close to his chest, and apprehend them all together.

That is, if Ontario was their destination. Trust your instincts, he learned from his instructors during Advanced Wildlife Officer training.

He did not want things to escalate, so he had not called the Border Services Agency. Instead he would meet face to face with the officers at International Falls, and alert them to a potential problem with undocumented wildlife. He would not mention the name of Luna Burke.

As far as he knew, she, Warren Trask, two Bald Eagles, and possibly Ned Harrelson were the players. He would add himself, several border patrol officers, and, with Warren in the game, maybe two officers from the Ministry of Natural Resources and Forestry, Canada's version of Fish and Wildlife. As for Adam Matheson, the morning's *Chicago Tribune* reported that he had been attacked and robbed by two men in his own townhouse. There was a chance he knew where she was going, but it didn't seem likely.

He would recover the two eagles, take her into custody, and return her to the United States. Before they crossed the border, he would arrange for a good lawyer to meet her at the airport. And that, he concluded, was the most and the best he could do for her.

• • •

The summer sun was close to the horizon when the caravan began.

The first car to roll away from the cabin was Stanley's Subaru, as he and Sean were heading home. "Be careful of that arm," Stanley told Luna with mock severity. "Don't mess up my nice work."

Following them was the hearse. Elias and Wizzie sat in the front, Ned and Luna In the pop-up seats behind them, and Mars and Banshee in their crates in the back. Before they left, Banshee had eaten all of Mars's fish.

Next was Warren in the silver Mercedes, which he had wiped free of fingerprints and would eventually leave at the edge of a field. Last to join were Beck and Flagler, who packed up their camp, loaded their Jeep, and locked the gate. One by one, the four cars turned onto the county road and headed for the highway.

CHAPTER 27

Hélène de la Croix rose each day at dawn.

At night she climbed the three flights of stairs to the attic room where she had moved after the death of her husband, despite the protests of her children and staff. One of the volunteers had installed a large window so daybreak would rouse her. From her bed she could see the sprawling sanctuary she had built and run for the last sixty years.

Each morning Hélène dressed and made her way down the stairs. In the summer, pale light bathed her house in a soft glow. In the winter, a single lamp she left burning through the night illuminated her path. Daily she stood at her kitchen window, sipped black coffee, and watched the early volunteers arrive. She anticipated a day filled with intakes, releases, tours, treatments, and on-site surgeries. She readied herself for the never-ending battles over the fate of the natural world.

This day was no different. At six o'clock Hélène bid the remaining volunteers goodnight, and walked to her house alone. Tonight would be very different. She hadn't seen Luna in three years.

Hélène entered her kitchen and poured herself a glass of merlot. Normally she would sit on her porch for a half hour, enjoy the evening air, then return to the kitchen and prepare dinner. Instead, she walked to the living room, paused before a wall of photographs, and remembered a night nearly thirty years before.

It was standing room only in the auditorium of the University of Michigan, as people had traveled far and wide to hear the words of the famously taciturn and short-tempered Hélène de la Croix. She spoke for an hour about wildlife conservation, the calamitous effects of toxins, and the need for stricter regulations in both the United States and Canada. She described her renowned eagle sanctuary, now in need of additional funding. When she finished, hands shot up all over the room. She answered question after question, reeling off statistics and stories, until she pointed to a woman in the third row.

First I want to thank you, said the woman, a volunteer from the Western Pennsylvania Wildlife Center. And then I want to ask: what sustains you?

Hélène had scowled and nearly replied, Certainly not circuses like this one. But the woman's face was open, her gaze gentle but inquiring, and Hélène felt an unexpected kinship. The eagles, she replied. My family. And a few close friends.

After she left the podium, she made her way through the admiring crowd and found her. Hélène touched her on the back, and the woman turned around with a warm smile. Hello, she said, and offered her hand. I'm Rose. And this is Harry.

Hélène stared at one of the photographs on her wall. Rose and Harry stood beaming, both wearing hats, gloves, and heavy coats. Between them, holding a Golden Eagle, was Luna. Hélène? Luna had said not two weeks ago, her voice barely audible through the phone. Can I come up?

Chérie, she replied. Come home.

She took a sip of merlot. Since then Esther had called with daily updates from her bat lab in Georgia, using an international burner phone so it couldn't be traced. Hélène had not spoken again to Luna, whose world had gone mad.

Hélène turned away from the photograph. She wished it were as simple as getting Luna and her eagles across the border, providing them with a safe haven, and letting justice prevail. But nothing was ever that simple, and justice was a slippery thing.

• • •

Luna stared out the window as Elias drove north. Eventually she shifted in her seat and glanced at Ned. He met her eyes, and for a moment she didn't react. She didn't instantly smile, or look away and pretend she hadn't seen his gaze. She simply sat still, regarding him, her face expressionless. It was like looking at Mars, Ned thought, and realized he never really knew what was going on in the heads of either one of them.

But then she smiled, as if suddenly she recognized him. Her pale cheeks turned pink, her eyes a deeper blue. He smiled back, and she returned to the window.

He tried to think realistically. She had fallen for Adam Matheson once, she could do it again. And if America's potential environmental messiah was caught crossing the border with a small arsenal and two stolen eagles, she'd certainly need his lawyers. An online tabloid had featured a photograph of Ned, Luna, and an eagle, all enclosed in a pink heart. Matheson must be livid, he thought. He closed his eyes and rubbed his temples.

"This is from envirowacko at gmail dot com," said Wizzie, reading from Elias's phone. "They wrote, 'The girl's gone rogue!' And then carnivorous at northwest dot net wrote, 'Hallelujah!'"

"Put that down," ordered Elias.

"But Pop, there's, like, three hundred of them! Wait, here's one from bluestreak at juno dot com. Isn't that Carlene? The one in Florida with the blue hair who does songbirds? She says, 'Time for our mutual friend to permanently delete that dickweed.'"

Wizzie raised her eyebrows at Warren. "'Dickweed,'" she repeated, enunciating the unfamiliar word.

"It's like 'pissbrain,'" he explained.

"Give me that phone," said Elias, pulling it away and slipping it into his pocket.

"But who's the mutual friend, and who's the dickweed?" asked Wizzie.

"Never mind!"

"Pull up behind that truck," said Warren, and pointed to a blue pickup with a black cover over the bed, waiting by the side of the highway. "I'm getting out."

Elias coasted to a stop behind the pickup. Beck and Flagler stopped their Jeep behind the hearse. "But we're an hour away!" said Luna. "Where are you going?"

"Same place you are, just a different route. Now listen. Once you get through the border, you'll have Canada's finest in two squad cars waiting to escort you. If your dearly beloved does show up, he'll have to get through four cops. Okay?"

"Cops!" said Ned. "Since when?"

"Since a text I got a half hour ago from Hélène."

"If we have a police escort," said Ned, "then Luna doesn't need those two little items!"

"What two little items?" asked Wizzie.

Warren turned around and looked at Ned. "Yes...she...does," he replied. "Where's the paperwork?"

"Here," said Elias, patting a manila envelope in the door's side pocket.

"All right, you good people," said Warren, raising his hand. "It's been real." He grabbed a backpack from the floor, jumped out, patted the hearse on the hood, and climbed into the waiting pickup.

"I just love that Panther Man," sighed Wizzie.

• • •

Warren lay in the darkness beneath the cover of the pickup, listening to Chuck speak to the border guard in fluent French. Chuck was short, animated, and more than happy to trade goods and services. No problem, he had said when Warren called. I cross that bridge all the time. Besides, I think the guy on duty will be Lévesque, and he owes me money.

After Warren climbed into the truck they averaged about eighty, then stopped before International Falls so Warren could climb into the back. They crossed over the bridge, then stopped at the Fort Frances Border Station on the Canadian side of the Rainy River. Warren heard the conversation cease, and felt the pickup roll forward. A minute later it slowed and stopped again. Chuck dropped the tailgate, and Warren slid out. "I didn't know you spoke French," he said.

"Of course I speak French," said Chuck. "I moved here in '64 — you think I don't pay attention?"

Chuck's phone was ringing when they climbed back into the pickup. "Yup," he said, and listened to the chattering voice as Warren opened his backpack, loaded his Glock, and double checked the Beretta strapped to his calf.

"Thanks! Appreciate it!" Chuck said, and disconnected. "So, the jet landed a couple hours ago. Falcon 2000X, right? White with blue pinstripes?"

"That's the one. How many?"

"Three passengers. Rented a car and left the airport. Sounds like Matheson and two security. Both white guys. No Roland Edwards."

"No shit!"

"Yeah, no shit, because Roland Edwards came in on a commercial flight this afternoon, and right now he's sitting in an SUV on 532 behind the billboard for Swiss Chalet."

"Chuck!" grinned Warren, slapping him on the back. "I owe you big time! Do me a favor and take me to 532 behind the billboard for Swiss Chalet."

"You got it. So, what's with Edwards?"

"He's had a few personal disruptions lately. He's either going to be my best friend or my worst enemy, I can't tell which. I'm also undecided as to how to go about extracting this information, given my time frame."

Chuck rubbed his jaw. "Maybe you could ask him nicely," he suggested.

• • •

Roland Edwards was sitting in the driver seat of his rented Ford Expedition when almost simultaneously he heard the back door open, saw a flash of motion, and felt a pain so excruciating it seemed survival was unlikely, if not impossible. He clawed at his throat but the rope had sunk into his skin, hard and unforgiving as iron. Thrashing his fists he tried to turn in his seat, but the rope held him fast against the head rest. As his heart pounded, desperate for oxygen, his trachea compressed and his vision began to swim. He raised his furious eyes to the rearview mirror, determined not to die by the hand of Ortega or Paszkiewicz; but instead, illuminated by the light of the dashboard, was a bearded man he'd never seen before. His eyes widened, and instantly the pressure let up enough for him to take a precious gulp of air.

"Talk," said the man.

Roland gasped, coughed, and tried to pull the rope away, but it held him like a vise. He took another breath, and the man tightened the rope. "All right!" Roland managed, his voice raw. "I quit him!"

"Convince me."

"My family was…in the car with Luna!"

"Who's with him?"

Roland coughed, and the rope loosened again. "Two security."

"He trying to grab her again?"

"Yeah. This time she won't get away."

The bearded man's voice hardened. "Why are you here?"

Roland grimaced and held his gaze. "Payback."

The rope vanished, and the man stood beside him. "Go around," he ordered. "I'll drive."

Roland staggered out of the car, weak and light-headed. "Wait a minute," he said, squinting at Warren as he slid into the passenger seat. "You the shooter?"

"Game on," said Warren.

"Shit!" rasped Roland disgustedly, and rubbed his throat.

• • •

Just before the exit for International Falls, Beck and Flagler flashed their lights. Elias took the ramp as the Jeep continued down the highway, raised fists protruding from both windows.

"Aren't they coming?" asked Wizzie.

"No," said Elias.

"Why not?"

"They can't go into Canada."

"Why?"

"Don't know."

"What did Warren say?"

"He said, 'They can't go into Canada.'"

He drove through International Falls, over the Rainy River, and stopped at the Fort Frances Border Station. Ahead of them a uniformed officer stood beside a single car, inspecting the driver's identification papers. The officer eyed the hearse.

"I hate to drop you and run," said Elias, "but I'm going to follow directions. Don't forget, we'll be at the Silver Lake Motel until tomorrow morning."

"Good luck, you guys!" whispered Wizzie. "Call us!"

The Border Services officer waved the car through. "Good evening," he said, as the hearse stopped beside him. "Identification, please."

"Evening," replied Elias. "I'm not crossing. I'm just providing transportation for these two people and their cargo."

Ned lowered his window. Flagler had explained that a random search of their names in the Border Services database would produce a list of their recent criminal activities, so it was wiser to say as little as possible until Hélène's people took over.

"You are the two people crossing?" asked the officer, whose name tag read LEVESQUE. "Identification, please."

"Our IDs were lost in an accident," said Ned.

Officer Lévesque squinted at him, then looked pointedly at the hearse. "Turn around, sir," he ordered Elias. "Canada does not accept…"

"Officer, we're taking two eagles to the Port Clyde Eagle Sanctuary," Luna interrupted. "Hélène de la Croix is expecting them."

The man frowned, as if debating his next move, then raised his walkie-talkie. "It's Lévesque," he said. "I need a trolley."

• • •

There were less than a dozen people in the Fort Frances Border Station at 12:48 a.m. The room was brightly lit. Cleaners wielded mops and vacuums, and the few people waiting slouched in their chairs. Among them was Gunderman, who wore jeans, a short-sleeved shirt, and a baseball cap. He watched Officer Lévesque enter the building, followed by Luna Burke, Ned Harrelson, and a maintenance man pulling two large animal crates on a trolley. They crossed the room and stopped at a table, behind which stood Officer Tremblay. Carefully they placed the crates on the table. Tremblay lifted each cover, and briefly peered inside.

Gunderman lowered his head and pretended to read his magazine. Late that afternoon he had called Canada Border Services, then stopped by and explained the situation to Officers Lévesque and Tremblay in person. He also called Ministry of Natural Resources and Forestry, and spoke to two more officers on the phone. All had been helpful and cooperative, even when he said he was working on a hunch, even when he explained that the situation was so delicate he could not reveal the names of the people involved until they had been apprehended.

And not only had the hearse arrived, as he predicted, it had arrived sooner than he hoped. The two Natural Resources officers were on their way. It was a public place, and there was no sign of Warren. All Lévesque and Tremblay had to do was stall things until the Natural Resources officers arrived, then Gunderman could step forward and make a textbook arrest.

"You have no identification at all?" asked Tremblay. "Why would you think we would let you into this country?"

"People from the Port Clyde Eagle Sanctuary are meeting us here," said Ned, glancing at the entrance.

"Documentation is your responsibility, not that of any Canadian citizen," Tremblay replied. "Where are your permits for these eagles?"

Luna handed him Elias's manila envelope, and Tremblay pulled out the documents. "This paperwork is not acceptable," he said. "Your Form 3-177 is incomplete."

"I see no reason to bring eagles to Canada," said Lévesque. "We have enough eagles." He turned to Tremblay. "I'm going to call security."

"Wait!" said Luna. "The Port Clyde people have our…"

"You are their colleagues?" interrupted Tremblay. "Both of you? You handle these birds yourselves?"

Luna and Ned nodded.

"I would like you to demonstrate this. Take one of them out."

Luna blinked, taken aback. She hesitated, then reached into her duffel bag and pulled out a leather glove.

"Not you," said Tremblay. "You." He nodded at Ned, and gestured to one of the covered crates. "Take that one out."

Gunderman watched, surprised by the officer's stalling strategy. The two fugitives struggled to appear composed, with Luna Burke succeeding far better than Ned Harrelson. Gunderman had no idea whether Harrelson knew how to handle an eagle. He took the glove, fumbling, and Gunderman had his answer: Harrelson was terrified.

• • •

Please be Banshee, Ned prayed.

He attempted to force his features into a semblance of insouciance as he pulled the cover away from the crate and glanced inside. It was not Banshee, with whom he had no history. It was Mars, the great god of war bird, the lethal predator who haunted his dreams and made him question his manhood, who held the heart of the woman he loved in a scimitar-taloned grip.

Luna's deadpan expression slid into place. She gave the entrance a final glance, then focused on him. Ned straightened his duct-taped glasses, and opened the crate.

He's okay with you, Stanley had told him the day after Luna had been kidnapped, when the two of them were desperate for something to do that might help her once they were reunited. Remember when he landed on the tennis ball? If you were the kind of man he hates, that ball would have been you.

This is not making me feel better, Ned replied.

But he had done it. In the quiet flight cage, coached by Stanley and ready to run if required, he had done it. But that was then.

Ned pulled on the glove. He reached toward the sleepy bird, trying to keep his heart from accelerating, remembering when the police arrived at Carlene's songbird sanctuary and Mars had nearly lifted Luna off the ground. "Please, buddy," he said, in the quietest, friendliest undertone he could manage. "We both need this." He tucked the leather jesses under the thumb of his glove and nudged the hard yellow foot, the dagger beak inches from his eyes. The eagle stepped onto his glove, and Ned took him out of the crate. He held his arm steady, and Mars raised his wings. Every person in the room looked up and caught their breath. The huge bird gripped Ned's glove, surveyed the area, then lowered and folded his wings. Ned turned toward Luna, and saw her poker face had failed.

• • •

"You can put the bird back," said Tremblay, and Gunderman watched Ned return the eagle to its crate. The Natural Resources and Forestry officers were still nowhere to be found. He continued to monitor the scene, ready to change his plan if they were delayed much longer.

A grey-haired, uniformed officer strode down a hallway toward the group, accompanied by a young man in khakis and a short-sleeved shirt. Lévesque looked at the officer in surprise and snapped to attention. "Sir!" he said. "We weren't aware you were in Fort Frances!"

"Good evening," he replied. "Do we have a problem?"

He glanced inside the crates. Lévesque grabbed the manila envelope from the table and extended it toward him. The man took the envelope and pulled out the paperwork.

"They have no personal identification, sir," said Lévesque.

The man frowned. "Do you know how tired we are of you Americans?" he asked. "Why do you think rules don't apply to you?"

Gunderman rose and moved quickly toward the group. "Thank you for your cooperation, officers," he said to Lévesque and Tremblay, as he flashed his U.S. Fish and Wildlife badge. Ned and Luna regarded him incredulously.

"Sir," he addressed the grey-haired man. "I am Federal Wildlife Officer Erik Gunderman, and these eagles are under the protection of the United States government. I am here to impound and return them. I have alerted two of your officers from Ministry of Natural Resources and Forestry, and they're on their way."

The man extended his hand. "Officer Gunderman," he said. "I am the Regional Supervisor for the Canada Border Services Agency. This problem falls under my jurisdiction, but the Canadian government very much appreciates your help. Tomorrow morning my office will coordinate with Natural Resources, and we will send you a full report."

"Sir, the birds are going to the Port Clyde Eagle Sanctuary!" said Ned. He glanced at Luna, who was strangely quiet in the face of adversity. "They should be here any minute!"

"You mean Hélène de la Croix?" the supervisor replied, with a look of aggravation. "Talk about someone who doesn't think the rules apply to them!" He turned to the young man in khakis. "We'll take the birds to quarantine. Put the crates on the trolley."

"Supervisor!" said Gunderman. "Both these birds have been taken illegally from a federally licensed wildlife center, which is a felony violation in the United States! I am here to recover the birds, and arrest these two perpetrators!"

The supervisor regarded him. "Thank you, Officer Gunderman. The birds will be in our quarantine facility and available to you after proper procedures have been followed. Meanwhile, I will contact Ontario Provincial Police myself, and they will place these people in temporary custody."

Gunderman's face flushed. "I strongly request you turn them over to me immediately!"

The supervisor cocked his head. "Are there extenuating circumstances?" he asked, and all eyes turned to Gunderman.

Gunderman hesitated, then focused on Luna. He expected her to look back at him with anger, with defiance, maybe in triumph. Instead she regarded him with compassion, an opposing team member who knew she had won by a lucky shot. She looked fragile and exhausted.

Gunderman's eyes moved to the silver nameplate on the supervisor's chest. DE LA CROIX, it read. He looked up and met the man's unwavering gaze. "Please call me in the morning, Officer Gunderman," he said. "And thank you for your diligence."

The young man in khakis reached for the trolley. The small crowd vanished down the hallway. Lévesque and Tremblay went back to work.

Gunderman stood alone. The air softened. He could almost feel the breeze as it skimmed the mudflats, slipped through the Spanish moss, and swept across the River of Grass.

•••

There were few cars in the parking lot of the Fort Frances Border Station. Ned and Luna followed the trolley toward a large green SUV waiting at the edge of a spotlight. A young man in jeans stood by the open rear door.

"Hey!" he said with a grin, his voice low. "Welcome to Canada! I'm Chris, guess you've met Philipe!"

The young man in khakis nodded as they transferred the crates from the trolley to the car. The supervisor wrapped his arms around Luna. "It's good to have you back, Luna," he said. "We've missed you."

"I've missed you too, Guillaume," she said, returning his hug. "Thank you!"

The supervisor extended his hand to Ned. "Guillaume de la Croix," he said, and scanned the parking lot. "There should be two police cars here. Just go, I'm sure they'll catch up. *Maman* is waiting for you." He nodded at Chris and Philipe, and returned to the building.

The side of the car was adorned with the graceful logo of the Port Clyde Eagle Sanctuary. Chris opened one of the back doors. "Hop in!" he said.

"Hold on," said Ned, trying to decide whether or not to follow Warren's instructions. Common sense told him he should leave the knife and the gun wrapped in the towel beneath Mars's perch. Inconceivably, however, he, Luna, and the two eagles had made it to Canada, so he was reluctant to deviate from the script. He hesitated as long as he could. "Luna needs to check something," he finally blurted.

Moments later they were on the road. Chris and Philipe chatted with them quietly and briefly, under strict orders from Hélène not to rouse the sleeping eagles and to give the human refugees time to rest. Ned replayed the last hour in his mind, still trying to understand how they had managed to thread the needle into Canada. "What would have happened if those other officers had shown up?" he asked.

"They were never going to show up," said Philipe. "They were Natural Resources officers."

Luna saw Ned's blank expression. "Hugo is the head of Natural Resources," she explained. "Hélène's other son."

Chris piloted the SUV carefully down the highway. "You must be wrecked," he said. "Take a nap, and we'll be there before you know it."

He and Philipe conversed in an undertone. Their hushed voices lulled Ned and Luna to sleep, until a gentle turn awakened them. Ahead was a narrow country road. Shafts of moonlight appeared through the heavy trees.

"Ned?" Luna whispered.

"Uh-huh?"

She laced her fingers through his, and gave him a look that made his heart pound. "I…" she began. "I…"

"You what?" asked Ned.

She hesitated, and the car slowed down. "Is it an accident?" asked Philipe.

"What's going on?"

"There's a car parked sideways on the road."

They eased to a stop, and Chris and Philipe shielded their eyes from the bright beam of a flashlight. "Where are those police cars?" said Philipe, his voice rising.

Luna's door opened, and a man reached for her arm. "Paz!" she cried. "What are you doing?"

She clutched at Ned's hand as Adam's security man pulled her out. Ned scrambled after her and Paszkiewicz opened his jacket, revealing a pistol tucked into a shoulder holster. "Stay put," he said.

Luna struggled but Paszkiewicz expertly twisted her arm behind her back, using just enough pressure to propel her toward the parked car. He steered her through the open back door, then slammed it shut. On the other side of the seat sat Adam, wearing suit pants and a pinstriped shirt. The look of contrition he had worn in Chicago was gone, replaced by one of intense determination. Ortega waited in the driver seat. Paszkiewicz slid into the passenger seat, and shut his door.

"Luna," said Adam. "I'm about to change my life for you."

The doors locked with a heavy click.

"Two miles past the bird place," said Ortega to Paszkiewicz, as the car jerked forward. "We'll take 623 and loop back to the airport."

A wave of exhaustion swept away what little fight Luna had left. "You must be so tired," said Adam, his voice warm and quiet. "All this running. Let me take you away, and make it all better."

It's a mirage, she thought. A safe place with teeth. But it was a place where she could close her eyes, where she could finally rest. The last of her defenses fell, and she sank against him. His arm closed around her. "Remember?" he said, and kissed her forehead. "When you're with me, you can fly."

Her consciousness started to slip away. Ortega's voice was distant. "There it is," he said. Inside her something stirred, and with enormous effort she opened her eyes. Ahead was a familiar sign. It grew larger as the car approached.

Chérie, Hélène had said. Come home.

Luna stiffened and sat up. She watched the sign pass and fade into the night. "Stop!" she cried. Adam frowned, startled. Ortega lifted his foot from the gas, his eyes on the rearview mirror. Paszkiewicz began to turn around.

Luna seized the kitchen knife from her cargo pants pocket and jammed it beneath Adam's chin. A drop of blood slid down the steel shaft. "Unlock it!" she screamed, her voice cracking. "I swear to God I'll cut his throat!"

There was another heavy click, and she yanked the door open and hurled herself out of the moving car. She hit the ground rolling, skin burning, stitches popping, feeling twin blasts of pain and adrenaline as she scrambled to her feet. Tires shrieked behind her as she raced down the road, past the sign, and onto the mile-long dirt driveway of the Port Clyde Eagle Sanctuary.

CHAPTER 28

Roland studied the small metal box on his lap. "This is high tech," he said. "I could use something like this."

"Maybe I know a guy," said Warren. "She on track?"

"Yup. Pulling onto 517."

"This road'll intersect with theirs a couple of miles from Hélène's. Meanwhile, no point in interfering with Canada's finest."

Three tones emerged from Warren's backpack. "Black phone," he said.

Roland rummaged through the pack. "How many goddamned phones have you got in here?" he asked irritably. "Hello?"

"Who is this?" shouted Ned, his voice clearly audible. "Where's Warren?"

"What's the problem?" demanded Warren.

"They got her! They dragged her out of the car and there's no cops! What do we do now?"

Warren slammed his foot on the accelerator. "On the way," said Roland, and disconnected.

• • •

Gunderman drove his car along a dark Canadian road, unable to comprehend his own motivation. There was nothing to be gained.

But he had tracked Luna Burke, Ned Harrelson, and their stolen eagle for almost 2,300 miles, and he could not accept that he had truly lost them. Everything he believed in was burning, his carefully maintained life about to collapse. He headed north, looking for an answer, knowing he wouldn't find one. He couldn't rectify the night's events, nor could he look past them into his empty future. He drove toward the Port Clyde Eagle Sanctuary without a plan. I've never done this in my life, he thought, and kept driving.

• • •

A wide shaft of moonlight illuminated her path. The knife, she thought as she ran down the dirt driveway, picturing it lying on the road where she had dropped it. But she still had the gun, strapped snugly to her calf. She heard the roar of an engine, and the area around her was flooded with light.

Memory slipped through her panic. The cairn. Deep in the woods was a safe place, a fortress. She searched the side of the driveway as she ran. She spotted a balanced stack of rocks, and beyond it, a trail. She plunged into the forest, and the car screeched to a halt behind her.

When we get to Hélène's, we'll take you on an Owl Prowl! Rose had told her.

It's a bunch of nutty people wandering around the woods at night, calling to the owls! added Harry.

The tremulous cry of a screech owl joined the chorus of crickets and katydids. She followed the trail, enveloped by the smell of pine and earth, out of the glare of headlights and into a world where she could slip into shadows. She glanced behind her and saw flashlight beams. She skirted the moonlight, searching for the fort. She had helped to build it.

Something rumbled in the distance. Thunder had a physical presence, she remembered, and soon it would crash over the forest. It could lift her into the air. It could find her when she hid.

She leaned against a huge white spruce and paused to catch her breath. Tentatively she touched her thigh, which had taken most of the impact when she landed on the road. Her pant leg stuck to her skin.

She heard the crunch of footsteps. Behind her was Ortega, his flashlight sweeping the darkness. She edged to the other side of the tree, and briefly pressed herself against the trunk. She pushed forward, and Ortega's footsteps grew softer.

"Luna!" called Adam. "Where are you?" His voice had lost its warmth. Stress crackled around its edges. She straightened the holster around her calf, and hurried deeper into the woods.

• • •

Warren skidded onto the driveway of the Port Clyde Eagle Sanctuary without slowing down. He slammed on his brakes behind Adam's car, jumped out, and spotted the cairn. "Come on," he said. "I know where she's going."

"Dammit," said Roland, scowling at the dark wall of trees. Unwillingly he pulled his Glock from its holster and followed. The forest floor crackled beneath his feet.

"Keep it down!" snapped Warren. "You sound like a rhino!"

"Luna!" called Adam in the distance. Two flashlights flickered, and Warren paused.

"We gotta take these guys out," he whispered, "but they'll hear you coming. Stay on this trail, follow her, and I'll catch up."

"Got it."

Warren angled toward a single beam of light, which swept methodically back and forth. The man holding the light was tall and solid, and held a pistol in his other hand. Warren hugged the shadows and circled behind him. He glided closer, and in one fluid motion lunged forward and locked an arm around the man's throat. Paszkiewicz squeezed the trigger, and his silenced weapon coughed. The bullet ricocheted off a nearby pine.

"Paz?" called a voice. Paszkiewicz went limp, and Warren followed the voice.

Ortega was on the alert. He swept his flashlight once, twice, then quickly turned and shone it behind him. He spun slowly, encasing himself in a protective circle of light. "Paz!" he called again.

Warren hovered out of the flashlight's range, watching its nervous route. This situation requires an accelerant, he decided, so he took a deep breath, slid his left hand upward, and squeezed his own throat enough to slightly compress his larynx. He let out a hoarse, wheezy yowl that fell in pitch and tone until it ended in a deep, resonant rumble. The moving beam came to an abrupt halt. Warren repeated the call. *Owwooooo.*

"Holy shit," breathed Ortega. His beam darted back and forth, jerky and sporadic. Put a man alone in the woods, thought Warren, add the sound of a very big cat, and watch how fast thousands of years of civilization grind to a halt. He let it loose again, and the man gasped and dropped his flashlight. He bent to retrieve it, and as he straightened a right cross caught him squarely on the jaw. Warren watched him drop, then set off in the direction of Luna's trail.

• • •

Luna spotted a rock shelf beside a split hickory. She was close.

There had been more than twenty of them, she remembered, all ages, all hauling wood. Everyone was friendly and kind. She had just turned sixteen, and never experienced anything like it. Are you Harry and Rose's granddaughter? a man asked her. Silently she smiled back at him, afraid to break the spell.

"Luna!" called Adam. She could feel the electricity in the air. A storm was coming. A pot of water boiled on the stove. Where is that little bitch?

She slowed, puzzled by the denseness of the forest. How could they have driven a truck with lumber and doors and locks all the way back here? She didn't know why she couldn't remember. But they had built a safe house, strong and impenetrable. When they were done, a happy six-year-old boy had turned to her.

It's our castle! he cried. Our fortress!

It stood in a clearing, partially illuminated by moonlight. Luna stopped, her heart pounding, and stared at the structure before her. Many hands had fashioned tree limbs, branches, and vines into a one-room stick fort. Part of the roof had collapsed. A few of the vines had sprouted leaves. All expression vanished from her face.

"Luna?" called Adam, somewhere behind her.

• • •

The forest darkened as clouds drifted in front of the moon. "Come on, babe," called Adam, using his calm voice. "We're wasting time!"

He saw an outline in a clearing. He held up his phone, and its flashlight illuminated a crumbling fort. The clouds dispersed, bathing it in a silvery glow, and he leaned in the door. Abruptly she appeared beside the fort, ghostly in the moonlight, and he stumbled backward in surprise. She slid the safety off, and aimed the Ruger at his chest. "Go away, Adam," she said, holding her arms straight.

He flinched, then recovered. "You're not going to shoot me," he said.

The bullet tore past his shoulder. "Jesus Christ!" he cried, as the report echoed through the woods. "What the hell are you doing?"

Footsteps crackled, and Roland appeared out of the darkness. Luna gasped and pointed her pistol at him.

"Roland!" said Adam, with relief. "I thought you…"

"I don't work for you anymore," said Roland.

"Bullshit!" cried Luna, aiming the gun from one to the other and back again. "I'll shoot both of you! That last one was just a warning!"

Roland raised his hands. "No! Wait for Warren!"

She grimaced, confused. "Luna!" called Warren's voice, seconds ahead of Warren himself. "We're good," he said, and rested a hand on Roland's shoulder. He looked at her encouragingly, and held out his other hand. "You did it. Birds are safe. Let me take that."

She kept the pistol pointed at Adam's chest. "No!" she said. "It will never end! He won't let me go!"

"Yes, he will. Come on. You've completed your mission."

"She's my wife!" snapped Adam.

Luna pointed the gun at his face, and Warren lowered his voice. "Listen to me," he insisted. "You can do anything you want, but not if you shoot him."

Her hands trembled. She felt the fort against her back. She heard the rustle of leaves, and two figures approached. She squinted as she kept her pistol on Adam, trying to identify them, knowing it must be Paszkiewicz and Ortega and that her time was almost up. Instead, two Canadian police officers moved toward her. Their guns were drawn. Their handcuffs glinted in the moonlight. "Drop the weapon!" one called.

The ground rose beneath her. Darkness and hunger and breaking glass. Whirling red lights and a dead end. Cornered. There she is!

Warren positioned himself between her and the officers. "They're not here for you," he said urgently.

"Of course they're here for you!" Adam shouted. "And I'm the only one who can help you!"

Luna swallowed. She looked at Warren, at Roland, at the two police officers with their drawn guns, and at Adam, with his hard stare. Coming closer were more footsteps. She couldn't see the stars.

She leaned against the fort, the ebb of adrenaline and flood of despair so familiar it was almost a comfort. She slid down and sat on the ground, knees to her chest, the Ruger in her hand. Warren started toward her, and she raised the gun to her head. Warren stopped as if he had hit a wall. Adam froze. The police hesitated.

There it is, thought Luna. Harry and Rose's pond. It was dark and soft and would cradle her and sing her to sleep. From its depths came fireflies, glittering like tiny crystals as they made their way to the surface. They're not fireflies, she realized, they're stars. She had found the stars again. Her forefinger tightened.

Ned rushed through the crowd, fell to his knees, and wrapped her in his arms. The gun fell and exploded, taking out the remaining section of roof. A ragged cry emerged from Luna's chest and she clutched him, sobbing, as her tears soaked his shirt.

"It's okay," Ned whispered. "It'll be all right."

CHAPTER 29

T he Ford Expedition climbed a rise in the dirt driveway. The trees thinned, the sky widened, and the moon hovered above an expanse of open land. To the right was a weathered old Cape with a porch. To the left were massive slatted flight cages.

"Jesus," said Roland.

"No kidding," said Warren, in the driver seat beside him.

Ned sat in the back, his arm around a sleeping Luna. That night the town of Port Clyde had experienced an almost unprecedented crime wave: a shootout at a local bar. Backup arrived shortly, but it delayed Luna's police escort long enough for Paszkiewicz to pull her from the car.

Ned had called Warren. Chris and Philipe called Hélène and the police. They drove down the sanctuary's driveway, stopped behind Adam's and Roland's cars, and moments later the first police cruiser screeched to a halt. Two uniformed officers jumped out, spotted the cairn, and both of them vanished down the trail. Soon another police car appeared, siren wailing. A black-haired policewoman barreled out, sprinted by, and Ned followed her into the woods.

They all emerged from the forest long after Chris and Philipe took the eagles to the sanctuary. They found Ortega and Paszkiewicz seated in the back of a cruiser, a fourth officer standing guard. Undeclared firearms, Sergeant, said the officer.

The black-haired policewoman glanced coldly at Adam. Mr. Matheson and his employees will accompany us to the station, she replied. Ned's eyes dropped to her nameplate. DE LA CROIX, it read.

Adam watched grimly as Ned helped Luna into the back of Roland's car. Roland slid into the passenger seat without a backward glance. Warren stood for a moment, his eyes on Adam, and Adam felt a chill.

"I don't get this animal thing," said Roland, as Warren pulled up in front of the weathered Cape.

"That's because you haven't seen mine," said Warren.

Luna stirred, awakened, and saw the house. She slid out of the car and Ned followed, steadying her as she paused dizzily. Chris, Philipe, and three other volunteers sat on the front steps. Above them, a woman stood regally on the porch.

She was small and wiry. Her feral eyes slanted over high cheekbones. Her thick white hair was swept into a chignon, and her hand rested on the head of an eagle carved into a wooden cane. When her eyes met Luna's, she looked at her with a love so fierce Ned felt its heat.

"Luna," she said, in a husky half-whisper.

Luna rushed up the stairs and wrapped her arms around Hélène. They stood together, then Hélène held her at arm's length. *"Mon Dieu, oisillon,* look at you," she rasped, taking in Luna's bruises, the dirt in her hair, her torn and bloody clothing. "Go with Sharon," she added, gesturing to a young woman on the stairs. "She is a nurse."

In the driveway, a door slammed. Gunderman stood beside his car, his shoulders slumped, his expression unreadable.

He had found his way to the Port Clyde Eagle Sanctuary, not knowing what he would do when he arrived. He spotted three vehicles on the driveway, the last one a green SUV with a graceful eagle logo. The police cruisers arrived, the dark-haired policewoman sprinted into the woods, and Harrelson rocketed after her. Gunderman hurried out of his car and trailed them to the old stick fort. Hidden by darkness, he saw it all unfold. Afterward he was the last to leave, hanging back and walking alone.

Now he stood facing the group. Hélène narrowed her eyes and stepped to the edge of the porch. Gunderman waited, feeling the heavy gaze of those who believed, despite his life's work, that he was the enemy.

Slowly Hélène raised one hand. Luna raised hers, as well, and the others followed. Haltingly, Gunderman raised his in return. He straightened his shoulders, gave them all a single nod, then he climbed into his car and drove away.

"Gentlemen," said Hélène. *"Merci.* You have my gratitude. Come, you look like you could use a drink."

Luna went inside with the nurse. Roland followed Chris and Philipe into the house. Warren started up the stairs, and stopped when he reached the porch. *"Ma belle Hélènne!"* he rumbled, eyeing her with a grin. "The patron saint of wild things!"

Hélène tilted her head and gazed up at him, her brows drawing together like storm clouds. Suddenly she smiled, and Warren cradled her face between his hands and kissed her on the lips. Ned, two steps behind him, let out an audible gasp. Hélène turned, pinned Ned with her dark eyes, and nodded at Warren. "This little bastard didn't tell me he was seventeen!" she said.

"'Course I didn't," Warren retorted. "What do you say, Ned? You're thumbing rides across Canada, and a black-haired bird sorceress picks you up — would you tell her you were seventeen?"

• • •

Ned opened his eyes, sat up, and found himself alone in another unfamiliar bedroom. Light seeped through the edges of the blinds.

The night returned in hallucinatory pieces. He had shared a drink with Roland Edwards in the living room of Hélène de la Croix. Volunteers scrambled eggs as the sky turned lavender. Luna emerged, pale and bandaged, and fell asleep on his shoulder. Roland carried her effortlessly up the stairs to one of the bedrooms. As he slid in beside her, Ned thought, this time it's really over.

He dressed, went downstairs, and found three-quarters of a cup of coffee left in the pot. The house was empty. He wandered to the office, to the clinic, and to the small auditorium, but no one seemed to know where to find Luna. Eventually he ran into Philipe, who led him to one of the flight cages. In the far corner, Hélène sat in an ornate wicker chair.

"They're unreleasable," said Philipe, gesturing to the great dark creatures watching him from various perches. "Half of them are education birds. They're used to people. You can walk right through."

Ned thanked him and regarded his latest obstacle course: a slatted airplane hangar filled with a dozen free-flying eagles. He snorted, closed the door behind him, and walked determinedly toward Hélène.

"Good morning," she said.

"Good morning," he replied. "I'm having trouble finding Luna."

"She's not here."

"Where is she?"

"She left."

"What do you mean, she left? Where did she go?"

Hélène regarded him steadily. "She needs some time." She shifted her eyes to the eagles, as if signaling the end of the conversation.

"But I need to talk to her." When he received no response, his voice rose. "Where is she?" he demanded. "Are you hiding her from me?"

A flash of contempt crossed her face, and Ned felt a swirl of disorientation. "I just want to make sure she's all right!"

The contempt disappeared. "You are a good man," said Hélène. "You have my respect and support. You are welcome to stay here as long as you like. Whenever you wish to leave, one of the volunteers will drive you to the airport."

"But what about Luna?"

"I'm not hiding her, Ned. I am respecting her wishes. You would do well to do the same."

• • •

Gunderman sat in the Falls International Airport, waiting for his flight home. Ned entered the room and stood uncertainly, his clothes rumpled, his taped glasses at a slight angle. When he saw Gunderman he sighed, trudged over, and sat beside him.

"Matheson's plane was here, but now it's gone," said Gunderman. "Is she staying at the sanctuary?"

"I don't know where she is."

Roland appeared, carrying a leather overnight bag, and spotted the two of them. He frowned and glanced around, as if searching for alternatives, then he crossed the room and sat on the other side of Ned. "Where's Luna?" he asked.

"He doesn't know," said Gunderman.

"Where's Warren?" asked Ned.

Roland shrugged. "I don't think he uses public transportation."

They sat in silence. "Thanks to this, I've got no job," said Gunderman finally.

"I've got no job and no family," said Roland.

"I've got..." Ned began, then stopped as two uniformed marshals appeared before him.

"Ned Harrelson?" said one. "We are authorized by the government of the United States of America to return you to the State of Wisconsin, where you are wanted for crimes against the persons and property of both state and federal officers."

Ned rose, and the second officer pulled his hands behind his back and snapped the handcuffs shut.

"I've got nothing," Ned finished, as they escorted him toward the door.

• • •

The plane touched down in Chicago. No town car, SUV, or limousine waited for him, so Roland waited in line until a battered cab pulled up. He climbed into the back seat. The springs were shot.

A block from his building, he told the driver to stop. He entered the park, sat on a bench, and stared at Lake Michigan. He had been sitting on the same bench, swigging Jack Daniels and replaying his doctors' words, when Adam called him for the second time. He pulled out his phone and turned it off.

Nearly an hour later he picked up his overnight bag and walked to his building. He rode the elevator to the top floor, and pulled out his keys. The door was unlocked. Instantly he tensed and pictured his Glock, disassembled and in a case in his bag. He turned the knob slowly and silently, until the slimmest beam of light shone through.

"Yeah, finally!" came Lyllis's voice. "He's been sitting on that goddamned bench for an hour. Yep, okay! I'll tell him."

He opened the door and found Michael sitting on the easy chair, grinning, his sister Selma dabbing her eyes. Lyllis leaned on her crutches, trying to look happy instead of triumphant. "Warren wants to know wassup?" she said, and tossed her phone onto the couch.

• • •

The air was warm and humid. Gunderman stood in his cabin, wondering what breathing would be like in the next place he lived. Maybe his lungs would burn in the dry heat. Maybe they would smart from the sharpness of the cold. As long as they don't ache from air conditioning, he thought, as he tried to be pragmatic.

The television chattered in the corner. The news shows were grasping at straws, churning out increasingly outlandish stories about Adam Matheson, his runaway wife, and his shadowy trip to Canada. Gunderman started toward the television, intending to turn it off. "In a related story," said the newscaster, "we go to the Western Pennsylvania Wildlife Center, where this story began."

Celia appeared before a bank of microphones, even paler than usual, flanked by Wizzie and Elias. Wizzie reached out and tapped one of the microphones. "Is this thing on?" she asked.

Celia bit her lip, and Elias placed a hand on her shoulder. "Last night our missing eagle was returned to us," she said determinedly. "Our bonded pair of Bald Eagles are together again, and it is thanks to…to the outstanding work of Wildlife Officer Erik Gunderman. We want to thank him. And we want to thank Daniel Whittaker, Chief of Law Enforcement for U.S. Fish and Wildlife Service. In this day and age, it's rare to find such dedicated public servants. Both of them have the grateful thanks of all of us who care about the wild creatures of America."

Everyone smiled and clapped. Gunderman stared at the screen, confounded. She might have just saved my job, he thought.

• • •

Ned sat in his office, staring unseeing at his computer screen. He had been in variants of the same position for a week. Once again, he reached for his phone.

bluestreak@juno.com Baby you all right? We're still up here in Tallahassee if you want to visit

stanleykw@outlook.com Hang in there Ned. Come help with the turtles if you need a break

chiroptera@gmail.com I have a bottle of bourbon with your name on it.

iris@bluemoonwildlife.org hello sweetheart why don't you come back and let me give you another makeover? You probably need a touch up by now LOL

Ned had arrived at the airport in Wisconsin flanked by marshals, wearing an orange jumpsuit and shackles. His mother stood at the gate with tears in her eyes. He could read his father's lips: No, Neddo, no.

An op-ed piece in the Milwaukee Journal-Sentinal wove a Shakespearian tale of forbidden love, corporate tyranny, and freedom in America, and was picked up by media outlets all over the country. This is what you want me to spend the taxpayers' money on? shouted the prosecuting attorney, an avowed enemy of Adam Matheson, pushing Ned's case to the top of his list. You have a rich and powerful figure who routinely pays fines instead of following the law, who started this whole thing by stealing a protected eagle, and you want me to try to max out a kid with an otherwise spotless record? I won't do it!

Ned had been given fines, probation, and community service. He spent two days with his parents, then returned to his empty apartment. At work he found a large framed photo of himself wearing shackles, "Employee of the Week" emblazoned above it.

The sequence he was working on might as well have been written in hieroglyphics. He rose from his chair and looked out his window. He returned to his desk and typed **Luna Burke** into his search engine. There was nothing new. He typed **Port Clyde Eagle Sanctuary**. Nothing. He envisioned the afternoon Gunderman and the police had closed in, and felt a small, blessed surge of adrenaline. He thought of Trish and Angelica's house, with its undulating hobbit roof.

They left me the house but I couldn't live in it, Luna had said. I had nowhere to go.

He typed **Prattsville PA real estate,** and an hour later his office manager looked at him in surprise. "What?" she said. "You're leaving again?"

• • •

Ned drove steadily, his arm out the window of his rented car, listening to the swell of cicadas in the afternoon heat. He drove past rolling, sun-drenched fields, glancing into the rearview mirror at the clouds of dust swirling behind him. He turned off a country road and passed a mailbox.

At the top of the hill stood a farmhouse, and behind it a barn. Ned pulled up by the house and turned off the engine.

The front door was covered with graffiti. Three windows were broken. The barn's sliding door hung haphazardly from its hinges, held in place by a large padlock. Of all the fool's errands he'd been on, he thought, this was by far the most idiotic.

"I can work remotely," he said into his cell phone, as he sat on the top step of the back porch.

"Are you out of your mind?" demanded Earl, leaning against a '74 Trans Am in his garage in South Carolina. "You haven't even talked to her! She's officially a Missing Person! *And* she already told you she didn't want to live in that house!"

"I know. But she left it a long time ago. Maybe if I changed it around a little, she'd feel…"

"What's wrong with you, man? Why don't you go out and get laid? You're a celebrity — you can have anyone you want!"

"I'm not a celebrity, and I don't want anyone else!"

"What do you think the odds are of this working?"

"The kind I'm used to," said Ned. "Two hundred billion to one."

CHAPTER 30

Harper closed her laptop, slid it into her bag, and stepped out into the brilliant sunshine of Cielo Azul. She walked past the pool and the tennis courts to the formal garden, where she picked a single red hibiscus and slid it into her hair. When she reached the zoo, she performed a final patrol.

She had found homes for all of them. Good homes, too, not mere holding pens where they would languish. The camels, the kangaroos, the flamingos, the spiders, every one of the 38 different species in Adam Matheson's zoo had been carefully placed. The pairs would be kept together, and all would receive the best of care and enrichment.

The property had sold in a day. The wife was a romantic, and wanted to erase all trace of its multi-married former owner and re-create her honeymoon villa. The husband was a germaphobe, and wanted to erase all trace of the zoo so there was no possibility of bird flu. The bulldozers would arrive on Monday.

Harper closed the gate behind her, and Carlos emerged from the house. They walked toward each other, and met in the middle of the luxurious green lawn.

"Good morning, Miss Harper," said Carlos.

"Good morning, Carlos," she replied. "Have you decided where you're going?"

"Yes. I am going to Orlando, to join my brother's landscaping company. And you? Will you go to live with the dolphins?"

"I hope so. I'm looking for a way."

"Good luck to you, Miss Harper."

"Good luck to you too, Carlos."

They bumped their fists together, and parted ways.

• • •

These clowns in Washington are slicing the shit out of my budget, Whittaker had said.

Gunderman glanced at the neat row of locked canoes, and continued down the North Trail. The late afternoon sun shone behind him. He heard a rattling call, and paused to watch an anhinga soar past him and land in a cypress tree.

I can't afford to fire you to prove a point, Whittaker had continued. I don't know what kind of stupid shell game went on with those eagles, but if the public thinks we're heroes, fine. This is a crazy time, Gunderman. Any minute I'm expecting the fuckers in this administration to start selling licenses to shoot endangered species to the highest bidders.

Gunderman passed the visitor center, and continued to his cabin. He had made peace with it all. Three unreleasable eagles would live out their lives in luxury, doted on by volunteers. Once he would have fought this breach of law and order, but while tracking Luna Burke he had begun to realize that sometimes delicate colors appeared in the crevices between black and white.

He grabbed a beer from his refrigerator, went out to his porch, and sat down. He thought about Celia, Wizzie, and Elias, even though there was no point. He had spoken to Celia after the news segment, a short and stilted conversation filled with awkward silences and overlapping attempts at banter. She was rooted firmly in Pennsylvania, he in Florida. There was no more to be said.

His reunion was next month. He would attend, reconnect with his fellow wildlife officers, and catch up on all the years he had missed. He would swap stories and feel the camaraderie. Maybe, he thought, I'll track a couple of them down this weekend.

The knock on the door startled him. When he opened it Celia gave him an inquiring smile, and Wizzie raised her hand in greeting. Both were in shorts and t-shirts. For a moment, he was too surprised to react.

"You see?" said Wizzie. "I told you we should have called first!"

"We're on vacation," said Celia. "Wizzie wanted to come to Florida, but I didn't want to impose on you, you know? So I thought we'd just say hello, and then we'll go."

"But you can come with us if you want," added Wizzie, "and give us a tour."

Gunderman grinned. "Come in," he said, and he tumbled into a world of primary colors.

• • •

Roland let himself into his apartment and found Lyllis emerging from the bedroom in a scarlet evening gown, a blaze of diamonds around her neck.

"Holy mother," he said, his eyes sweeping her from head to foot. "You are one fine woman." He crossed the room, his eyes widening at her necklace. "Where'd you get that? *Now* what have you done?"

"Oh, stop it," she retorted. "It's Luna's. She was wearing it the night she showed up in the rain. Will you hurry up? We're going to be late."

"Did she give it to you?"

"Nah, she just left it. I'm keeping it for her, because someday she's going to come back from wherever she went and need some money."

"Maybe she won't want it."

"She'll want it after I get through with her. It's her fee for being kidnapped and manhandled and everything else. If there was any justice in this world, me and Michael would have one, too. I'm wearing it tonight, then I'll put it in the safe deposit box in the bank." She pushed him toward the bedroom. "Go. Get dressed. How's the team?"

"Good," he replied, and smiled. "They're good kids."

Lyllis smiled back at him. After a moment he blinked, as if something had startled him into motion. "Sorry," he said. "I'll be five minutes. It's just…sometimes I don't want to do anything but stand still and look at you."

She beamed. "Go," she said. "You can look at me when we're not late."

He peeled off his clothes in the bedroom. His phone rang, and he glanced down.

"Yeah?" he said, guarded.

"Roland," said Adam. "You have a minute?"

"I'm on my way out."

"This won't take long. Listen. Now that some time has passed, I just want to tell you how sorry I am. Especially about the car. You know that wasn't supposed to happen."

"I know."

"Things got out of hand. It was temporary insanity. Anyway, I'm sure you've heard I'm done with Luna."

"I gotta go."

"What do you say we get past it? Why don't you come work for me again?"

"No."

"You've said that to me before."

"This time I mean it," said Roland, and hung up.

• • •

Adam regarded his phone. Roland will change his mind, he thought. The driver opened the door, and Adam sent Darcy a quick text.

adam@matheson.com Change of plan. Back next Wednesday.

Paszkiewicz accompanied him to the private elevator, then to the penthouse. He took a seat in the bar, and Adam continued into the dining room. The restaurant was booked a year in advance, but one of his assistants had called that morning and reserved a table next to the window. It was set with antique china and crystal. His favorite champagne rested in a silver bucket. The lights of Manhattan sparkled below.

Waiting for him was Sophie König, whose latest film had just won the Palme d'Or at Cannes, whose agent was currently negotiating her first big-budget American picture, and whose career was on a nearly vertical climb. She was there unbeknownst to her boyfriend, a German actor with whom she had been living for the past four years.

Sophie talked about her childhood, career, and ambitions, and Adam smiled, nodded, and thought about the shit storm he had faced when he returned from Canada. His marketing and PR people were hysterical, investors were jittery, and the media was all over him. He answered his phone the second day and heard the voice of Joe Reiner, his mentor, frequent business partner, and friend. Adam, he said. Come have dinner with me tomorrow night. Seven o'clock.

Adam arrived at the cavernous apartment and followed a woman to the roof garden, where Joe sat holding a gin and tonic and looking out over the city. Adam sat beside him, and a young man handed him a Scotch on the rocks. Adam, said Joe. What are you doing?

It's complicated, said Adam.

No, it's not, said Joe. Bottom line is she's making you look like you're not in charge. We can't have that.

Joe listened patiently, and at the end a kindly smile appeared on his heavily lined face. Are you on drugs? he asked.

Of course I'm not on…

Then what are you talking about? Even if things were going well with Luna, which they're not, have you ever spent more than a week on an island? I didn't think so. Look. I know you love her. But what is marriage, really? In your case, it's a piece of paper with dollar signs all over it. If you've managed to find the one woman in the world who doesn't want any of them, then get on your knees, thank God, and run with it. Tell the media you're divorcing her and she's not getting a penny. It'll show the world you've wised up, and then maybe you won't end up with another…what was that last one's name, again?

Shannon.

Right. Shannon. Anyway. Divorce her, get back in charge, and then do whatever you want. Am I making sense?

"I love America!" exclaimed Sophie, in her charming accent.

"It's the land of opportunity," said Adam.

"And what about your wife?" asked Sophie. "Are you divorced yet?"

"It's in the works."

She wasn't at the eagle place. He had hired a Canadian private investigator to stake it out, and there was no sign of her. She wasn't with Harrelson, who had returned to Key West after his trial. She wasn't at the Western Pennsylvania Wildlife Center. She wasn't at Starfish Key. She wasn't with any of the animal people on her phone list.

"There is a chance I will move to Los Angeles," said Sophie. "Do you have a house there?"

She was stunning. Heads turned when she entered a room. "I certainly do," he replied. "Would you like to see it?"

He thought of the day he crossed the wide lawn of Cielo Azul to meet his new zookeeper. She stood waiting in the sunlight, her curly hair auburn, her eyes Caribbean blue. She wore khakis and a white sleeveless shirt. Hanging from a leather cord around her neck was a silver bead, and inside was the downy feather of an eagle.

"Adam?"

Lilac-colored silk. Stars in a summer sky.

"Adam?"

He looked up and smiled. "This has been a most enjoyable evening," he said. "My apartment is not far from here. Would you like to go there for a nightcap, or shall I take you back to your hotel? I leave the choice to you."

She returned his smile. "A nightcap would be lovely," she replied.

• • •

Luna wandered along the ridge and slept beneath the stars. She cooked over a fire, and when it rained she moved her sleeping bag into the cabin. Twice a week a pair of Hélène's volunteers appeared with supplies.

She had left Ned as he slept and hiked up the mountain, accompanied by five of the volunteers. They readied the site for her, and spent the night. In the morning, at her insistence, all five returned to Hèlène's. For a week her mind and body closed ranks, her body absorbing its remaining adrenaline while her mind shut its door and allowed her to sleep. She rose so she could eat and use the camping toilet, then she returned to her sleeping bag.

As she healed, her system loosened its protective grip. She spent fewer hours asleep. The stitches in her arm began to itch. The road burn on her thigh scabbed over. Memories returned, vying for space as she hiked. When she ejected them, they appeared at night in a form far worse. Not Ned, though. When she banished him from her waking hours he slipped between her nightmares, piloting one of his carefully restored cars or holding Mars on a glove, allowing her a moment of respite before her dark dreams returned.

She knew the farther the distance between them, the better it was for Ned. They had been thrown together by chance, not choice. Besides, relationships were fleeting and destructive, and she was still married to Adam. Ned had moved on, she was sure, and she was safe on her mountain. But each time the volunteers appeared with supplies she held her breath, hoping, until it became clear Ned was not with them.

Warren arrived long after time became irrelevant. He emerged from the forest, a steak dinner in his backpack, singing "People Are Strange" in a voice uncannily like Jim Morrison's. He gave her a hug, kissed her forehead, and stretched out by the fire pit. "Ned's fixing your house up," he announced.

She flinched, as if his words had cut her. "I don't know what to do with this information," she said.

"You could just consider it," he replied.

He chopped a stack of wood, cooked their meal over the fire, and removed her stitches with his multitool. When he left in the morning, she lay on her back and stared at the clouds. She pictured Ned at Starfish Key, brown-haired, pony-tailed, slouching and looking noncommittal. She replayed their journey north, from Warren's all the way to Hélène's.

It's the eagle courtship ritual! she told him at Esther's, fumbling with the CD.

Not the courtship ritual! he gasped, in horror.

Otherwise known as the Death Spiral!

They sure got *that* right!

They were on the same page, she thought. Fixing the house was just a nod to the past, a way to channel his remaining adrenaline. She couldn't live at Harry and Rose's, but maybe he could. Maybe she could give him the house, as a way to thank him for all he had done.

• • •

At the top of the hill stood a farmhouse, and behind it a barn. The classic red Chevy was parked near the front steps. Clustered around it it were two cars, a pick-up truck, and a van.

Ned had flown to Kentucky and stopped at the Blue Moon Wildlife Center. He retrieved his car from Iris's brother's barn, then he drove to Pennsylvania. He spent one night in a roadside motel, feeling a sweet, fleeting moment of anticipation when he woke up alone in an unfamiliar room.

He tracked down the executor of Harry and Rose's will, a retired lawyer who kept the title to their home in one of his files. So you're the famous Ned Harrelson! the white-haired man said. He drew up a contract stating Ned expected no financial return for repairs on the Burke's house, barn, or property. I hope you can get her to come back, he added.

Ned sat at the kitchen table, attempting to respond to the email his office had sent him that morning. On the table before him were invoices, receipts, and a nearly completed master list. The cleaners, carpenters, painters, and decorator had been working for two months. "I know, Francine, I'm on it, " he said, answering his phone without checking the screen.

"Wassup?" asked Warren. "How you doing, man? I hear you're fixing up her place."

"Uh, yeah, I am," Ned managed, taken aback. "I'm good. You?"

"Good."

"Have you seen Luna?"

"Saw her yesterday."

"Where?"

"She was in her own space."

Ned knew trying to cross-examine Warren would get him exactly nowhere, so he tried a different tack. "How is she?"

"Okay."

"Can I see her?"

"She needs a little more time."

"How much more?"

"Sorry, man, I really wish I could tell you. Listen, I gotta go. I just wanted to check in and tell you she's all right. You need anything, just call me."

"Right. Black phone."

Autumn turned the fields to burnished gold, the oaks and maples to a fiery blaze, and Ned wandered through the restored house. It was beautiful and serene. It was the kind of place that made him wistful, that made him long for the kind of complete and happy life its occupants must surely live. He sat in the living room on the edge of the couch, thinking, why did I do this?

• • •

The air was chilly when he arrived. The sky was streaked with purple. Hélène sat on her porch wearing a heavy wool cardigan, holding a glass of red wine. On the table beside her was the bottle and another glass. She watched him approach, her face impassive.

"I must have called you two dozen times over the last few months," he said, sitting beside her. "I've talked to everyone here but you."

"Have some wine," she replied.

Ned let out an exasperated sigh. He spilled a few drops as he poured, then he set the bottle down and raised his glass.

"To the birds of the air," said Hélène, in her insinuating whisper.

"Where is she?" he asked.

Hélène gestured to a ridge in the distance. "She lives in the forest. Like in your fairy tales."

"There's a house up there?"

"It depends on your definition of a house."

"Can I drive up and see her?"

"There's no road. It's a three-hour hike."

"Can I call her?"

"There's no service."

Ned drained half his glass. "Why won't she see me?"

"She believes she has done you harm. And any further contact will cause you more. "

"Do you know how she's caused me the most harm? By disappearing on me!"

"Harm is relative."

"No, it's not!" He glanced at the ridge. "Is she staying up there so she can be 'free?' Because that's bullshit! If she won't leave that mountain then she's not free, she's just living in a really big cage!"

Hélène regarded him implacably. Ned forced himself to meet her eyes, even though he felt he was tempting fate just by sitting next to her.

"Mars and Banshee have joined the group of unreleasable eagles," she said, turning toward the flight cages. "Each day I go out and sit with them. I would never do that with the wild ones."

Ned threw caution to the winds. "Are you trying to be metaphorical?" he snapped. "Are you trying to tell me Luna is a wild bird, and I should keep away from her?"

"You're not as smart as you think you are."

"I think I'm the biggest idiot who ever lived! If I were smart, I would never have left Florida!"

"Then why don't you learn?" said Hélène. "Everything changes. Birds. People. Times. Egg to chick. Predator to prey. You may try to slow it down, but you can't stop it. And only rarely can you hurry it along."

Ned glared. "Why are you so casual about all this? Aren't you supposed to be passing her your torch? Isn't she supposed to be the new environmental savior? Because that's what all the rehabbers say!"

Hélène waved her hand, as if the whole subject irritated her. "Maybe she doesn't want my torch. Did any of you ever think of that?"

She gestured to the bottle, and Ned poured again. "Are you the same man you were when you met her?"

"You know I'm not!"

"Did she ask you to to change? No. You did it on your own, even when you were afraid. She gave you the room you needed. And when the stakes were the highest, you raised an eagle on your glove."

Ned rested his elbows on his knees. He removed his glasses and wearily rubbed his eyes. "Hélène," he said. "She didn't even say goodbye."

CHAPTER 31

Chris and Philipe arrived at the cabin, flushed and damp from their brisk three-hour hike. "Hi, Luna!" called Philipe.

"We brought you more food," added Chris, "and Hélène wants to talk to you!"

She pulled on her boots and jacket and followed them down the rocky trail. She found Hélène in a flight cage, sitting on her wicker chair. On a high perch, Mars preened the feathers on Banshee's neck.

"Some people can live in solitude," said Hélène, when Luna was seated on a folding chair beside her. "Not all of them."

"Ned's fixing the house," Luna replied, and her eyes filled with tears.

"Why does that make you sad?"

"I don't know. How should I feel?"

Hélène's hand closed around Luna's. Her grip was firm. "'Should' is a ridiculous word," she said. "And you've been sad long enough. Try another feeling."

"I need to get back to the cabin," said Luna, still holding her hand.

"Safe travels, *chérie*," Hélène replied. "But before you go, Ned is moving to Portland on Thursday."

• • •

A gust of wind sent bright leaves spinning onto the surface of the pond. Ned sat on the Burke's back porch, watching a car roll slowly up the driveway. The three of us used to sit on the dock and watch fireflies, Luna once told him. Rose said the bravest ones fly so high they turn into stars.

He answered his ringing phone. "Inter-nedt!" said Earl. "You're not still going to Portland, are you?"

"Yeah, I am."

"Aww, why don't you move here? Julie Marie's friends are all hot for you! Did those people come back to see the house?"

"Yeah. They just drove in again. The agent says they're going make an offer."

"You're keeping some of that money, right?"

"Just what I put in. The Burke's lawyer will put the rest in a trust for her."

"But that was months of work!"

"Shut up, Earl."

• • •

Luna felt a painful tightness in her chest as she parked beside the Chevy. The barn door was new. The paint was fresh. There was a swing on the porch. Fall flowers lined the walkway.

Quietly she entered the house. She picked up the photograph of Harry and Rose, beaming beside her as she held a Golden Eagle. Heat rose in her throat. She put down the photograph, and continued into the living room.

The couch had been reupholstered. The overstuffed chair by the window was now in front of the fireplace. Hanging from a formerly empty wall was an antique wooden painting of an eagle, wings outstretched, arrows clutched in its feet. SPIRIT OF '76, read the banner. Luna teetered, not knowing which way she would fall.

"No, it's fine," said Ned, his voice coming through the screen door. "They must have gone into the barn."

She paused in the kitchen. The rooster-shaped pitcher was the same, the new microwave was not. The sun shone through the windows. "Because I want to see Portland," said Ned's voice.

Luna climbed the stairs and hovered in the doorway of Harry and Rose's room. Everything was the way they had left it, and tears spilled down her cheeks. She wiped her face on her sleeve, picked up a pillow Rose had embroidered, and cradled it as she sat on the bed. She closed her eyes, wondering how she had survived all these years without keeping a single thing that belong to them.

She continued to the guest room, where Ned's bags were packed. She almost started down the stairs, but forced herself toward the last room. She could almost hear the mirror shatter, see the hurled cup break, and feel the silver stars crumple as she ripped them from the ceiling. Bracing herself, she stood in the doorway.

The room was still. The cataclysm had passed. The clothes were back in their drawers, a new mirror gleamed on the wall, and a blue flowered cup rested on the table. Her collages were framed. Her acceptance letter from Cornell was taped together and tucked into a basket. Luna raised her eyes to the ceiling, where the stars had returned to the sky.

• • •

The turquoise water slid past her like silk.

Harper undulated her body and long flippers, moving with the easy grace that propelled sea creatures for miles without effort. Through her mask she could see shafts of sunlight illuminating the Porkfish and the French Grunts, the Indigo Hamlets and the Queen Angelfish, all of them glowing against the coral bed below. She had been searching for a dolphin pod for hours. She climbed into her boat, headed for land, anchored a hundred yards offshore, and dove back into the water. When the sun began to descend there was still no sign of them, so she sighed and swam toward her boat.

She had spent days writing her proposal, titled it "The Differences in Communication Patterns Between Spinner and Bottlenose Dolphins," and sent it to Luna's contact at the Senzimir Wildlife Foundation. Two weeks later their response arrived in the mail. Harper, always proud of her sang-froid, pulled out the check, dropped the envelope, and sat down heavily on the floor. Eight days later she moved to a two-room cottage in the Bahamas, bought a 10-year-old Triumph with a Yamaha outboard, and set up her sound equipment.

Luna was off the grid, so she emailed one of Hélène's volunteers. Can you get a message to Luna? she wrote. Tell her this: Your debt for the birdnapping is paid.

She was fifty yards from her boat when the pod found her. There's something behind me, she thought, then the tranquil sea turned dark and muscular. She pumped her legs, trying to keep up, as the dolphins sliced through the water on both sides and beneath her. One jumped over her head, twisted in the air, and knifed back into the depths. Another peered into her mask, steadily and inquiringly, then surged forward. They tightened around her, closer and closer, until she thought her heart would burst from the joy of their acceptance; then they all slipped away, a few shooting upward and falling back into the sea.

Harper slowed, breathless, as the last of the pod glided past her. She looked to the side, hoping for a final moment of contact, and saw an eye hovering above a wet expanse of beard. "Dammit, Warren!" she cried, yanking off her mask. "You scared the shit out of me!"

"But I thought you *liked* sea monsters!"

"How did you find me?"

"I asked the dolphins, of course."

Harper grinned, treading water. "I suppose you're going to invite yourself to dinner."

"Actually, I've invited myself for a week."

"A week! Well, hmm. You might come in handy."

"I'm pretty good in the water. Want to see how long I can hold my breath? I'll go down, and you start counting. Go ahead, start."

Warren disappeared, and Harper counted out loud.

"One. Two. Three. Whoa!" She grinned and splashed, trying to maintain her composure. "Four. Five. Nine! Twenty-five! Ohhhh! Twelve! Fifty! Ahhhh! A hundred and sixty-seven!"

She threw back her head and cackled. "Submerging!" she cried, and vanished beneath the sea.

• • •

Ned sat on the top step of the back porch. "No, I never heard from her," he said. "I know. Listen, the buyers are here. Talk to you later."

When Luna appeared he stayed seated, too astonished to rise. He saw her reddened eyes and damp cheek, and for a moment he looked concerned. He steadied himself, resumed staring at the fields, and Luna sat on the step beside him.

"Thank you," she said.

Ned glanced at her, then looked away. "You're welcome."

"For everything."

He waited, his eyes straight ahead.

"If it weren't for you, I would never have made it out of Florida. I owe you…"

"You don't owe me anything," he said, and rose. "The files are on the kitchen table. Your lawyer said it made more sense to sell the house than to abandon it again. If you want to keep it, just take it off the market."

"Wait!" she said, scrambling to her feet. "Don't go!"

He turned to face her. "You disappeared," he said. "Not even a message. Not one word!"

"I know. I'm sorry."

He reached for the door. "I'm really sorry!" she said.

He opened it, then shut it again. "You know something?" he demanded. "Once I calculated the odds of you and me living happily ever after, and you know what I came up with? Two hundred billion to one!"

She nodded, and her eyes held his. You've been in this situation before, he told himself. Don't do it.

"I know," she said. "I know. It's just that…some people might say those odds aren't so bad."

He rolled his eyes. "Like Warren?" He opened the door.

"Ned," she said. "Please don't go."

He ordered himself to ignore her, grab his bags, and drive away. Just don't look at her, he thought. He met her crystal gaze, and once again he was nine years old. Fighting terror, vertigo, and common sense, he peered over the edge of the quarry to the glowing green water below. Go on, you chicken! shouted his brother. It won't kill you unless you land flat!

"It's too late!"

"But what if we could have a normal life?"

"A normal life!" he said, inching toward the edge. "Oh, sure! You're a Missing Person! You're in legal trouble!"

"Stanley could help me - he's good with legal issues!"

"Adam's not done with you!"

"Yes, he is! He filed all the papers!"

"You're impossible to sleep with! Do you still have those dreams?"

"Sometimes. Are you still scared of Mars?"

He snorted. "Totally!"

"Ned?" she said, and her expression changed to one he had never seen her wear before. "I..."

"What?"

"I...I..."

"For God's sake! What?"

"I love you," she said. "Stay with me in our house."

Ned flung himself into the bright air. Gravity reached for him, but he eluded its grasp.

"All right," he said, and kissed her.